THE BONE SEASON

SAMANTHA SHANNON

Praise for THE BONE SEASON Series

Sunday Times Bestseller

New York Times Bestseller

Asian Age Bestseller

USA Today Bestseller

Indie Bestseller List

Daily Mail Book of the Year

Stylist Book of the Year

Huffington Post Book of the Year

Nominated for a FutureBook Innovation Award
Bookseller Ones to Watch

Today Book Club Pick

GoodReads Choice Awards Fantasy Nominee

Amazon Rising Star

"There is no question over whether or not you should pick up *The Mime Order*. It is a MUST." —*The Guardian*

"Gripping, edge-of-the-seat plotting." —*The Daily Mail*

"*The Mime Order* picks up a scant half-hour from the end of *The Bone Season*, thrusting readers back into the world of Paige and a more detailed journey through future London. The novels are hugely imaginative." —*Independent on Sunday*

"A gripping sequel." —*US Weekly*

"*The Mime Order* . . . is, if anything, more accomplished and imaginative than *The Bone Season* . . . I'm left wondering where Paige and Shannon will go next . . . Wherever she does go, I will follow." —*Scotland on Sunday*

"Shannon's ability to take classic tropes, such as forbidden love and dystopian societies, and give them a well-knuckled twist is to be admired—books one and two have demonstrated that she looks set to become a trailblazer for young talent." —*Independent*

"Shannon's haunting dystopian universe is rich in detail, consistent, suffused with familiar afternotes. Just when the bloodshed seems over the top, she turns to shimmering descriptions of Paige's dangerously illicit tie to Warden. When Paige seems toughest, Shannon reminds us of her empathy for the downtrodden. 'Hope is the lifeblood of revolution,' Shannon writes. 'Without it, we are nothing but ash, waiting for the wind to take us.' Like Paige Mahoney, Shannon now has proven staying power. Her fans will be calling for more." —NPR.org

"London already has a long history of memorable ne'er-do-wells—Jack the Ripper, anyone?—but author Samantha Shannon adds dark, shady corners and an amazingly rich and unruly underworld to the city in *The Mime Order*." —*USA Today*

THE
MIME
ORDER

AUTHOR'S PREFERRED TEXT

The Second Book in The Bone Season Series

SAMANTHA SHANNON

BLOOMSBURY PUBLISHING

NEW YORK · LONDON · OXFORD · NEW DELHI · SYDNEY

BLOOMSBURY PUBLISHING
Bloomsbury Publishing Inc.
1385 Broadway, New York, NY 10018, USA

BLOOMSBURY, BLOOMSBURY PUBLISHING, and the Diana logo
are trademarks of Bloomsbury Publishing Plc

First published in 2015 in Great Britain
First published in the United States 2015
This author's preferred text edition published 2024

ISBN: HB: 978-1-63973-459-7; PB: 978-1-63973-346-0; EBOOK: 978-1-63973-540-2

Library of Congress Cataloging-in-Publication Data is available.

2 4 6 8 10 9 7 5 3 1

Typeset by Integra Software Services Pvt. Ltd.
Printed and bound in the U.S.A.

To find out more about our authors and books visit www.bloomsbury.com
and sign up for our newsletters.

Bloomsbury books may be purchased for business or promotional use.
For information on bulk purchases please contact Macmillan Corporate and
Premium Sales Department at specialmarkets@macmillan.com.

For the fighters – and the writers

Author's Note on this Edition

The Mime Order was originally published in 2015.

The Author's Preferred Text you're about to read has been significantly revised. It follows roughly the same course of events, rewritten with a bit more experience under my belt.

I hope you enjoy this series as much as I've loved working on it for the last decade.

Samantha Shannon, 14 February 2024

Mimes, in the form of God on high,
Mutter and mumble low,
And hither and thither fly—
Mere puppets they, who come and go
At bidding of vast formless things …

EDGAR ALLAN POE

Contents

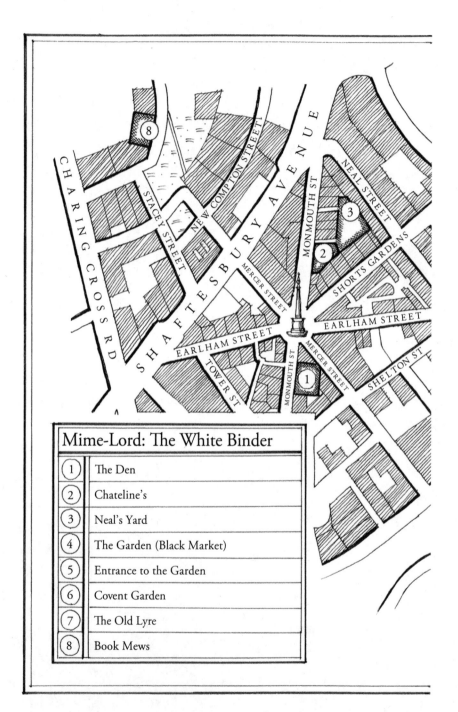

	Mime-Lord: The White Binder
1	The Den
2	Chateline's
3	Neal's Yard
4	The Garden (Black Market)
5	Entrance to the Garden
6	Covent Garden
7	The Old Lyre
8	Book Mews

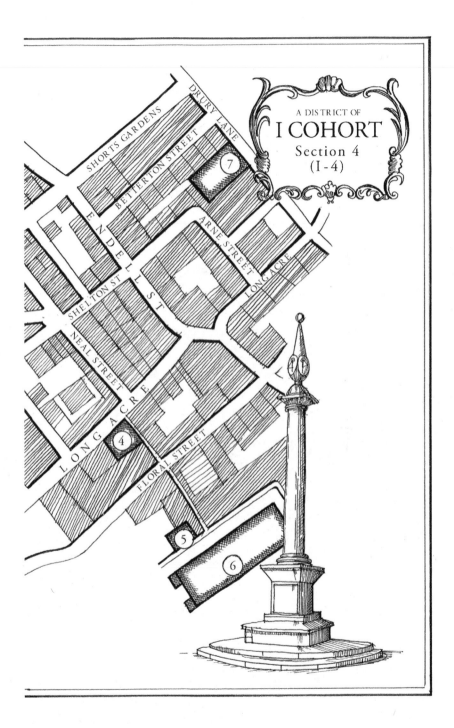

A DISTRICT OF
I COHORT
Section 4
(I-4)

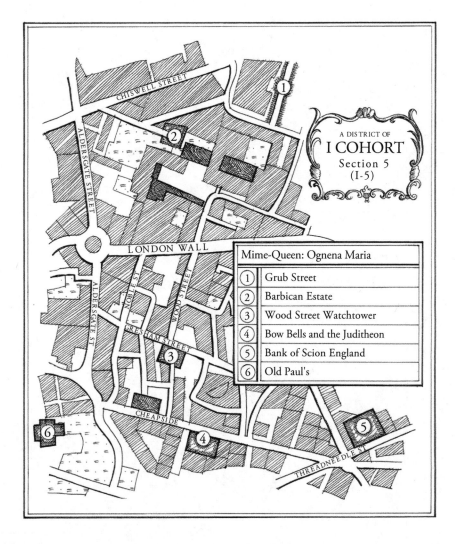

A DISTRICT OF
I COHORT
Section 5
(I-5)

Mime-Queen: Ognena Maria	
①	Grub Street
②	Barbican Estate
③	Wood Street Watchtower
④	Bow Bells and the Juditheon
⑤	Bank of Scion England
⑥	Old Paul's

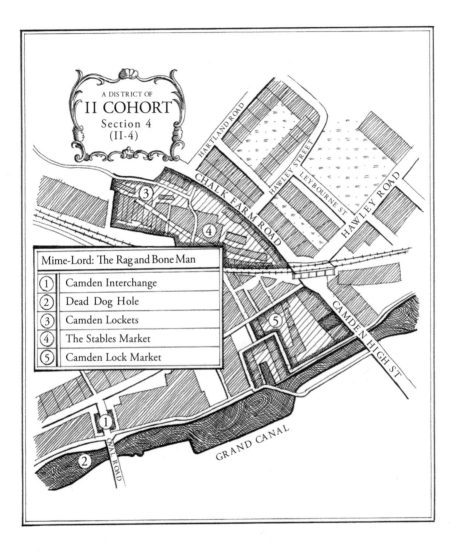

A DISTRICT OF
II COHORT
Section 4
(II-4)

Mime-Lord: The Rag and Bone Man

①	Camden Interchange
②	Dead Dog Hole
③	Camden Lockets
④	The Stables Market
⑤	Camden Lock Market

The Unnatural Assembly

– 2059 –

I COHORT

1. *Haymarket Hector and his esteemed mollisher, Cutmouth*
2. *The Abbess*
3. *Mary Bourne*
4. *The White Binder*
5. *Ognena Maria*
6. *Spring-heel'd Jack*

II COHORT

1. *Jimmy O'Goblin*
2. *The Glass Duchess*
3. *Ark Ruffian*
4. *The Rag and Bone Man*
5. *Bloody Knuckles*
6. *The Wicked Lady*

III COHORT

1. *The Bully-Rook*
2. *The Mudlark Prince*
3. *Madam Speaker*
4. *The Fifth Sister*
5. *Tom the Rhymer*
6. *The Glym Lord*

IV COHORT

1. *Redcap*
2. *The Buried King*
3. *The Pearl Queen*
4. *Faceless*
5. *The Lord Costermonger*
6. *The Heathen Philosopher*

V COHORT

1. *The Wretched Sylph*
2. *The Faithful Raven*
3. *Charley Truthteller*
4. *The Guy*
5. *Captain Card-Sharp*
6. *The Ferryman*

VI COHORT

1. *Seer Green*
2. *The Hare*
3. *The Lady of the Manor*
4. *Slyboots*
5. *Jenny Greenteeth*
6. *The Winter Queen*

Please note that a Record of the esteemed Mollishers of London can be located elsewhere in the Private Library of

The Spiritus Club

PART ONE

THE ROGUE DIAL

Here I am once more in this Scene of Dissipation and vice,
and I begin already to find my Morals corrupted.

– JANE AUSTEN

I

TRAITORS' GATE

It's rare that a story begins at the beginning. In the grand scheme of things, I really turned up at the beginning of the end of this one. After all, the story of Scion started centuries before I was born – and human lives, to Rephaim, are as fleeting as a heartbeat.

Some revolutions change the world in a day. Others take decades or centuries or more, and others still never come to fruition. Mine began with a moment and a choice. Mine began with the blooming of a flower in a secret city on the border between worlds.

You'll have to wait and see how it ends.

Welcome back to Scion.

---

2 September 2059

The train was upholstered in the style of a luxurious parlour. Red carpets, rosewood tables, and the anchor – Scion's symbol – stitched in gold on every seat. Baroque music drifted from a hidden speaker.

At the end of our carriage, Jaxon sat with his hands folded atop his cane, staring ahead without blinking. Across the aisle, my best friend, Nick Nygård, gripped a metal hoop that hung from the ceiling. After six months away from him, seeing his face was like looking at a memory.

Danica was nearby, hunched at a table, while Nadine and Zeke were in the next carriage. The last of us, Eliza, had stayed behind in London.

I sat apart from them, watching the tunnel rush past. There was a fresh burn on my skin where Danica had disabled the tracking device in my arm.

The events of the night seemed like a hallucination. Somehow, Warden and I had pulled off our ambitious plan to stage a jail-break from Oxford. He had trained me for the Bicentenary, helping me to hone my gift – all so I could hold my own against Nashira Sargas. I had survived her attempt to execute me in front of the Scion emissaries. Together, we had ruined her grand celebration.

Oxford was burning in my wake, and he was still there.

Run, little dreamer.

The golden cord stretched out between us, linking his spirit to mine. I gave it a tug, but there was no answer. I tried not to imagine why.

Warden could look after himself. For now, I had to think of the people on this train. My head was in agony, even with the scimorphine Nick had given me, but I had no time to rest. This night wasn't over.

Scion would be waiting for us on the other side, expecting the emissaries. The survivors on this train each carried a historic secret – one that could sink the whole empire. If we didn't escape, Scion would send us straight back to our prison. That or shoot us on the spot.

'We need to do a headcount.' I stood. 'Nick, where did you board the train?'

'Whitehall,' Nick answered. 'There's a station right under the Archon.' Seeing my confusion, he shook his head. 'We'll explain later.'

'What do we do?'

Nick glanced down the train. Even with his ski mask, I could tell he was rattled.

'I'm not sure,' he said. 'We had a way out, but with this many people—'

Jaxon was making a point of ignoring my existence. I tried not to look at him.

His plan had been for the six of us to escape Oxford. By insisting on bringing the other survivors, I had lowered our chances of survival.

I refused to regret it.

'There has to be another exit.' Nick took a deep breath. 'Any ideas, Dani?'

Danica pressed a cloth to her temple. One of the Vigiles had fetched her a solid blow.

'The Pentad Line divides in London. One branch has two stations, the first of which is Whitehall. That is no longer an option,' she said. 'There is one station on the other branch.'

'That could be our escape route,' I said. 'Where is it?'

'The Tower of London.'

The odds had always been stacked against us, but this was worse than I could have imagined.

'Dani,' I said, 'are you sure we can't reach the surface from this tunnel?'

'The Banqueting House was our access point,' Danica said, 'but it's *past* the hidden station at Whitehall. If we had kept to the original plan, the six of us could have made it, but this group would be too slow and conspicuous.' She seemed to think. 'I could … manually divert the train to the other branch. On a line this old, there should be a lever.'

'Would Scion notice the diversion?'

'I don't know. I'm an engineer, not an Underguard,' she said, her tone clipped. 'But if we stop the train early and walk the rest of the way, it may take Scion some time to locate it. The longer we can stall them, the better.'

'The Tower, then. We'll try,' Nick said. 'Just tell me it's not impossible, Dani.'

Danica took a while to reply. Her eyes were ringed with bruises.

'No,' she concluded. 'Not impossible.'

I stood. 'I'll let the others know.'

'Find something to set on fire,' Danica said. 'If I can't stop the train, we'll have to use the smoke alarm.'

I left them to prepare. Jaxon turned his face away when I stopped beside him.

'Jaxon,' I said, 'do you have a lighter?'

'No,' came the peevish answer.

'Fine.'

He definitely had a lighter. I went through the sliding doors to the next carriage, where Nadine and Zeke were leaning on each other, half asleep.

In the carriage after that, a crowd of exhausted faces looked up at me. I had clung on to hope Julian might have boarded the train, but there was no sign of him. Even if he and the other performers survived the night, Nashira would have them all trimmed at the neck by sunrise.

In all likelihood, the rest of us would be dead by then, too.

'Where are we going, Paige?' Lotte said. She was still wearing her bloody costume from the masque. 'Whereabouts in London, I mean?'

'About that,' I said. 'Was anyone awake when they put us on the train to Oxford?'

'I was,' a scarred augur said. 'I used to smoke regal. I'm pretty resistant to flux.'

'So there *is* a station at the Tower?'

'Yeah.' He paused. 'That isn't where we're going, is it?'

Even as he spoke, the train came to a gradual halt. Danica must have spotted the lever.

'We don't have a choice,' I said. 'It's either that or Whitehall, and Scion is expecting the train to arrive there.'

Felix swallowed.

'The good news,' I went on, 'is that we cut their only line of communication with Oxford. If our luck holds, the confusion should give us just enough time to pull this off.'

'We'll die,' Charles said hoarsely. 'The Tower is full of elite Vigiles.'

'They don't know we're coming. That means we have a small window of opportunity to escape.'

'We can make it.' A performer stood up. 'Where should we go, Paige?'

'Head for the back of the train. I'll meet you there.'

While they helped each other up, I counted them. Not including me and the gang, there were sixty-one survivors. Some of them would barely remember the citadel, or what it was like to live beyond Oxford. All they had done for years was serve and fear the Rephs.

And I had thrown my job away, scotching my best chance to help them find a livelihood in London. Even if I went to Jaxon and grovelled for all I was worth, he would not forgive me lightly for insulting him, or for disobeying his order to leave the other prisoners behind.

In hindsight, I probably shouldn't have told him to get fucked.

I pushed the thought away and sat beside Michael Wren, who was sitting a few seats away from the others.

'Hey.' I touched his shoulder. His cheeks were blotched and damp. 'Michael, are you all right?'

He nodded.

'We're going to be okay,' I said. 'You know Warden wanted you to leave.'

Another nod. Michael wasn't quite mute, but he used words sparingly.

'You don't have to go back to your parents, I promise. I'll try to find you a place to live.' I looked away for a moment. 'If we make it out alive.'

Michael wiped his face with his sleeve.

'I wish Gail and Fazal had come,' I said quietly. 'Maybe they were scared of leaving what they knew, after so long. I can't blame them.'

'Liss,' Michael whispered.

He reached for my hand. I pressed his fingers, clenching my jaw.

Liss would have wanted me to save as many people as I could. For all our sakes, I couldn't let her loss sink in.

'Warden kept a lighter in the Founders Tower,' I said, using a calm voice. 'I don't suppose he gave it to you?' He dug a hand into his grey tunic and pulled out an engraved silver lighter. I took it. 'Thank you.'

Also sitting alone was Ivy, the palmist. I pocketed the lighter and sat opposite her.

'Ivy?'

Her nod was barely visible.

'You know we can't take you to a hospital,' I said, 'but my friend can help you. He's a medic.'

Ivy said nothing.

Thuban Sargas had suspected she was in the syndicate. That was part of why he had been torturing her. After a moment, I said, 'Do you have a gang?'

She looked at me. 'What?'

'You broke out of Corpus by picking the lock. Were you in the syndicate?'

'No.' Her voice was a wasted husk. 'I mean, not really. I was … a gutterling.'

'You're too old to be a gutterling now.'

'I just did odd jobs.'

I clasped my hands on the table. Old moons of dirt sat under my fingernails.

All I wanted was to offer Ivy somewhere warm and safe to stay, but Jaxon would never have put up with strangers invading his den, even if I hadn't just ended our working relationship. Somehow, I would need to find places for everyone, whether in the syndicate or a dosshouse.

'Is there no one at all you can trust there?' I asked. 'A friend, a contact?'

Ivy dug her fingers into her arm, stroking and grasping. After a few moments, she said, 'Agatha Lamb. She owns a jewellery shop in Camden Market.'

'What's it called?'

'Camden Lockets.' Blood seeped from her bottom lip. 'She hasn't seen me in a while, but I … think she would help me get back on my feet.'

'I'll send one or two of the others with you. We're not leaving anyone on their own.' I took in her many bruises. 'I'm sorry we didn't get you out of Corpus sooner.'

'You couldn't have,' she said. 'Thuban would never have let me go.'

Her gaze was on the window, far away.

Warden and his allies had stayed to fight for Oxford. I could only hope one of them would destroy Thuban before he came after us for revenge.

The train started to move again. I led Ivy after the others, to the rear compartment, where my gang had gathered up their weapons and supplies.

'That's the White Binder,' someone whispered.

Jaxon stood to one side, grasping his cane. His silence was unnerving.

'I stopped the train for long enough to divert it,' Danica told me, 'but I must have tripped a defence mechanism. It's locked me out of the controls.'

I flashed the lighter. 'Just say the word.'

Danica kept an eye on her watch. When she gave me a nod, I snapped the lighter open. Before I could go for the upholstery, Michael tapped my shoulder and offered me his grey tunic.

The uniforms would make us too conspicuous. I placed his tunic on a seat and held the lighter to it. Without a word, some of the other survivors took off their outer layers as well, leaving them in their undershirts. Before long, a pile of tunics and gilets had formed, and the small flame I had set was spreading.

'*Emergency*,' said the voice of Scarlett Burnish. '*Fire detected in rear compartment.*' There was a drone as the train glided to a halt. '*Please move towards the nearest exit and alight with caution. A life-preservation team has been dispatched to your location.*'

'They'll probably be on foot.' Danica spoke over the murmurs. 'I doubt Scion has another train waiting.'

'Then we have time,' I said. 'Let's get the hell out of here.'

Nick opened the door at the end of the train, which was home to a small platform with a guard rail.

'Pass a torch,' I said to Zeke. When he did, I aimed the beam at the ground. 'Okay. There's room to walk next to the tracks. Everybody off.'

Keeping a wary eye on the third rail, I let go of the platform and dropped on to the ballast. Zeke started to help the other survivors down.

'Paige.' Jos caught up with me. 'What will happen to the others, like Julian?'

'I don't know,' I said.

'Warden will protect them, won't he?'

'I'm sure he'll try.'

Jos nodded, but his eyes filled. Julian and Liss had looked out for him in the Rookery. I drew him to my side, and we made our way into the dark.

Our group set off in single file, giving the rails and sleepers a wide berth. My filthy boots crunched through the trackbed.

We pressed on in a tense silence, quickening our pace. Nick stopped to help Ivy, who was so weak I marvelled that she had reached the train at all.

The tunnel was vast and unlit. We had five torches between us, one with a flagging battery. Shivering in my coat, I stayed close to the wall and concentrated on avoiding the tracks, making sure Jos was doing the same.

As soon as Scion found the empty train, they would try to contact Oxford. When that failed, they would alert the support outpost, Winterbrook. We had to be out of here before they caught wind of the rebellion.

At last, our torches lit a platform. I stepped across the rails and pulled myself on to it, my muscles throbbing as I lifted the torch to eye level. The beam cut through the crushing darkness, revealing white stone walls and a rack of folded stretchers – a mirror image of the station on the other end.

At some point, I had been here, though I had no memory of it. The smell of disinfectant lingered. Did the Vigiles bleach their hands once they had dumped us on the train, scared clairvoyance might rub off on them?

So far, there were no guards. A sign was bolted to the wall, with the name of the station written across it in tall white lettering.

TOWER OF LONDON

Beneath the sign was a small tablet. I leaned closer, blowing dust from the embossed letters, which read PENTAD LINE. A map showed the five secret stations: Oxford, Winterbrook, Whitehall, Lambeth East, Tower of London.

Nick came to stand beside me.

'Is this where they sent you?'

'They keep some voyants in the Tower for years. I was … lucky.'

He laid a hand on my shoulder.

'Come on,' he said. 'We have to go.'

When I nodded, a gust of tiny spots crossed my vision. I pressed my fingers to my temples.

Warden had given me a few drops of amaranth, which had healed most of the damage to my dreamscape, but a faint sense of malaise hung around my head, and my vision kept faltering. I had never felt so exhausted.

There were two exits. One was a lift, big enough to accommodate several stretchers at a time; the other was a heavy metal door marked FIRE EXIT. Nick opened the latter and glanced out.

'Looks like we're taking the stairs,' he said. 'Anyone know the layout of the Tower?'

'I do.' Nell raised her hand. 'Some of it.'

Nick turned. 'What's your name?'

'Nell.' She resembled Liss enough to have been her understudy – long black hair, sylphlike build – but her face was made of harder lines, her skin a deeper olive. 'I was here for three years. If those stairs come up near the elevator doors, we're going to be right behind the Traitors' Gate.'

Of course they had sent us through there.

'It will probably be locked,' Nell said. 'They'll shoot us like fish in a barrel.'

She raked back her curls, baring more of her gaunt face to the light. Her eyes were raw and weary. Liss had been one of her closest friends.

'I can deal with locks.' Nadine held up her pouch of picks. 'And Vigiles.'

'We're not dealing with Vigiles.' Nick looked at the low ceiling. 'We need to move in small groups. Paige and Bell, we'll go first. Nell, you're with us. Binder, Diamond, you stay here and keep an eye on—'

'I hope very much,' Jaxon said, 'that you are not presuming to give me orders, Red Vision.'

In the blur of getting off the train and finding the station, I had scarcely noticed him. He was standing in the shadows, his hand on his cane, straight and bright as a new candle.

After a moment, Nick said, 'I was asking for your help.'

'You chose this way,' Jaxon said coldly. 'I will stay here until you clear a path.'

'That's exactly what I was—'

'It's fine,' I cut in. 'Diamond, you all right?'

'Yes,' Zeke said. One of his hands was clamped over his shoulder, the other wrapped into a white-knuckled fist. 'Let us know when to move.'

I gave Jaxon a final look before I followed Nell. He returned it with no discernible emotion.

Even after this long night, Nell was quick as a bird. I found myself struggling to keep up, every muscle burning. Our footfalls were too loud, echoing above and below us. Nell slowed down and cracked open another door.

'All clear,' she whispered.

I tried to check the æther, but my head throbbed, forcing me to stop. Behind me, Nick took out his syndicate phone and held it to his ear.

'Eliza parked near Whitehall,' he murmured to me. 'I need to tell her we're here.'

'Just send her an image,' I said.

'I have.'

Only the gang would fit in the car. I would have to stay behind and help the others.

The entrance to the station was opposite the elevator doors. To our right was a wall of enormous bricks, sealed with mortar. To the left, built under a sweeping stone archway, was the Traitors' Gate – a solemn black construction, used as an entrance during the monarch days. A flight of stone steps rose beyond it, with a narrow ramp for stretchers.

'Muse.' Nick clutched the phone to his ear. 'Muse, can you hear me?' He ducked back into the stairwell.

'Most of the Guard Extraordinary live in the White Tower,' Nell muttered. 'They do regular patrols.'

'How do we get out?'

'We'll have to climb over the battlements.'

'Won't they be able to see us?'

'There's an interior wall between the Traitors' Gate and the White Tower. That will help us. If we stay low and quiet, we should make it.'

As she spoke, footsteps came up the path by the Traitors' Gate. We flattened ourselves against the walls, but luck was on our side, and the Vigiles moved on. Nell slid to the ground.

I tried opening the gate, to no avail. The chains were held together with a padlock. Seeing it, Nadine took a tiny flathead screwdriver from her belt. She slid it into the keyhole, then pulled out her picks.

'This could take a while,' she said. 'The pins feel rusty.'

'We don't have a while.'

'Stop distracting me, then.'

I returned to the stairwell. Nick was removing the battery from his phone.

'Eliza will bring the car to Harp Lane. She's on her way now,' he said. 'Don't ask me how, but she persuaded Spring-heel'd Jack to help us. He's sending a group of his best footpads to distract the Vigiles.'

Spring-heel'd Jack was the mime-lord of the next section. He was also completely unhinged, which might be working in our favour.

'That could save us,' I said. 'How long will they be?'

'Ten minutes.'

'What about Ognena Maria?'

'Eliza is trying to contact her. She'll understand the need to work together here.'

'You should get the others, then.'

'Take this.' He removed something from his backpack. 'Just in case.'

My revolver, along with its holster. I accepted it.

Nick went down the steps. I stepped back outside, tensing when a light shone through the Traitors' Gate. Nell drew away from it, her eyes narrowed against the glare.

'I don't know if that's normal,' she murmured. 'I don't remember.'

'Whitehall would have got the empty train by now.' I watched the light. 'Scion might have put the other stations on alert. Bell, how long?'

'Just shut up and let me concentrate.'

Nadine was working at an awkward angle, given that the padlock was on the other side of the gate, but her hands were steady. I took a slow breath.

'Paige.' Nell looked up at me. 'When we get out, where are we going?'

I thought fast as I buckled on my holster.

'We should head north,' I said. 'There's an empty building I know in Candlewick. We'll rest there. In the morning, we can see who has contacts.'

'I thought *you* had contacts.' Nell frowned. 'Aren't you a mollisher?'

I couldn't bring myself to answer.

Somewhere in the citadel, sirens began to drone. I stiffened, readying the revolver.

Zeke emerged from the stairwell with a flock of nervous survivors behind him. I motioned for him to stay where he was.

At the gate, Nadine sprang the padlock. We helped her draw the chains from the bars, careful not to let the links make too much noise. Together, we pushed open the Traitors' Gate. It scraped against gravel, its hinges groaning with disuse, but the sirens drowned out the sound. Nell stole up the steps and we followed.

The outer wall of the Tower of London was much lower than I had expected. Another flight of steps led up to its battlements. I signalled to Nick and Zeke to bring the others, then went after Nell. When I reached a gap between the battlements, my chest tightened.

There it was. That shatterbelt of metal, glass and lights, all glittering with promise.

London.

After six months of captivity, I was back.

Ahead was a steep bank and a final wall to the Thames. To our left was Tower Bridge. To reach Harp Lane, my gang would need to go right.

'I'll go first,' Nick said. 'You help the others down.'

I looked over my shoulder, scanning for snipers. There were none to be seen, but I sensed dreamscapes.

Nick squeezed between the battlements and gripped one in each hand, turning to face the wall. His feet sought purchase against the stone, dislodging small fragments. He shot me a reassuring smile before lowering himself and dropping the last few feet, falling straight into a crouch.

It made me uneasy that a wall now stood between us.

I held out my hands for the first survivor. Michael was there with Nell, both supporting Ivy. I took her by the elbows, guiding her to the battlements.

'Up here, Ivy.' I shucked my coat and buttoned it around her, leaving me in my red dress from the Bicentenary. 'Give me your hands.'

Between us, Michael and I got her over. Nick reached up for her, lowering her on to the grass.

One by one, the survivors went over the wall. First Ella, then Lotte, then a shaken crystallist and an augur with a broken wrist. Each one stayed close to where they landed, guarded by Nick. As I held out a hand to Michael, Jaxon swept him aside and tossed his cane over the wall. Before he climbed, he leaned down to whisper in my ear.

'You have one more chance, Paige. Come back to Seven Dials,' he said, 'and I will forget your insolence. We can put this night behind us.'

He sounded just like a Reph.

'Thank you, Jaxon,' I said, keeping my gaze dead ahead. 'I'll think about it.'

Jaxon stepped on to the battlements and was gone. I turned back to Michael.

'That's it.' I took him by the wrists. 'Almost there, Michael.'

Michael managed to hook a leg over the wall. His fingers dug into my arms.

Nell suddenly gasped. Even in the dark, I could see the bloodstain cutting through her trouser leg. She looked up at me, her eyes wide.

'Get down,' I shouted over the sirens. 'Everybody over the wall, now—'

There was no time for anyone to obey. A torrent of bullets tore through the line of people on the steps.

A piercing scream rang out. Michael slipped between my fingers. I threw myself down behind the balustrade and covered my head with my arms.

Containment would be paramount: kill on sight, don't ask questions.

If we escaped, so did the secret.

Nick was roaring from below, telling me to move, to jump, but I was paralysed. My perception narrowed until all I could hear was my heart, my shallow breathing, the muffled gunfire. Then hands were grasping me, lifting me over the wall, and I was falling.

The soles of my boots slammed against earth, jarring my legs to the hip, and I pitched forward a few more feet. With a dull *whump* and a grunt of pain, someone else landed beside me – Nell, her teeth clenched tight. She dragged herself upright and limped as fast as she could. I crawled in the same direction until Nick pulled my arm around his neck. I twisted away from him.

'No,' I heaved out. 'I can't leave them—'

'Paige, come on!'

Nadine had made it over the wall, but the other two were still climbing the battlements. A fresh barrage of gunfire had the survivors running in all directions. Danica and Zeke jumped for their lives.

An amaurotic woman went down, her skull blown open like soft fruit. I sensed the sniper above us, taking aim from the Byward Tower. Michael almost tripped over the body. The sniper set their sights on him.

Warden had trusted me to get the prisoners away. I had failed to keep them all safe, but I could save Michael Wren. With the last drop of strength I had left, I homed in on the sniper and seared right through their dreamscape, sending their spirit into the æther and their body tumbling from their post. As the empty corpse hit the grass, Michael vaulted over the wall to the Thames. I screamed his name, but he was gone, and Nick was pulling me away.

My feet moved faster than my thoughts. The cracks in my dreamscape were straining open.

Nick kept hold of my hand. When my knees buckled, he somehow got me into his arms.

There were the blue streetlamps, the cars. The guns boomed from the keep. We ran and ran until I thought I would die from the pain. And then came the roar of an old engine, and the blinding glare of headlights. Nick bundled me into the front seat, and Eliza Renton was staring at me, hands tight on the wheel. Nadine shouted frantically at her, and she slammed on the accelerator.

And then we were gone into the citadel, like dust into shadow, leaving the sirens to howl in our wake.

2

LONG STORY

S he appeared at 6 A.M. She always did.

My hand snatched my loaded revolver, almost of its own accord. The theme for ScionEye was playing – a sweeping, theatrical composition, based around the chimes of Big Ben.

I waited.

There she was. Scarlett Burnish, the Grand Raconteur, white lace frothing from the top of her black dress. She looked the same as usual – like some hellish automaton – but on occasion, when some poor denizen had fallen prey to a cruel unnatural (apparently), she could exude manufactured distress. Today, however, she was smiling.

'*Good morning, and welcome to another day in the Scion Citadel of London. Good news as the Guild of Vigilance announces an expansion of its Sunlight Vigilance Division, with at least fifty more officers to be sworn in this Monday. The Chief of Vigilance has stated that the New Year will bring new challenges to the citadel, and that in these perilous times, it remains critical for the denizens of London to—*'

I switched it off.

There was no breaking news. No faces. No hangings.

The revolver thudded on to the table. I had been on the couch all night, staring at the ceiling. My muscles were stiff and painful. Every time the pain began to ebb, a fresh wave came, surging from a bruise or cut. I rolled my shoulders and tried to work out the dull ache in my back.

I should be heading for bed, as was my custom at dawn, but I had to get up, just for a minute. A glint of natural light would do me good.

Once I had stretched my legs, I switched on the music player. 'Guilty' drifted out, sung by Billie Holiday. Nick had dropped off some of my illegal records on his way to work, along with my rent money and a pile of books I hadn't touched. I didn't miss very much about Oxford, but I did miss the gramophone in Magdalen. You could get used to being lullabied by the lovelorn crooners of the free world.

It had been three days since the escape. My new home was the Lily Shallow, a dosshouse in Soho. Most such establishments were hardly fit to live in, but the landlord – a cleidomancer, who had probably opened a dosshouse just so he could finger keys for a living – had kept this one in a decent condition. Nick hadn't told him who I was; only that I was a voyant who needed to be kept out of sight, as a Vigile had beaten me and might still be looking to finish the job.

Unless I returned to Jaxon, I would have to keep moving between these sorts of lodgings as long as I remained in London. It must be costing Nick a fortune, but it would keep Scion from tracking me down.

If Jaxon was vengeful, he might force me to pay syndicate rent, or throw me off his turf altogether. So far, he hadn't. I didn't even know if Nick had told him where I was.

With the blinds down, no light entered the room. I opened them, just a little.

The dosshouse was on Sutton Row, close to Soho Square. A pair of amaurotics walked past, probably on their way to work. On the corner, a foolhardy soothsayer was already on the lookout for querents. The streetlamps glowed blue, as they would until sunrise.

In short, London was exactly the same. It was as if I had never been gone.

I closed the blinds again. For six months, I had been nocturnal, forced to sleep when the Rephs did. That might not change in a hurry.

Oxford had been dark and still, its rooms lit by candles and hearths. London was deafening in comparison. It must have always been this loud, but I kept flinching awake whenever cars or motos passed.

The Rephs had wrapped the lost city in amber, preserving it as it had been when they claimed it. Now that amber had cracked open, and I was the frail thing inside it, desperately trying to flutter back to life.

I reached for the water on the table and gulped it down with two Nightcaps. The pills were meant to help reset my body clock, but I found myself necking them even by day, just to shed the tension I was holding. I curled up on the bed and wrapped my arm around a pillow.

And I replayed it all again. Nashira Sargas trying to kill me. Liss Rymore dying in my arms. The bloody escape from the Tower of London.

My dreamscape was still fragile. During our confrontation at the Bicentenary, when Nashira had intended to steal my gift, her fallen angels had damaged the barrier of my dreamscape. I had also over-used my ability. Even after Warden had given me amaranth – the nectar that healed spiritual injuries – I couldn't shake the lingering headache.

Thinking of him tightened my chest. I pressed my face into the pillow.

I must have dozed off for a while. When I woke, my skin felt too warm.

It was still only half past ten in the morning. I sensed a dreamscape outside and sat up.

After a while, there was a light knock. Slowly, I picked up my gun and held it behind my back. With my free hand, I cracked the door open.

Clement Rush, the landlord, was holding out a tray. His numen – an antique iron key – hung on a chain around his neck. He never took it off.

'Morning,' he said.

'Lem,' I said, wary.

'I've just made some coffee. Thought you might fancy a cup.'

'Oh.' I took one. 'Thanks.'

When Nick had first brought me here, I had worried. Everyone in this section reported to Jaxon. By a stroke of luck, however, I had never met Lem. I had collected his syndicate tax, but he always left it in a dead drop. As far as I could tell, he had no idea I was the Pale Dreamer.

'I just wanted to warn you that there's going to be a séance in the room above yours tonight. They'll be using a table,' he said, looking weary. 'The lodger twisted my arm, but I'll make sure it's over by ten.'

'It's all right. I don't sleep much.'

'Well, you're looking much better today, if I may say so.'

'Thank you. Did my friend call?'

'He said he'll be here at seven. Do give me a bell if you need anything.'

'I will. Have a good day.'

'And you.'

For a dosshouse owner, he was strangely helpful. I closed the door and locked it, then sank to the floor and rested my brow against my knees.

I had to get this under control.

It was some time before I stood. When I could draw a steady breath, I put the revolver down and went to the airless bathroom, where I peeled off my nightshirt to inspect my injuries. Most visible were the deep gash near my temple, closed with stitches, and the shallow wound that curved across my cheek. Both were from Nashira – one from the knife she had thrown at me, and one where she had shoved me to the floor, having seen me with my bare hands on her consort.

I shook the thought away, lifting my gaze back to the mirror. Every part of my body looked worn and whittled. My fingernails were flimsy, my skin was dry and sallow, and my ribs and hipbones bulged.

During my first weeks in Oxford, I had only been able to clean myself with icy water from a sink. Now I stepped into the shower cubicle, cranked up the pressure as high as it went, and scrubbed shampoo into my hair. I breathed out as warmth poured over my shoulders.

A door slammed.

My hand swiped a hidden blade from the soap dish. My body pitched itself from the cubicle, straight against the opposite wall. I concealed myself behind the door, holding the blade to my chest.

It took a minute for my heart to slow down. I peeled myself from the wet tiles, slick with sweat and water.

It was nothing. Just another lodger going to their room.

Shaking, I grasped the sink. My hair hung in damp coils around my face, brittle and dull.

I looked my reflection in the eye. My body had been treated as property in the colony, dragged and grabbed and beaten by red-jackets and Rephs. I turned my back to the mirror and ran my fingers over the little threads of scar tissue on my shoulder. That brand would be there for as long as I lived.

But I had survived, as I had in Dublin.

I had survived, and the Sargas would know it.

I slept until late in the afternoon. When I opened the door to Nick for the first time in two days, he drew me into a gentle embrace, minding my slices and bruises.

'Hey,' he said.

'Hi.'

'I brought supper.' He picked up two paper bags. 'Has Lem been feeding you?'

'I've not had much appetite, but he's offered.'

'You need to eat, Paige.'

'Trust me, it's not for lack of trying.'

To show willing, I laid the table, while Nick pulled up a blind and opened the windows. A wind blew in the familiar smells of autumn – smoke from buskers' fires, leaf fall, a hint of petrichor – but the scent from the boxes was stronger. Tiny hot pies stuffed with chicken and ham, fresh bread, golden chips scattered with salt – Nick had brought a feast. He pushed a nutrient capsule across the table.

'Go on,' he said. 'Not too fast.'

The pies were glazed with melted butter and poured out a thick, rich sauce when cut. Dutifully, I placed the capsule on my tongue.

'Can I see your arm?'

I nodded. Nick took it in his hands and peered at the circular burn.

'I'll take the tracker out at some point,' he said. 'How's your wrist?'

'It's stiff, but I can live with it.'

'I wish I could give you a scan.' His face grew overcast. 'What about your side?'

'It's fine.'

'I'm so sorry. I should have realised it was you.'

It had been three months since Nick had stabbed me, thinking I was an agent of Scion. I grasped his hand and gave it a reassuring squeeze.

'You were under attack,' I said. 'I don't blame you, Nick.'

He grimaced. 'Did it really hurt?'

'Yes, but I appreciate your precision.' I reached for a slice of crusty bread. 'Still nothing on ScionEye.'

'They're keeping quiet,' he said. 'Very quiet.'

We were quiet, too. The sacks under his eyes betrayed the sleepless nights. The wondering. The waiting. I ate slowly, looking out of the window.

If the others had survived, they would be sleeping rough. Even if they had found enough coin to afford a penny hangover, the Vigiles checked those places.

If I was going to find them, I would have to get used to daylight again. It was too dangerous to go out after dark, when night Vigiles were on duty. If they spotted my aura, there would be no second chances.

'For you.' Nick placed a burner phone on the table. 'If you do need Jaxon, we've switched to a new call box. The number is in here.'

'Is yours, too?'

'Yes. Did Scion get your old phone, the one you used to call for help?'

'They did. Warden told me.'

'Warden,' Nick repeated. 'He came with us to the station.'

'Yes.'

'Are you ready to talk about it?'

Nick hadn't pushed the subject of what we had all seen in Oxford. His curiosity must be driving him spare.

'I want to,' I said. 'I'm just afraid you won't believe me.'

'I saw things in that city I can't wrap my head around. Whatever you're going to say, I believe you.'

'Okay.' I breathed out. 'Let me just … think of how to explain it.'

'Take your time.'

I crowned the bread with butter. 'How was work?'

'Just a normal day. Nobody said a word.' He palmed the stubble on his jaw, a nervous habit. 'I called in sick to go to Oxford. If anyone guessed—'

'You'd already be on the Lychgate,' I said. 'You kept your mask on. It would have looked suspicious if you hadn't gone back, but you did.'

'True.' He watched me glance out of the window. 'What are you thinking?'

Suddenly I had no appetite again.

'We lost a lot of people at the Tower,' I said. 'I told them I'd get them all home.'

'Paige, you'll destroy yourself if you think that way.'

I didn't answer. He came to kneel beside my chair.

'Sweetheart, look at me,' he said, keeping his voice low. 'None of this is your fault. Scion took you away from us. You did whatever you could to survive.' He wrapped an arm around me. 'If they're alive, we'll find the other prisoners. I promise.'

We stayed like that for some time. I rested my head on his shoulder, eyes closed.

'I'm sorry about your other friends,' he said. 'The ones we left behind.'

I nodded.

Warden must have known he could be sending us all to our deaths. Everyone had been aware of the risks, but there had been no other way. The Bicentenary had given us one shot, and we had both agreed to take it.

Once we had eaten, Nick cleared away the leftovers. Another knock at the door had me reaching for my gun again, but Nick held up a hand.

'It's okay.' He opened the door. 'I called a friend.'

I looked. A familiar woman was standing in the corridor.

When Eliza came in, she rushed straight over with a look that said she was going to sock me in the face. Instead, she yanked me into her arms.

'Paige, you idiot.' Her voice was thick with anger. 'You bloody idiot. Why did you take the Underground that day when it was after dark?'

'I took a chance.' I patted her back. 'I was stupid.'

'At least you admit it. Why didn't you just wait for Nick to drive you home?' she pressed. 'We thought Hector had bumped you off, or Scion had—'

'They got me. I'm okay.'

Nick detached her from my neck. 'Careful. She's got bruises on bruises.' He steered her to the opposite couch. 'I thought more than one of us should hear this, Paige. We need as many allies as we can get.'

'You *have* allies,' Eliza said, exasperated. 'Jax is worried sick about you, Paige.'

I huffed. 'Is he?'

'Yes. He's been sulking in his room for days, smoking like a chimney. Why are you staying in a dosshouse when you have a home?'

'Eliza, he's not worried, he's raging,' I said. 'I've left the gang.'

'Zeke told me, but you can't mean it.'

'I do.'

This was news to her. She looked between us. 'But Jaxon got you out,' she said. 'Why would you want to leave us?'

I ground my jaw. Nick came to sit beside me.

'Paige,' he said gently, 'if you're ready, maybe you could tell us what happened.'

After a moment, I nodded.

'I'll get us something to drink,' Eliza said, softening. 'It's cold in here.'

She went downstairs. Nick drew the curtains, while I switched on the television.

'She's never going to understand,' I said. 'She adores Jax.'

Nick said nothing.

'*Vigile numbers are expected to double in I Cohort over the next few weeks, with the instalment of a second prototype Senshield scanner, the only technology known to detect unnaturalness, expected before December*,' Scarlett Burnish said. '*Denizens should expect an increase in the number of spot checks on the Underground, the bus network, and in Scion-authorised taxis. If you have nothing to hide, you have nothing to fear. Now, moving on to this week's weather.*'

'They're trying to find us,' I said. 'I don't understand why they haven't said anything.'

'That might not be the reason they're recruiting Vigiles.' Nick came to sit beside me. 'They always boost security around Novembertide. And this year they're inviting the Grand Inquisitor of Paris.'

'Aloïs Mynatt was at the Bicentenary. If he's dead, I doubt Ménard will be in a festive mood.' I watched the screen. 'Senshield will change everything. Has the Unnatural Assembly made any contingency plans?'

'Not that I've heard.'

'Hector has no idea what to do,' I said. 'No one does.'

'Dani heard the prototype is erratic. It will be a while before they fine-tune it.'

'Not long enough.'

After a few minutes, Eliza returned with drinks from a local coffeehouse. Soon we were seated in the gloom, sipping from cups of creamy saloop.

'Before I tell my story, tell me yours,' I said. 'How did you get to Oxford?'

Nick rubbed his forehead. He must be getting a migraine.

'The night you called for help, I wanted to go to you,' he eventually said, 'but Jaxon was afraid I'd be arrested, too. He said he'd told you to make for the Thames. Eliza went to find you in the morning.'

'I didn't get that far,' I said.

Nick nodded. 'We hoped you'd gone to ground. After a few days, I decided to ask your father if he'd heard from you, but Colin had stopped coming to work. That's when I knew something was wrong.'

I closed my eyes.

'Jaxon ordered a search,' he said. 'Hector refused to help, but some of the mime-lords and mime-queens agreed to keep an eye out, and Maria sent couriers to watch the Lychgate. After a month, we had to accept that you had probably been detained. We had no ransom notes from the other gangs, no evidence that you'd been killed.'

'We even paid for a few readings from soothsayers and augurs,' Eliza said, 'but they kept saying cryptic things – that you were in the limen, among giants. You can see why Jax gets annoyed with them sometimes.'

I had to tamp down a shiver.

'We couldn't find any record of your arrest,' Nick said, 'but Jaxon concluded that you were dead. He tried to go back to business as usual.'

'Like getting in touch with Antoinette Carter,' I said.

'Right.' He paused. 'How did Scion know we would be meeting her, and where?'

'Scion can use the æther. It gave you away,' I said. 'Why risk meeting her in the open?'

'Jax didn't know if he could trust her. He wanted to see her on his own turf, but not in one of our hideouts,' Eliza said. 'He had voyants on standby around Trafalgar Square. That's how we got away so quickly when Scion attacked.'

'Yes,' Nick said. 'But a few people were detained in our stead.' He looked back at me. 'You told me where you were that night. Finally, we had a lead.'

'As soon as Jaxon knew you were alive, you were his only focus,' Eliza said, with a pointed look. 'He was obsessed with getting you back.'

I believed it. Losing his prized dreamwalker would have been infuriating, even humiliating – but I still wouldn't have expected him to risk everything to save me. That was the kind of sacrifice you made for people, not property.

'We weren't sure how to establish what was happening in Oxford,' Nick continued. 'Jaxon was the one who found the missing piece, a rumour of a tunnel under Whitehall. Dani looked into it and unearthed some maintenance records. Only a special unit of engineers was allowed in this tunnel, which connected to the Banqueting House.'

That was a heritage site, the former home of several Grand Inquisitors of England. Scion had turned it into a museum.

'Dani found the entrance,' Nick said. 'There was a train down there, waiting in Whitehall. She worked out that it was due to leave on the morning of the first of September. We decided to take a chance and infiltrate it.'

'Even Jaxon,' Eliza said. 'I said I'd stay behind to be the getaway driver.'

'It's not like Jax to get his hands dirty,' I said.

'He cares about us, Paige. He'd do anything to keep us safe. You most of all.'

Eliza had always thought the world of Jaxon. A few months ago, I was the same. And then I had spent half a year away from our employer, befriending people he despised, and seen him for what he was.

Jaxon was *capable* of kindness, but he wasn't kind. He could *act* like he cared, but it would always be an act. It had taken me years to wake up and see it.

'Sounds like Dani was the hero of the hour,' I said.

'She was incredible,' Nick agreed. 'At the end of August, she got us all down to the Pentad Line and accessed the train. By the time the Scion emissaries boarded, we had sealed ourselves into a storage compartment.'

'You're mad.' I shook my head. 'How did you get off on the other side?'

'We waited until everyone left. Someone locked the station, but we found a maintenance hatch, which took us to the street. We knew from the emissaries' conversations that there was some kind of party, so we followed them at a distance and scoped out the building.'

'We had to get you back, Paige,' Eliza said. 'Jax was willing to try anything.'

'Jax is not stupid,' I said. 'Putting a ragtag group of criminals on a secret train without a clue what to expect at the other end *is* stupid.'

'Well, maybe he got bored of sitting in the den.'

'You're safe now. It was worth the risk.' Nick leaned forward. 'Your turn.'

I hesitated. 'It's a long story.'

'Start with the night you were taken,' Eliza said.

'That's not where it starts,' I said. 'It starts two hundred years ago.'

They looked at each other.

It took a while. I told them about the night of my arrest, when I had finally unlocked my gift and killed two Underguards with my spirit. I told them how, later that night, Scion had sent a detainment unit to arrest me. Days later, I had been transported to the lost and quarantined city of Oxford.

And then I got on to the rest of the story.

I told them about the Rephaim – immortal beings who resembled humans, and came from a realm called the Netherworld. How their home had fallen into ruin after the breaking of the ethereal threshold, when the number of drifting spirits on Earth had torn the veils between the worlds. How they had come to Oxford and created Scion.

'Paige,' Eliza said slowly, 'I really don't want to sound patronising, but—'

'I'm telling the truth, Eliza.'

'I saw them. We all did,' Nick said. 'Ask the others.'

Eliza looked as if she couldn't decide whether to be angry, worried or curious.

'Okay,' she said, with clear difficulty. 'What are they, these Rephs?'

'They're humanlike,' I said, 'but their skin looks a bit like metal, they're tall, and their eyes are yellowish. Except when they feed on aura.'

'Sorry?'

'They need our auras to sustain themselves. That's why Scion hunts voyants,' I said. 'They also need us to fight the Emim.'

'The what?'

'They overran the Netherworld and forced the Rephs to come to Earth. We called them Buzzers,' I said. 'They feed on spirits and human flesh.'

I hadn't thought it possible for Nick to be any paler, but he managed.

'This is ridiculous,' Eliza said flatly. 'Be serious, Paige.'

'Look, I'm aware it sounds mad, but do you really think I would come up with a story this convoluted and expect you to take it seriously?'

'No, I think you're winding us up. That or you've been smoking regal.'

'Will you just let me talk?'

She released a long, slow breath. I took that as a reluctant agreement.

I told them about the pact between the Rephs and the Victorian government, which had led to the establishment of Scion. About the garrison in Oxford, meant to keep the Emim away from citadels like London.

I told them about the Bone Seasons – a decadal harvest of voyants and amaurotics, given to the Rephs every ten years. About their leader, Nashira Sargas, and how she had coveted my gift. How I was given to her consort, Arcturus Mesarthim, also known as Warden.

I explained the hierarchy of Oxford. The red-jackets, who served as guards and soldiers; the performers, cast into the slum, used as a source of aura and entertainment; the amaurotics, held in cells when they weren't being worked to death. I told them how the Rephs would beat and feed on humans, evicting them if they didn't pass their tests.

At some point, our drinks turned cold.

I told them about the first test, and how I had trained on Port Meadow with Warden. I told them about Gallows Wood; about Julian and Seb; about Liss. I told them how the Rephs had discovered the meeting with Antoinette Carter.

'Nashira suspected I was the Pale Dreamer,' I explained. 'She wanted me to detain Jaxon.'

Nick was frowning. 'Why were the Rephs so interested in him?'

'I still don't know.'

'You didn't arrest us,' Eliza said, a question in her tone.

'Of course not. I did everything I could to ruin the assignment,' I said. 'After that, the game was up. But then I realised Warden had always been on my side.'

My throat was starting to ache, but I told the story to the end. Everything but the fine print of my relationship with Warden. From my abridged description, he was a reticent creature with whom I had rarely spoken, who had suddenly agreed to help me.

'So he went against his own consort,' Eliza said.

'He didn't choose to be with her,' I said. 'There's an older conflict between the Rephs that I don't know about. I assume Warden sued for peace. He tried to organise a jailbreak twenty years ago, but a human betrayed him. That's why he didn't trust me at first, but he was training me to fight Nashira.'

By the time I stopped talking, it was the middle of the night. The séance upstairs had stopped.

'You escaped from Oxford,' Nick said. 'That means the secret is in danger.'

I nodded. 'They need to wipe out everyone who knows.'

'And then, what, another Bone Season?'

'I assume so. They're already building Sheol II in France.'

'Can Warden and his allies stop it?'

'They stayed behind to fight for Oxford. If they succeeded, then maybe.'

Nick searched my face. 'Can we be sure he's on our side?'

My brow creased. 'I'd say so,' I said. 'He helped me. He let us go.'

'He also used you as a weapon to settle a personal score,' Nick said. 'He risked your life repeatedly. Does that sound like an ally, Paige?'

I looked away.

In the warmth and gloom of Magdalen, it had been easy to forget the complexities of working with Warden. I told myself he had done everything he could, but I could see how Nick would have doubts.

'I might never see him again,' I said quietly. 'It doesn't matter now.'

I couldn't tell Nick about the kiss. He would think I was off the cot. I wasn't even sure I could explain it to myself, let alone someone else.

'Thank you for sharing all this,' he said. 'We're lucky to have you back in one piece.'

'She's in one piece because of Jaxon,' Eliza said. 'You will come back to Seven Dials, won't you, Paige?'

'I quit,' I reminded her.

'Jax will take you back.'

'I called him a stretched weasel and told him to get fucked. You don't come back from that, Eliza.'

'You've cracked your gift, like he always wanted. He'll forgive you,' Eliza said, her tone beseeching. 'Please. Seven Dials is the safest place for all of us.'

'He abuses us,' I bit out, startling her. 'Yes, he might forgive me, but I'll only be in his good books for so long. What happens when I start to lose my shine again?'

'You're being so ungrateful.'

'You didn't hear the way he spoke to me in Oxford.'

'He was *stressed*, Paige. Do you realise how close you all came to dying?'

'Jax wanted me to leave the other prisoners to die.'

'To protect us. To give *you* a better chance.'

'Are you saying I should have done it, Eliza?'

'We're criminals. We protect our own,' Eliza said, her voice strained. 'Since when did you care this much about morals?'

'Since I had to choose a side.'

'This isn't helping.' Nick looked at me. 'We need to get you out of London. There are too many cameras and Vigiles. If Scion arrests you again—'

'I'm not leaving. Where would I go?'

'We could get you back to Ireland.'

'I can't *do* anything from Ireland, Nick. I haven't lived there since I was eight. Everyone I knew could be dead,' I said curtly. 'We need a solid plan.'

Eliza blinked. 'What do you mean?'

Nick gave her a puzzled look. 'Eliza, something has to be done about the Rephaim. We can't just let them carry on with the Bone Seasons.'

'Paige is safe now. It's over,' Eliza said. 'Can't we just get back to work?'

I stared at her. 'What?'

'You said Sheol II was in France. If we keep our heads down, we'll never—'

'Eliza, you don't seem to understand what I'm telling you. Scion exists because of the Rephs. Nashira was after Jaxon, and now she's going to be after me,' I said, feeling my temper start to fray. 'We have to bring the syndicate together, before they introduce Senshield.'

'To do what?'

'Fight back.'

Eliza sighed. 'Paige, come on. The Unnatural Assembly would never agree to it.'

'I'll ask for an audience with Hector.'

'And you think he'll believe you?'

'Well, you believe me, don't you?' When her expression changed, I stood. 'Don't you?'

'I didn't see it,' she said weakly. 'You said you were fluxed a lot, and it just sounds—'

'Eliza, stop it,' Nick cut in. 'I was there, too.'

'I have not been hallucinating for six months,' I hissed.

'I'm not saying that, Paige, I just—' Eliza rubbed her eyes. 'I'm sure you really were imprisoned in Oxford. But maybe something awful happened to you there, something that you had to block out, and you told yourself this story to make it easier. I've heard that can happen.'

'Get out, Eliza.'

She flinched.

In all my time in the gang, Eliza and I had never come to blows. She was my friend – perhaps the closest person I would ever have to a sister.

For a long time, nobody spoke. Eliza picked up her scarf, looking shaken.

'I'll tell Jax you'll come back soon,' she said. 'I hope I'll be telling him the truth. You won't last long without a gang, Paige, and you know it.'

She closed the door behind her. I waited until her footsteps had receded before I let loose.

'I can't believe this,' I snapped. 'What the hell does she think is going to happen to the syndicate when they put Senshield on the streets?'

'She's in denial.' Nick heaved a sigh. 'Eliza has never known anything but the underworld. She was dumped on the street. When she got in touch with Jaxon, he recognised her talent. He gave her expensive paints, a safe place to sleep, muses beyond her wildest imagination. The day she turned up at the den, she was so overwhelmed she broke down in tears. All she wants is to keep us together.'

'If she was captured tomorrow, Jaxon would replace her in a day. He doesn't care about us. Just our gifts.' I stopped for breath. 'Nick, I know this is terrifying. But we can't do nothing.'

Nick seemed to think.

'The Rephs know the syndicate is a threat,' I said. 'It's a monster they inadvertently created, one they can't control. We have hundreds or thousands of voyants. If we could organise and fight, instead of fleecing and killing each other, we might stand a chance against Scion.'

'Paige, it's a criminal organisation. Most thieves don't want to save the world.'

'The world as we know it will not exist if Nashira gets her way. She won't stop until Scion is everywhere. I have to speak to the Unnatural Assembly.'

'How? Hector hasn't called a meeting in—' He paused. 'Hector has never called a meeting.'

'I can ask for one.'

'Can you?'

'Any mime-queen, mime-lord or mollisher is entitled to send a summons to the Underlord. He's duty-bound to call the Assembly,' I said. 'If I write one, could you deliver it to the Spiritus Club?'

'Why the Spiritus Club?'

'Hector's dead drop will be full. The Club can send a courier to deliver it in person.'

'Jaxon will be furious if he finds out.'

'I don't answer to Jaxon now.'

'Your power depends on your place as his mollisher,' Nick pointed out. 'Eliza *is* right, Paige. You need a gang, or the syndicate will shut you out.'

'I have to do this.'

'No. You've been through a difficult experience, and you're in a vulnerable position. If you send this summons, Hector will laugh in your face.'

'I'm not afraid of Hector, now I know there's worse than him out there.'

'Even if he believes you, this won't happen overnight. You're up against decades of tradition and corruption. If you put your head above the parapet—'

'I might lose it. I know.' I folded my arms. 'The Rephs need to feed, and they just lost most of their voyants. Sooner or later, they'll come for us. I don't know if we can beat them, but I can't lie down and let Scion decide how my life will look. I can't do it, Nick.'

There was a brief silence.

'No,' my best friend said at last. 'I don't think I can do it, either.'

3

THEN THERE WERE FIVE

The next day was the same. And the next. Sleeping from daybreak until dusk. Waking after it was dark, when I couldn't go out.

There was no word from the Unnatural Assembly in response to my summons. I would give it a week before I sent another. The Spiritus Club was fast, but Hector might not look at the note for days.

I could do nothing but wait. Without knowing what was happening in the Archon, I couldn't make much of a plan. For now, the board belonged to Nashira.

On my seventh day in the dosshouse, I ran a low fever. As I tried to sleep it off, I saw the chapel where Seb died. The twisted slum of the Rookery. Duckett's house of mirrors, where my face grew monstrous and misshapen and my jaw snapped off, brittle as old ceramic.

Find Rackham, a bleeding man whispered. *He is the one who hunts. Find him.*

Then Liss, dead in the Guildhall, seven cards scattered around her. I reached for them, straining to see the last one – the outcome, my ending – but as soon as I touched it, it screamed in a tongue of fire. I jerked awake at dusk, my cheeks damp and burning hot. My lips tasted of salt.

I sat in the dark for a long time, tears seeping down my face, arms wrapped around my knees. Outside, a car sounded its horn, making my heart beat faster.

Liss had almost made it. After a decade of imprisonment, losing hope with every year, she had been ready to reclaim the life Scion had stolen from her.

The reading she had done for me still played on my mind: Five of Cups, King of Wands inverted, the Devil, the Lovers, Death inverted, Eight of Swords. She had never reached the seventh card, the end of the reading.

Whatever happened next, I would not let Gomeisa Sargas forget what he had done. Liss had mattered; so had the other humans who hadn't reached the train. No matter how long it took, I would make sure they were avenged.

After ten days, I assessed my injuries. My bruises from the escape had ripened to a dark purple, while most of the small cuts were healing. After checking the news – still nothing of interest – I slowly ate the buttered toast and poached eggs Lem had brought me.

My mind drifted back to my last meal in Magdalen. I was sitting by the fire again, listening to the gramophone while Warden wrote in his journal.

He risked your life repeatedly. My stomach tightened. *Does that sound like an ally, Paige?*

I could dwell on Warden later, when my life was back under some degree of control. For now, I sipped my coffee, willing it to keep me awake.

When I had finished the cup, I lay on the couch. Even though it helped with healing, I had avoided withdrawing into my dream-scape, afraid to see the damage Nashira had caused – but if I was going to fight the Rephs, I couldn't let my gift get rusty.

When I finally immersed myself, I was standing at the edge of my sunlit zone. In the distance, lightning flickered. There were faint cracks in the sky over my poppies. That must be where the barrier was damaged.

Only time would strengthen it. Until then, I would have to be careful in spirit combat.

I knelt beside a poppy. At the touch of my hand, it changed, its petals reforming. A deeper red, a smaller bloom – the windflower, which harmed the Rephs. They broke across my dreamscape like a wave.

The flower that grew from the blood of Adonis, blossoming in the soil of my mind.

I didn't try to dreamwalk. Even with the amaranth Warden had given me, my barrier looked shaky. It would be a while before I could enter the æther.

Still, I hadn't escaped Oxford to do nothing. I was going to bring Nashira Sargas down, no matter how long it took.

By now, she must know some of us had escaped. She would be plotting her next move.

I thought about my options. There was a good chance that Hector would ignore my summons. That meant I would have to strike out on my own.

There were two serious problems: money and respect. More specifically, my lack of them.

If I left the Seven Seals, I would need a steady income, beyond thieving. Assuming Nick was up for it, he and I could try starting our own gang. If we pooled our savings – his money from Scion, mine from Jaxon – we might have enough to secure a den in one of the outlying cohorts, if nothing else. Then we could start looking for allies.

I gazed out of the window. The only thing money couldn't buy was respect. I wasn't a mime-queen. Without Jaxon, I wasn't even a mollisher.

There were rules. If Nick and I were to form our own gang, we would have to seek permission from the mime-lord or mime-queen in our chosen section, and the Underlord would have to approve. If we did it anyway, we would have our throats cut, as would anyone we had been foolish and selfish enough to employ.

Perhaps it would be easier to join another gang. Given the rarity of my gift, I had been approached with offers of work before, as had Eliza – but I'd always turned them down, fearing what Jaxon would do if he found out. Most mime-lords and mime-queens would consider it a betrayal worthy of expulsion, if not a death sentence.

Ognena Maria often joked that I should be working for her, since my legal residence was in her influential and wealthy section. Perhaps I could persuade her to let me join her gang, the Firebirds.

Except that Jaxon wouldn't take that lying down. In fact, anyone who employed me openly would make a lifelong enemy of him.

If I stuck to my guns, he would ensure I was locked out of the underworld and shunned by other voyants. When Frank Weaver put a bounty on my head, which he would, those voyants would be falling over themselves to sell me out to Scion.

There was another option. Frustrated, I turned away from the window.

I had seen things in Jaxon I couldn't unsee. I had spent three years craving his approval, forgetting I was anything but his creature, the Pale Dreamer. In Oxford, I had started to discover who I was without him.

To him, you are nothing more than quick flesh grafted to a ghost; a priceless gift in human wrapping.

Warden was right. Just from glimpsing a few of my memories, he had known.

Yet Jaxon might be my only hope of having a voice in the syndicate. The easiest choice *was* to swallow my pride and move back to Seven Dials.

I thought of all the cruel barbs, the manipulation. Having to crawl back with my tail between my legs, after finally standing up to him, would be a humiliating defeat. But if there was one thing worse than having Jaxon as an employer, it could be having him as an enemy.

Before I gave Jaxon any more thought, I meant to get a few things done. Ivy had said she knew someone at Camden Market. If she had survived, that was where she would be.

Nick had bought me some new clothes. I belted on a black woollen coat, turned up the collar, and bundled my hair into a peaked hat. I pulled on a pair of gloves, hiding the scar on my left palm. Finally, I wound a scarf around my neck, so I could shroud part of my face.

In Oxford, Warden had given me a strange pendant, which could deflect poltergeists. I fastened the chain around my neck and held the wings between my fingers. The metalwork was like filigree, complex and delicate. It would protect me while my dreamscape was healing.

Once, I had loved throwing myself into the labyrinth of London. Even at night, I had sometimes risked it. It was easy enough to walk unnoticed: avoid the cameras, keep a safe distance from sighted Vigiles, don't stop moving. Head down, eyes open, as Nick had always taught me.

Now Scion knew I was voyant. Even if I wasn't yet a known fugitive, there would be people looking for me.

Camden Town was a good forty minutes' walk. If I left now, I could get there and back again before dusk.

I almost lost my nerve. But then I looked at the couch and the bed, where I had been paralysed with terror, waiting for Scion to break down the door. If I didn't go out now, I might never go out again.

Lem caught me in the corridor. 'Leaving, are you?'

'I need some fresh air.'

'What about the Vigile that beat you?'

'He won't be on duty yet,' I said. 'He was voyant.'

'I don't know how they can do it.' Lem shook his head. 'Be careful, won't you?'

'I will.'

Nick was definitely paying him a sweetener.

I went down the creaking stairs. When I opened the front door, cold wind clawed at my face. For a minute, I just stayed there, staring at Soho Square.

The first tremor hit me. I gripped the doorframe. The dosshouse was safe. I shouldn't leave it.

But the streets were my life. I had fought tooth and nail to get back to this citadel. I knew the location of every security camera in this section. I would be fine. I closed the door behind me and walked, taking each step as though it were my last.

As soon as my boots hit the pavement, I looked over my shoulder, reaching for the æther. A couple of mediums stood beside a phone booth, talking in low voices, one wearing dark glasses. Neither of them looked at me.

My fingers worked under my cap, tucking every strand of blonde away.

People brushed past, talking and laughing.

I stepped on to Tottenham Court Road, where engines roared. White cabs, white buses, white velotaxis, white pedicabs with patent black seats. Skyscrapers loomed above me, many draped in Scion banners. Below it, huge screens were stacked on top of the local Underground station, showing off an electronic spectrum of advertising and propaganda. Brekkabox and Floxy held the top spots, while smaller screens showed off the latest data-pad programmes, like KillKlock, which notified the user of upcoming executions.

One monitor scrolled through a series of messages from Scion: BEWARE OF CIVIL INATTENTION. NIGHT VIGILES WILL BE ON DUTY AT 18:00. ALERT THE GUILD OF VIGILANCE IF YOU SUSPECT UNNATURAL BEHAVIOUR. PLEASE STAND BY FOR PUBLIC SECURITY ANNOUNCEMENTS.

I knew these streets like the back of my hand. For the first time in years, they unnerved me. Everything was too bright, too loud, too fast. The clamour was incredible: snatches of music, engines and motors, talking and shouting, voices from the screens, the rattle of rickshaws.

In three hours, the streetlamps would glow blue. Glym jacks would come to stand beneath them, holding their green lanterns, offering protection from unnaturals. By then, I had to be safely indoors.

I had planned to use the backstreets to get to Camden Town, but it would slow me down. Instead, I hailed a rickshaw. They were safer and cheaper than the Scion-approved white taxis and pedicabs.

When a rickshaw stopped, I clambered in, keeping my head down. The roofed cab behind the driver would be perfect for avoiding cameras.

'Camden Market, please,' I said, using my best English accent.

The driver pedalled up Tottenham Court Road. My blood rushed in my veins. Here I was, riding through the heart of London, bold as brass, and no one seemed to notice.

I couldn't allow myself to get cocky. One misstep, and every death in Oxford would have been for nothing.

As the rickshaw neared Camden, I cooked up my cover story. On the whole, voyants stuck to their own turf. There were places in London I couldn't go, where Jaxon had enemies – Whitechapel, for example – but as a mollisher, I would usually be received with courtesy.

Soon enough, I was paying the driver and stepping into Camden Market. Built into old stables on the Inquisitors' Canal, it was a hotbed of illicit activity, thronged with voyants. Here, costermongers sold numa and aster hidden inside hollow fruit. Hawkers came past on their boats every day, bringing merchandise and food from other citadels. It was also home to an underground cinema, the Fleapit.

The sky had cleared, covering the market in sunlight. With my face tilted down, I walked past tattoo parlours, art galleries, shops of all kinds. Open-air stalls jostled for space, mostly selling clothes and trinkets. It had been over a year since my syndicate work had last brought me here.

The Rag Dolls were the dominant gang in this section. They were one of the few to have invented their own distinctive uniform, favouring pinstriped blazers and skull brooches. Only a handful of people had ever laid eyes on their mime-lord, the elusive Rag and Bone Man.

Ivy had said her friend worked at a place called Camden Lockets. As I crossed the footbridge over the canal, a man with a lemon-yellow ponytail caught my eye, smoking on the towpath. In this district, voyants often dyed their hair or painted their nails to match their auras.

When I approached, he clocked me at once. I went to stand beside him.

'You busy?'

He looked me over, assessing my aura. Even his eyes were yellow, changed with contact lenses. It gave me an unpleasant reminder of the Rephs.

'Depends,' he said. 'Who are you?'

'The Pale Dreamer.'

The corner of his mouth twitched.

'Yeah,' he said. 'I'm busy.'

Eyebrows raised, I stood my ground. His face was carefully blank. Most voyants would have jumped to attention at the sound of my alias.

'You've some grievance with the White Binder,' I said. When he ignored me, I stepped closer. 'I'm busy, too, sensor. Are you planning to waste my time?'

'You're not a mollisher any more,' he said, shooting me a dirty look. 'Word is that you and Binder have fallen out. He's sacked you.'

A sickening cold went right through my body.

Jaxon really had made good on his word.

'I'm afraid you've been misinformed.' I tried to sound unmoved. 'Binder and I don't disagree.'

'You would say that, wouldn't you?'

My heart was hammering. I would usually have used my gift to put some pressure on him, but the cracks in my dreamscape were too wide.

'I've been away for a while,' I said, keeping calm. 'If the White Binder had cut me loose, he'd have chosen another mollisher. Has he?'

His eyes narrowed a little, assessing me.

'Get on with it, then,' he said. 'The Rag Dolls don't have no issues with your lot, but you're on thin ice, Pale Dreamer. I want you gone by sundown.'

'I'll overlook your tone if you can point me in the right direction,' I said. 'I'm looking for Camden Lockets. It's run by a voyant called Agatha Lamb.'

'Stables Market.' He folded his tattooed arms. 'Anything else?'

'Not right now. Thanks,' I said. 'The White Binder will know how helpful you've been.'

He grunted. I ducked under a brick archway and forged back into the market.

Jaxon was already destabilising my position in the syndicate, trying to force me back to him. I should have known he wouldn't wait long.

If the White Binder had made an explicit announcement that I wasn't his mollisher, no amount of threats would have budged that sensor. Instead, Jaxon had chosen rumours, meant to poison my reputation. This was a warning shot. He was reminding me to return to Seven Dials.

The Stables Market was a short way north. I passed two narrowboats on the green water of Camden Lock, each crewed by a costermonger.

'Hot pies, toss or buy,' one cried.

'A tenner apiece for an apple and white!'

'Roasted chestnuts, three pound for a cone!'

My ears pricked at that one. I shouldn't risk stopping, but it had been a while since I'd last indulged in my favourite delicacy.

The boat was a deep red, trimmed with plum and swirls of gold. It must have been beautiful once, but now the paint was peeling and faded. The chestnuts roasted on a stove. When I approached, the costermonger smiled down at me with crooked teeth.

'A cone for you?'

'Please,' I said.

She filled a paper cone with chestnuts and smothered them with butter and coarse salt. I passed her the right coin and moved on quickly.

I picked at my chestnuts as I walked, soaking up the comforting and familiar sounds of humans going about their business. There had been none of this lively chatter in Oxford, where most of the prisoners had made themselves quiet and small, hoping to avoid the Rephs.

Camden Lockets was a tiny shop on the edge of the Stables Market. The windows glistened with fake gemstones.

A bell tinkled above the door. A bony woman sat inside, wrapped in a lace shawl. I guessed she was in her seventies. To match her aura, she had gone fluorescent green in the extreme – green nails, green eyebrows, green lipstick, green hair in a razor cut. A speaking medium.

'What can I do for you, love?'

'I'm looking for Agatha Lamb,' I said.

'You've found her.'

To an amaurotic, she might have sounded like a chain smoker, but I could tell that rasp was from a throat ill-treated by spirits. I closed the door.

'We have a mutual friend. Her name is Ivy,' I said. 'I don't suppose she's visited?'

She regarded me. I waited, on edge.

'You must be the Pale Dreamer,' she croaked. 'They've been expecting you.'

As soon as she said it, I released my breath. I wasn't the only survivor.

Agatha led me towards a curio cabinet. When she moved one of the vases inside, it opened like a door. She led me down a rickety staircase.

'I used to store aster down here,' she said. 'Needed a false door in case the Vigiles came raiding.'

She had a scratchy cough, as if there were barbs in her windpipe. Some speaking mediums cut out their tongues to keep spirits from using them.

I followed her into a cellar, where a few lamps flickered. The walls were crammed with shelves of penny dreadfuls and dusty ornaments. Two mattresses vied for the remaining space, covered by patchwork quilts.

Ivy slept on a pile of cushions, skin and bones in a button-down shirt. Three more voyants shared the second mattress: Nell, Jos and Felix.

'Paige,' Jos said happily. He wore baggy dungarees over a jersey. 'Ivy said you'd come.'

'Hush, now. Don't wake her.' Agatha stroked her head. 'She needs her rest.'

Jos came straight over to me. I wrapped him into a hug.

'I'm so glad to see you all,' I said. 'Nell, you were shot. How are you?'

'Just a graze. I could still run,' Nell said. 'I expected more from the Guard Extraordinary. More like the Guard Mediocre, really.'

Felix gave me an awkward wave. Julian had persuaded him to deliver messages for the rebellion, but I had rarely seen him. He was tall and thin, with a shock of black hair and a smattering of freckles.

'We got a cab from the docks,' Nell said. 'There were two others with us, but they're both—'

'Dead.' Agatha held a cloth to her mouth and hacked from her throat. 'One had too many wounds. Found the other one in the canal.'

'Nate was one of the amaurotics,' Nell said quietly. 'Maya was a performer.' She shook her head. 'I don't understand. She seemed … fine.'

It took me a moment to digest the news.

'Just so I understand,' I said. 'Maya … went into the canal herself?'

'Must have,' Agatha said. 'Not to worry. I had one of the boats take her away.'

Jos sat back down. 'I liked Maya.'

'We all did.' Nell drew him close. 'You haven't found anyone else, Paige?'

'No. I'm not sure where to look.'

'Where are you based?'

'It's best you don't know. Are you all right here?'

'They're fine,' Agatha said. 'Don't you worry, Pale Dreamer. I shan't let them out of my sight.'

Felix gave her a tentative smile. 'We'll be fine for now. Camden seems okay. Besides,' he said, 'anything's better than … where we were before.'

I knelt beside Ivy, who didn't stir. 'I was her kidsman for a few years,' Agatha said. She took off her lace shawl and draped it over Ivy. 'When she disappeared, I had all the little horrors out searching for her, but we couldn't find anything. I knew Scion must have nabbed her.'

I tried to govern my expression. Kidsmen picked up young orphans and trained them to steal and beg, often giving them cruel injuries to attract sympathy. In that state, we called them gutterlings.

'I'm sure you missed her terribly,' I said.

If she noticed my tone, she ignored it. 'Ah, she's like a daughter, this one.' She stood and rubbed the small of her back. 'I'll leave you to your business. I've got my own to run.'

The secret door clunked shut behind her. Even then, I could hear her coughing.

'We told her we escaped from the Steel,' Nell said. 'I don't think she believes it, but she hasn't questioned us.'

Agatha was right to be suspicious. Coldbath Fields – otherwise known as the Steel – was an amaurotic prison, used in the rare event that Scion couldn't pin a crime on unnaturals.

'Paige.'

Ivy had opened her eyes. Jos helped her into a sitting position, propping her up with cushions.

'Ivy,' I said. 'How are you feeling?'

'Not my best. You know, we should really send Thuban an invitation to my deathbed. I'm sure he'd love to see the fruits of his labour.'

Nobody smiled. The sight of her bruises shook me to the core.

'You did well to get everyone here,' I said. 'Agatha was your kidsman, then?'

'I trust her. She's not like other kidsmen,' she said. 'She took me in when I was starving.' She pulled the lace shawl around her shoulders. 'She'll hide us from the Rag and Bone Man. She's never liked him.'

'Why do you need to hide from him?'

'He's violent.'

'Aren't they all?'

'You don't want to get on the wrong side of Rags. If he finds out there are fugitives in his section, he'll turf us out, if we're lucky. More likely he'll just kill us.'

As she spoke, I glimpsed a missing tooth.

'Look, Paige,' Felix said, 'we ought to work out what to do. Nashira will send Scion after us soon, given what we know.'

'I've called a meeting of the Unnatural Assembly.' I folded my arms. 'I'm going to warn them about the Rephs.'

Nell let out a hollow laugh.

'You're off the cot,' Ivy said. There was a tremor in her voice. 'You think Hector would do anything about it? You think he would care?'

'I hear he doesn't even care about Senshield, and that's a threat he can actually see,' Nell said. 'Hector doesn't have a scruple to his name. Friend of mine tried to report a murder to his gang once, and they beat him senseless for bothering them. That was twelve years ago.'

'The amaurotics, then,' Felix pressed. 'We'll tell *them* what happened to us.'

Nell snorted. 'Sorry, remind me why the rotties would give a rat's ear?'

'You seriously don't think they'd be interested to know that the whole empire is being run by clairvoyant giants?'

'It's not a bad point,' I said. 'Scion has always taught its denizens to hate clairvoyance. I doubt they would warm to the Rephs, if they knew.'

'Anything we say would be dismissed as unnatural lies,' Nell said, a stubborn jut to her chin. 'We can't exactly sell our story to the *Descendant*.'

'Then we'll try the penny papers,' Felix insisted. 'You could show some optimism, Nell.'

'Oh, yes, the constant executions and propaganda make me *really* optimistic. We have no proof but our word, and our word counts for absolutely nothing in Scion. So there goes that brilliant plan.'

You could tell they had been stuck in a small room for a while.

'There is some proof,' I said. 'There's the tunnel under London, for one thing. My friend knows an unguarded entrance. We could show Hector.'

'Exactly. Anyway, there are five of us,' Felix said, looking confident. 'Surely *some* of the Unnatural Assembly would hear us out.'

'You really don't know them,' Ivy said.

'We could show them a Reph,' Jos piped up. 'Warden will help us, won't he, Paige?'

I hesitated. 'Jos, I don't know if he made it out of Oxford.'

The golden cord had been silent. Then again, I still wasn't too good at using it.

'We shouldn't work with Rephs.' Ivy looked away. 'We all know what they're like.'

'But he helped Liss,' Jos said, frowning. 'He got her out of spirit shock. I saw it.'

'Give him a medal, then,' Nell said, 'but I'm not working with them again, either.'

I didn't try to argue. Nell had been imprisoned for at least a decade, while Ivy had known nothing but violence from her keeper, Thuban Sargas.

'I'm going to do my level best to gather evidence and allies,' I said. 'Nell, you're a summoner. The syndicate must have snatched you up.'

'I used to work for the Bully-Rook,' Nell confirmed. 'Is he still a mime-lord?'

'I haven't heard otherwise.'

'Well, don't bother trying to befriend him. If I told him about the Rephs, he'd throw me out to beg with cuts on my arms, seeing as I was such a good liar.'

'Right.' The Bully-Rook was as much of a brute as his name suggested. 'Felix?'

'I wasn't a syndie,' he admitted. 'I don't even know how you join.'

I sighed. 'Jos?'

'I was a gutterling. My kidsman won't help us,' Jos said. 'I don't want to go back to him.' He sat beside Ivy. 'Will we have to stay here, Paige?'

'For now. Is Agatha asking for money?'

'No, but she'll expect us to work for our keep,' Ivy said. 'We can't sponge off her.'

'You still need time to adjust. Nell, you've been away for years.'

'I'm just grateful she's putting us up.' Nell leaned against the wall. 'Getting back to work will do me good. I'd almost forgotten what it was like to be *paid* for doing a job,' she added. 'You said you would help us find somewhere in London. Would the White Binder employ us?'

Her limpid green eyes were sharp. She had sensed the discord between us.

'He might hire you, Nell.' Ivy smiled grimly. 'Not me.'

'I'm going to talk to him about it,' I said. 'Even if he can't, I'll be in touch.' Upstairs, the door opened. 'Keep Agatha in the dark. I want the truth to be heard for the first time at the Unnatural Assembly, or they'll think it's just a story that's spun out of control.'

'Paige, *don't* tell the Assembly.' Ivy sat up, arms shaking. 'You didn't say anything about fighting back or going public. You said you'd get us home. We need to either stay hidden or find a way to leave London.'

'I don't want to stay hidden,' Jos said. His voice was small, but firm. 'I want to make it right.'

Agatha returned just then, bearing a tray of food. 'Time to leave, Pale Dreamer,' she said to me. 'Ivy needs her rest.'

'If you say so.' I glanced at her four charges. 'Agatha, do you have a phone?'

'No, but I shall send a courier if we need you.'

'It's fine. I'll come back soon.'

I gave Ivy a final glance before I left. She lay back down and closed her eyes.

On my way up the creaking stairs, I swallowed the knot in my throat. Nate, the amaurotic, must have been hurt during the escape – Agatha couldn't have saved him – but Maya, who I hadn't known, played on my mind. Had she not seen a future beyond Oxford?

At least the other four were safe, with a place to sleep and other voyants to protect them. That was more than I could have hoped to gain from this excursion.

All the survivors were eyewitnesses. If I could persuade them to testify before the Unnatural Assembly, it might force Hector to listen.

By the time I left Camden Lockets, the sky had clouded over. I bought a cheap umbrella – a cunning way to elude the cameras – before I returned to the canal, tempted by the wealth of street food. Shiny buttered peas, steaming in paper ramekins; masses of fluffy mashed potato; sausages spitting in cast-iron pans. When I passed a tray of drinking chocolate, I couldn't resist. It was silky sweet, and it tasted like winter. Everything I ate and drank was another way to spite Nashira.

It soon sat oddly on my stomach. Liss would have given anything for a sip of this.

A shoulder knocked against mine, sending the rest of the cup flying.

'Hook it.'

The voice was deep and gruff, belonging to a burly medium. I almost retorted, but the sight of his blazer, brass knuckles and skull brooch stopped me dead. This time, I had run into one of the Rag Dolls.

'I don't recognise you,' he said. 'What's your business here, oracle?'

'Just browsing,' I said. 'I'll be out of your hair.'

'Good. Watch your back.'

That had been too close a shave. I left before he could decide to pick a fight.

Thanks to the rickshaw, I had plenty of time to get back to Soho. I headed out of Camden Market and hailed another ride on Oval Road. As soon as I was in the cab, exhaustion came down on me like a wall.

The voyant driver took me back on to Tottenham Court Road. I had asked to be dropped off near Seven Dials, in case she recognised me. I needed to maintain the façade that Jaxon and I were perfect friends.

I closed my eyes for a while. When I opened them, the rickshaw had stopped, but not in Seven Dials. Instead, I was in an alleyway with clean white walls.

'This isn't where I asked to go,' I said.

'Get out,' the driver said.

Slowly, I did as she said, wishing I had brought a weapon. As I looked around, I started to recognise my surroundings. This was Cravens Passage, which cut through a wealthy residential district in Westminster.

I had to get out of here.

The damage to my dreamscape had made it hard to use my gift – even in its passive form, sensing the æther at a distance. I didn't sense them coming until I was surrounded. The rickshaw left without a sound.

'Well,' an oily voice said. 'Look who returned from the dead, just as the White Binder always claimed she could.'

My stomach plummeted into my boots. Tragically, I knew that voice.

That was the voice of Haymarket Hector.

4

GRUB STREET

The Underlord was not someone I had seen very often. Each time had been a painful or nerve-racking experience. The last time had been shortly before I killed two Underguards, changing the course of my life for ever. Before that, in February, our gangs had met for a friendly game of cards.

It hadn't stayed friendly for long.

Hector smiled at me, his eyes black and cold. As usual, he wore his bandolier of expensive blades. His gang – the Underbodies – clustered around me, forming a tight circle.

I should have known better than to get into a rickshaw with a voyant driver. She must have recognised me and tipped someone off. Three years in the underworld, and I could still make thoughtless mistakes.

Tensed in preparation, I looked at each of them in turn. The most notorious was the Undertaker, a powerful binder, recognisable by his top hat. His right arm had been hewn with so many names, it was little more than a sleeve of scar tissue. He was pinched and deathly pale, with grey eyes.

Beside him was the muscle of the group, the Underhand, who I had always thought was tall until I saw Warden. I had been at the mercy of his iron grip before.

I was far too close to the Westminster Archon. Hector stepped towards me.

'Welcome back.' He gripped my chin. 'How wonderful to see you again.'

'I'd love to say the same for you,' I said. 'Mind getting your grimy fingers off me?'

'Your time away hasn't changed you. Jaxon was looking everywhere.' His long nails bit into my skin. 'Did you run away from him?'

'None of your business.'

'Everything that happens in this citadel is my business.' A thin smile. 'I understand the two of you have quarrelled.'

'That's news to me.'

'Then why is he allowing you to make such foolhardy decisions?'

'We were just on our way to have a word with him.' Magtooth grinned at me, showing teeth inked to resemble the tarot. 'But then a little bird told us that *you* were back in London. I did miss our games, Pale Dreamer.'

He was a dab hand at tarot games, Magtooth. The best cartomancer I had ever played. The only way to beat him was to cheat him, and I surely had.

'I'd hate to deprive you of my company for too long,' I said. 'To what would the White Binder have owed the pleasure of yours, Hector?'

'I wanted to ask my old friend a question,' Hector said. 'I wanted to know why his wayward mollisher has taken it upon herself to demand a meeting of the Unnatural Assembly. Do you deny it?'

'It's my right to call meetings. Why would I deny it?'

'You sent a courier.'

'You never check your dead drop.'

'Of course not. Imagine if I were to address *all* the petty complaints that land in my lap, Pale Dreamer,' Hector said. 'I would never be doing anything but listening to my voyants' woes.'

'Their woes might be important. Isn't it your job to take an interest?'

'Look at her, telling us how to do our jobs.' Magtooth laughed. 'She thinks we're her lapdogs, boss.'

'Yes, Magtooth, it seems she does. How presumptuous of her.' Leaning close, Hector whispered to me: 'The courier paid for your insolence. Now it's your turn. You are on my turf, and I have every right to punish you for trespassing.'

'Binder will never believe I came here of my own accord, and you know it.'

'I'm not convinced he'll care. I think you and Jaxon *have* fallen out, else your little summons would have come from both of you. And if Jaxon has cut you loose, what's to stop me doing what I like with you?'

The courier was probably dead. If I had any hope of getting out of this situation alive, I needed Hector to believe I still had Jaxon's protection.

'I have something to say to the Unnatural Assembly. I'd like Jaxon to hear it with the rest of you,' I said. 'That aside, Scion is about to crush us with Senshield. I want you to do something about it.'

'Senshield is a lie, concocted by Scion to frighten the weak.' He grasped my throat. 'That's why it works on you.'

In the past, I might have been shaking at this point. After six months in Oxford, however, I was almost immune to threats of violence.

'Don't act like a king, Hector,' I said. 'You know what Scion does to kings.'

As soon as I said it, the æther gave an ominous tremor. I stiffened as a poltergeist seeped from the wall and slunk up to the Undertaker.

'This is the London Monster,' Hector said. 'He walked these streets in the eighteenth century, splitting the skin of young ladies like you.'

That blot in the æther was enough to cover me in goosebumps. Then I remembered the pendant, and courage sparked inside me.

'I've seen worse,' I said. 'That thing's a cheap Ripper knock-off.'

Roundhead, another lackey, let out a ghastly snarl. Like Agatha, he was a speaking medium.

'Blast your eyes, you damned bitch,' he barked. The poltergeist was borrowing his vocal cords. 'I will murder you and drown you in your blood!'

The Undertaker crooked a long finger. Reluctantly, the poltergeist retreated. Roundhead choked out a handful of ugly curses before falling silent.

'Any other party tricks,' I said, 'or can I get back to my own section now?'

'I know a trick or two, Pale Dreamer.'

The words came from a woman in a fitted navy coat and polished boots. She was several inches taller than Hector and styled her copper hair in a French braid.

Her mouth was drawn into a permanent sneer, thanks to a thin scar that slashed upward from her lips to her cheek. It had appeared on her face about six months after I joined the syndicate.

'Let me show you.' She drew a curved knife from under her coat and touched its tip to the corner of my mouth. 'I think they'll make you smile.'

I held still. Cutmouth could only be a few years older than me, but she was already as cruel as Hector.

'A mollisher should have scars.' She traced the scab on my cheek. 'How did you get this one?'

'That's my concern,' I said.

'I understand. You probably tripped,' Cutmouth said. 'Nothing but a chair warmer. You and your gang make me want to spit.'

And she did. The others burst out laughing, save the Undertaker, who never made a sound.

'Now that's out of the way' – I wiped my face with my cuff – 'maybe you could tell me what you want.'

'To know where you've been for the last six months,' Cutmouth said, keeping her blade on my face. 'You disappeared. Where did you go?'

'Nowhere near your foul excuse for a den, if that's your issue.'

Cutmouth thumped me hard enough to knock the breath from me. Pain exploded from my old injuries, doubling me over like a snapped twig.

'I'll ask you again,' she said. 'Where have you been?'

'I'll tell the Unnatural Assembly,' I forced out. 'Just call a meeting.'

'The only thing we're calling for you is an ambulance.' She aimed a kick at my knee, bringing me to the ground. 'Look at you. You're no mollisher.'

'She's a charlatan,' said their wiry blond summoner. 'Thought she was supposed to be a dreamwalker?'

'Well said, Mr Slipfinger.' Cutmouth pressed her blade against my throat. 'We're honour-bound to get rid of charlatans, so you'd better open that trap of yours and talk. Where have you been, Dreamer?'

I clutched my ribs, teeth gritted. 'I will tell the Unnatural Assembly.'

She gave me such a smack across the face, my ears rang.

Hector stood by, looking at the pocket watch he always carried. There was no way I would win this fight – not with the injuries I was hiding.

I also didn't want Hector to know how much my gift had changed. As far as he knew, I was just a radar, good for nothing but counting dreamscapes. When he learned what I could do, I wanted it to come as a surprise.

'Oh, she won't talk. Give us your coin,' Slipfinger said to me. 'We'll buy something more fun.'

'And that pretty necklace.' His companion, a thickset woman, grabbed my collar. 'Is that silver?'

'It's plastic,' I said, grasping it.

'Liar. Give it.'

The metal tingled against my palm. It might deflect poltergeists, but I doubted it would protect me from this lot.

Warden had given me this pendant. It was my only real proof that he had existed. I refused to hand it over to a bunch of witless crooks.

'I'm on your turf.' I pulled away. 'You've a right to defend your own property, but stealing mine is a different matter. Binder won't be happy.'

Hector fixed me with the empty gaze of a predator considering a wounded deer.

'We'll let her keep her trinket, Slabnose,' he said. 'But we *will* take her coin.'

'I don't have any,' I said.

'Don't lie to me, Pale Dreamer, or I may have to ask Bloatface to search you.'

My gaze snapped to the man in question. He was bald, with greedy eyes and an absence of expression I had once found terrifying, before I had spent months among Rephs. Otherwise known as the Maggot, Bloatface was the one who did the really dirty work. If Hector wanted someone dead, this man was the one he sent. I dug into my pocket and threw my last few coins at Slipfinger.

'Consider that payment for your life,' Hector said. Slipfinger picked up the coins. 'Cutmouth, we've had our fun. Time to put the knife away.'

'She hasn't talked yet.' Cutmouth stared at him. 'You just want to let her go?'

'The White Binder is a bore. I am in no mood for his complaints.'

'He's given her the boot. She's lying to save her worthless hide.' When he turned away, she followed. 'You ordered her to tell us where she's been. You said—'

Hector turned on his heel and struck her. One of his rings caught her cheek, drawing blood.

'Are you questioning me, Chelsea?'

Hair had come loose from her braid, falling over one side of her face. She caught my eye, then looked away. 'I ask forgiveness, Underlord.'

'Granted.'

The Underbodies looked at each other, but Magtooth was the only one smiling. All of them, I noted, had small scars on their faces. With a last look at me, Hector took Cutmouth by the waist and guided her away. I couldn't see her expression now, but her shoulders were tense.

'Boss,' Magtooth called. 'Forgetting something?'

'Oh, yes.' Hector glanced back. 'You cheated us in February. This is for your insolence, Pale Dreamer. Bother me again, and you are bound for Flower and Dean Street.'

The Underhand parted the others. Before I could duck, his fist smashed into the side of my face, then into my stomach. Sparks flew from the centre of my vision. The ground lurched up to meet my palms. If he had been a smaller man, I would have at least tried to land a punch, but if I pissed him off, he might just kill me. I had fought too hard to live to let that happen. He gave me a few kicks for good measure, spat on me, and went like a dog after his mime-lord.

Pain leapt from the roots of my teeth. I wheezed and coughed.

Gutless bastards. Magtooth had been itching for a fight since that tarocchi match, although setting the Underhand on me hardly counted as a fight. It seemed so downright *stupid* now, to shed blood over a game.

Then again, Hector Grinslathe had made a game board of the whole underworld. He would cling to power until Senshield broke the syndicate, and then he would move on to another citadel, flush with coin.

I needed to get of sight, in case they really had called an ambulance. Pulling my scarf back up my face, I limped out of Cravens Passage.

Jaxon and I might not be talking, but I still felt safest on his turf. To get there, I needed to cross the Strand, one of the busiest thoroughfares in the area. I walked a short way up the street and waited at the lights, like a good denizen. As soon as I was on familiar ground, I slipped into Bull Inn Court, an alley that was usually deserted.

It killed me to do it, but I was going to have to warn Jaxon. I took the burner from my jacket and dialled the number, letting it ring four times.

I counted my breaths as I waited, pacing. Ten long minutes passed before my phone vibrated, and I held it to my ear.

'What do you want?'

His voice was cold and flat. In the main, he was all charm on the phone.

'Hector ambushed me. My rickshaw diverted to his turf,' I said, mirroring his stiff tone. 'I thought you should know.'

We had never been quite sure if Scion monitored our calls. As always, I kept to the point, trying not to use specifics.

'The rickshaw,' Jaxon said. 'Where did you hail it?'

'Camden.'

'I won't ask what the blazes you were doing there.' Pause. 'Are you hurt?'

'Not badly. I just wanted to warn you that they might be coming.'

'You must be near the den.' When I was silent, Jaxon said, 'This childish behaviour is beneath your dignity. I have already been forced to inform the nearest sections that you and I have had a disagreement.'

'I'm aware of that.'

'Then come back, and we'll talk this over.'

'I'm not ready,' I said. 'I don't know if I'll ever be ready.'

This time, the silence was much longer.

'Well,' Jaxon said, 'I await your *readiness*. In the meantime, perhaps I shall begin my search for another mollisher. Bell has shown great promise in your absence.'

The dialling tone pierced my ear.

Jaxon would never make Nadine his mollisher, but he could hold the possibility over both our heads. I called the other number in the phone.

'It's me,' I said. 'I need a favour.'

—————

Nick sent a bob cab to collect me. When it stopped at the entrance to Bull Inn Court, I climbed in, keeping my face as hidden as possible.

There would be no meeting of the Unnatural Assembly. Even trying had been foolish, but part of me had thought Hector might have a morsel of respect for syndicate law. Apparently even that was too much for him.

I would have to get word out some other way, but I couldn't go shouting about the Rephs on the street. In the unlikely event that I wasn't arrested on the spot, people would think I had lost my mind.

Perhaps this was why Frank Weaver hadn't bothered to make us fugitives. Our story was simply too hard to believe.

I couldn't fight the Rephs alone. They had the whole empire of Scion behind them. The sheer size of the enemy seemed insurmountable.

If I didn't have the syndicate, I had nothing.

It had started to rain by the time the rickshaw dropped me off at Grub Street. I raised my hood and walked beneath a stone archway lit by two iron arms holding lanterns.

Grub Street was home to many artists and intellectuals of the voyant underworld, who generally broke the law without violence. It was more of a district than a single street – a seam of sedition in the heart of I-5.

It was also right beside the Barbican Estate, where my father lived. He came here for coffee now and again, unaware of its secret other side.

I wished I could extend my perception far enough to see if his dreamscape was still there. Even if my own dreamscape hadn't been fragile, my body was in too much pain to let me concentrate on the æther.

Parlour music drifted from a printery. The architecture here was an eccentric mix of Georgian, mock Tudor and modern – all crooked foundations, cobblestones and leaning walls. Shops sold every treasure a wordsmith could desire: thick paper, moonbows of ink, bejewelled pens and old collectors' tomes – the sort with metal clasps, making them seem like doors to other worlds. Alongside the bookstalls, there were at least five or six coffeehouses and a solitary cookshop. Above those, bibliomancers and psychographers dwelled in musty garrets, with only their muses and novels for company.

Short alleys twisted off the main street, each leading to a small, enclosed court. I walked into one, heading for a ramshackle doss-house. A sign hung over the door, with letters spelling out THE GOLD CUSHION. As I got closer, I sensed Nick.

His worried face appeared at the garret window. I waited until he came to the front door.

'What happened?'

'Hector,' I said, by way of an explanation.

'You're lucky to be alive.' He kissed the top of my head. 'Quickly. Inside.'

'Did you already pay the driver?'

'Yes.'

I stepped into the dosshouse. Nick led me into a firelit parlour, lined with bookshelves, where a large man was smoking a pipe. He was perhaps sixty, of sallow complexion, wearing a corduroy suit and a turtleneck. A ducktail beard, shot with grey, started below his fleshy nose.

'Alfred.' Nick stopped. 'Is that you?'

The man started so violently, the chair let out a gunshot crack.

'Nicklas, my friend.' He had a genteel English accent. 'How are you?'

'Fine. I thought you lodged above the Potboiler,' Nick said. 'Why are you here?'

I smiled a little. He could never resist checking on people.

'Well, that's rather a tedious story. In short, Minty is looking for me.' The man heaved a sigh. 'And what are *you* doing in a doss-house, Red Vision?'

'I stay here now and then.'

'You live near Jaxon, don't you?'

'I can walk to work from here. It's convenient.' Nick took a key from his pocket. 'Why don't you get out of Grub Street for a few days, take a break?'

Alfred scoffed. 'No fear. Your mime-lord would throw a fit, for one thing. He likes me to be available at all hours. Not that he's in my good books, if you'll pardon a literary pun. Still owes me a blasted manuscript.'

'*On the Machinations of the Itinerant Dead*, I take it.'

'Yes. His deadline was five years ago.' He adjusted his pince-nez with a gnarled finger. 'And who's this you're sneaking into your room?'

'This is the Pale Dreamer.'

Alfred peered at me. 'Not *the* Pale Dreamer?'

'The very same.'

'My word.' Alfred chuckled. 'How do you do?'

'Alfred is a literary scout,' Nick told me. 'He's also the only agent in London who represents voyant writers to Grub Street. He discovered Jaxon.'

'I see,' I said. 'You helped him publish *On the Merits,* did you?'

'Indeed,' Alfred said. 'I've heard a great deal about you from your mime-lord, but he never deigned to introduce you.' His bushy eyebrows furrowed. 'You look as if you've been in the wars, dear heart.'

'Hector.'

'Ah, yes. Our Underlord is not the most peaceful of men. Why we voyants fight each other so passionately, yet do nothing to fight the Inquisitor, I shall never know.'

I studied his face. This man was partly responsible for the publication of *On the Merits of Unnaturalness,* the pamphlet that had turned voyant against voyant and created fault lines that still fractured the syndicate. The pamphlet that had forced us all into a hierarchy.

'It is strange,' I said.

Alfred looked curious. His downturned eyes were blue, underhung by pouches of skin.

'So, Nick. Tell an old man the latest Scion scandals.' He folded his hands on his stomach. 'What sort of devious new experiments are they performing?'

'Nothing too devious in my department. We do low-priority medical research,' Nick said. 'There's an overarching goal to understand the cause of clairvoyance, but it seems like an exercise in futility.'

'I'm astonished that they've never detected you.'

'It's easier than you'd think, but I'm on borrowed time.'

'Ah, yes, Senshield. You're not being forced to work on it, are you?'

'No, that's mostly left to SciORE.'

'And how is your Danica faring around that?'

I was almost certain Danica had never met this man. Jaxon must have told him about us, trusting him with our real names. The idea of Jaxon having a friend was fascinating.

'Dani mostly does Underground maintenance,' Nick said. 'She's heard Senshield can only detect certain types of clairvoyance in its current state, in any case.'

Danica only worked part-time for SciORE, but I was willing to bet that she had reported for her shift after the rescue. I still needed to think of a way to thank her for everything she had done to get me out.

'Still, a frightening prospect,' Alfred said. 'For myself, I prefer to avoid technology.'

'If only we all could.' Nick steered me towards the staircase. 'I should get Paige some painkillers. Good luck with Minty.'

'Not worry. *Fortune, seeing that she could not make fools wise, has made them lucky.*'

'Shakespeare?'

'Michel de Montaigne.' Alfred returned his attention to his book. 'Farewell, halfwit.'

'Goodnight, Alfred.'

The Gold Cushion was a gloomy place, more dilapidated than my dosshouse in Soho. We creaked up the stairs to the top floor, where the carpet was threadbare and the walls were the dull brown of an old bruise.

'Alfred and Jaxon go back a very long way.' Nick unlocked a door. 'He's remarkable – probably the most talented bibliomancer in the citadel. He claims he can read anything and just *sense* if it's going to sell.'

'Has he ever been wrong?'

'Not to my knowledge. That's why he's the only scout in the underworld. He put all the others out of work.'

'What does he do for Jaxon?'

'Pitches his pamphlets to the Spiritus Club, for one thing. He made a small fortune from *On the Merits.*'

I didn't comment.

Nick switched on the light. The room was a little cosier than the corridor, furnished with a mirror, a sink, and a plain double bed. A few essential items from his apartment were dotted around the place.

'I didn't know you stayed here,' I said.

'Sometimes I'm too tired to drive after work.' He put his keys down. 'Other times, I need to be away from Jax. Call it a holiday home.' He picked up a face cloth and went to the sink. 'Tell me what happened with Hector. Did he find you in the dosshouse?'

'No. I went to look for the others.'

'You shouldn't have done that, Paige.'

'I can't stay indoors for ever.'

'You've been through a traumatic experience. You need to give yourself time to recover.' He soaked the cloth in hot water and offered it to me. 'For your face.'

'Do I look a state?'

'I'm afraid so.' When I took it, he said, 'Did you find the survivors?'

I nodded. 'They were in Camden.'

'How many of them made it?'

'Four, including Nell.' I blotted my split lip. 'On the way back, I told the driver to take me to Soho, but she took me to Cravens Passage. Hector was waiting there with the Underbodies.'

'Why didn't you hop out of the rickshaw?'

'It sounds absurd, but I dozed off.'

'This is why you need to get your strength up.' Nick sighed. 'What did the Underbodies want?'

'To beat the stuffing out of me. For daring to send them a summons.'

Nick grimaced. 'No meeting, then?'

'Of course not.' I used the cloth to clean the rest of my face. 'I called Jax to tell him what happened. Is he going to make Nadine his mollisher?'

'Nadine pushed for it once we'd given up hope,' Nick said. 'They've been having private meetings, and he's let her do a lot of your work – collecting rent, auctions, that sort of thing. It will stop if you go back, but Nadine won't be happy about it.'

'He's always made it clear he thinks Nadine is the weakest link. He's told her so himself,' I said. 'Nick, is he toying with her?'

'I'm not sure. Either way, she's going to get hurt.' Nick paused. 'Do you really want to quit?'

'Yes.' I sank on to the bed. 'But I'm not sure I can.'

Nick sat beside me. When I rested my head on his shoulder, he wrapped an arm around me.

'Jaxon sent a few couriers to spread the word that you'd left the Seven Seals,' he said. 'It's not official. He's just seeding rumours, but—'

'They're spreading.' I looked up at him. 'I know Jax is your friend, but he manipulates us all. You saw how he was treating me last year; how he's treated Zeke and Nadine. You heard how he spoke to me in Oxford.'

'I did, and I was angry with him.' He breathed out. 'If you're going to leave, you'll need money. I'll support you for as long as you need, but Scion does check its employees' bank accounts – there's a risk I'll be questioned about my withdrawals. Say what you like about Jax, but he pays.'

'Yes, he pays me to bid on captive spirits and bully the people who don't pay their rent.'

'It's your job, Paige. It's how we've survived,' Nick said. 'What else can we do?'

'If not for the Rephs' creation of Scion, we'd have other choices. We wouldn't need to be criminals. If we can oust the anchor, we could live openly as voyants – but the only way we're going to do that is if we change the syndicate. Turn it into something that could fight an empire.'

Nick waited for me, always patient.

'It starts with Hector,' I said. 'If he was gone, we could do something.'

'Not quite. Both the Underlord and the mollisher supreme need to be gone before a scrimmage can be called,' he reminded me. 'If Hector died, Cutmouth would become Underqueen, and she's no better. Hector is only in his fifties. He won't be heading to the æther for a while.'

'Unless someone gets rid of them both.'

He drew back.

'You couldn't,' he said, his voice low. 'Even if you got away with it, the Unnatural Assembly still wouldn't fight. Hector is only part of the problem.'

'A big part.'

'I'll give you that.' He reached for a flask. 'Here. You look freezing.'

I sipped the hot coffee. He moved to the window seat and watched the rain freckle the panes.

'I've been having visions since we got back,' he said. 'It's probably nothing, but one of them—' He shook his head. 'It's so vivid.'

Nick had many visions. Most of the time, they seemed random and meaningless. He had a theory that the æther shed dust, like a body – tiny fragments of unrealised futures, which landed on him every so often.

Now and again, it would be something else. Something that did come to pass.

'It's all right,' I said. 'What did you see?'

'A waterboard.' His jaw worked. 'There's a wooden clock on the wall behind it, with flowers carved around the face. When midnight strikes, a tiny metal bird springs out and sings an old song from my childhood.'

'Have you seen a clock like that before?'

'Yes. It's called a cuckoo clock,' he said. 'My parents had one in Småland.'

'It still might not be for you. You didn't solicit the vision, did you?'

'No, but sooner or later, Scion will find out what I am. We like to think we're brave, but in the end, we're only human. People break bones trying to get off the waterboard.'

'Nick, stop it.'

'Sorry.' He pressed his brow to the window. 'Whatever happens next, I have to stay there, Paige. Now more than ever, we need people on the inside.'

I had always admired his courage. Jaxon hated the fact that his prized oracle worked for Scion, but Nick had always insisted that he would keep the day job, and he was happy to share his earnings when he could.

'You can still leave,' Nick said. 'Even if you don't go back to Ireland, there must be ways to reach the free world. In the end, Scion will give up.'

'You haven't met Nashira.' I glanced at the window. 'Only five people definitely survived the escape. Out of those people, I have the most sway in the syndicate. I have the best chance of changing things.'

'So we stay.'

'Yes. We stay and change the world.'

His face lifted in a tired smile, but it looked like hard work. I couldn't blame him. The prospect of going up against Scion wasn't exactly cheering.

'There's a good cookshop here,' he said. 'I'll get us supper. Don't answer the door.'

He shrugged on his coat and headed outside. I closed the heavy curtains.

In Oxford, the performers had been convinced to fight back after years of pain. With the right reasons, at the right moment, even the most beaten and broken of people could rise up and reclaim themselves.

The mime-queens and mime-lords of London were not broken. They had simply grown comfortable in the shadows. Somehow, they had to be persuaded that overthrowing Scion would give them better lives, *and* that it was possible – but while Hector lived, he would always silence me. He would always have more power. I went to the sink and washed my neck, as if I could get his finger-prints off.

Nick seemed to think Hector was untouchable, but when I looked at my puffy cheek, I wondered. He represented everything that had rotted the underworld: greed, violence, apathy. His syndicate hurt the very people it was meant to protect. He must have angered many voyants.

Quite a lot of murder went unpunished on the streets. Hector got rid of plenty of us. Had part of him not feared Jaxon, I had no doubt he would have bumped me off without a second thought.

But killing the leader of the syndicate was another matter. You could kill someone on your own level and get away with it, but you couldn't defy your superiors. It was our equivalent of treason.

Once I had dried my face, I lay on the bed and closed my eyes, drained to the marrow.

I knew what I was going to have to do.

Warden hadn't come for me. I had waited for him for almost two weeks, to no avail. He must have been killed or captured. I was on my own.

To turn the syndicate against Scion, I had to be close to the Unnatural Assembly – close enough to command a degree of respect, and to be privy to its workings. I needed to know that if I got them on their own, they would listen.

I needed to be a mollisher.

But underneath the Pale Dreamer, I would keep looking for a way to spur the syndicate to action, even if I had to convince each voyant individually that we had to fight. Unless Warden returned, giving me proof of the Rephs' existence, I would have to do it without a shred of evidence. For the first time in days, I reached for the golden cord.

You needed me to start this, I thought. *I need you to help me end it.*

No answer.

Just the same grave silence.

FUGITIVE

Nick let me sleep at the Gold Cushion. By the time I woke, he had left for work. I rubbed my eyes and squinted at the note he had left.

Don't leave Grub Street.

He would see me back to Soho. Stiff all over, I got up, wincing at the tension in my stomach where the Underhand had socked me. When I saw myself in the mirror, I pursed my lips. Once again, my face was a mess.

It was already midday. I ventured out to buy a coffee and a chocolate pastry, then returned to the dosshouse.

I dozed for most of the afternoon, my body protesting the latest round of bruises. When I woke again at five, I took a long shower, then dressed in my trousers and one of Nick's shirts.

My stomach was growling. As I set off to find something else to eat, I passed a voyant beggar, wrapped in filthy blankets.

He was an augur. Thanks to *On the Merits* devaluing their abilities, augurs and soothsayers were the ones who often ended up on the streets.

Liss and her parents had been like this man, locked out of the underworld. To save the syndicate, I was going to have to work inside it, but it would be a bitter pill to swallow.

Oxford had changed me. For years, I had been happy with my position in the syndicate, able to close my eyes to the suffering it caused others. I wasn't sure how long I could pretend to be that person again, but if I was going to keep the Pale Dreamer alive, she had to be convincing.

We all do what we must, Liss had said.

I held those words close. In the weeks to come, I was going to need them.

It was strange to be back in this part of the citadel. Before I had joined the Seven Seals, I had spent my weekends exploring the green spaces between the skyscrapers of south Islington. My father had rarely stopped me. So long as I kept my phone on, he had been content to let me wander.

When I reached the dead end of Grub Street, I spotted an arched door and stopped, wondering. The sign above that door read BOBBINS COFFEE.

My father was a man of habit. He often liked to have a coffee after work. More than once, he had asked me to meet him for supper at Bobbins. I had made my excuses, because Jaxon hated me seeing my father.

It was worth a try. I could never approach him publicly again, but I had to know that he was alive. After everything I had endured, everything I had learned about Scion, I wanted to see a face from before.

Bobbins was crowded, the air thick with the smell of coffee. Glances came in my direction – sighted glances, assessing my red aura – but nobody seemed to recognise me. The voyants of Grub Street considered themselves to be a cut above syndicate politics. I still chose a seat behind a screen, feeling as if I had been stripped.

When I was sure no one had identified me, I bought some cheap soup, careful to use an English accent and keep my head down. The soup was thick and hearty, made with barley and garden peas, poured into a hollowed loaf of bread. I ate it at my table, savouring each mouthful.

The jukebox played 'The Java Jive' when someone dropped a coin in it. Most people were reading: plays and chapbooks, deckled tomes. No data pads, of course. To blend in, I took a penny dreadful from the shared bookcase. Every building on this street was also a small library.

As I opened it, I cast a glance at a bibliomancer. Behind his newspaper, he was thumbing through a well-worn copy of *Love at First Sight; or, the Seer's Delight* by Anonymous.

At least, Didion Waite liked to *think* he was anonymous. We all knew who had written the dreary collection of poems, since he addressed them to his late spouse. Jaxon was waiting on tenterhooks for the day he tried to write erotica.

The thought made me smile until a bell clanged above the door, diverting my attention from the book. The new dreamscape was familiar.

An umbrella was hooked over his arm. He put it in the stand and stamped his loafers on the mat. Then he was walking past my table, waiting in line for a coffee.

He really had come.

In the last six months, his auburn hair had greyed at the temples. I saw no scars, but he seemed older and smaller, his clothes too big for him. Someone changed the song on the jukebox, and several voyants concealed their books, subtly enough that you could blink and miss it.

The waitron asked my father for his order.

'Black coffee,' he said, concealing his accent. 'And a water. Thank you.'

It took all my willpower to stay quiet.

My father sat at a table by the window. I stayed behind the screen, watching him through a crack. Now I could see the other side of him, I noticed a mark on his neck.

I had a matching flux scar on my back, from the night I was detained.

Another clang, and a stout amaurotic came into the coffeehouse. She caught sight of my father and went straight to join him.

I wasn't close enough to eavesdrop, nor to read their lips. When the woman shook her head, my father seemed to lose control. He dropped his forehead into his hand, and his shoulders slumped and shook. The woman placed both hands over his free one, which was balled into a fist.

'Are you okay?'

The waitron had appeared over my shoulder. She was drying a glass with a dishcloth.

'I'm fine,' I said.

'Don't worry about them.' She kept her voice low. 'The rotties have no idea.'

I nodded, and she left.

My father and the woman spoke for a quarter of an hour. She was about his age, with brown skin and greying black hair. I couldn't put my finger on where I had seen her before.

At six, I watched them leave together. Fighting down a thickness in my throat, I forced myself to remain at my table, rather than run after my father like a frightened child. I couldn't put him in any more danger.

He was alive. That was all that mattered.

'Penny for your thoughts, Pale Dreamer?'

The voice startled me. I found myself looking at a concerned face with heavy jowls.

'Alfred,' I said, surprised.

'Yes, that tragic fool.' Alfred examined me. 'You look rather glum this evening. In my experience, that means you haven't had quite enough coffee.'

'I haven't even had one.'

'You are clearly not a member of the literati.'

'Evening, Alfred.' The waitron raised a hand, as did some of the patrons. 'Haven't seen you in a while.'

'Hello, hello.' Alfred raised his hat, smiling. 'Yes, I'm afraid the anchor has been nipping at my heels. Had to pretend I had a real job, the muses forbid.'

A round of good-natured laughter went up before the voyants went back to their drinks. Alfred placed a hand on the chair opposite mine.

'May I?'

'Of course,' I said.

'You're very kind. It can be quite unbearable to be surrounded by writers every day. Ghastly lot.' He sat down. 'Now, what can I get you? Café au lait? Noisette, glacé, gourmand?'

'Just a saloop, please.'

'Oh, dear.' He placed his hat on the table. 'Well, if you insist. Waitron, bring forth the beans of enlightenment!'

It was easy to see why he and Jaxon got on so well. They were both off the cot. The waitron almost ran to fetch the beans of enlightenment, leaving me to face the music.

'I hear you work at the Spiritus Club,' I said.

'I have a modest office in their building, but they don't employ me. I show them pieces of paper, and occasionally, they pay for them.'

'Seditious pieces of paper, I hear.'

Alfred chuckled. 'Yes, sedition is my field of expertise. Your mime-lord is a fellow connoisseur. *On the Merits of Unnaturalness* remains the one true masterpiece of voyant literature.'

Debatable. 'How did you find him?'

'He sent me a draft of the pamphlet when he was about your age. A prodigy if ever I saw one, but possessive. Still goes into fits of rage whenever I take on a new client.' Alfred shook his head. 'He's a brilliant wordsmith – fiercely imaginative. I wonder why he gets himself so worked up about these things.' The waitron delivered a tray. 'I knew there were risks in publishing such a pamphlet, of course, but I've always been a gambler.'

'You're a soothsayer,' I said. '*On the Merits* ranked your order lowest. Did you not mind?'

'Oh, poppycock. Jaxon never said any such thing. The hierarchy was based on the *rarity* of each order, not objective worth,' Alfred said. 'That misconception twisted his point about soothsayers' weakness – that is, our reliance on numa. A reasonable opinion, in my view.'

'The Spiritus Club still withdrew the pamphlet.'

'A gesture of goodwill. Far too late by then, of course. *On the Merits* had already been pirated by every halfwit with a printer from here to Harrow. It's back in print now, as you know, and sells briskly to this day.'

I nodded. 'Jax is working on the next edition.'

'Don't remind me. I told him to stop tinkering with it, but he never learns.'

'You want him to write something new.'

'We need his voice. Literature is our most powerful tool, one Scion has never mastered.' He nodded to a bibliomancer at a nearby table. 'Behold, its living power in our midst. Isn't it wonderful, how words and paper can enthral us so? We are witnessing a miracle, dear heart.'

The bibliomancer was reading a penny dreadful, *Tea from a Tasser*. Her gaze followed the printed words, ignoring everything outside them.

She was lost in a story that would seem insane if you heard it on the street. In her mind, in this moment, that story was utterly real.

'Of course, we must be careful what we publish, even in the shadows.' Alfred sipped his coffee thoughtfully. '*On the Merits* taught me that. A single word or sentence can set a fire that roars out of control.'

I stirred rosewater into my saloop.

'If you could go back in time,' I said, 'would you do it again, Alfred?'

'I would. As I said, *On the Merits* is a cornerstone of our hidden society,' Alfred said. 'That aside, nothing has ever been so successful. Not to sound callous, Paige, but I could use the coin. Even though the Spiritus Club continued to publish the pamphlet, they docked the price considerably. Now the poor scout lives in squalor in his rented garret.'

'You must take a cut from your other clients.'

'True. Every pamphlet and chapbook in this underworld is one of mine – apart from Mr Waite's romances, which are no loss to me, or indeed, to literature.'

I smiled. 'Who represents Didion?'

'Why, he represents himself, of course. Who else would be so foolish?'

All at once, the screen above the counter turned white, then showed an anchor. Every head came up as the anthem of Scion filled the coffeehouse.

The waitron swiftly turned off the lamps, so the screen was the only source of light. Two lines of black text had appeared.

'Oh, my,' Alfred murmured.

The anthem tightened my throat. We had been ordered to sing 'Anchored to Thee' almost every morning at school. As soon as it ended, the anchor disappeared – and then Frank Weaver took its place.

The Grand Inquisitor was rarely seen outside the Westminster Archon. His face was a blunt oblong, framed by greased sideburns, and his thinning hair lay flat across the top of his head, the grey of cast iron.

Scarlett Burnish was poised and expressive; her lips could soften the worst tidings. Weaver was her polar opposite, always cutting straight to the unvarnished point.

'*Denizens of Scion, this is your Inquisitor,*' he said. '*It is with grave news that I address you here in London, stronghold of the natural order. I have just received word from the Chief of Vigilance that eight unnatural fugitives are at large in our capital.*'

Sensation drained away. The urge to run screamed through my blood, beating at my frozen muscles.

'*In the early hours of this morning, these criminals escaped the Tower of London and vanished. Those who failed to prevent this have been relieved of their public duties.*'

He was lying about the time of the escape. They must have needed a few days to coordinate a response.

'*These unnaturals have committed some of the most heinous crimes I have seen in all my years in the Westminster Archon. They must not be allowed to remain at large,*' Weaver continued. '*I call upon you, the law-abiding denizens of Scion, to ensure that these fugitives are detained. We must also identify any individuals who have abetted them. If you suspect a friend or neighbour of unnaturalness, report immediately to a Vigile. Clemency will be shown.*'

He was lying about that, too.

'*At present, only five of these criminals have been named. Until they are apprehended and executed, the Scion Citadel of London will be placed under red-zone security measures. Please pay close attention to*

76

the following photographs. Together, we will make sure that there is no safer place than Scion.'

With that, he was gone.

The slideshow of the fugitives was silent, except for a mechanical voice stating each name. The first was Felix Samuel Coombs; the second, Eleanor Nahid; the third, Michael Wren. Next came the fourth, Ivy – no surname – with her old haircut. Her photo was against a grey background, rather than the white of the official database.

And the fifth – the most wanted – was mine.

Alfred didn't even pause for breath. He didn't wait to read my crimes, or to check my face against the woman on the screen. He swept up both our coats, gripped my arm, and led me towards the door. By the time it swung shut, the coffeehouse had erupted into speculation.

'There are voyants in this district who would sell you to the Vigiles.' Alfred hurried me along. 'Ognena Maria never would, but I doubt she'll want a fugitive in her territory. You should get back to Jaxon at once.'

I baulked at the idea of returning to him so quickly, but it seemed the choice had been taken from me. Surviving in the syndicate without Jaxon would have been hard. As a fugitive, it would be impossible.

'Keep your head down,' Alfred muttered. 'There are no cameras in Grub Street, but there are plenty around the Barbican Estate.'

'I know,' I said. 'I used to live there.'

My father must be seeing the broadcast. Within the next few hours, Scion would come to question him again, suspecting him of harbouring me. He would be watched for the rest of his life.

I'm sorry.

Alfred opened his umbrella and drew me under it. We rounded the corner, heading for the archway. My heart was pounding in my throat.

It was past sundown. The safest course of action would be to hide until morning, but Alfred was right about Maria. She was a fair-minded woman, but would rightly see me as a threat to her voyants' safety.

I closed my eyes for a moment, my breaths coming short. This felt just like the night of my arrest. Same part of the citadel, same considerations.

This time, I couldn't make the same mistakes. I had to elude the dragnet.

'What's going on, Alfred?'

It was the augur who had been sleeping outside the coffeehouse. 'Oh, er—' Alfred pulled me a little closer. 'I'm in rather a hurry, Doris. I do apologise. Pop in for some tea in the morning, won't you?'

Without waiting for a reply, he kept walking. I could hardly keep up with his strides.

We left Grub Street. All around us, London was a wasps' nest, stirring. People moved towards the Barbican, where a public transmission screen played the Inquisitorial broadcast again. Their dreamscapes overwhelmed me. Beneath my jersey, I was sweating cold rivers.

When a gap emerged in the tide of human bodies, Alfred pulled me off the street and into a doorway, where I fought to regain control of my sixth sense. He took out a handkerchief and mopped his brow.

Away from the crowd, a strange calm came over me. Little by little, I tuned out the æther. All I had to do was focus on my body: my shallow breaths, my beating heart. The opposite of what Warden had taught me.

'I will take you to the border of this section,' Alfred said. 'From there, you can take the rooftops to Seven Dials. Jaxon says you're quite the climber.'

'You shouldn't risk being caught with me, Alfred. I'll manage from here.'

'And have you telling Jaxon I abandoned you?' He clicked his tongue. 'No, dear heart. I insist on escorting you as far as Farringdon Street.'

It was easier to agree than to argue. The man was braver than he looked.

'The section border will be guarded. They'll be expecting us to panic,' I said. 'We should move towards the river. There aren't so many cameras there.'

'Very well,' Alfred said. 'Do lead on.'

We strode away from the Barbican. I couldn't have been caught in a worse area. This section housed the Guild of Vigilance, the Bank of Scion England, *and* the Tower. It was lousy with cameras and Vigiles.

I thought back to the night of my arrest. Jaxon had advised me to head for the river.

The Thames was relatively neutral ground. Maria wouldn't be thrilled if I was found on her stretch of it, but she wouldn't legally be able to kick me off, either. If I couldn't make it back to Seven Dials, I would spend the night in a derelict barge I had spotted near Broken Wharf.

Alfred and I picked up our pace. There was only so much time until the broadcast stopped. Without the magnetic influence of the screens, vigilantes would gather all over the citadel, hunting for traitors.

By the time we reached Burgon Street, Alfred was puffing like a locomotive. I didn't sense an aura until it was too late, and a Vigile stepped out in front of me.

Armoured knuckles smashed into my stomach, sending me sprawling to the ground. When I got a good look at my assailant, hot fear surged through me.

The Vigile lifted her rifle. 'Freeze,' she shouted at Alfred. 'Hands where I can see them!'

'I *am* sorry, Vigile, but I fear there's been a mistake.' Alfred was red in the face, but his smile was perfectly congenial. 'We were just on our way to—'

'Hands *up*, unnatural, now.'

'All right, all right.' He raised his hands. 'May I ask what we've done amiss?'

The Vigile ignored the question. Her visor snapped up, allowing me to see her sighted eyes. Her gaze darted all over me, assessing my aura.

'Jumper,' she whispered.

There was no greed in her expression. She wasn't like the Underguards on the train, imagining the reward they would get for me. No, this was a serious anchorite.

'On your knees,' she barked. 'On your *knees*, the pair of you!' I did as she ordered. With difficulty, Alfred followed suit. 'Hands on your heads.'

We obeyed. The Vigile took a step back, but her rifle was trained on my face.

'You're going straight to Inquisitor Weaver, Paige Mahoney,' she said. 'Don't think I won't send you, murderer.'

She might have known the Underguards I killed. Maybe she had been there when they found the second man, salivating garbled pleas for death. Satisfied with my silence, the Vigile reached for her transceiver.

I looked at Alfred. To my shock, he *winked*, like he got detained in the street every day.

'Perhaps,' he said, reaching into his pocket, 'I can tempt you with this. You're a cyathomancer, aren't you?'

He held up a small gold cup, about the size of a fist, and raised his eyebrows.

'This is 521,' the Vigile said into her transceiver, ignoring him. 'Requesting immediate backup on Burgon Street. Paige Mahoney is in custody; I repeat, Paige Mahoney is in custody. Send all available units.'

'*This is 515.*' The transceiver crackled. '*Approaching your location. Detain suspect until our arrival.*'

'You're unnatural, too, soothsayer,' I said quietly. 'You need a numen.'

Her rifle snapped back up. 'Shut your mouth before I put a bullet in it.'

'How long do you have before they exterminate you? Noose or nitrogen asphyxiation, do you think?' I said. 'Do they give you a choice?'

'One more word, and I'll break your legs.' The Vigile reached for the handcuffs on her utility belt. 'Hold out your hands, or I'll break those, too.'

Alfred swallowed. The Vigile grabbed my wrists with one hand, making the left one twinge.

'Bribes won't help you,' she told Alfred. 'If I bring this one to Weaver, they'll give me as many cups as I like.'

My vision shook.

The Vigile sniffed thickly. Her nose was bleeding. As she raised a hand to her face guard, I gritted my teeth, remembering everything I had learned. My dreamscape was still fragile, but I had no choice.

I flung my spirit into her body.

Her dreamscape was a sterile office, lit by stark white lights. She tidied every thought and memory into filing cabinets. It was easy for her to separate what she did at work from her own identity as a clairvoyant. There was colour in here, but not a great deal. Self-hatred had diluted it.

I shunted her spirit out of the way. It fell without fighting, taken by surprise.

A feeling like falling into a chasm. I opened eyes that weren't my own. When I looked down, I saw the hollow shell of Paige Mahoney, crumpled on the ground. Alfred was shaking it with both hands.

'Speak to me.' A lavender aura swirled around him. 'Paige, can you hear me?'

I gazed at my body, transfixed.

My fist clenched around the transceiver. It felt heavy as a dumbbell, but I raised it.

'This is 521.' My voice came out as a slur. 'Paige Mahoney has escaped. Heading towards Smithfield Market.'

That market had no voyant presence. The Vigiles would find nothing of use.

I heard the reply as if from a distance. The silver cord was drawing me away from my host. Her eyes were failing to see, rejecting the foreign body behind them.

All at once, I was expelled. I almost headbutted Alfred as I sat up and took a breath, or tried. Suddenly I felt as if my head was in a noose.

This had never happened with Warden. I clawed at my collar and clutched at my throat, eyes widening. Alfred slapped me on the back, and I took a gasping breath, my face slick with sweat or tears.

'Good gracious, Paige,' Alfred said, staring at me. 'Are you all right?'

'Fine,' I heaved.

My head was aching, like a hand had gripped the front part of my skull, but it was a tolerable pain. The Vigile lay unconscious, blood leaking from her nose. I pulled her pistol from its holster and pointed it.

'Don't shoot her,' Alfred said. 'The poor woman is voyant – traitor or otherwise.'

'I won't.'

I crouched and pressed two fingers to her neck. A faint pulse ticked above her collar.

'I'm not far from I-4,' I said. 'Thank you, Alfred. I'll take it from here.'

'If Vigiles bleed at your command, far be it from me to stand in your way.' Alfred smiled, but I could see he was shaken. 'Good luck, Paige.'

He left, his umbrella shielding his face. I went in the opposite direction. Gathering my courage, I all but ran to Fetter Lane – the section boundary, according to syndicate maps – and then I was in I-4. From here, voyants were duty-bound to defend me against Vigiles.

The freezing wind made my bruises ache. I shot down Rolls Passage, vaulted a gate, and dashed up a fire escape to the rooftops, putting me out of sight of the night Vigiles. I refused to fall at this last hurdle.

On the roof, I surveyed the scene. Lincoln's Inn Field, a public square, was full of Vigiles. The lights of their vehicles flashed at its edges. Scion must have spread them out to coincide with the announcement, hoping to catch us as we panicked, like rabbits startled by a gunshot.

I took a steeling breath. Unlike last time, Scion had no idea of my starting point. If I kept a level head, I could make it back to Seven Dials.

There were several cameras around the square. To avoid them, I moved as far north as I could on the roofs before I descended back to the pavement. I didn't stop for breath until I reached the concrete playground of Stukeley Street, where Nick had trained me to climb. There were wheeled bins and railings and walls in abundance.

My palms burned as I dragged a bin across the road and used it to reach a ledge. Once I had my balance, I jumped and pulled myself on to a roof, my shoulders protesting. From here, I would stay off the ground for as long as I could. Whatever I did, I could not lead the Vigiles to Jaxon.

By the time I reached my own district, I was drenched in sweat and sore all over. I descended and strode along Earlham Street, then turned left at the sundial pillar – the pillar I had loved and missed, welcoming me back.

When I reached the right building, I knocked hard. There were no lights in the windows, but I was sure I could feel a dreamscape.

I glanced over my shoulder, tense. Swallowing hard, I knocked again, hearing sirens in the distance. I couldn't go back to the doss-house in Soho, or even the one in Grub Street. Both landlords had seen my face.

If Jaxon didn't let me in, there was nowhere left to run.

My legs were close to buckling. I prepared to beg, just as the Rephs had wanted.

And then the red door cracked open, and a pair of strong hands pulled me into the den.

SEVEN DIALS

As I crossed the threshold, my knees almost gave way. I heard the door shut behind us before Danica Panić got me upstairs, into an upholstered chair. My nose was streaming, my ears ached, and my cheeks burned with cold.

'You're blue,' Danica said.

I managed a laugh, though it sounded more like a cough.

'It's not funny.' She gave me a flat look. 'You're probably hypothermic.'

'Sorry,' I said.

'I don't know why you're apologising. You're the one who's probably hypothermic.'

'Right.'

My legs shook. My boots had rubbed my heels raw. I had often travelled on foot between sections, but Grub Street was a considerable distance from Seven Dials. I hadn't dressed for that journey.

'Thank you,' I said. 'For letting me in.'

'Okay,' Danica said.

Ever the conversationalist. I looked around, eyes watering. Save for a single lamp, the den was dark – every curtain drawn, every light out – but it was wonderfully warm. Someone must have fixed the boiler at last.

'The others are searching for you,' Danica said. 'Except Nick. He's at work.'

'Jaxon went, too?'

'Yup.'

That was surprising. Jaxon rarely did legwork ('I'm a mime-*lord*, darling, not a mime-peasant'), but suddenly he was leaping to my rescue every other week.

Danica took a seat on the footstool and pulled a familiar machine towards my chair.

'Here.' She unhooked the oxygen mask. 'Take a few breaths. Did you drift?'

'I dreamwalked.'

'You can do it now?'

'Sometimes.' I lifted the mask to my face and inhaled. 'With the right incentive.'

'Jax will be over the moon.'

As she turned her face towards the light, I noticed the long cut where the Vigile had struck her, held together with a series of thin stitches.

'That looks better,' I said. 'Are you all right?'

'As *all right* as you can be with a mild traumatic brain injury. Nick thinks I was concussed,' she added, seeing my frown. 'It doesn't hurt so much now.'

'Have you been back to work since we got back?'

'Scion would have been suspicious if I didn't go. I did a job the next day.'

'While concussed?'

'Didn't say I did a *good* job.'

I took another breath from the oxygen mask. A botched job by Danica Panić was probably still a lot better than what most engineers could manage on top form.

'I will get you a blanket, or something.' She got up. 'Don't turn anything on.'

As soon as she was gone, the æther flickered at eye level. Pieter Claesz – one of our muses – was beaming deep reproach at me.

'Hi, Pieter,' I said.

He floated into the corner to sulk. If there was one thing Pieter hated, it was people leaving him for months without a word of explanation.

'I'm sorry,' I said gently. 'I didn't mean to disappear.'

Pieter ignored me. I nestled into the chair, blowing into my chilled hands.

Danica returned with the blanket. I gathered it around my shoulders.

'Thank you,' I said. 'Do I still have a bedroom?'

'Yes. We needed the space, but Nick didn't let us touch it.' She considered me, as if I was a problem to be fixed. 'Now I will boil the kettle.'

'Okay.'

Danica was not the nurturing sort. If she was being this attentive, I must look awful. Looking down, I saw the greyish stain in my fingertips – a sign that I had overtaxed myself. Possessing that Vigile had been necessary, but it would set my recovery back.

The smell of the den fell like dust around me: tobacco, paint, rosin, cutting oil. As I unlaced my boots, I took in the familiar study. I had spent most of my first year working at the desk by the window, doing research into the history and spirits of London, perusing *On the Merits of Unnaturalness*, sorting out syndicate rent and tax.

Now I was safe and comfortable, my eyelids felt heavy. Little by little, I started to nod off.

My heart caught at the sound of keys in the lock. Boots thundered on the stairs, and for a terrible moment, I was back in my father's apartment.

Nadine Arnett stepped into the room, stopping dead when she saw me. She had cropped her hair in the last fortnight, so it just covered her ears.

'Wow,' she said. 'I *ran* all over Holborn to find you, and here you are, with your little blanket.' She dumped her coat. 'Where have you been?'

'I came from Grub Street.'

'On foot?'

'I couldn't think of what else to do.'

'We could have sent a cab. You could have called,' Nadine said, incredulous. 'Why have you been acting like we don't exist since Oxford?'

I was saved from answering when the door slammed again, and Zeke came charging up the stairs.

'Still no sign of her,' he said, out of breath. 'If you call Eliza, we can head over to—'

'We're not going anywhere, Zeke.'

'What?'

Nadine pointed. When he saw me, Zeke came straight over and wrapped me in a tight hug. The gesture took me by surprise, but I returned it.

'Paige, we were so worried,' he said, muffled. 'Did you come here by yourself?'

'Yes. I'm fine,' I told him. 'Thank you both. For looking for me.'

'We didn't have a choice.' Nadine unzipped her boots. 'As soon as Scion made you a fugitive, Jaxon sent us out to scour the whole section for you. You're damn lucky he pays me, or I might be irritated.'

'Stop it,' Zeke murmured. 'You were just as concerned as the rest of us.'

Nadine kicked off her boots without comment.

'We split up to search,' she said. 'Eliza went to Soho, and Jaxon covered Piccadilly. No idea when they'll be back.' She looked between the curtains. 'I'll keep an eye out for them.'

'I can do it,' I said.

'Paige, you're clearly about to keel over. Just get some sleep.'

I nodded, but didn't move from the chair. My legs were killing me.

Zeke opened the doors of his box bed (so Jaxon called it, though it looked remarkably like a cupboard) and sat on the quilt to pull off his shoes. 'Have you seen Nick?' he asked me. 'He said he's been checking on you.'

'I saw him yesterday,' I said.

'Okay.' He paused. 'Do you think they suspect him, after Oxford?'

'If they did, he would have been on the screens, too.'

'What if they detained him at work?'

'Quit spiralling,' Nadine said to him. 'Nick will be fine. He's always fine.'

Zeke lay on the quilt and closed one of the doors, gazing at the photographs and posters he had pinned inside the box. They were mostly of free-world musicians, with a single shot of him and Nadine. None of the rest of their family, or any friends from back home.

Nadine stayed by the window. While Jaxon and Eliza were out there, any night Vigile could spot them.

Danica returned with a steaming mug. I took it gratefully.

'The kettle is boiled,' she said to the others. 'I am not making any more.'

'Good for you,' Nadine said, not looking at her.

I sipped my tea. 'Anyone mind if I check ScionEye?'

'Knock yourself out.'

I turned on our small television. Jaxon hated us watching it, but even he liked to keep an eye on what Scion was saying.

The screen was split down the middle, with Scarlett Burnish on one side and a reporter on the other. This one was standing outside the Tower of London, her red coat whipped and battered by the wind.

'... *say the prisoners escaped by using their unnatural influence on the newest addition to the Guard Extraordinary, who had no idea what to expect.*'

'*A very unfortunate state of affairs,*' Burnish said. '*That was Victoria Huntington, speaking to us from Tower Hill.*' She clasped her slender hands. '*The Chief of Vigilance reports that the most dangerous of these individuals, whose capture is paramount, is Paige Eva Mahoney, an Irish immigrant from Munster, which now lies within the Inquisitorial region of the Pale.*'

The Pale was where Scion had total control. These days, it covered most of Ireland. In the tiny pockets that lay beyond it, Scion claimed that rebels still conspired against the natural order.

Part of me wished the story were true. A wiser part knew that it must serve a purpose, like making sure the hatred of the Irish never faded.

'Mahoney is nineteen and a former student of the Ancroft School in Bloomsbury. She is charged with murder, sedition, and high treason. Her father is Colin Mahoney, born Cóilín Ó Mathúna, a key worker at the Organisation for Research and Science,' Burnish said. *'The Chief of Vigilance has confirmed that Dr Mahoney holds a trusted position at SciSORS, and is being treated as a valuable witness. His supervisors have vouched for his innocence, as well as his dedication to Scion. Until his daughter is in custody, he will be held in the guest wing of Coldbath Fields for his own protection.'*

They showed a live clip of my father being escorted from the Barbican Estate. It was strange to hear Burnish say his birth name. He had anglicised it shortly after our arrival in England, as well as changing my middle name from Aoife to Eva.

Nadine watched the screen. 'You okay?'

I managed a stiff nod.

'He'll be fine. They don't execute amaurotics.' She glanced at me. 'You're not planning another jailbreak, are you?'

'No. He's survived Scion for this long,' I said quietly. 'If I try to get him out and fail, I'll only implicate him.'

'He really didn't know, did he?'

I shook my head.

All my life, my father had been distant. The night of my arrest, he had shown me some warmth for the first time in years – offering to make me breakfast, using my old nickname. The memory tightened my throat.

His shoulders had been shaking in the coffeehouse. The woman had met him in secret to comfort him.

Nadine was wrong. Scion did occasionally execute amaurotics, for misprision of treason. To avoid a death sentence, my father would have to publicly disown me. To deny he had ever seen my clairvoyance.

Did he hate me for what I was, or Scion for bringing us here?

———

My bed at the den was piled with throw cushions. Gauzy drapes hung above and around it. To the left was a window with wooden shutters, which looked down on the beautiful courtyard behind the building.

The room was small. Other than the bed, there was just enough space for a chest of drawers and a bookcase. The latter held a magic lantern, an electric fan, and a portable, leather-bound record player. Along with the lights I had strung across the ceiling, these were atmospheric tools, designed to put me in a fit state for dreamwalking.

Jaxon had tried everything to unlock my gift. In the end, only Warden had succeeded.

I lingered in the doorway, looking at it all. My old room, with its crimson walls, its ceiling painted with constellations. When I was in Magdalen, I had longed to be standing here. Now it represented a defeat.

Jaxon had me right back where he wanted me.

I shut the door. I wanted a hot bath, but I would only doze off in the tub. Instead, I knelt by the bed and drew out the chest where I kept my collection of trinkets from the black market. I brushed a thin layer of dust from its lid.

Next, I opened the chest of drawers. There was my pillbox, rattling with painkillers. There were my nightshirts, pressed and folded. I chose a grey one, climbed into bed, and fell straight to sleep.

When I woke, Jaxon Hall was sitting on the edge of my bed.

'Well, well.' His face was half in shadow. 'The sun rises red, and a dreamer returns.'

He wore his favourite lounging robe, made of green brocade, with a gold sash.

'I understand Alfred brought you back,' he said.

I sat up. 'Some of the way.'

'Sagacious man. He knows where you belong.'

'I don't know about that.'

We studied each other. For the first time in a fortnight, I was facing Jaxon Hall – the White Binder, the King of Wands. The man who had made me his sole heir, giving me unparalleled respect, when I was only sixteen years old. The man who had given me a chance, taken me into his home, and saved me from Scion.

The man who demanded obedience.

The man who would have gladly left the performers and amaurotics to die.

'You and I have our differences, Paige.' He crossed one leg over the other. 'I sometimes forget what it was like to be almost twenty years old, drunk on the prospect of independence. When I was the same age as you, my only friend was Alfred. I had no mime-lord, no mentors, no gang. I started my life under the cruel gaze of a kidsman.'

I watched him. 'You were a gutterling?'

'Oh, yes. My parents were hanged when I was four. Probably blockheads,' he said airily. 'They left me alone in this citadel, penniless. I couldn't always afford fine clothes and famous spirits, my mollisher.'

Once, I would have been overjoyed that Jaxon was confiding in me. Now I could see it for what it was – an attempt to manipulate my emotions.

Still, I could listen to this story, for old times' sake. That aside, I was curious.

'My kidsman worked with two others. All three were osteomancers,' Jaxon recalled. 'Together, they controlled a flock of sorry gutterlings. We picked bones and cloth, paper and glass. We sang on the streets and stole for our keep. Any money I earned was taken from me; in return, I was tossed scraps of food. I had always dreamed of going to the University, of being a man of letters – some great, scholarly clairvoyant, like Nostradamus or John Dee – but all the trio did was laugh at my desires. They told me I had never been to school, and while I could pick pockets and beg for coin, I never would. But when I turned twelve, I felt an *itch*. An itch beneath my skin, impossible to reach.'

His fingers strayed to his arm, as if he could still feel it.

He always wore long sleeves. I had seen the scars before, alongside his boundlings' names – long white marks that ran from the creases of his elbows to his wrists.

'I scratched the itch until my arms bled and my fingernails broke. I would scratch my own face, my legs, my chest,' he said. 'My kidsman threw me out to beg, thinking my wounds would attract public sympathy. Indeed, I never made as much coin as I did when I was itching.'

'That's awful,' I said.

'That's London, darling.' His fingers tapped his knee. 'By the time I was fourteen, nothing had changed, except that I carried out more dangerous crimes for mouthfuls of bread and sips of water. Once gutterlings reach a certain age, they make less coin, you see. I was losing my value to the kidsmen.

'Still, I knew my own worth, deep in my bones. I burned for independence, for *vengeance* – and for the æther. Though I was sighted and had an aura, the precise nature of my gift had never revealed itself to me. If I only understood my clairvoyance, I would think, I could make my own money and keep it. I could read palms or cards, like the buskers in Covent Garden. Even they laughed at me.'

He said it all with a faint smile, as if this were no more than a bedtime story.

'When I was seventeen, I was struck down with cholera,' he said. 'That was the final straw for my kidsmen, who cut me off from the syndicate, unwilling to waste one more resource on me. I found myself dying of thirst, ripping at my itching arms. I was close to shouting out my clairvoyance to the world; to begging the Vigiles to take me to the Lychgate, ending my suffering at last – until a woman knelt beside me and whispered in my ear, *carve a name, sweet child, a long-dead name.* And with those words, she disappeared.'

'Who was she?'

'Someone to whom I owe a great debt. I can only assume she, too, was a binder.' His pale eyes were in the past. 'I knew no long-dead names – only the names of those I *wanted* dead, which were plentiful – but I had nothing else to do but die. I walked four miles to Nunhead Cemetery.

'I had never learned to read, but I knew the marks on the head-stones were names. I chose a grave, cut my fingertip, and traced the letters on my inner arm. I soon felt the spirit come to my side. I spent a long, delirious night in that cemetery, sprawled among the revenants, racked by joy and agony. And when I woke, the itch was gone.'

Jaxon in his cemetery, learning how to bind. A little girl in a poppy field, reaching for a poltergeist. I had been younger when my gift first stirred, but until I had met Jaxon, I hadn't known I was a dreamwalker.

'I asked the spirit to guide me to someone who needed his services. He took me the New Cut, where I sold him to a medium. The spirit I had chosen was a valuable muse,' he said. 'With coin enough to eat and rest, I recovered from the cholera. I paid a bookseller to teach me to read. And I resolved to rise in the syndicate.'

'I've heard kidsmen don't like to let their investments go. They crawl out of the woodwork when their gutterlings are older, claiming unpaid debts,' I said. 'Did yours come after you?'

'Later,' he said, 'I went after them.'

I could only imagine the sorts of deaths he must have given those three kidsmen.

'After I mastered my letters, I began my research on the strains of clairvoyance. I was determined that no voyant should be ignorant of their own gift, as I had once been,' Jaxon said. 'And I found out what I was. A binder.'

There was a long silence.

'I told you this because I want you to know that I understand. I also empathise with that burning desire for independence,' Jaxon said, softer. 'But I am not a kidsman, Paige. I am a mime-lord, and I consider myself a generous one. You are allowed a little coin for your own uses. You are given bed and board. All I ask is that you follow my orders.'

He really was sounding like a Reph now.

'I've followed your orders for three and a half years. I've always done it gladly.' I held my nerve. 'But you asked too much of me in Oxford.'

'I lost my temper. I suppose you did, too,' Jaxon said. 'It was a fraught situation, to say the least.'

'You wanted me to leave the other prisoners. You called them an unwashed rabble,' I said. 'You claim you wrote *On the Merits* to help voyants. You know what it feels like to be rejected and belittled by your own kind. But you still meant to leave those people to die.'

'Only because *you* were my priority. Perhaps I was too concerned about my Seven Seals to care about the others,' Jaxon said. 'Still, it was beastly of me to threaten you, and I fully deserve your displeasure.'

It wasn't quite an apology, but this was as close as Jaxon had ever come to admitting fault.

'The Tower was a bloodbath,' he said. 'Fortunately, none of us perished, but others did. Was I wrong to recommend a more cautious approach?'

There he went again, making cruelty sound like reason. I looked away.

'I do appreciate you coming for me,' I finally said. 'We wouldn't have made it without you.'

'Anything for my dreamwalker.'

There was a brief silence. I swung my legs out of bed, so I sat beside him.

'The night I came to London, you were meeting Antoinette Carter,' I said. 'Why?'

'I heard about her prophecies and wanted to study her gift,' he said. 'Minty publishes her work here, so we extended a joint invitation through Leon. Alas, I have not been able to contact her since Trafalgar Square.'

'The Rephs had voyants scrying to establish where you were. That's how we knew you'd be there,' I said. 'Their leader is after you, Jax.'

His eyebrows leapt. 'Why should they be interested in me, of all mime-lords?'

'I don't know.' I paused. 'Did Nick tell you what happened to me?'

'Some of it, yes. I hardly know what to make of it.'

'The Rephs are coming, Jax. We can't let them carry on with the Bone Seasons.'

'Darling, I don't doubt your tale, but your lamp-eyed friends have suffered an embarrassing defeat. It will be some time before they rally.'

'No. They're already building another city in France.'

'That means they are no longer our concern. The grand ducs can deal with the matter.'

'This is *all* voyants' concern,' I said, frustrated. 'We have to warn the Parisian syndicate, and then we have to fight. If we don't pull together—'

'Paige, Paige. Your passion is to be commended, but let me remind you that we are not revolutionaries or freedom fighters. We are the Seven Seals.'

'The syndicate will fall apart when Senshield is installed. It will mean the Rephs can round up every voyant in London. No one else will be able to fight them,' I said. 'Jax, all of us are living in their lie.'

'A lie that sustains the syndicate, that gave birth to it. You will never change its character, Paige.'

'You did,' I said. 'Your pamphlet did.'

If I had to appeal to his ego to make him listen, I was not above doing that.

'That was quite a different set of circumstances.' Jaxon held my gaze. 'There is a reason I forbid you all to take long-term partners. I require your absolute commitment to the underworld. I cannot have a mollisher whose mind is wandering. Do you understand that, Paige?'

I didn't understand at all. I wanted to grab him by the lounging robe and shake him.

'No,' I said. 'I really don't. How can you think anything is more important than the Rephs?'

'Nick tells me these creatures have been here for two centuries. So far, they have only bothered us once. Senshield is still nascent, whatever Scion claims,' Jaxon said. 'You have had a terrible experience, but time heals all wounds. You will forget Oxford, as you forgot your life in Ireland.'

'I never forgot that,' I said, very softly. 'I'm not going to stop, Jaxon.'

'If you want to keep your place in the syndicate, you will.' He gave me a long look. 'There is one thing you clearly gained during your time away from Seven Dials. You realised your potential for leadership.'

'I don't know what you mean.'

'Don't play the fool. You organised a revolution in that cage they put you in.'

'With help,' I said. 'I couldn't do what you do, Jax. I'm happy as a mollisher.'

'Ah, modesty. It's a vice. True, you might have struggled without your friends, but on that final night, you were a queen. I understand you even made a little speech. And words, my walker – well, words are everything. Words give wings even to those who have been stamped upon, broken beyond all hope of repair.'

I wished I had words now.

Eliza, I could understand, but Jaxon had seen the Rephs for himself. He was still acting as if they were figments of my imagination, dreamed up in a haze of flux and regal.

They both had to be in denial. I had no other explanation for their apathy.

'Do you know how old I am, Paige?'

The question took me by surprise.

'Um,' I said.

'Forty-eight,' Jaxon said. I couldn't help but stare. 'As an unnatural, I do not want or expect to grow old. The day I join joyfully with the æther, you will come into possession of this section. You will be a young, capable and intelligent mime-queen, part of the highest order, with many loyal voyants at your beck and call. London will fall at your feet.'

I tried to imagine being a mime-queen. Deciding where the money would go. Commanding my own gang. Knowing that every voyant in the section would obey and follow me. Having a voice too loud to silence.

It was a tempting picture.

Jaxon held out a hand. I looked at it, my heart thudding.

'A truce,' he said. 'Forgive my loss of temper, and I will give you everything.'

King of Wands, inverted, Liss whispered from my past. *You're afraid of him.*

I was a wanted fugitive. Without his protection, I would be fair game for every voyant who had ever thought about selling information to Scion. Everyone else would simply pretend I wasn't there. I would be as vulnerable as Jaxon had been as a child, left to the mercy of the streets.

To him, you are nothing more than quick flesh grafted to a ghost; a priceless gift in human wrapping.

Jaxon was my only link to the syndicate, and the syndicate was the only organised force of voyants that could possibly stand against Scion. I had no intention of being silent, but for now, I would play along.

I shook on it.

'You have made the right decision, Paige.'

'I hope so,' I said quietly.

'To your reign.' His grip tightened. 'Until then, you remain my mollisher.'

I forced myself to nod. His little smile returned as he released my hand.

'Now, we ought to discuss this wretched fugitive situation.' He stood and ushered me across the landing. 'If we are to continue eluding the eye of Scion, we must take a few precautions.' He rapped on the ceiling with his cane. 'Danica, wake up and send for my darlings. We are having a *huddle*, and we are having one forthwith.'

Without waiting for a reply, Jaxon led me into his study. His *boudoir*, as he called it. It had made sense when I realised it meant *sulking room* in French.

Heavy curtains fell past the windows. Behind the chaise longue was the cabinet where he kept his absinthiana, along with a few blacklisted novels. The room smelled of tobacco and rose oil. A Victorian lampshade covered the floor in shards of colour, like a handful of shattered jewels: amethyst and sapphire, emerald and citrine, orange garnet and fire opal, ruby – the rainbow of clairvoyance.

Jaxon sank into his armchair and lit a cigar. I sat across from him, silent.

He wanted me to pretend to forget. The Rephs were still out there, lying in wait, and I seemed to be the only one who gave a damn about it.

Danica trudged into the room, still in a crumpled set of night-clothes. 'Jaxon,' she said in a flat voice, 'it is not even six in the morning.'

'Well observed, my Chained Fury.'

'Why am I awake?'

'Because we have our huddles before you and Nick go to work.' Jaxon struck a match and used it to light a cigar. 'Your request, if I recall.'

'It is Saturday, Jaxon. Saturday is my day off.'

'Oh, do forgive my ignorance of your amaurotic schedule, which changes on a weekly basis. Shall I consult Scion next time I need you?'

Danica sat, rolling her eyes.

Half a minute later, the other three appeared. Nadine curled up on the chaise, hair wrapped in silk, while Zeke sat beside her and stifled a yawn. Seeing me in my old place, Eliza grinned.

'Knew you'd come back.'

I forced a smile. 'Couldn't keep away.'

'The æther led her back to us, just as I said it would.' Jaxon waved her in, trailing smoke. 'Come, my precious trinkets. We have matters to discuss.'

I still couldn't believe he was forty-eight. There was scarcely a line on his face.

'First of all, recent payments – starting with yours, Nadine.' With a flourish, he handed her an envelope. 'You've brought us good coin in Covent Garden. There's also a small cut from the last spirit we sold.'

Nadine rubbed her eyes before taking it. 'Thanks.'

'For you, Ezekiel,' Jaxon said. 'You've done your tasks superbly, as usual.' Zeke caught his packet with a grin. 'Danica, I'm withholding your pay until you make progress.'

'Fine,' she said. 'Can I go back to sleep now?'

'And finally, Eliza. My dearest.' Jaxon held out the thickest envelope. 'We received an excellent sum for your last painting. Here, as always, is your cut.'

'Thank you.' She tucked it into the pocket of her skirt. 'I'll put it to good use.'

I tried not to look at those envelopes, full of precious notes. If I had returned to Jaxon sooner, I could have had some money under my belt.

'On to more sobering business,' Jaxon said. 'As there is a wanted fugitive living under my roof, we must establish some rules.' He tapped away a sprinkle of ash. 'Scion has declared a red zone. This has happened only twice in my lifetime. While it lasts, security will be much higher than usual. There may even be sighted Vigiles on duty in the day.'

Zeke bounced his knee. 'How can we avoid them?'

'First and foremost, you are not to use the Underground. We must learn from what happened to Paige. If you need to travel to another section, I will personally arrange for a cab or rickshaw to deliver you.'

Eliza looked up. 'Can we go on foot?'

'So long as you tell Nick in advance. He will ensure there are voyants on your route, ready to assist you.'

That sort of thing would usually have been my job. I was going to have to get used to keeping a low profile.

'For the next two weeks, the hunt will be at its most intense,' Jaxon said. 'After that, we should be able to lower our defences, but let us not be lax. For the time being, only leave the den when necessary. Our underlings can risk their necks.'

'So we don't have to go to Didion's auctions?' Nadine said, looking pleased.

'Auctions are safe, as is the black market.' Jaxon reached over to pat her hand. 'I abhor the very air he has the nerve to keep inhaling, darling, but we must invest. Besides, now Paige is back, she will take over the bidding, along with her other duties as mollisher.'

Nadine glanced at me.

'Right,' she said. 'Good.'

I raised an eyebrow. Jaxon sent a quick, incisive glance between us.

'If you do have to go outside, take an umbrella or wear a hood,' he went on. 'Cover as much of your lovely faces as you can – you especially, Paige – and check every street before entering it.' He drew on his cigar. 'We know that plainclothes Vigiles often visit the Garden. Never let your guards down, even there.'

'Jaxon,' I cut in, 'the Rephs could work out where we live at any given moment. Should we have an escape plan?'

Eliza stiffened. 'How could they?'

'I told you. They had voyants scrying for us,' I said, arms folded. 'It's only a matter of time until the æther serves up another few pointers.'

Jaxon raised his gaze skyward. He might not want to discuss the Rephs, for whatever absurd reason, but he couldn't just brush them under the carpet.

'Paige,' Nadine said, 'has Scion identified any of us?'

'Not as far as I know.'

'But they did find us before,' Zeke said. 'Paige is right. We should have a plan.'

'Oh, the Inquisitor take you all.' Jaxon snatched up his cane. 'To soothe your paranoid young minds, allow me to show you something. Follow me.'

He led us downstairs, to the hallway of the den. There wasn't much to see – just a wall-sized mirror, Zeke's bike, and a back door, which led out to the courtyard. Jaxon indicated the narrow space under the stairs.

'These floorboards are a trapdoor.' He gave them a smart rap with his cane. 'It leads to our bolthole.'

Eliza blinked. 'We have a bolthole?'

'Indeed.'

Nadine leaned against the wall. 'We've all lived here for years, and you never thought to share this life-saving information with us, Jax?'

'Where was the need?' he pointed out. 'You and Zeke are presumed dead as doornails, and Scion never cared about the rest of us until this year.' He looked at us. 'If the Vigiles *were* to come here, we would descend into this bolthole. It leads to a network of forgotten vaults and tunnels, which once connected the public houses of Seven Dials.'

He removed the blade from the end of his cane and used it to work up the trapdoor. We all leaned in for a look at the square opening.

'There,' he said. 'Are you satisfied?'

'Yes,' Zeke said.

'Good.' Jaxon snapped his fingers. 'You now have a quarter of an hour before the working day begins. Get ready. Paige, you come with me.'

Nadine gave me a sour look as I left. She had gone out to the courtyard before I could ask why.

Back in the study, I waited for orders. Jaxon swept a pile of paperwork from his desk.

'To business, then,' he said. 'Nadine has done a fair job as your interim, but she isn't you, and *you* were rather good at filling my coffers. With you at my side, I can send Nadine back to her usual duties.'

'She might not like that, Jax.'

'She did them before, didn't she?'

'Yes,' I said, as patiently as I could, 'but I doubt she'll appreciate having her salary cut out of nowhere. Were you paying her my wages?'

'Well, you didn't need them, did you?' he said. 'She's a whisperer, Paige. Let her busk for her keep.'

'She's busking?'

'Yes, she suddenly remembered how to play her violin in June. I would usually disapprove, but she's been charming the coins out of the amaurotics of Covent Garden, and we need every penny we can get.'

'Do we?'

'We are losing income. Unless you wish to watch our money roll away like water off a crystal ball, you will have to work harder than ever.' He whipped a scroll of paper from a drawer. 'An invitation to the next auction. I'm sure Didion will be *delighted* to see you.'

I took it. 'Not losing your touch, are you?'

'What?'

'This has always been a wealthy section of London. What changed?'

'Never blame a mime-lord for the failures of his dogsbodies.' Jaxon leaned against his desk. 'Several of our best voyants have been detained and hanged. Two lucrative establishments have closed down, while another has failed to pay syndicate tax. On top of that, the entire section has turned bone idle since you were taken. I need you to get them back in line, darling.' He cocked his head. 'I do hope your absence wasn't for nothing. Did you learn any new skills in Oxford?'

I kept my face carefully blank. 'What makes you think I would have?'

'Nick said you were being trained.'

'Not in possession. The Rephs wouldn't have wanted to give me that ability,' I said. 'I've got a little better at spooling, but they kept me weak.'

Jaxon looked at me for some time, still with a burning hunger in his eyes.

'Pity,' he said.

He had spread rumours about me. I knew some of his subjects believed that I could read their minds, or find them anywhere. Neither of those rumours had been too far off the truth. I might not be able to read minds, but I could sense them. Now I could walk in them, too.

I didn't want to admit that I had learned possession. First, because I had barely got the hang of it. It had taken months of training to control Nashira.

Second, because he would force me to use it, to cow people into doing his bidding. Even before Oxford, I had known I didn't want to be his weapon. Alfred might tell him the truth, but he wouldn't hear it from me.

'I meant to ask,' I said. 'Is Bill all right?'

Jaxon poured a glass of wine.

'No,' he said. 'I neglected to tell him to stop paying you. Scion must have noticed.'

'They did. That's why I asked.'

'Now you know how we lost one of our key establishments.' Jaxon unlocked a cabinet and sifted through a line of bottles. 'One more thing. We can't have you walking around looking like that.'

'Like what?'

'Like *you*, O my lovely. That hair of yours is far too easy to spot.' He held out a glass bottle and a small container. 'There. You have the tools,' he said. 'Make yourself invisible.'

7

MOLLISHER

17 September 2059

'Do I hear one hundred?'

A white candle burned in front of us, casting the only light in the crypt. Wax dripped as the flame swayed in a draught, watched by a stone cherub with stumps where its wings had once been. I sat among the bidders, a length of red silk concealing the lower half of my face.

A few moments passed before a paddle was raised.

'One hundred to the gentleman from IV-3.' Didion Waite cupped a hand around his ear. 'Do I hear two hundred?'

Silence.

Didion always dressed like he was off to court in the eighteenth century, as if he was daring Scion to question his unusual taste in fashion. He sauntered across the stage in his tailcoat and steel-buckled shoes.

'Can I tempt you with one hundred and fifty?' he cajoled us. 'This is no day for cheese-paring, my friends. You'll earn back your investment in good time, I promise you. Ask the good sergeant for his secrets, and you might just bag yourself a Ripper lady. And if you bag yourself a Ripper lady, who knows? You might just bag yourself a Ripper.'

Another paddle went up.

'A believer,' Didion declared. 'One hundred and fifty from VI-5. You've come a long way to claim this prize, sir. Anyone for two hundred, mollishers and mobsters? Ah, two hundred? No, *three* hundred! Thank you, III-2.'

Jaxon never liked me to lowball Didion. While I waited, I considered the room. Usually it was just mollishers who went to auctions, but this one had drawn a few mime-lords and mime-queens.

The Juditheon had been established before I joined the syndicate. Named after the late Judith Gower, a talented Welsh cleromancer (who Didion had somehow convinced to marry him), the auction house was hidden in the crypt of Bow Bells, a derelict church on Cheapside.

The lot was Edward Badham, a sergeant of H Division. They had been the law enforcers of the monarch days – the forerunners of V Division, the early Vigiles. Any spirit connected to H Division, which had once policed Whitechapel, could provide a solid lead to the Ripper.

That was why this auction had attracted a full house. Along with the Screaming Queen and the Crushing Force, Jack the Ripper would be a valuable spirit. That sort of prize would solve our financial problems.

Ognena Maria wore a tight smile, as she always did at auctions. Hector allowed Didion to hold them on her territory, but she received no tax from them. I was sure she attended them all out of spite.

She wasn't the only voyant who had a few bones to pick with Didion. Everyone knew he poached spirits from other sections and auctioned them to fill his own pockets, slipping Hector a generous cut. My first assignment for Jaxon had been to contain Sarah Metyard, a poltergeist Didion had unleashed while trying to purloin her.

Still, we all wanted the Ripper, either to sell or wield, so here we sat.

I had to wonder what Nashira Sargas was doing while I was bidding on a dead man. Oxford seemed like years ago, and it had only been two weeks.

A paddle went up, held by the Highwayman, the hard-faced mollisher of II-6. I had never heard of him missing a Ripper auction. I tried to stay on cordial terms with other mollishers, but the Highwayman despised Jaxon, thanks to his long feud with the Wicked Lady.

Auction by the candle was always tedious. The damn thing never seemed to burn down. When Didion called for six hundred, I raised my paddle.

'Six hundred to—' Didion twirled his gavel. 'I-4. Yes, six hundred to the Pale Dreamer. Or perhaps we should call you *Paige Eva Mahoney*.'

I stiffened.

Perhaps I should have expected it. Didion and Jaxon had been at war since they first met, jabbing at one another with pamphlets and insults. Didion despised Jaxon ('the most discourteous sir I ever did meet') for selling more pamphlets than he ever would; Jaxon despised Didion ('a useless, pigeon-hearted fribble') for sharing his gift, and for having terrible teeth. This had gone on for over a decade.

Hearing Didion say my real name still hit me like a punch to the stomach.

'Will we be auctioning *you* off next, madam,' he continued, plainly enjoying himself, 'given your standing with Scion?'

Murmurs blew from ear to ear, and several people turned to look. My skin prickled as I slid a hand into my jacket, grasping my revolver.

Didion Waite had unmasked me.

'I wouldn't be surprised, Didion,' I said, recovering. 'Why not hawk the living as well as the dead?'

A few grim chuckles rose, making Didion bristle.

'You look like your mime-lord's double,' he said. 'Is the White Binder so in love with his own reflection that he's painted it on to his mollisher?'

I had dyed my hair black and cut it so it was level with my chin, baring the length of my neck. My contacts were hazel, not pale blue, but I took his point.

'Binder knows that one of him is quite enough for you to handle,' I said. 'We wouldn't want to damage your fragile constitution, Didion.'

I was too shaken for much wit, but Spring-heel'd Jack let out such a hoot of mirth that the Pearl Queen started. Didion turned from pink to puce.

'Order,' he snapped. 'I am working on a new pamphlet, thank you very much – one that will wipe that rag *On the Merits* from the pages of history, mark my words.'

'Get on with it, Didion,' Maria drawled. 'I don't want to die of old age down here.'

Jimmy O'Goblin, sitting beside me, shook with laughter as he drank from his hip flask.

A light tap on my shoulder made me turn. Jack Hickathrift, a fellow mollisher, draped an arm over the back of my seat. He smelled of nutmeg. Eliza fancied the strides off him, as did about half the syndicate.

'Hello, Pale Dreamer,' he said. 'You're really the one Scion is after?'

I crossed my arms. 'No idea what he's talking about.'

'Show us your face, then.'

'Oh, I'd be embarrassed. I'm not as pretty as you, Jack.'

He grinned, showing a rakish dimple. 'Still resistant to my charms, I see.'

'That must be devastating for you.'

Didion cleared his throat, glaring at us.

'The proceedings will continue,' he declared, as if he hadn't been the one to interrupt them in the first place. 'Do I hear eight hundred for Sergeant Badham?'

'That pompous bastard,' muttered old Dobrev, cracking his knuckles. He was one of the Firebirds. 'We have your back here, Dreamer.'

I gave him a nod, hoping he was right. At least no one had rushed off to report me. The syndicate lacked honour, but rats were always killed.

Jaxon would be raging for at least a year when he found out about this. Although the Pale Dreamer was well known in the syndicate, my face and real name were not. Many syndies abandoned their legal identities, but the other half still held on to respectable jobs, forcing them to hide behind masks and aliases.

To protect my father, I had always led a double life. Nick had advised me to conceal my face when I was the Pale Dreamer, but over time, I had grown careless. Didion must have been waiting for the perfect opportunity to stick the knife in me.

Still, this was low, even for him. The mood in the room had soured even further.

As the candle burned lower, the price of Sergeant Badham climbed. Soon there were only six of us bidding. I watched for the telltale burst of light. As the candle winked out, I snapped up my paddle.

'Nine hundred,' I called.

'One thousand,' came a voice from behind me.

Heads turned. That was the Monk, mollisher of I-2. As always, a black cowl shadowed his face.

'One thousand to the gentleman from I-2,' Didion proclaimed. That would keep him in powdered wigs and ill-fitting trousers for a while. 'The candle is extinguished, and the spirit of Sergeant Edward Badham belongs to the Abbess. Commiserations to everyone else!'

Groans and curses filled the crypt, along with the bitter mutterings of those from poorer sections. I pursed my lips.

'That should have been yours,' Jack Hickathrift said. 'You've a sharp eye for the candle, Dreamer.'

'For all the good it does me.' I stood up. 'See you around, Jack.'

'I do hope so.'

Yet another waste of time. At least I had been able to get out of the den for a few hours.

Before I could even put my coat on, the Highwayman stepped forward, shoving his chair to the floor. The sound of it silenced the room.

'Enough of this charade, Waite.' His voice boomed. 'That spirit is the property of II-6. Where did you get it?'

'This spirit came into my keeping legally, sir, as they all do.' Didion bristled. 'If this spirit belongs to II-6, why did I find it in my territory?'

'You're a macer and a crook.'

'Can you prove these allegations, sir?'

'One day,' came the acidic reply, 'I will find the Ripper, and you will regret your thieving, Waite.'

'I hope that is not a threat against my person, sir, verily I do,' Didion said, all of a quiver. 'I shall not endure that sort of talk in this auction house. Judith would never have allowed such wanton verbal abuse, sir.'

'Where's her spirit, Didion?' a medium shouted. 'Shall we auction her off, too?'

Didion purpled like a bruise. You knew things were getting serious when Didion Waite ran out of *sirs*.

'Enough.' Ognena Maria rose. 'I won't have you throwing a tantrum on my turf, Highwayman. Hector is the one who allows these auctions. Either cry to him, or look to your own streets for your Ripper.'

The Highwayman stormed from the crypt. Spring-heel'd Jack ran off as well, laughing to himself, while Jenny Greenteeth growled. Didion approached the Monk, but he was already halfway up the steps.

'I'll take it,' a young woman said. Her red hair was arranged in a braided bun, with an ornate comb to hold it in place. 'I serve the Abbess.'

'Of course.' Didion handed her a token. 'Tell her to send her binder when she pleases.'

The woman gave him a gracious smile. 'I'll see to it that you have your money within a few days, Mr Waite.'

The Abbess was certainly flush with coin these days. Most of the central leaders were wealthy, but I wasn't convinced that many of them had a spare grand to throw at a spirit.

'Pale Dreamer?'

Ognena Maria had come to my side. Her short auburn hair was slicked into a pompadour, and she wore two sets of gold earrings. I touched three fingers to my brow, as was expected around the Unnatural Assembly.

'Maria,' I said. 'How are you?'

'I was about to ask you the same question. Binder had me mount a search for you in March,' she said, her brow furrowed. 'What happened?'

'Scion caught me. I slipped the noose, but I went to ground for a while.'

'How did you escape from the Tower?'

'They put me in a building with lax security,' I said, not missing a beat. 'My father works for Scion. I guess it was their idea of a courtesy.'

'Well, I'm glad you're still breathing, even if your situation is less than ideal.' Maria clapped me on the shoulder. 'Good to have you back.'

'Thanks.' I swung on my coat. 'I didn't know you were a Ripper hunter.'

'I really have no interest in the Ripper. I just like to remind Didion who he's stiffing.' She sent a dark look in his direction. 'I can't believe he unmasked you. Rest assured, he'll be punished for it.'

'No point now. The horse has bolted.'

'You *are* Paige Mahoney, then?'

'You know I am. You've seen my face.' I picked up my satchel. 'I'll get off your turf.'

'No immediate hurry. While I appreciate your caution, I trust that you can avoid night Vigiles.' She nodded to the steps. 'Join me?'

We made our way up the steps of the crypt. Didion had discovered it years ago.

'I didn't think you'd be this understanding,' I said. 'You've always been protective of your voyants.'

'As I always said, you *should* be one of mine,' Maria said, giving me a thin smile. 'I'll allow it. Just don't bring the anchor down on our heads.' The brooches on her jacket clinked. 'Did Binder come with you?'

'No, he's in Seven Dials.'

'I'd like a word with him. An opportunity has arisen, and I think he might be interested,' she said. 'I need a few spaces filled in Old Spitalfields.'

'I thought you were full until January?'

'We've had a few arrests. If Muse is interested, I'd love to see her work.'

'I can ask him,' I said. 'Sorry about the arrests.'

'I suspect it's only a small taste of what will happen when Senshield arrives.'

I glanced at her.

We emerged into the shell of Bow Bells, one of the few religious houses in London that Scion hadn't gutted and repurposed. It had been disfigured in the early twentieth century, like all things associated with the afterlife or the monarchy – the wings carved off the angels, the altars destroyed by republican vandals – but its bells still hung.

The place reminded me of Oxford. A remnant of an older world.

A woman stood near the remains of the altar, talking to the Monk. Tall and slim, she wore a blouse of needle lace (which must have cost a fortune) and a dark pillbox hat, pinned over furls of chestnut hair.

That had to be the Abbess, mime-queen of I-2. She had turned up to meet her mollisher.

'Maria,' she called. 'How are you?'

Her voice put me in mind of a match being struck, soft and clipped with a smoky edge.

'Congratulations, Hortensia,' Maria said. 'A good prize.'

'You're very kind. I don't have as fine a collection of spirits as some, but I do occasionally like to bid.'

'I do hope this won't be a case of the winner's curse. Badham couldn't find the Ripper while he was alive. Let us hope he's a little sharper in death.'

'Quite. How are you coping with the red zone?'

'Well enough.' Maria patted my back. You know the Pale Dreamer, don't you?'

The Abbess regarded me through a birdcage veil. I could make out her light brown skin, long nose, and crimson feather of a smile.

'I don't believe we've ever met in person. What a pleasure,' the Abbess said. 'The White Binder has always spoken highly of his prodigy.'

I gave the salute. 'Abbess.'

As well as being a mime-queen, the Abbess ran the Chanting Lay, the largest night parlour in London. After three and a half years in the underworld, I had yet to set foot in there, but I knew enough.

Maria was toying with her lighter. She was a pyromancer, able to use flames to scry.

'I'd love to stay and chat, Hortensia,' she said, 'but I've a section to manage.'

'I want a word,' the Abbess said. 'Do you have a moment?'

'No. I'm expected at Leadenhall.'

'Tomorrow, then, at noon. Meet at the Gilded Anchor.'

Maria walked on with a curt nod. I followed her through the doors to Cheapside.

'Apparently, the Abbess has endless time for chin music,' she remarked, checking the street for Vigiles. 'Sadly, she's bosom friends with Hector, so I must indulge her. That man is the bane of my life.'

'What do you think she wants?'

'Probably more nightwalkers. She seems to think I'll let my voyants moonlight if she asks nicely.' Maria turned up the collar of her coat against the wind. 'You keep your nose clean, Dreamer. See you soon.'

'Maria,' I started. When she raised her eyebrows, I lost my nerve. 'Never mind.'

'All right, sweet. You know where I am.'

I watched her walk away, grinding my jaw.

Maria believed in the danger of Senshield. She also had a deep grudge against Hector. If I played my cards right, she could be a useful ally.

My bob cab waited on Milk Street. I climbed into it, sighing in defeat.

'The Garden,' I said to the driver.

'Binder said you're to go to Soho,' she said. 'To chase up some missing syndicate rent.'

'I thought Bell was handling that?'

'I've got my orders, Pale Dreamer. I'll take you to the Garden once you've done it.'

I closed my eyes and breathed out. 'Fine.'

London was still in the thick of its red zone. Underguards lurked at station turnstiles round the clock, and there were twice as many Vigiles.

As the cab passed a transmission screen, my face appeared yet again. To a stranger, this face would look hostile: unsmiling, with chill grey eyes and the pallor of a corpse. It was not the face of an innocent.

The cab stopped on Silver Place, a dingy alley in Soho. I got out and approached the right building, my chest tightening with every step. Even when I had enjoyed serving Jaxon, I had never grown used to this part of the job. I tapped the knocker and took a step back.

A physical medium answered the door. Tara was one of our thieves, small and wiry, with a head of dark curls. She stiffened at the sight of me.

'Tara,' I said. 'How are you?'

'Pale Dreamer,' she said in a faint voice. 'We didn't know you were back.'

'The White Binder says you're behind on your rent. I thought I'd drop by.'

'It's been a hard few months.' Her fingers blanched on the door-frame. 'I don't know if the Silent Bell told you, but Effy lost her job in July. I've been trying to busk, but there are so many more Vigiles.'

'That's why you need our protection.' I used a forbearing tone, meant to unsettle her. 'These are dangerous times, Tara. If the Vigiles raided Soho, you two wouldn't want to be on your own, would you?'

'No, of course not.' She was shaking now, reaching into her pocket. 'I'll get the rent to you, I promise. Give me another week or two.'

In the past, I would have been able to follow the script. I had been able to divorce myself from what I was doing, knowing it was what Jaxon wanted, and turn the screw until I had the money in my grasp.

Now I looked at Tara, and all I saw was Liss.

'It's fine,' I said. 'I'll let you off this once, Tara. See you in October.'

Now it was my voice that threatened to shake. Before she could say a word, I was gone.

Back in the cab, the driver glanced at me. 'Did you get the money?'

'That's between me and Binder.' My voice was cold. 'The Garden, please.'

The driver said nothing more after that. At least today couldn't get any worse.

When I got out in Covent Garden, I slammed the door a little too hard. Now I was going to have to use my next pay packet to cover for Tara.

The Pale Dreamer had been able to intimidate her fellow voyants, even if she had found it hard to stomach. I needed to step back into her skin, but I couldn't see when it would end. All I could do was keep saving money and hope that I eventually worked out what to do with it.

Warden, where are you?

No answer. If he wasn't dead, I expected a damn good excuse for why he had left me high and dry here, without a clue what Nashira was doing.

If you never see me again, it will mean all is well. I remembered his voice, soft and deep. *But if we fail tonight, and Nashira still holds power by dawn, I will come to warn you.*

Find me either way, I had told him.

Somehow, I doubted all was well.

Zeke was waiting for me under the stone archways. He had scrubbed up nicely, as he always did on selling days: silk brocade waistcoat, neatly parted hair. The thick-rimmed glasses, however, were new.

'How are you today, Paige?'

'Chipper. Nice glasses.' I hitched up my red silk. 'What's the story?'

'Eliza has finished touching up the painting. Jax wants them all sold by the end of the night. The spoils from the burglary, too.' He fell into step beside me. 'We've missed you at the Garden. I'm terrible at selling.'

'You'd be better if you didn't think you were terrible. You say Jax wants us to sell the lot?' I said. 'Does he need another Parisian absinthe fountain, or something?'

'He claims we're low on money.'

'I'll believe that when he stops buying wine and cigars.'

'He hardly stopped drinking while you were away.'

I glanced at him. 'Was Nadine looking after the finances while I was gone?'

'Yes. I'm sure she would be happy to talk to you about it.'

'I feel like she's giving me the cold shoulder.'

'No, no. I think she was just shaken by everything that happened in Oxford,' he said. 'Nick told us your story. It's … kind of incredible.'

Behind the eccentric lenses, his eyes were bloodshot. He must not have been sleeping.

'Zeke,' I said, 'if you were me, what would you do about the Rephs?'

'I really don't know.' He adjusted the glasses. 'I was talking about it with Nick the other day, and I thought we could do some kind of broadcast, but how do you tell people what you know they won't believe?'

I hadn't realised Zeke was that ambitious. Much as I liked the idea of exposing the Rephs, I couldn't think of how a bunch of thieves could pull it off.

'We can't run before we can walk,' I said. 'If we're going to do something, I think we need to start with the underworld.'

'Yeah. I guess it would be hard to make a broadcast, anyway. Scion has too much security.' He cleared his throat. 'By the way, did Nick tell you—?'

'Tell me what?'

'Uh, forget it.' He straightened his collar. 'Did you get the spirit at the auction?'

'No. The Monk snatched it. But what were you going to—?'

'It doesn't matter. I don't think Jax really cares about H Division,' he went on, looking resolutely at anything but me. 'I'm sure he only sends you to auctions to remind everyone how wealthy he is.'

'Right, because apparently he's now impoverished.'

'You really should talk to Nadine.'

'I will.'

We followed the colonnade until we reached a lantern. Instead of the muted blue of the average streetlamp, its panes were tinged with green, hard to see unless you knew to look for it. It hung above the door to a clothes shop.

The amaurotic shopkeeper nodded us straight through. A winding staircase took us into the basement. There were no customers down here; just mannequins in second-hand coats. Zeke looked over his shoulder, then pulled one of the mirrors open like a door. We sidled through the gap into a tunnel.

The Garden extended under Covent Garden and Long Acre. A massive underground cavern, it had been the hub of illegal trading for decades.

Some voyants earned their flatches in the amaurotic markets, but this one was solely for us. The night Vigiles had never surrendered its location to Scion, since so many of them still bought their numa from its stalls. Scion gave them food and shelter, but no means of touching the æther. It was a wretched life they led, fighting their own natures.

The cavern was poorly ventilated, thick with the heat of hundreds of bodies. In the Spirit Hall, stalls sold every sort of numa, the objects many voyants needed to reach the æther. Mirrors: handheld, cheval, framed. Crystal balls too heavy to lift. Smoked-glass shew stones, small enough to fit inside a palm. Cases of small blades and needles. Tarot decks of all designs. Lots for casting. Dust and oak ash. Teacups and cast-iron kettles, keys for locks that no longer existed – whatever their numa, soothsayers could barter or beg for them here. Then there were the augurs' carts, where flowers and herbs were sold in abundance. I breathed in the scent of bay leaves and roses.

The aster dealers had a stand to themselves. White for amnesia, blue for comfort, purple for a deadly high, and pink, the aphrodisiac. A few apothecaries sold drugs to mediums – muscle relaxants, mood stabilisers – and helped them with the physical hardships of possessions.

Tiny luthiers' workshops made instruments for whisperers. There were pens for psychographers, books for bibliomancers, pomanders to block out the strange odours that plagued sniffers. One stall offered ornate notebooks, meant for recording visions and prophecies.

Beyond the stalls that served our needs, the Stone Hall offered even more. Forbidden imports from the free world. Lost treasures from the days before Scion. I had spent endless hours in this section, poring over curios, scavenging for American records.

Jaxon got a fair cut of the money from this place, since he protected its entrance. He liked us to drop in every so often – hence our stall, which appeared once a month. It sold funerary art, human ashes, winding sheets, and other morbid luxuries for the well-heeled voyant. No cheap trinkets here. Most of it came from our thieves and tomb looters.

Zeke put his mask on. I did the same, realising how much I had missed this place.

Behind the table, Eliza was a vision in a green velvet dress. Her golden hair fell in polished ringlets down her back, and lacework spidered up her arms. She was talking to an augur, who was admiring her new painting. He left with a longing glance when she saw us.

'Interested parties already,' I said.

'He can't afford it.' Eliza brushed a speck of dust from the frame. 'I've worked for two years on this one. Make it worth my time, won't you?'

'We'll do our best.' Zeke rolled his sleeves up. 'Do you want a coffee?'

'Yes, please. A strong one.' She dabbed her brow. 'And some cold water.'

'You need to be out of sight,' I told her.

'Yes, yes, I know.'

I steered her to the back of the stall, where she took out some paperwork. She needed to be here so we could consult her, but if anyone saw an art medium near our paintings, they would put two and two together at once. I took off my coat and smoothed my blouse.

Zeke soon returned. 'Here,' he said, handing Eliza a coffee. 'Are you all right?'

'I'm fine,' she said, unusually curt. 'Just make sure we sell these, Zeke.'

With a slight frown, he went on his way. I unloaded human skulls from a box. Eliza was often in a foul mood after a possession, riddled with tics and aches.

'Eliza,' I said, 'be honest with me. How long have you been awake?'

'I slept a bit on Sunday night.' Her eyelid twitched. 'Jax sent me here as soon as I finished with Pieter.'

'Let's not sell the art today, then. Surely it can wait until October.'

'Jax said he needs the money.'

'Eliza—'

'I'm *fine*, Paige. Can we drop it, please?'

'For now.'

I couldn't blame her for being short with me. By rights she ought to be asleep in a dark room after a trance. Trying not to worry, I went out and started arranging the candles. Nadine arrived as I lit the last one, formally opening the stall.

'I'll do the rounds,' she said. 'Any objections?'

'Not from me.'

She piled some of our smaller wares on to a platter. I covered two of the paintings with cloth. Zeke gave me a nod, and we started to sell.

I soon got back into the swing of the market. Not everyone who came to the Garden belonged to the syndicate, but those who did often stopped at our stall, to pay their respects to the White Binder. A few of them had heard of my return and welcomed me back warmly.

No one seemed to know about my unmasking. Maria must have tried to keep it under wraps.

A dispute soon broke out on the opposite stall, where a pair of palmists were offering readings. The querent was an acultomancer, and seemed to be unhappy with what his palm had told him.

'I want *all* of my money back, charlatan!'

'Your palms are your enemies, friend, not me. If you want your own version of the truth,' the palmist said, eyes hard as flint, 'perhaps you should try knitting it.'

'You what, you dirty augur?'

A *crunch* as the palmist snapped, breaking his nose. The nearest voyants stamped and jeered. The acultomancer fell into the table, then lunged at the palmist with a roar, sending them both to the ground.

The ensuing brawl was short and brutal. Most palmists were good with their fists, but the acultomancer was stronger, winning with an uppercut. The second palmist made a spool and hurled it at him with a scream, only for him to throw a sharp awl, which struck her in the throat.

'Should have stayed in Jacob's Island,' he snarled at her. 'Anyone else?'

The nearest voyants broke out into rowdy cheers. Eliza shook her head and withdrew, while I gazed at the dying woman, my jaw so tight it hurt.

A gathering of vagabonds is no threat to the Republic of Scion, Nashira had told me.

At this point, I could hardly argue.

The mess was cleared away. Business as usual. I had sold three watches and a finger-sized hourglass by the time Zeke came back from his break, his vintage glasses clouded by the heat.

'Did you hear about the fight?'

'We saw it,' I said.

'There was another one near the cake stand. The Crowbars and the Threadbare Company again.'

'Surely there are better things to do near a cake stand.' I raked my damp curls away from my face. 'We've sold about half the stock. Let's attract some art dealers.'

Eliza leaned out again. 'Zeke, did the apothecary have any waking salts?'

'No, sorry. They sold out.'

She was swaying on her feet. 'I think it's your turn for a break,' I said, taking the paperwork from her limp hand. 'That's an order, Eliza.'

'But the paintings—'

'If we're going to sell them, you can't be this tired. Rose will let you nap at the Gallant until five.'

'Yes. You should rest.' Zeke moved her away from the stall. 'No arguing, okay?'

'Fine, but you two have to get your facts straight,' Eliza said, exasperated. 'Philippe was Brabançon-born, but he was from the Duchy of Brabant. Brabançon is not a place. And Rachel used *liquor balsamicum* when she helped her father. Do not say *balsamic vinegar* again, Paige, or I swear on the æther, I will break a vase over your head.'

She picked up her knitted bag and was gone. Zeke looked at me and blew out his cheeks.

'Skellet bell?'

'Let's do it,' I said.

I searched under the table for the heavy medieval bell, which had once been used for funeral processions. As I unwrapped it, Nadine returned with her platter of wares, slamming it on the table. I stared at her.

'You didn't sell anything?'

'In the twist of the century,' she said, 'nobody wants table junk.'

'They're never going to want it if you call it *table junk*.' I picked up one of the skulls, checking it for breaks. 'You have to make them tempting.'

'Tempting? *Oh, good afternoon, madam – would you like to buy the skull of some plague-addled churl for the price of a month's rent?* Make it tempting, Paige.'

'Don't use my name here,' I said under my breath. 'I know you're good at this. What happened?'

'Maybe I'm distracted.' She took a sip of water. 'We're showing the art now, right?'

In answer, I offered her the skellet bell. She moved in front of the stall and rang the bell with all her might, startling a sensor. Even with so much noise in the cavern, the clanging made scores of people look up.

'Good voyants of London, do you remember your mortality?' She offered a rose to the sensor, who laughed nervously. 'Scion is always watching us. Among the boneless dead, it's easy to forget that *you* are flesh and blood.'

'Sometimes,' Zeke said, 'you need a gentle reminder. He aquí, the lost masterpieces of Europe!' He dramatically revealed the paintings, one after the other. 'Pieter Claesz, Rachel Ruysch, and Philippe de Champaigne!'

'The finest vanitas paintings, brought to you from France and Holland, courtesy of the White Binder.' Nadine rang the bell again. 'Vanitas for your very own lodgings! Roll up for your next investment!'

'Private viewings begin at half past five,' Zeke called, hands cupped around his mouth. 'Once the slots are gone, they're gone!'

Soon we had attracted a large crowd. Zeke fielded the first rush of questions, but he would need Eliza during the private viewings, to make sure our trick held up under scrutiny. Other than racketeering, ethereal forgery was our best source of income.

Nadine took over the stall with a smile. She lavished praise on the paintings, making up boxes of ashes and bones to offer to people with lighter pockets. Meanwhile, I handed out flowers and Zeke charmed people with stories of his old life in Oaxaca de Juárez. In the safety of the Garden, he liked telling people that he came from the free world, far beyond Scion. They clung to him like flies to honey, hungry for tales of Mexico, a place where voyants could find peace.

His sister was less forthcoming. If people asked about her accent, Nadine usually pretended she was French. While they charmed our visitors, I counted our coins.

And I wondered what Warden would think of me now, after everything we had done.

He had risked everything to help me escape. He might have died so I could stand here, right back where I started. I had crawled back to my petty treasons with my tail between my legs – hawked stolen trinkets, submitted to Jaxon, and cursed Hector where he couldn't hear me.

Yellow-jacket, I thought to myself.

———

At quarter to five, I was done for the day. The night Vigiles would soon be on duty, and Jaxon had insisted that I was back by then. Given the short walk to the den, the others would stay later. The Garden was open until ten on Wednesdays.

'I'm off,' I said to Nadine. 'Are you all right to carry on?'

'If you can get Eliza back,' she said, scanning the room. 'Where did she go?'

'She's having a quick nap in the Gallant.'

'Wow, a nap. I'd love one of those.' She checked her watch. 'The Greek dealer said he would come back at six. She needs to be here before then.'

'I told her to head down by five. You'll be grand.'

'I hope you're right.'

Ethereal forgery was one of the few ways we conned our fellow voyants. It wouldn't go down well if the deception was uncovered.

'Zeke says you were keeping an eye on the coin when I was gone,' I said, buttoning my coat. 'Jax claims we're losing money. Any idea why?'

'I really don't know what he's talking about. There *was* a drop in profits while you were away – Oxidate and the Clock House were raided and shut down, and people were definitely slacking off – but honestly?' she said. 'It's nothing like as bad as what he's making out.'

'Could someone be embezzling?'

'I would have noticed that.' She flashed me a smile. 'Anyway, it's not my problem now, is it?'

'No.' I sighed. 'See you in the morning.'

My head ached from hours of noise and concentration. Suddenly I was ready to drop. I wove through the crowds of people, keeping my mask in place.

I stopped beside a stall that specialised in metal numa: needles, small blades, bowls for cottabomancy. The vendor looked up when I approached.

'Hello,' he said. 'You're no soothsayer.'

'I'm looking to sell.' I lifted the chain from around my neck. 'How much would you give me for this?'

'Give it 'ere.'

I placed the pendant into his palm. He squeezed a loupe against his eye and held it to the light.

'Interesting,' he said. 'What metal do you say this is?'

'I was hoping you could tell me.'

'Looks like silver, but—' He shook his head. 'Weird charge coming off it, like a numen. Never heard of a pendant being a numen.'

'It repels poltergeists,' I said.

'You what?'

'Well, so the previous owner told me. I haven't tested it,' I said. A sigh escaped him, somewhere between relief and dismay. 'How much would you give me for it if it did?'

'Hard to say. If it *is* silver, then a thousand, give or take.'

'Only a thousand?'

'I'd give you a few hundred for your average bit of silver.'

'Come on. If it protects the wearer, it must be worth a lot more than a grand.'

'With all due respect, I don't know what macers' tricks have been used on this. I'd need to take it away and give it a closer look. If the metal's sound and it works, and I can twig exactly *why* it works, I could give you a fair bit more.' He handed the necklace back to me. 'Depends if you want to part with it. I could get it back to you in a week.'

I tucked it into my pocket. Warden had given me this necklace for my protection, and I had a feeling he wouldn't want me to sell it.

'I'll think about it,' I said.

'As you like.'

At the entrance to the Spirit Hall, I pulled back the velvet curtain and strode into the tunnel. I was aching for a shower and a rest.

'Thought you might be here, Pale Dreamer.'

I turned on my heel, knife in hand. Cutmouth was leaning on a crate of supplies.

'Paige Mahoney,' she said. 'That's your real name, then, is it?'

Cutmouth rarely visited without her gang in tow. For once, her long red hair was loose, covering one side of her face.

'Maybe.' I kept the knife up. 'Should I be concerned for my safety, Cutmouth?'

'No more than usual. I don't give a shit what your name is,' Cutmouth said, 'but I am sick of seeing your miserable face on every fucking screen.'

'I'm honoured you'd remember it,' I said. 'You last saw it two years ago.'

'I remember my enemies.'

'What do you want?'

'I want you to do something useful, for once.' Cutmouth held my gaze. 'Tell me where Ivy Jacob is hiding.'

I tensed. 'Ivy?'

'You heard me. Where is she?'

'You think all the fugitives know each other personally?'

The briefest flicker of uncertainty crossed her face. She glanced at the doorway to the market, then stalked towards me, one hand clenched.

'I'm not playing, Dreamer,' she said. 'I need to speak to her.'

'Why?'

'None of your concern.'

Cutmouth was only in her twenties, not much older than me. Perhaps we had been in the same situation – two young voyants discovering their gifts, running to a charming mime-lord for protection and guidance. After a moment, I slotted my knife back into its sheath.

'Cutmouth,' I said, 'drop the act for a minute.'

'What act?'

'The mollisher act.' I lowered my voice. 'Does Hector really not care about Senshield?'

Cutmouth pressed her lips together.

'He's voyant,' I said. 'He's not going to survive this just because he's Underlord.'

'Are you *frightened* of Frank Weaver, Paige?'

'Of course I am. Why aren't you?'

'Hector has everything under control. He promised me we're safe with him. When he dies, I'll be there to take over,' Cutmouth said. 'I'll fix this syndicate.' All at once, her scarred face looked naked and vulnerable. 'If you won't tell me where Ivy is, I can still find out.'

I saw the switchblade a second too late.

Cutmouth shoved me against the wall and clamped her fingers over my mouth. When I raised a hand to push her back, the blade flashed across my palm. A shallow wound, not meant to maim.

She was a haematomancer. If she was any good, she could use my blood to scry for information about me. I wanted her to know about the Rephs, but on my terms.

As soon as the pain registered, my spirit whipped out. Cutmouth reeled away from me with a scream of agony. I got a glimpse of her dreamscape – a misty dock, rotten boats floating on greenish water – before I returned to my body. In the instant she was dazed, I knocked the knife from her grasp and wrenched her arm behind her back.

'Fuck,' Cutmouth gasped out.

'You trying to spy on me?' I hissed into her ear. 'Tell Hector to keep his nose out of my business. Next time I'll send you back as a shell.'

Cutmouth twisted free and took off. Her knife lay on the floor, lined with my blood. I waited for my eyes to stop watering, then took a cloth from my pocket and wiped the blade clean before stowing it.

Ivy wasn't telling me something. If Cutmouth knew her, she must have been more than a gutterling.

At least I could use my gift again. My head ached in protest, but the barrier of my dreamscape was just strong enough to allow me to jump.

I slipped out of the clothes shop. As I crossed the street, I nearly kicked a bollard in frustration. I could sell baubles and paintings all day long, but I couldn't think of how to rally the syndicate, or how to get a message out.

Back at the den, I took a hot bath. Danica and Jaxon had gone out, leaving me to my own devices. Once I had dried off and dabbed some fibrin gel on my palm, I changed into my nightshirt and took out my knife.

Ever since Jaxon had first employed me, I had kept my savings hidden in my room. I unpicked a few stitches on my pillow and extracted a roll of money. In silence, I fanned it out, counting the notes.

Jaxon had always paid us well, but not well enough for us to be financially independent of him. Any money we made ourselves was handed to him for redistribution. We had to spend a good chunk of our wages on little things for the section, which he conveniently forgot to reimburse: couriers' fees, supplies for the den, cabs between districts.

The æther shivered, distracting me. The muses were hovering at my door in a pointed manner.

'We got someone interested in yours, Pieter,' I said. 'Yours, too, Rachel.'

The spirit at the back quivered.

'Don't worry, Phil. You're a luxury.'

I could sense his doubt. Philippe was prone to melancholia. The trio lingered, drawn to my aura like flies to a lamp, but I shooed them back to the painting room. They were always restless when Eliza was away.

Outside, night was drawing in. I carried out the checks – lights off, curtains drawn – then returned to bed and slotted my bare legs under the covers.

The only sound was the record player, sighing out 'Elegy' by Fauré. I listened with my eyes closed, remembering the gramophone at Magdalen.

The longer I was away from Warden, the more I thought of the Guildhall. All those weeks of mutual distrust, and suddenly I had been wrapped in his arms, not wanting to leave him. I still didn't quite understand when things had changed between us.

Against my will, I relived the gentle precision of his touch. His hands in my hair, framing my face. His lips on mine, and the heat of his skin.

I opened my eyes and fixed a hard gaze on the ceiling. Warden was clearly not coming back. There was no point in thinking of what could have been.

To take my mind off him, I switched on the magic lantern. There was already a slide inside. I angled the mirror towards the ceiling, directing a beam of light through the painted glass, and a scarlet field of poppies appeared. This was the slide Jaxon had used when I was learning to enter my dreamscape. It was so detailed you could believe it was real, as if the ceiling opened out into the meadow in Arthyen.

But my dreamscape was different now. This was the dreamscape of before.

I flicked through a box of slides until I found one Jaxon had shown me when I was about seventeen, when I had first confessed my interest in history. An older slide, with fine black text:

The Destruction of Oxford, September 1859

As I adjusted the lens, a familiar skyline materialised. Black smoke choked its streets, and fire whipped at its daunting spires. This was the lie Scion had told, only for our rebellion to make it true, two centuries later. I fell asleep with the lost city burning above me.

8

THE DEVIL'S ACRE

'Paige?'

The voice drew me from a heavy sleep. It couldn't be time for the night bell yet. I turned on to my side, blinking.

'Warden?'

A familiar chuckle answered. I opened my eyes to see Jaxon above me, framed by the blazing city on my ceiling.

'No, my sleeping walker,' he said. 'You're not in Oxford any more.' A light floral smell hung on his breath, eclipsed by the scents of white mecks and tobacco. 'What time did you return here, Paige?'

It took a few moments to remember where and when I was.

'When you said.' My voice lolled behind my thoughts. 'About five.'

'Was Eliza here?'

'No.'

'How odd.' Jaxon switched off the magic lantern, plunging the room into darkness. 'Sleep, darling. I shall wake you if the situation escalates.'

The door closed behind him. I curled into the warm bedding and dozed off again.

The next time I woke, someone was shouting. I sprang up, ready to sprint to the bolthole.

'... *selfish*, we wouldn't have—'

That was Nadine. I held still, listening. Her voice was raised, but not in fear. I followed it to the floor below, where I found Zeke, Nadine, and a drawn Eliza. Her hair was a mess of wet tangles, her eyes puffy.

'Nadine,' I said, 'what's going on?'

'Ask *her*,' Nadine snarled. Her left cheek was swollen. 'Ask her, go on!'

Eliza wouldn't meet my eye. Even Zeke was looking at her with something close to exasperation. His lower lip resembled a split grape.

'Hector and the Underbodies came to the Garden,' he told me. 'They interrupted our meeting, warning the dealer our paintings were fake. It made her ask very difficult questions. Eliza wasn't there to help.' With a wince, he reached for his side. 'Hector confiscated the Champaigne for testing. His gang took the rest of our wares, too. We tried to stop them, but—'

He gestured to his bruised face.

This was a delicate situation. Philippe was going to hit rock bottom when he found out his painting had been stolen, but that was the least of our problems if any local voyants learned that we sold forgeries. We had always selected our targets with care, favouring smugglers and unscrupulous dealers, but if Hector exposed us, the game would be up. Jaxon was going to flip his lid.

'I'm sorry.' Eliza looked close to collapsing. 'I'm sorry, both of you. I was just ... so tired.'

'Then you should have told us so we could get out of there,' Nadine bit out. 'Instead, you left us on our own. You're supposed to be there to advise us.'

'Eliza,' I said, 'tell me what happened.'

She crossed her arms tight. 'I fell asleep outside.'

'Where?'

'Hop Gardens. I wanted some fresh air,' she said dully. 'I woke up in a puddle.'

'You're a liar.' Nadine pointed at her brother. 'On top of the damn painting being taken, Zeke has a cracked rib. How are we going to get that fixed?'

Now the spotlight was on me. As mollisher, it was my job to handle disagreements when Jaxon was away.

'Eliza,' I said, trying to sound reasonable, 'I did tell you to go to the Gallant. Rose would have woken you.'

'I know,' Eliza said, her cheeks blotchy. 'As soon as I came round, I ran to the Garden, but it was too late.'

'You left the gang vulnerable, yourself included. We could have just postponed the sale and left the Garden early.'

'Jax said—'

'I'd have interceded with Jax. That's my job,' I said. 'But I can only help you if you're honest with me.'

There were some voyants who wouldn't take a lick of criticism from someone four years their junior, but Eliza had always respected my position. She brushed her sleeve across her face and took a deep breath.

'You're right,' she said. 'I'm sorry, Paige.'

There was such defeat and exhaustion in her expression, I couldn't bring myself to lecture her for any longer.

'Don't let it happen again,' I said. 'Let's just work out how to rescue the painting.' When Nadine stared, I folded my arms. 'Nadine, she obviously isn't well. What do you want me to do – put her on the waterboard?'

'I want you to do *something*. You're supposed to be our mollisher,' Nadine burst out. 'We got the shit beaten out of us, but Eliza just gets away with it?'

'It isn't her fault. Hector picked on you because he hates Jaxon, and he gets a kick out of throwing his weight around. I wish someone would fucking kill him and be done with it,' I said bitterly. 'You know how much time Eliza spent on that painting. Isn't that punishment enough?'

'Yeah, must be exhausting to go into a trance while poor Philippe does all the work.'

'Just as hard to play the violin and get money thrown at you, like a rottie.' Eliza squared up to her. 'What do you contribute to this section, Nadine? What would happen if Jaxon threw *you* out tomorrow?'

'At least I do my own work, puppet princess.'

'I make Jax the most money out of any of us!'

'Pieter makes Jax money. Rachel makes Jax money. Philippe makes Jax—'

'You're only here because of Zeke,' Eliza shouted. 'Jax didn't even want to hire you!'

'Enough,' I snapped.

Eliza dissolved into tears. Nadine just stood there, stunned into silence.

'Yes,' a deep voice said. 'That *is* enough.'

Jaxon was in the doorway, his face bloodless. Even the whites of his eyes seemed paler.

'What in the æther,' he said dangerously, 'are you all caterwauling about?'

I stepped in front of Eliza. 'I've sorted it, Jax.'

'Eliza abandoned us, all our goods have been stolen, and Zeke has a cracked rib,' Nadine said hotly. 'How exactly have you *sorted it*, Mahoney?'

'Nick will take a look at Zeke. I'm not going to punish Eliza for being overtired, Nadine.'

'I will make that decision, Paige. Thank you.' Jaxon held up a hand. 'I heard what happened in the Garden. Eliza, explain yourself.'

'Jax, I'm so sorry. I just—'

'You just what?'

'I was so tired,' she said, still on the verge of tears. 'Paige let me go outside for a break. I went for a quick walk, and—'

'You didn't manage to find your way back to the Garden.' His voice was as sleek as a ribbon. 'Am I correct?'

'She collapsed on the street, Jax,' I said. 'You know she needs rest after a possession.'

For a long time, Jaxon said nothing. Then he stepped towards Eliza, wearing an odd smile.

'Jax,' I warned, but he didn't even glance at me.

'Dear, sweet Eliza.' He took her chin in one hand, hard enough to make her tense. 'On this particular matter, I must agree with

Nadine.' His grip on her chin tightened. 'I will not have any indolence in this den. If you feel I am too demanding, leave. You may have to leave either way. If we are unable to sell your art on the black market, you are as useful to me as a crystal ball to a summoner.'

The silence was terrible. From the look on her face, he couldn't have hurt her more if he had stabbed her in the heart.

'Jaxon,' she whispered.

'I have heard enough.' Jaxon pointed his cane at the door. 'Go to the garret. Reflect on your fragile position in this organisation. And hope, Eliza, that we can resolve this dilemma. If you decide you would like to keep your job, inform me before sunrise, and I will consider it.'

'Of course I want my job.' She looked ill with fear. 'Jaxon, please, you can't—'

'Try not to snivel, Eliza. You are a medium of Seven Dials, not some importunate beggar.'

Eliza backed away from him. Jaxon watched her go upstairs with not so much as a drop of discernible emotion.

'That was cruel, Jax,' I said.

He might have been a well-dressed piece of wood, for all the response I got.

'Nadine,' he said, 'you are excused.'

Nadine didn't quite looked ashamed of herself, but she didn't look triumphant, either. The door to her room slammed behind her.

'Zeke.'

'Yes?'

'Your box. Go to it.'

'Was that true, Jaxon?' Zeke said softly. 'That you only gave my sister a job because of me?'

'Do you see many whisperers living in my home, Ezekiel? What use do you suppose I had for a violinist with a panic disorder?' He pinched the bridge of his nose. 'You're giving me a headache. Get out of my sight.'

For a while, Zeke just stood there. He opened his mouth, but I shook my head at him. Jaxon was in no mood for debate.

Defeated, Zeke took off his broken glasses, picked up a book, and shut himself away.

'Come upstairs, Paige,' Jaxon said. 'I have something to tell you.'

I followed him, hot around the eyes. The gang hadn't had such a terrible argument since last December, the night my world had fallen apart.

In his study, Jaxon directed me to an armchair. I stayed on my feet.

'Why did you do that?'

He looked at me. 'Do what?'

'You know they all depend on you.' I wanted to box his ears. 'Eliza was beyond exhausted. You know she hasn't slept since Sunday?'

'Oh, she's fine. I've heard of mediums going for up to two weeks without sleep. It causes no lasting damage.' He waved a hand. 'I shan't fire her, in any case. We can always relocate the stall to another market, if we flatter Maria. But Eliza has had the morbs of late. It's tedious. She needed a good shake, to bring her up to snuff again.'

'Maybe you should ask her why she's been down. There might be something wrong.'

'Matters of the heart are quite beyond me. Hearts are frivolous things, good for nothing but pickling.' He steepled his fingers. 'The stolen painting is an attack on my authority. Hector may decide to bribe an expert to testify that the paint is fresh, which could be irritating. I want it returned to Seven Dials – or, failing that, thrown into the Thames.'

'What makes you think he'll hand it over?'

'I'm not that naïve, darling. A carrot must be offered to the ass.' He took something from his desk. 'I want you to take a carrot to the Devil's Acre.'

He showed me.

In a leather-bound case was a solitary knife, about eight inches long, cradled in a bed of crimson velvet. When I reached for it, Jaxon grabbed my wrist.

'Careful,' he said. 'When numa are left without a voyant for a long time, they may not respond well to being handled. This one has been orphaned for at least a century. Only someone from the appropriate order has a chance of touching it without a shock to the dreamscape.'

'Whose was it?'

'No idea.' He snapped the case shut and handed it to me. 'I have no use for it, but Hector is a macharomancer. He should be thrilled with a blade for his collection. An *expensive* blade, I should add.'

It didn't look too special to me, but far be it from me to question Hector's taste. 'You think that's why he did this?' I asked. 'He wants a sweetener?'

'Almost certainly. He does like to remind me who is Underlord.'

'He lives next to the Archon,' I said. 'I shouldn't go at night.'

'Therein lies the quandary. If I send anyone less than my mollisher, it will wound his pride. If I send the others to accompany you, he will accuse me of trying to browbeat him into handing over a forgery.'

'I met Cutmouth on my way out of the market. She tried to get some blood from me.'

'Hector must want to know where you've been.'

'She could try again if I go there.'

'Cutmouth is a vile augur. Her so-called *art* is unrefined.' He drummed his fingers on the desk. 'Still, I won't have my mollisher bled. A cab will take you to Westminster. From there, I will arrange for a glym jack to escort you to the Devil's Acre. He'll be waiting for you on the steps of the Thorney. Make sure Hector knows he's there.'

There was no getting out of this.

'I'll get changed,' I said, defeated.

In my room, I laced on steel-capped boots and found the stab vest Nick had stolen from a Vigile. I had to be ready for Hector this time. More likely than not, one of the Underbodies would give me a hefty thump for being in Westminster, even if I was there for a reason.

On the other side of the landing, the door to the painting room was closed. I knocked and leaned against it.

'Eliza?'

There was no reply. When I opened the door, the smell of linseed floated out. Tubes of oil paint littered the floor, spilling colours on to the dust sheet. Eliza was sitting on her bed, knees drawn up to her chin.

'He won't fire me, will he?'

She sounded like a lost child. The three muses hung like clouds above her.

'Of course not,' I said gently.

'He's never looked at me like that.' She rocked back and forth. 'I deserve to go.'

He has looked at you like that. I almost said it out loud. *He's looked at all of us like that.*

'Jax wasn't being fair,' I said. 'I'm going to talk to Hector now. I'll get the painting back.'

'He won't give it to you.'

'Yes, he will.'

'I don't want you to get hurt, too.' Tears seeped to her chin. 'Please, be careful, Paige.'

'I will. Just get some sleep,' I said. 'If you need to talk later, you know where I am.'

She nodded and lay down on her side. Giving the muses a warning look, I switched off the light and closed the door.

Last year it was Nadine that Jaxon had chosen to pick on. Now it was Eliza. And so it went, on and on. Only Nick ever escaped his wrath.

I zipped the stab vest over my blouse and covered it with a black jacket. Next, I loaded my revolver. I had no intention of hurting Hector, but I didn't trust him to surrender the painting.

Finally, I tucked the numen into my bag. Even in its case, it gave me an unpleasant chill. The sooner it was with Hector, the better.

The Devil's Acre, home of the Underlord, was in the shadow of the Westminster Archon. The Underlord considered himself to be the other leader of the citadel, with every right to settle in I Cohort, Section 1.

It was the last place in the world a fugitive should be heading.

The cab drove along the Thames Embankment. I got out near Westminster Bridge, where the river heaved and splashed. From there, I went on foot, keeping my hood up and my eyes peeled for Vigiles.

Once known as Palace of Westminster, the Archon was the heart of Scion. Its most distinctive feature was the Gothic tower that housed Big Ben. The clock face shone volcanic scarlet, indicating the security level.

Nashira could be in there. I wished I could look, but I dared not dreamwalk into that place.

The Archon stood by the former Westminster Abbey, where the kings and queens of old had been crowned. These days, it was the Inquisitorial Hall, reserved for important ceremonies, currently enclosed by scaffolding. I still wasn't sure why locals called it the Thorney.

As promised, a glym jack waited on its steps. He was all muscle, hooded, with a green lantern in one hand. Their job was to escort amaurotics to their destinations at night, ensuring protection from unnaturals, but Jaxon had one or two in his service.

'Pale Dreamer.' He inclined his head. 'Binder says I'm to escort you to the Devil's Acre.'

'Fine by me,' I said. 'What's your name?'

'Grover.' He walked beside me, close enough for him to look like a bodyguard. 'Stay close and keep your head down. I'm charged with keeping you alive.'

I wondered how much Jaxon was paying him. What price he placed on the life of his dreamwalker.

'You're amaurotic,' I said. 'How long have you worked for the syndicate?'

'Ten years. My daughter was voyant.'

I could guess what had become of her.

Before Scion, the high lords of Westminster had intended to demolish the overcrowded rookeries of London and replace them with modern, sanitary dwellings. Those plans had been shelved when unnaturalness arrived on the scene. Although some attempts at clearance had been made, there were still a number of slums in the citadel.

The Devil's Acre had once been the smallest, confined to a few marshy streets. The Golden Baroness – the first and only Underqueen – had claimed the slum as her residence and cleaned it up as best she could. Hector had let things slide since then. I had only been to his sanctuary twice, but I still remembered the damp reek of it.

Westminster was heavily guarded. As we made our way down Victoria Street, a squadron of night Vigiles appeared. The glym jack ushered me into an alley before they could spot my aura.

Hector lived in a large building on Old Pye Street. I approached the rusted entrance, where the gatekeeper would usually stand. There was no one there.

'Gatekeeper,' I called.

Nothing.

'It's the Pale Dreamer.' I hardened my voice. 'The White Binder sent me. I demand an audience with Hector.'

Still nothing.

Grover gave me a sceptical look. There was no way I was going back to Seven Dials without the painting. Eliza wouldn't sleep until it was recovered.

'Wait here,' I said to Grover. 'I'll find a way in.'

'As you will.'

Hector had made it difficult to infiltrate his sanctuary, streaking its walls with oily paint. Coils of razor wire would tear my hands to shreds. I made a few rounds, searching for gaps, but it was a fortress. I was about to admit defeat when I spotted the maintenance shaft, and the rose engraved on its cover.

The rose was an old symbol of the syndicate. I heaved the cover to one side and switched on the torch I had brought with me. Instead of the small access chamber I had expected, a tunnel ran under the wall.

This must be the bolthole. Strange that Hector hadn't put a padlock on it.

The tunnel was lined with soiled cushions and foam so caked in dirt it looked like stone. I duckwalked along it. If Hector caught me in here, I was worse than dead.

At the end of the tunnel, I found a trapdoor. I checked the æther, trying to pinpoint Hector. Oddly, there were no dreamscapes or spirits at all.

Hector had a vast array of spirits, from poltergeists to wraiths and shades. Perhaps the Underbodies had gone out again, or hadn't come back at all, but I couldn't imagine why the spirits would have left.

Whatever the reason, this was my chance. If the painting was here, I could grab it and sneak out again.

I surfaced in a small courtyard, where the air smelled of rot. This district was built on low, wet land, and Hector clearly had no idea how to maintain it.

The nearest building had once been a townhouse. I approached its doors. This was where Hector had let us in, the night he had invited us to play a game of cards.

In the hallway, the walls shone with blades of all kinds. Some of them were imported from the free world, bought on the black market. To the right of the staircase, another set of doors was ajar. Warm light flickered across the carpet, but there was no sound.

I pushed open the doors. I saw the drawing room, and I saw what was inside it.

Hector and his gang were here, all right.

They were all over the floor.

9

THE BLOODY KING

Hector Grinslathe lay on his back in the middle of the drawing room, legs splayed wide, with his left arm resting across his abdomen. Dark blood was spilling from his neck, and no wonder. His head was nowhere to be seen.

A row of red candles had been lit along the mantelpiece. Their dim light made the lake of blood look like crude oil.

Eight bodies were lined up in pairs, like couples in bed, with their feet pointing east. The Underhand was beside Hector – head still attached, eyes glazed, mouth open.

The insides of my ears tingled. I looked back through the doors and reached for the æther, but there was no one else in the building.

The painting had been placed against the wall. Blood dripped down the canvas. The stench of iron reached my nostrils, mingled with urine and shit.

Run.

The word drifted through my thoughts. I gripped the doorframe to stop myself, my mouth dry as dust. I had to get the painting and take note of what was here.

First, the corpses. From the spray, they must have been killed here, not moved. I had seen bodies before, some in the late stages of decay, but these identical positions were grotesquely theatrical. Streaks of blood led up to each body. They must have been dragged around the room like dummies before being posed. I pictured gloved hands propping up legs, lifting arms, tilting heads to the desired angle.

Each face was resting on the left cheek. Each right arm lay on the floor by the torso. All the furniture – armchairs, a séance table and a coatrack – had been shunted against the walls to make room for them. I pushed up my sleeves and crouched beside the nearest corpse.

Magtooth. It seemed impossible that he had been taunting me a few days ago, eyes alight with amused malice. His cheeks had been hacked with a knife, most of his nose was missing, and small cuts split his eyelids.

The perpetrators must have known that Hector was never alone. There had to have been more than one killer, to take down the entire gang.

I checked the corpses: Hector, the Underhand, Slabnose, Slipfinger, Bloatface, Magtooth, Roundhead. All of them had been stabbed in a frenzy, either before or after their throats were slashed. At the bottom right corner of the arrangement, next to Magtooth, was the Undertaker. That explained why the spirits had fled.

Cutmouth was the only one missing. Either she had escaped the attack, or she had never been here.

As well as arranging the bodies, the killer had left a calling card. Each body held a red silk handkerchief in its right hand. A few of the gangs had calling cards – the Threadbare Company left a handful of needles, the Crowbars a black feather – but I had never seen this one.

Magtooth was still warm. His watch was stuck at quarter past one. A sharp chill bolted down my spine. I had to get the painting and leave.

The Underbodies needed the threnody to release them from the physical world. If I denied them that mercy, they would almost certainly develop into poltergeists, but I didn't know most of their names. I stood over the decapitated body.

If I banished Hector, he would never be able to offer any information about his killer. He would also not be able to say I had been here.

'Hector Grinslathe,' I said, my voice strange, 'be gone into the æther. All is settled. All debts are paid. You need not dwell among the living now.'

There was no response from the æther. I turned to Magtooth.

'Ronald Cranwell, be gone into the æther. All is settled. All debts are paid,' I said, a bit louder. 'You need not dwell among the living now.'

Nothing. I focused, straining my perception until my temples ached. I had thought their spirits might be hiding nearby, but they didn't emerge.

Something else did.

The æther had been very still. Now it began to vibrate. Like water touched by a tuning fork, it stirred around me, shaking the whole room. I ran between the corpses, heading for the painting, but my presence had been scented. The candles blew out, the ceiling bowed, and a poltergeist burst into the drawing room. It hurled me against the floorboards, dazing me. At once, I realised my mistake – the pendant was still in my pocket, not around my neck. Before I could reach for it, the London Monster had seized my arm.

When the agony came, so did a gut-wrenching scream.

It had been ten years since a poltergeist had last touched me. The rush of hallucinations came: a cry, a torn and bloody dress, a spike concealed by mock flowers. I gasped for air, twisting away, but the breacher had its claws in me, and every breath seemed to freeze in my lungs.

Somehow, my fingers got to my pocket. I slammed the pendant on to my chest, where my collar was open. The spirit dug into my dreamscape. I thrashed like a hooked fish, my neck straining, but I kept the necklace pressed to my skin, like salt to a wound, until the poltergeist let go. It took off through a window, showering the room with glass. I curled into a ball on the floor, shuddering and covered in blood.

My right arm was beginning to stiffen. I had thrown it out to protect myself. Slowly, I got back to my feet, my boots sliding on blood. With gritted teeth, I hung the pendant around my neck, then grabbed hold of the painting and concealed it under my coat. Abandoning the bodies, I limped back to the bolthole and climbed down.

Grover had found my entry point. When I reached it, he took my hand and pulled me up. I clutched the painting close.

'Done?'

'He's dead,' I said, heaving. 'Hector, he's—'

I could hardly speak. Grover dropped my hand and looked at his own.

It was smeared with blood.

'You killed him,' he said, stunned.

'No.'

'You've got blood all over you.' He stepped away. 'I'll have nothing to do with this. Binder can keep his coin.'

He snatched up his lantern and broke into a run.

'Wait,' I shouted after him. 'It's not what it looks like!'

Grover was already gone.

Beneath my stained coat, my heart drummed. Grover had been meant to get me out of here. Now I would have to walk back to Seven Dials.

Birdcage Park was close, and Vigiles rarely patrolled it. If I left the district that way, l could wash some of the blood off in Palmerston Lake. I shed my coat and forced myself to start moving.

I dumped the painting, along with my coat, in a skip on Caxton Street. Eliza could retrieve them later.

Birdcage Park was one of the largest green spaces in London. Now, in late September, tawny leaves scattered its paths. When I reached the lake, I splashed my face. I couldn't feel a thing above the elbow; my forearm was in agony. I came to the cold realisation that I was about to pass out.

There was a payphone at the edge of the lake. I took a coin from my pocket, then remembered I hadn't brought my burner. No one would be able to answer my signal. I rang anyway, hoping the courier Jaxon paid to watch the call box might pick up. No such luck.

I had to hide before I collapsed. Dripping wet, I stumbled into the undergrowth and curled up in a bank of fallen leaves, shivering. I thought I heard laughter before I blacked out.

───────────

Pain welled behind my eyes. Even before I opened them, the smells of rose oil and tobacco told me where I was. Jaxon had tucked me up on his chaise longue.

I started to turn over, but every limb was stiff. Even my jaw was locked. When I tried to lift my head, my neck protested.

Jaxon opened the door to his study. Seeing that I was awake, he let the others in.

'Paige.' Eliza placed a hand on my clammy forehead. 'What happened?'

'Hector, presumably.' Jaxon brushed her out of his way. 'My poor dreamwalker. I suspected our Underlord might lash out at you, but not that he would leave you insensible in Birdcage Park. He will suffer for it.'

I managed to speak: 'You found me?'

'Well, I collected you. Dr Nygård sent me a vision of your location. Into a bob cab I leapt, only to find my mollisher in a heap of leaves, without her coat.' He sat down beside me. 'It seems another poltergeist has left its mark on you.'

Trying not to move, I looked. On my inner forearm, four cuts formed a distinct M. The sight of the wound made me sick to my stomach. The marks were darker than the scars on my left palm, and broken veins spidered around them, stark against the pallor of my skin.

Jaxon studied it. His keyhole pupils swelled, heightening his spirit sight.

'This is a phantom blade,' he said. 'The work of the London Monster.'

Sweat poured off my forehead. Nadine leaned in for a look. 'There's a *blade* in there?'

'In a manner of speaking. I trust you are all familiar with the concept of a phantom limb,' Jaxon said. 'The itch in a severed arm, the ache in a pulled tooth – the sensation that an absent part is not just present, but in pain.'

'Chat mentioned that to me,' Nadine said. 'He felt it when he lost his hand.'

'A common occurrence. Some people even feel pain from limbs that never existed at all.' Jaxon took me by the wrist, lifting my heavy arm into the light. 'A small number of poltergeists can inflict phantom sensations, often related to their past lives. It's a sinister breed of apport, the force that breachers use to affect the physical world. A strangler might leave phantom hands around its victims' necks, for example.'

'You're saying Paige has … an invisible knife in her arm.' Zeke grasped my good shoulder. 'Right?'

'In essence.' Jaxon put my arm back down. 'Did Hector set the Monster on you, Paige?'

'No,' I rasped. 'He's dead.'

The news hung in the air.

'Dead,' Jaxon echoed. The others stared at me. 'Hector Grinslathe, Underlord of the Scion Citadel of London. That particular Hector is dead?'

'Yes,' I said.

'Deceased.' He weighed each of his syllables, like each one was pure gold. 'Silver cord severed. Lifeless. No longer. Is that what you are telling me, Paige?'

'Yes, Jaxon.'

'What about his spirit?'

'It wasn't there.'

'Pity. I would have loved to bind that miserable churl.' A low chuckle escaped him. 'Drink himself senseless and fall into the fireplace, did he?'

'No,' I said. 'He was beheaded.'

Jaxon raised his eyebrows.

'Paige,' Eliza said, breaking another hush, 'please don't tell me you killed the Underlord.'

'Of course not. They were dead when I arrived.'

'The whole *gang* is dead?'

'Only Cutmouth wasn't there.'

'Interesting.' Nadine leaned against the doorway. 'What was that you were saying earlier, about wishing someone would kill Hector?'

'Don't be ridiculous. I couldn't have taken down the Underbodies by myself.'

'Maybe you *weren't* by yourself.' She lifted a shoulder. 'Your friends in Oxford looked quite strong.'

'What?'

'I do hope you are not the responsible party, Paige,' Jaxon said, his voice soft. 'We tolerate many crimes in this syndicate, but murdering the Underlord ... I doubt even I could protect you if that charge were ever proven.'

'I would never have killed anyone like that,' I said quietly. 'Not even Hector.'

'No.' Jaxon tapped his knee. 'Did you find the painting?'

'I dumped it in Caxton Street.'

'Good. Did anyone see you leave?'

'Grover,' I said. 'He thinks I killed Hector.'

'Ah, the glym jack.'

Jaxon went to stand beside the window. We all watched him.

'Nadine,' he eventually said, 'you will monitor the gossip. If Grover has talked, we can find a way to sully his reliability. Zeke, Eliza, go to Caxton Street. Destroy the painting.'

'My coat is there, too,' I said, while Eliza turned away. 'It had blood on it.'

'Just so I understand,' Zeke said, 'are we going to cover up the fact that Paige was there?'

'That would be far too much of a headache. We are simply taking precautions,' Jaxon said. 'As soon as you have the painting, I will report the murders to the Abbess. Until then, do not breathe a word.'

The others filed out, all shooting me looks. Zeke and Eliza were clearly shaken, while Nadine was harder to read. Danica and Nick must both still be at work.

Jaxon sat with me again. He considered me, then brushed a hand over my hair. I could hardly remember the last time he had been tender.

'I understand,' he said, 'if you felt you couldn't tell the truth in front of the others. I will ask you once more, darling. Did you kill Hector?'

'No,' I said.

'But you wanted to kill him.'

'There's a difference between *wanting* to kill someone and actually killing someone, Jax.'

Which is why you're not dead yourself, I thought at him.

'True.' The corner of his mouth quirked. 'You're certain Cutmouth wasn't there?'

'Not that I could see.'

'Fortunate for her. Not so fortunate for London,' he said, 'if she claims the crown.' His eyes were bright as jewels, and two spots of colour glowed on his cheekbones. 'Her absence is conspicuous. That may work in our favour. All it would require is a rumour that she did the deed, and the sheer weight of suspicion will force her to flee for her own safety. You, meanwhile, will be out of the firing line.'

I sat up, cradling my arm. 'Maybe she actually did it.'

'I doubt it. She was devoted to Hector.' He looked thoughtful. 'Were they all beheaded?'

'Just him. The others were carved up,' I said. 'All of them were holding a red handkerchief.'

'Intriguing.' He stroked his chin. 'There's a message in the murder, Paige. And I don't think it's simply a reference to Hector running around like a headless chicken for the last eight years.'

'Mockery,' I ventured. 'He was getting too big for his boots. Acting like a king.'

'Quite. A very Bloody King.' He sat back. 'Whoever did it had good reason. Hector needed to die. Ever since Jed Bickford fell, we have watched his successor turn the syndicate into a nest of boors and sycophants. He was lazy and brutish, unworthy of the Rose Crown. Yet he *was* clever enough to win his scrimmage.

And now … well, if Cutmouth does flee, someone must be clever enough to win the next one.'

Only then did it sink in.

We were getting a new Underlord.

'Then change is coming,' I said. 'For better or worse.'

'Hector was rock bottom. The only way from here is up.' He stood and procured a cane from the cabinet. 'Use this, darling. You're going to find it hard to move.'

A mollisher knew when she was dismissed. As I opened the door to my room, I stopped dead.

Jaxon Hall was laughing his head off.

PART TWO

A HOTBED OF VILLAINY

And in the lowest deep a lower deep …

– JOHN MILTON, *PARADISE LOST*

INTERLUDE

Ode to London Under the Anchor

The old steeple rose pale and cold against the darkened sky. All across the citadel, the homeless were scattering dirt on their fires, while the Vigiles returned to their barracks, back from a long night of hunting their own. Still they seemed no closer to finding Paige Mahoney.

On the Lychgate, three corpses swayed in the breeze. An urchin climbed up to steal their shoelaces, watched by crows with bloody beaks.

On the banks of the Thames, mudlarks crept from their tunnels and dug into the ancient dirt, hoping for glints of the old world.

The amaurotics filed like soldiers to the Underground. They read the *Descendant* over their coffees, looking at the faces on the cover without seeing them. With silk nooses around their necks, they counted the coins that glutted the empire, unable to see the strings that entangled them.

And somewhere, a god was in chains again, waiting for a golden thread to lead the dreamwalker to him.

On the night of
November the first, 2059,
the Spiritus Club shall exhibit

A SCRIMMAGE

FOR DOMINANCE OF
THE LONDON SYNDICATE

N.B.—Venue to be confirmed closer to the Date.
All Participants shall be matched in close Combat
within the Confines of the Rose Ring.

A Memorial Bell will be rung for our erstwhile
Underlord at Dawn on the first of October.

Let the Signs of the Æther guide your Way.

Minty Wolfson.

Secretary of the Spiritus Club, Mistress of Ceremonies

On behalf of the Abbess,
Mime-Queen of I-2,
Interim Underqueen of the
Scion Citadel of London

IO

A REVOLUTIONARY
BREAKFAST

In the darkness before dawn, a small crowd of voyants waited on Cheapside. Bow Bells would only ring for one reason – to acknowledge the death of the Underlord.

At daybreak, the first chime rang out. Traditionally, one brave voyant would steal into the church and ring the bells for as long as possible before the Vigiles came to investigate. Since Hector had been a macharomancer, the Abbess had chosen a soothsayer to do it.

Thirteen chimes later, sirens rose from the Guild of Vigilance. The gathered voyants melted away, slipping between the cracks of London. I wished I could do the same.

Today, I would face the Unnatural Assembly.

A silhouette darted across the rooftops. There went the bell-ringer. I hoped he would get away in good time. Nick, who had been watching in silence, sat down and poured three flutes of sparkling rose mecks.

'To Haymarket Hector,' he said, raising one towards Bow Bells. 'The worst Underlord the citadel has ever seen. May his reign be swiftly forgotten.'

Zeke helped himself to a flute. I leaned against the parapet, curling and uncurling my fingers. Nick had told me not to keep my arm still for too long.

Only he and Zeke had felt like going to the tribute. We had wrapped up some food and spent the night here, on the roof of the old tower on Wood Street, just for a break from the den. Sometimes it was easy to forget that we were all friends, despite our bizarre circumstances.

'Paige.' Nick was looking at me. 'Are you okay?'

'Just nervous. I'll be fine.'

He nodded and reached for a pear. Zeke gave me a concerned look.

Not long after I fled the scene, Jaxon had reported my grim discovery to the Abbess. Two days later, a letter had appeared in our dead drop, along with a sprig of hyacinth. Minty Wolfson, the Mistress of Ceremonies, had called for anyone with knowledge of the murder to report to the Chanting Lay and give evidence to the Abbess.

After a week, a second notice had been sent, giving Cutmouth three further days to present herself to the Unnatural Assembly. Finally, a third letter had appeared, to announce the date of the scrimmage.

Cutmouth had failed to answer the summons. Surely that meant she was guilty.

Hector had been laid to rest in the garden of Old Dunstan in the East, a ruined church near Tower Hill. Overgrown and beautiful, with a canopy of branches, it was where all syndicate leaders were interred.

The first light of October bathed us in a golden haze, burning away the mist and dew. The Vigiles searched Bow Bells, then retreated.

'Coast is clear,' Nick said. 'Shall we go?'

'Let's wait a little longer,' Zeke said, eyes closed. 'I'm enjoying it up here.'

Nick smiled. 'All right.'

On Monday evening, Jaxon and I had received a summons from the Abbess, who was now interim Underqueen. I suspected Jaxon had tried to silence Grover, but he must have evaded our cutthroats and talked.

If anyone believed his story, I would end up in the Thames. Not many people had liked Hector, but his death threatened all mime-lords and mime-queens. If one of them could be killed, then they all could.

'Zeke,' I said, 'were there any voyant organisations in Mexico?'

'Not that I heard about, but I didn't know what I was, back then.' He toyed with his shoelace. 'There weren't that many voyants in the city where I lived.'

I felt a small pang. It had been a long time since I had lived in a country where clairvoyance wasn't acknowledged in law, even as treason.

'Sometimes I wonder which is worse,' Nick said. 'Not knowing, or being defined by it.'

'Not knowing,' I said, with certainty. 'I'd rather understand what I am.'

Zeke rested his chin on his knees. 'I'm not sure.'

Nick glanced at me and shook his head. Something had happened to Zeke that had made him lose his original gift and become unreadable. Jaxon and Nadine knew, but the rest of us were in the dark.

'Paige,' Zeke said, 'there's something you should know.'

'What?' I said. He was looking at Nick, whose jaw clenched. 'What's the matter?'

'We dropped into the Minister's Cat yesterday,' Nick said. 'There was a group of voyants there, taking bets on who might have killed Hector.'

'Right.' I tried to sound calm. 'Who were the candidates?'

Zeke clasped his elegant hands. 'Cutmouth and the Highwayman were mentioned.'

'But you were the favourite.' Nick looked unhappy. 'The clear favourite.'

Grover had definitely talked.

'They've no proof,' I said. 'Have they?'

'No. We just wanted to warn you.' Nick stood. 'Come on. You don't want to be late.'

'You two do believe me, don't you?'

'Paige, of course we do.' Nick took me by the shoulder. 'I wouldn't care if you *had* killed Hector, but I know you didn't. Jaxon will protect you. We all will.'

Zeke nodded. I released my breath, wishing I had the same confidence.

As the sun rose, we packed up our camp. We had climbed up here from the street, but now we meant to make a leap to the nearest rooftop, so we could stay off the ground for a while. Nick went first. As soon as he touched down, he fell into a roll – a lithe turn of limbs, smooth and practised – and then broke straight into a run.

I was next. Just as I jumped, my right arm went rigid, the phantom blade twisting inside me. I landed badly and ended up sprawled on the roof, hissing in pain. Nick came straight back for me, his face white.

'Paige, are you all right?'

'Not really.' I clenched my teeth. 'It's the blade.'

'Don't move.' He crouched beside me. 'Can you feel your legs?'

'Yeah, they feel great.'

Nick checked for breaks before helping me up. I pushed up my sleeve and grimaced at the sight of the mark. It was weeping yet again.

'We'll bandage it.' Nick touched my back. 'It will be okay, Paige.'

I pulled my sleeve down. 'Only if Jaxon finds its name.'

'This is very high,' Zeke called. He was still grasping the parapet, white-knuckled. 'Why was I less nervous going up this thing?'

'You didn't look down.' Nick beckoned him. 'It's not as far as you think.'

'It looks really far, Nick.'

'I promise you, it's easier than climbing down. You can do it.'

Zeke blew out a breath and jumped. Not quite far enough. He grabbed the edge of the building, but his legs swung towards the street, kicking at nothing. I started towards him, my heart in my throat.

Nick got there first. With a strength born of many years of climbing, he grasped Zeke under the arms and lifted him away from a long fall. Zeke clamped a hand over his chest, laughing between gasps for air.

'I don't think I'm cut out for this.'

'You're fine.' Nick patted his shoulder. Their foreheads were close together, almost brushing. 'Paige and I have been doing this for years. Give it time.'

Zeke gave us a rueful grin. 'No offence, but I think you're both insane.'

'We prefer *intrepid*.' Nick smiled back at him. 'Seriously, it's a good skill to learn. If you can run the slates, you can move around London at night. That's as close to freedom as it gets in Scion.'

I had to agree. Knowing how to run and climb had almost saved me from detainment, that fateful day in March. If that flux dart hadn't caught me, I might have escaped without ever setting foot in Oxford.

We headed for the section border. Zeke was nervous about jumping again, but Nick was patient with him, just as he had been with me at the beginning.

After a while, we stopped for a rest. The wind picked up as I looked out at the citadel, letting it work its dark enchantment on my state of mind. From here, we could see the pale dome of the Inquisitorial Courts, where voyants were occasionally given televised sham trials before they were sentenced to death. The sight of it gave me a chill.

'The first time I came to London, I was terrified. All those layers of history and death – they made me feel like a morsel, swallowed whole by something that had never even seen me,' Nick said. 'After I moved here for good, I slowly came to realise that I didn't mind being devoured. If I could just be part of London, I felt as if I could be anything, *do* anything. All I had to do was let myself be swept away.'

He had a way of voicing what I could only feel.

'I'm glad I came here,' Zeke said quietly. 'Even if it scares me, too.'

Nick nodded. He wrapped his arms around us both, drawing us in close. I rested my head against his shoulder.

Nearby, the Bank of Scion England stood on Threadneedle Street, pumping money across the empire, keeping Nashira Sargas in extraordinary opulence. This was what I had to fight. The anchor and its riches against one young Irish woman and her pillow full of pennies.

But standing beside Nick and Zeke, I remembered I wasn't alone. And now Hector was dead, there might yet be hope.

When we reached the den, I headed up to my room to get ready. Taking slow breaths, I tidied my hair, then opted for a blazer over a cream shirt, a black jersey, and dark check trousers – smart, but not too showy.

Jaxon waited in the hallway with his rosewood cane. He wore a frock coat and a wide-brimmed hat.

'A fine morning for an excursion,' he said. 'Dr Nygård said you took a tumble.'

'The blade distracted me. I'm fine.'

'Indeed you are. The London Monster won't be tormenting you again.'

'You found his name?'

'Eliza did. Hold out your arm.'

Relieved, I rolled up my right sleeve. Eliza had been scouring our records for days, trying to find the real name of the London Monster.

Jaxon took out his binding knife. It was sharp as a scalpel, with a bone handle and a silver blade. He turned up his own sleeve, revealing the white scars on his forearm, where he had carved scores of names into his skin. He pressed the blade to the mark on my arm, then turned it on himself.

If Jaxon wanted to control a spirit for a short time, he daubed its name in blood on his skin, or made cuts that would heal. If he wanted to keep it, he left a deep scar. Some binders preferred tattoos, but not Jaxon.

He cut the letters without flinching, keeping the wounds shallow. The other names were all beautifully written, with painful-looking flourishes.

'I never asked you what would happen if you wanted to sell an older boundling,' I said, watching. 'How do you revoke the scarring?'

'I would simply allow the spirit to leave me,' he said. 'The scars that still hold boundlings are a little colder than the rest.'

'Lots of people have the same names.'

'That was precisely why I rested my blade on the mark. To make clear to the æther who I wish to bind.' His arm seeped blood. 'Let us hope this name works. It must be the one the Monster held closest.'

'How do you mean?'

'Well, if someone were to try to bind or summon my spirit with the name my distinguished parents foisted on me, my spirit would ignore the call. I abandoned that name. To control a spirit, I require its quick name – one it chose or accepted, and still heeded when it died.'

He carved the final letter. RHYNWICK WILLIAMS was written near his wrist bone, bleeding.

I sensed the London Monster coming. The mark burned cold as ice, and my knees wobbled. Jaxon steadied me. As the poltergeist hurtled towards us, he called out, 'That will be quite enough, Rhynwick.'

At once, the spirit was paralysed.

'Leave my dreamwalker in peace,' Jaxon said. 'Your reign of terror is over.'

Bound and obedient, the London Monster moved towards its new master. I leaned against the wall, breathing in sharp bursts, drenched in sweat.

'There. Mine,' Jaxon said, 'until I quietly sell him to a trader. We'll send him along a ley line to Europe.' His gaze flicked to the mark on my arm, which had turned grey. 'The scar, I'm afraid, will always remain.'

'Is there really no way to get rid of it?'

'Not to my knowledge. Daphnomancers say that essence of the bay laurel can allay the pain of spiritual wounds. Probably augurs' drivel, but I shall ask one of my couriers to fetch a bottle from the Garden.'

I doubted it was half as good as amaranth.

'Thank you,' I said. 'For binding the Monster.'

'It's what I do, darling.' He started to bandage his wrist. 'Hold your nerve today, and we'll be fine. The Abbess won't condemn you without evidence.'

'Hector was her friend.'

'Hortensia knows very well that he was a dangerous oaf. She will have to address what the glym jack saw, but she won't linger on the subject.' Jaxon held open the door. 'Come. Let's not keep the riff-raff waiting.'

One of our trusted drivers picked us up on Earlham Street. Though the Abbess lived in Kensington, the meeting would be held in II Cohort. All members of the Unnatural Assembly had been invited to attend.

'Not many will show,' Jaxon said. 'The centrals will, but those from outlying sections are unlikely to bother. Lazy, impertinent rogues.'

While he soliloquised about the various reasons he despised his fellow criminals, I sat in silence and nodded from time to time. The Abbess had seemed kind enough at the Juditheon, but she clearly had a firm hand. If she suspected me, I doubted she would show mercy.

By the time we got to Hackney, rain was pouring from dark clouds, sending water surging through the gutters. Jaxon opened an umbrella. A few voyants caught sight of our auras and touched their foreheads.

Usually, neither of us would be welcome here. The Wicked Lady hated Jaxon. I had lost track of the reasons, but she had banned us from her section on pain of a beating. The Abbess must have overruled her.

Haggerston Baths had been boarded up for over a century. When Jaxon rapped on its door, a dark-eyed medium cracked it open.

'Password?'

'Mother Shipton,' Jaxon said.

'Thank you, White Binder.' She opened the door. 'Welcome to Hackney.'

We stepped into the musty interior of the bathhouse. Jaxon folded down his umbrella. 'Tell me,' he said to the medium, 'how many of us have arrived?'

'Fourteen, along with twelve mollishers, but the Abbess expects more.'

'Not even half, but more than I thought.' He passed me the umbrella. 'Do lead the way. What a *delight* it will be to see all my old friends.'

Most of the Unnatural Assembly were recluses, choosing to stay holed up in their dens while their hirelings and cronies did their bidding. Maria and the Pearl Queen were among the rare exceptions, often walking the streets with their voyants. A few maintained loose friendships; more held grudges, some with roots in the gang wars.

Once the medium had secured the door, she led us into a large chamber. An arched white ceiling swept above us, painted with neat blue rectangles. The skylight that ran along it was filthy, turning the place as murky as dishwater. Candles flickered here and there, making the shadows dance. Top notes of sweet blossom were layered like petals over a grave, not quite overpowering the illicit reek of alcohol.

The Unnatural Assembly had gathered on the tiles where a deep pool must have been. The majority were in disguise, from simple hoods and scarves to threatening masks.

Even after Scion had seen him in Trafalgar Square, Jaxon showed his face wherever he went. I wore my red silk out of habit, though it wouldn't do much good, thanks to Didion.

While Jaxon straightened his cravat, I took stock of the auras in the room. Despite years of prejudice against the lower orders, our leaders displayed a wide range of gifts. Maria was among them, talking amiably with Jimmy O'Goblin, mime-lord of II-2. Their mollishers – Witcher Cully and Lady Godiva – stood nearby, both hooded.

I spotted Nell's old mime-lord, the Bully-Rook. He lurked in a corner with Jack Hickathrift, who shot me a winning smile. There was the Wretched Sylph, pale and mournful; there was the elderly Pearl Queen in her finery, the only syndicate leader to have come alone. I knew most of the others by sight, even if I had never spoken to them.

On a small balcony, the Abbess watched over her flock, wearing a tailored green suit. Her hair fell in sculpted waves down one side of her neck. Three members of her gang, the Nightingales – including the redhead from the Juditheon – were sitting around her, along with the Monk.

'What do you know?' The Glass Duchess examined us through a haze of smoke. A smirk crept up one side of her wide mouth. 'Assembly, behold! The White Binder has graced us with his presence.'

'Well met,' said her twin and mollisher, the Glass Dell. The only way you could tell them apart was by the wiry brown curls under their bowler hats; the Duchess kept hers much shorter. 'We haven't seen you in a summer, Binder.'

'And how we have missed his wisdom. Welcome, White Binder,' the Abbess called. 'And you, Pale Dreamer. Welcome.'

Heads turned to look at us: some with curiosity, others with open hostility. Jaxon ignored everyone but the Abbess. 'My dear Hortensia.' He touched his chest, making half a bow. 'It's been too long.'

'So it has.' She tilted her head. 'Why do I never see you at the Chanting Lay?'

'I have no particular uses for a night parlour,' Jaxon said, making the Glass Dell choke on her aster, 'but perhaps we could meet at a coffeehouse?'

'Of course.'

'Binder, you rancid old codger,' the Glym Lord boomed, slapping Jaxon so hard on the back that he almost dropped his cane. 'How are you?'

'How's life?' Tom the Rhymer appeared over his other shoulder, clapping down a liver-spotted hand. Jaxon pursed his lips. 'You know, next time somebody paints a tarot deck, they should stick you on the Hermit card.'

'If only,' Jaxon said. 'Then I might be left in peace.'

'Och, you're no fun.'

I smiled behind my red silk. Glym and Tom were in their seventies, both almost as big as Rephs. Seeing me, Glym flashed a grin that made his eyes twinkle, teeth white against his weathered brown skin. Greying locks fell to his muscular waist, and freckles dotted his nose.

Tom noticed me, too, and winked. A Scottish oracle with ruddy cheeks and short curtains of blue-rinsed hair, he was the only other jumper in the room. As always, he wore a trench coat and a hat with a wide brim. He and Glym loved nothing more than pranking other voyants.

'Leave him be, you two. Binder was good to come all this way,' the Abbess said. 'On that note, I do apologise for these grim surroundings. I would have invited you to Kensington, but I've heard troubling reports that the night Vigiles have been moving by daylight.'

I had barely noticed the graffiti on the walls, or the discarded bottles. Most of our hideouts were derelict places: abandoned buildings, closed stations. We gathered in the places Scion had forgotten.

'The same in my section,' the Wretched Sylph said. 'What are we to do, Abbess?'

'We will endure, as always,' the Abbess answered. 'This syndicate has held strong for almost a century. It will survive this red zone, Sylvia.'

I tried to read her aura. A physical medium – quite a rare gift. She had the sort of dreamscape that called out for spirits to seize control of her.

The Heathen Philosopher arrived in a cloud of perfume and white powder, trailing a lanky mollisher. Two voyants had to keep Didion Waite from entering, and we were treated to a volley of his pompous complaints ('I may not be a mime-lord, but I am a *valued* member of this community, Madam Underqueen!'). When the doors swung open again, the Wicked Lady marched in with the Highwayman. She was the brutal mime-queen of this section, presiding over several of the most notorious slums in the citadel, including Jacob's Island and the Frying Pan. She was a short and burly woman in her thirties, with a klaxon voice and lips purpled by aster.

'My dear friend,' the Abbess said. 'Thank you for allowing us to gather here.'

'No skin off my nose.' The Wicked Lady tossed her blonde curls over her shoulder. 'Half this section is falling apart. Scion won't come knocking here.' She gave Jaxon a poisonous look. 'Shall we get on with it?'

'I had rather hoped more would join us.' The Abbess looked around. 'Where is Mary Bourne?'

'Mary sends her apologies, Abbess,' said a whey-faced courier, curtseying low. 'She has a fever. Her mollisher thought it best to stay with her.'

'We wish her well. And Ark Ruffian?'

'Intoxicated, madam, the wretched scoundrel. So is his knave of a mollisher,' Jimmy slurred, waving a finger. 'Yesternight we raised a glass of moonshine to our Underlord. I says to him, *now, Ark, you know very well that Madam Abbess has called our names in her hour of need, perhaps you oughtn't to drink another*, but—'

'Yes, thank you, Jimmy. I believe I understand,' the Abbess said. 'Congratulations on arriving so clear-headed.' Her hands tightened on the railing. 'And what of the Rag and Bone Man? Does he consider himself too fine for these proceedings?'

A long silence followed her words.

'I don't think I've ever seen him,' Madam Speaker rasped. 'He could be dead, for all I know.'

'He lurks beneath the ground, as always,' the Lord Costermonger said. 'I hear the latest mollisher, La Chiffonnière, rules Camden in his name.'

'A sloven, as ever,' the Abbess said. 'He would sooner skulk in his squalid lair than answer the call of the syndicate.' She raised her chin. 'No matter. The room will smell less foul without him. Be seated, all of you.'

A few rickety chairs had been mustered. I sat beside Jaxon and tried to look calm.

'You will all have received the news that Hector, my dearest friend, was murdered,' the Abbess said. 'It now falls to me to command his beloved syndicate before his replacement is chosen by scrimmage. As part of my duties as interim Underqueen, I must investigate the circumstances that led to the deaths of Hector and the Underbodies. Pale Dreamer, would you present yourself to the floor?'

I glanced at Jaxon. He gave me the barest nod, and I stood.

'The White Binder informed me that you found our late Underlord,' the Abbess said. I walked to the middle of the room. 'Is this true?'

My legs turned to columns of ice.

'Yes,' I said.

'Why were you on the Devil's Acre?'

'That's what I'd like to know,' the Bully-Rook said, dealing me a nasty look.

'The White Binder sent me,' I said. 'Hector interfered with our business interests at the Garden. He confiscated a valuable painting from our stall, claiming it was a forgery. I went to negotiate its safe return.'

'By sneaking in and killing him?' the Glass Duchess asked, to murmurs of agreement. 'One of my best traders saw you arguing with Cutmouth.'

'I did speak to her,' I said. 'She wanted retribution for an insult from a while ago. I hope your trader saw her slice *me*, not the other way round.'

'Cutmouth was not among the dead,' the Abbess said. 'Could she have reached the Devil's Acre before you did?'

'Yes.'

'Disgraceful. Murdering her mime-lord in his own parlour,' the Pearl Queen groused. 'What has our underworld become?'

'We should have expected no less of a vile augur,' the Heathen Philosopher said darkly, earning himself an icy stare from Lady Godiva, a palmist. 'Until that woman is found, any of us could be next.'

'One thing at a time.' The Abbess looked down at me. 'When you arrived, did you find any trace of Cutmouth?'

'No,' I said. 'There were no spirits, either.'

'Not even the London Monster, which protected Hector?'

'Not that I saw, Underqueen.'

'That may be a promising lead,' the Heathen Philosopher said, stroking his ample chin. 'According to my records of poltergeists, the London Monster leaves a distinctive initial on the skin. Find it, and we find the killer.'

My fist clenched behind my back.

'Grover reported that you were covered in blood,' the Abbess said. 'Do you deny it?'

'Hector was beheaded,' I said. 'I checked the body to make sure it was him. I also looked for the painting, but the killer must have taken it.'

Eliza and Zeke had chosen to burn it. Over a year of work, up in smoke.

'Of course it was gone,' the Bully-Rook said, huffing. 'How very convenient. Now we can't test its authenticity. How did you obtain it, Binder?'

'For goodness' sake.' Maria sighed. 'Who *cares* if it was a forgery?' She lit a cigarette. 'We're criminals. What's a little mime-art among friends?'

'It's our problem if he's fleecing us.'

'Enough.' Jaxon stood, his eyes cold. 'I will not stomach further insults, Hortensia. The Pale Dreamer has behaved impeccably. I sent her to the Devil's Acre to retrieve my property, which Hector had seized for his own amusement. We all know he made a sport of such things. Tell me, who among you would have stood for what he did to me?'

Tom the Rhymer chuckled. 'You're not making her sound innocent, Binder.'

'What are you insinuating, Tom?' Jaxon turned. 'That I would *lie* to the Assembly?'

'No,' Tom said mildly. 'Just that you'd make a poor defence lawyer.'

'I take that as a compliment in this sham of a court.' Jaxon looked up at the Abbess, grasping his cane tight. 'The glym jack is amaurotic, Hortensia. When did we decide to accept rotten words as truth?'

'A good point,' the Pearl Queen said. 'All amaurotics' testimonies should be treated as hearsay.'

'Thank you, Margaret. I reported the murder as soon as I heard of it,' Jaxon said. 'If I had sent the Pale Dreamer to assassinate Hector, I assure you, none of you would ever have known she was there. A dreamwalker can kill in bloodless silence. No need for beheadings.'

There was a brief silence as they all considered me, their gazes wary and intrigued.

'My friend, I assure you, the Pale Dreamer is not a suspect,' the Abbess said. 'I only wanted to establish what happened that night, and to give her a chance to defend her integrity. If a mollisher has been falsely accused or framed, it is my duty to get to the bottom of it.'

I hadn't even considered the idea that someone could have framed me.

'Many of you will have heard that Scion is hunting the Pale Dreamer. She requires our protection, not our mistrust,' the Abbess continued. 'Cutmouth has ignored the call to serve as Underqueen. Her absence condemns her. She is our prime suspect. Is that understood?'

Tom muttered a few choice words, but shut up when Glym gave him a warning look. There were murmurs of assent from the others.

'On that note,' Jaxon said, 'will Didion be punished for unmasking my mollisher?'

'I've dealt with it, Binder,' Maria said grimly. 'Now Hector is gone, rest assured, Didion and I will be having more than a few words.'

'I will speak to you about that in due course, Maria. Thank you for your honesty, Pale Dreamer,' the Abbess said. 'You may be seated.'

I returned to sit beside Jaxon, heart thumping. He patted the back of my hand.

The Abbess leaned on the railing. Even through her veil, I could see the dark stains under her eyes.

'Cutmouth must be found before she kills again,' she said. 'In the meantime, keep watch for the mark of the London Monster. Maria, my dear,' she added, 'since you have so many contacts in the markets, I want you to search for the origin of the red handkerchiefs that were found with the bodies. They seemed to be of fine quality.'

Maria nodded, though she didn't look too pleased with being called *my dear*.

'Now,' the Abbess said, 'does anyone have any idea where Cutmouth might have fled?'

Nobody spoke. Before I knew it, I was standing.

'Abbess,' I said, 'I hope you'll forgive the intrusion, but there's something else the Unnatural Assembly needs to hear. Something that—'

'—had almost slipped my mind. My mollisher is as shrewd as ever.' Jaxon rose. 'Despite numerous attempts to keep her off my turf, Cutmouth was a patron of several gambling houses and night parlours in Soho. Perhaps it would be sensible to begin the search there.'

I bit the inside of my cheek. He knew very well what I had wanted to say. 'Quite,' the Abbess said, looking between us with obvious curiosity. 'Would you be offended if I sent my Nightingales to help you?'

'Of course not. We would be delighted to host them.'

'You are too kind. If there are no other points to raise, I shall let you return to your sections in peace. I hope to see you all at the scrimmage.' When the Abbess took a step back, her gang stood. 'Grub Street will take charge of proceedings. Until then, may the æther guide you.'

Everyone rose to leave. Outside, Jaxon pulled me under the umbrella, gripping my elbow a little too hard. 'You see?' he said. 'Cutmouth is the one they want. You have nothing to fear now, darling.'

I could hear the anger he was holding in his voice, like poison in a cup of sweet wine. 'Jax,' I said coldly, 'why did you cut me off just then?'

'Because you were going to tell them about Oxford.'

'Hector is gone. The Abbess seems different,' I said. 'Why shouldn't we try to get through to her?'

'Do use your common sense, Paige. We needed to ensure that you weren't killed for treachery. That was my priority, and so it will remain,' Jaxon said. 'Making yourself look insane will not help your case.'

'We could show her the entrance to the Pentad Line.'

'Scion has already sealed it.'

The news shocked me into silence. The tunnel to Oxford – the only solid evidence of my sanity – was now out of my reach for good.

'When?' I managed. 'When did they seal it?'

'The Banqueting House has closed for renovation. They must have worked out how we accessed the tunnel.' Jaxon rounded a corner, wrenching me with him. 'Nobody wants to hear about Oxford. Nobody cares about your giants. Disobey my orders again, and the Unnatural Assembly will see *this* little piece of evidence, Pale Dreamer.'

He dug his fingers into my arm, right where the London Monster had scarred me. I stiffened when I saw his face, blank and devoid of warmth. He had looked the same when he threatened Eliza.

Now I understood why he had bound the London Monster. So long as I was his Pale Dreamer, he would keep my wound from hurting. So long as I remained loyal to him, the syndicate would protect me. But if I ever challenged him, or tried to talk about the Rephs, he would expose the dirty secret underneath my sleeve. The scar kept me chained as fast as a boundling, preventing me from ever rising above him. He might as well have cut my name into his skin as well.

I should have shown the tunnel to as many voyants as I could.

I should never have returned to him.

'Now, back to Seven Dials.' He opened the cab door for me, switching the charm back on. 'The others are meeting us in Neal's Yard.'

Blackmailing, devious *bastard*. I could hardly get my answer out: 'Why?'

'To break our fast,' he said. 'Every revolution begins with breakfast, darling.'

———

Even a revolutionary breakfast – whatever that might be – had to be eaten at Chateline's. It was our favourite cookshop, tucked away in quaint Neal's Yard.

The others met us in our usual booth, tucked behind a screen. As always, I sat beside Jaxon, where a mollisher belonged. He ordered a spendthrift breakfast – everything on the menu, from buttered crumpets and French pastries to sausages, crisp bacon, and kedgeree with hard-boiled eggs.

Chat came to pour me a fresh cup of coffee. A burly, soft-spoken sniffer, he blotted out the reek of spirits with the scents of his own cooking.

'What's all this for, Binder?' he asked. 'Giving Hector a farewell toast?'

'In a fashion, my friend.'

'I can't say I'll miss him myself, but you do as you please. Any more drinks?'

Nadine reached for a bread roll. 'Could I get a citron pressé with syrup, Chat?'

'On its way.'

Chat returned to the kitchen. He had been a bare-knuckle fighter until a jealous rival had cut off his dominant hand. Since he had won Jaxon a small fortune in bets, Jaxon had lent him enough coin to open this place.

Fortunately for Chat, his food was good enough that he had cleared that debt with ease. If only it could be so easy to get Jaxon off my back.

Eliza served herself a slice of honey pound cake. 'How was the meeting?'

'Oh, tedious in the extreme. I almost forgot how insufferable they all are,' Jaxon said. 'Still, Paige convinced the Abbess of her innocence, so it served its purpose.' (*I'll bet it did*, I thought.) 'Devilled kidney, Danica?'

He offered her a hot plate. She gave it a surly look before taking it.

'This is the first time we've seen you in days.' Zeke slid a dish of sugared corn muffins towards her. 'What are you living on up there?'

Danica always looked out of her depth outside the den. Wild red hair tumbled from its bun, oil spattered her freckled cheeks, and a soldering burn had appeared on her right hand.

'Oxygen,' she said. 'Nitrogen. I could go on.'

Nadine popped a fried mushroom into her mouth. 'What are you *working* on, then?'

'I have set Danica a task,' Jaxon said. 'I want her to create a jamming device. Something that will stop Senshield from detecting our auras.'

Nick raised his eyebrows. 'Since when did you care about Senshield?'

'I've always cared about it, Dr Nygård. I simply choose not to make a song and dance about the matter.' Jaxon sipped his coffee. 'As mime-lord, I mustn't frighten my voyants.'

I spoke for the first time: 'Do you think you can do it, Dani?'

'In time,' she said. 'Scion is working on a handheld version of Senshield. I need to see a prototype, but my security clearance is too low. It will take more promotions to get there.'

'A handheld version.' Nick lowered his cup, his brow furrowed. 'I'd heard about that, but I didn't realise they already had prototypes.'

'It could just be a rumour.' Nadine sweetened her drink. 'Couldn't it?'

The development was still inevitable. If amaurotic Vigiles could be equipped with Senshield, Scion wouldn't need sighted eyes on the streets. No voyant would be able to openly work for the anchor again.

And I could do nothing about it. I wanted to break every plate on the table.

'Do eat,' Jaxon said to me. 'We have much to do over the coming weeks. You'll need your appetite and your wits about you.'

I took a bite of bread.

'You look better, Paige,' Eliza said. 'How's your arm?'

She looked a little better, too, now she had got some rest. Jaxon had given her the cold shoulder for a total of three days, in the end.

'It's grand,' I said. 'Thanks for finding the name.'

'We needed you back. There have been a few rainbow ruses in Soho,' she said. 'I could use some help from our mollisher, if you're up for it.'

Jaxon despised rainbow ruses, where amaurotic buskers pretended to be voyant. Most of the time, we chased them away. Now and then, however, he told us to punish them for their insolence.

'Don't concern yourself with fools, Eliza,' Jaxon said. 'We have more important matters to discuss. Matters that require us to look beyond I-4.' He paused, presumably for dramatic effect. 'Would you like to hear them, darlings?'

Zeke caught my eye and pulled a face. 'Yes, Jaxon.'

'Good. Gather round, then.'

We all leaned closer. Jaxon looked at each of us in turn, his eyes aflame with passion.

'I have been devoted to I-4 for almost twenty years. Together, we have kept this section prosperous,' he said. 'When Nick and I started the gang, we were two motes of dust on the floor of this citadel, barely maintaining Seven Dials. Just look at how we have risen since then.'

Eliza nudged Nick, who gave her a modest smile in return.

'You six are my magnum opus,' Jaxon said. 'And despite your occasional – well, regular – blunders, I have nothing but the greatest admiration for your skill and loyalty.' His voice dropped a note. 'But we can do no more with I-4. We are the best and brightest of all the dominant gangs in the citadel. Everyone wants to be us.

There is only one step to the top of the ladder.' His mouth curled up at one corner. 'I will take that step, my darlings. I mean to enter the scrimmage. I mean to be Underlord.'

Fuck.

'I knew it.' Eliza clapped, delighted. 'I *knew* you had this up your sleeve.'

'It could be dangerous,' Nick said. 'Don't candidates fight for the Rose Crown?'

'We held off an attack from Scion in Trafalgar Square,' Jaxon reminded him. 'I doubt a dust-up among thieves will hold a candle to that night.'

'We only got away because Paige was hindering Scion. You could be—'

'Paige will support me in this endeavour.' Jaxon took out his case of expensive cigars. 'Isn't that right, Paige?'

I mustered what I hoped was a convincing smile, even as I screamed inside.

'Absolutely,' I said. 'The only way from here is up.'

'You have faith that I can win, I trust.'

'Of course.'

Jaxon had the most ambition and cunning out of all the mimelords in London. Given how ruthless he could be, not to mention his mastery of binding and spirit combat, he had a high chance of winning. A *very* high chance. Nick looked as apprehensive as I felt.

'Good.' Jaxon took a cold draw of his cigar before lighting it with a long match. 'I shall be leaving some homework in your room – reading material, so you can learn the noble customs of the scrimmage.'

I nodded mechanically. While Scion and the Rephs plotted their next move, I would be doing my homework, like a good little mollisher.

'Wait.' I paused. 'What do you mean?'

'All contenders for the crown fight with their mollishers,' Jaxon said. 'You will be joining me in the Rose Ring.' He offered a wide smile. 'How could I be Underlord without my dreamwalker beside me?'

I exchanged a silent glance with Nick, who opened his mouth, then closed it tight. Nadine looked intrigued, while Zeke didn't seem to know what to think. Danica just sat there with her usual poker face.

'Right,' I said. 'I'd be … mollisher supreme.'

'It's such a risk, but imagine it,' Eliza said, flushed with exhiliration. 'Jaxon, we could really be—'

'The prevailing gang of the Scion Citadel of London.' Jaxon chuckled, his eyes twinkling. 'Yes, my faithful medium. Yes, we could.'

Eliza was basking in his good mood. I remembered that feeling so clearly.

'We'd be calling the shots.' Nadine traced the edge of her glass. 'We could tell Didion to blow up the Juditheon.'

'Or give all its spirits to us,' Eliza said. 'We could do *anything*.'

'Just the seven of us. The lords of London. It will be exquisite.' Jaxon breathed smoke. 'We must prepare ourselves. Paige,' he said, almost as an afterthought, 'fetch another rack of toast sandwiches, will you?'

It had been more than two years since I was the tea girl. I must not have shown enough enthusiasm. The whole gang watched me as I walked over to the bar and waited for Chat to emerge from the kitchen.

I should have known Jaxon would leap on this opportunity. Hector had lorded it over him for years, like the kidsmen who had tortured him as a child. This was his chance to balance the scales. To rule the entire underworld.

As mollisher supreme, I would be more powerful than most of the Unnatural Assembly, but still utterly dependent on Jaxon. Thanks to the wretched scar on my arm, he would always be able to blackmail me. I pressed my fingers to my temples, wishing suddenly that I could talk to Liss or Julian.

'… them all at the Garden that night.' I became aware of a gruff voice. 'I heard there was some quarrel with the French girl in the Seven Seals.'

'She's not French,' another voyant murmured. 'That's their whisperer, the Silent Bell. They say she's a free-worlder, like the Black Diamond.'

Chat emerged in his apron, his cheeks red from the heat of the ovens. 'Can I help you, Dreamer?'

'Just some more toast sandwiches, please, Chat.'

'Coming up.'

He returned to the kitchen. While I waited, I continued to eavesdrop, drumming my fingers on the bar.

'... saw her with Cutmouth. She was masked, but I'm sure it was her.'

'She's really back, then?'

'Aye. They're saying she was first on the scene,' the deeper voice said. 'I know the glym jack that went with her. A good man, he is – trustworthy as rotties come. He said she was covered in blood.'

'She's the one on the screens. Did you hear?'

'It's all over Cheapside. Maybe Hector sold her out, and that's why she killed him.'

It had been grim enough when Didion had unmasked me. This was all I needed. Sooner or later, a night Vigile would catch wind of these rumours at the market, and then Scion would know them, too.

So much for keeping a low profile. Chat returned with the rack of buttered sandwiches. I went back to my seat with them.

'The voyants in that booth,' I murmured to Jaxon. 'They're talking about us.'

'Are they, now?' He tapped his cigar into an ashtray. 'And what are they saying?'

'That I killed Hector, among other things.'

'Certain people in this section might wish to consider minding their tongues,' Jaxon said, loudly enough that everyone looked. 'I understand the White Binder does not tolerate slander. Least of all from his own voyants.'

There was a taut silence before three soothsayers rose from behind the screen, took their coats from the nearest stand, and left in a hurry, keeping their faces turned away from us. Jaxon watched them leave as everyone returned to their meals, their conversations hushed.

'One of them knows the glym jack,' I said. 'Grover is still talking, Jax.'

'You heard the Pearl Queen. The word of an amaurotic is rotten.' He raised his cigar back to his lips. 'Don't fret. You have me to vouch for you, darling. Once I am Underlord, these allegations will disappear.'

It took most of my willpower to nod and keep eating.

I tuned out the rest of the conversation. As I pushed my food around my plate, my ribs seemed to constrict. I was so close to surrendering. For all I tried, I couldn't see a way out of this corner. Perhaps I should give up the fight, accept the hand I had been dealt, and force myself to forget Oxford.

Goosebumps rose along my arms. I looked up slowly, sensing two dreamscapes just outside. Two unusual dreamscapes, horribly familiar.

My fingertips turned numb. I stopped breathing. A sour taste filled my throat, and chills prickled across my body, raising every fine hair.

No.

'Paige?'

Eliza was staring at me. Nerveless and leaden in my seat, I looked down at my broken mug. I had no memory of dropping it on the floor.

'Apologies, Chat,' Jaxon called idly. 'Excitement gives her butter-fingers. Do add the cost to our bill.' He frowned at me. 'What is it, Paige?'

'Nothing,' I managed. 'Sorry. I just need—'

Without finishing my sentence, I lurched up and headed for the bathroom. Jaxon would have to wait. I locked myself into a cubicle and promptly climbed through its window, scraping my arm and hip as I went.

It had to be a mistake. My fragile dreamscape, blurring memory and truth.

If not, I had just sensed two Rephs.

It was only a few seconds' run to the den. Every shadow grew taller; every streetlamp flashed like eyes. As soon as I was inside, I tore up the stairs and grabbed the backpack from under my bed. I ripped it open, almost breaking the zip, and crammed a blouse and trousers inside it.

Nashira must have tracked me down. I really should have gone back to Ireland. I should have run to the ends of the Earth. I yanked a coat from the back of the door and threw it across my shoulders.

When Nick came in, I was sitting on the floor, jamming on a pair of sturdy boots. My fingers shook on the laces, and my face was slick with tears.

'Paige—' He rushed straight to my side. 'Paige, what are you doing?'

'Rephs.'

'Where?'

'Here, in Seven Dials. They're after me.' I got up. 'I can't stay here. I'll go to a dosshouse and—'

'Paige, stop. They can't know for certain you're here.' Nick grasped my elbows. 'Are you sure they were Rephs?'

'Yes!'

'Then how do you know they're not on our side?'

'I can't risk it. They'll find you all.'

'We have the bolthole.' He kept hold of me. 'Leave again now, and Jaxon will never forgive you. This is the eve of his revolution, the culmination of everything he's ever worked towards. If you ruin it for him—'

'Nick,' I said, my voice cracking, 'can you hear yourself?'

Before he could reply, my bedroom door almost flew off its hinges. Jaxon barged inside, a strand of dark hair hanging over his forehead.

'What is the meaning of this, Paige?'

'Jax, there were Rephs here. Two of them,' I said. 'I have to go. We *all* have to go.'

'We are not going anywhere.' He shut the door. 'Explain yourself, quietly.'

A hollow laugh left me. 'Oh, you'd love me to be quiet, wouldn't you?'

'Dearly,' Jaxon said.

'Jaxon, *listen* to her,' Nick said firmly. 'She knows what she sensed.'

'She may think so, Dr Nygård, but we all know what recurrent exposure to flux can do.'

'I have *had* it with people telling me I'm hallucinating!' The shout erupted from me. 'Why the hell didn't you let me show *anyone* the Pentad Line, Jax?'

'Paige—'

'We could have shown the Abbess or Maria. Now it's too late. You just wanted me to shut up, like the Rephs did,' I said hotly. 'Well, congratulations, you shut me up. Now they're here, hunting us both. Do they need to have a rope around your neck before you believe me?'

'This was never a matter of disbelief.' Jaxon stared me down. 'As you pointed out, my dear, I can hardly deny what I saw with my own eyes.'

'Then why aren't you *doing* anything?'

'Paige, you don't need to understand my actions. You need to do as you are told.'

'If I'd done as I was told in Oxford, I would be dead now.'

There was a long silence.

'Explain this to me.' Jaxon stepped towards me, lifting a pale finger. 'You've always known that Scion is a growing threat. You tasted its brutality when you were only six. In your heart, you've always despised the inquisition into unnaturalness – but only *now* do you think we voyants should resist. Were you too complacent to strike when its corruption was only human? Were you enjoying yourself too much, darling?'

'I know why it exists now,' I said coldly. 'The Rephs made Scion. They oppress voyants because they need us. That means we can defeat them.'

'You naïve girl. Do you think fighting these creatures will bring a halt to the inquisition?' Jaxon looked pitying. 'Don't labour under the illusion that Frank Weaver and his fellow amaurotics will become devoted friends of yours if you destroy their masters. It's far too late for that.'

'We have to *try*, Jaxon.'

'What do you propose I do, precisely?'

'Tell the Unnatural Assembly what Scion is doing. Make them take Senshield seriously. Anything other than wishing this would go away.' I was about to rip my hair out. 'I protected you and Seven Dials. Nashira was after you, and I said nothing. They questioned me, they threatened me with torture, but I didn't crack. You *owe* me, Jaxon.'

'I see I underestimated what you endured in that place.' His tone became placating. 'When I am Underlord, we can return to this subject. Until then—'

'Oh, catch yourself on,' I said in disgust, losing the very last of my temper. 'I'm not sixteen any more, Jax. And you're not as clever as you think.'

'Be careful, Paige.' His face was losing colour again. 'You are treading a very fine line.'

'Fuck you.'

That did it. Jaxon shoved me into the bookcase with one arm, pinning me in place. He was much stronger than he looked. A jar of sleeping pills smashed against the floorboards.

'Jaxon,' Nick barked, but this was between mime-lord and mollisher. Jaxon gripped my arm where the mark was burned into my skin.

'Listen to me,' he said, very softly. 'I will *not* have my mollisher raving in the streets. Do you think the good unnaturals of London would support me as Underlord, Paige, if I were seen to be believing some fanciful tale of giants and walking corpses? Do you think they would take our word for it, or would they laugh and call us fools?'

'Oh, Jax,' I said. 'All these years later, and you're still afraid of people laughing at you?'

He smiled, a grim twist of his mouth.

'I consider myself a generous man,' he said, 'but this is your last chance, Pale Dreamer. You can stay and reap the benefits of my protection, or you can take your chances out there, where no one will listen. Let's see how long it takes the Unnatural Assembly to hang you from the nearest gibbet.'

'Let go of her.' Nick spoke quietly. 'Now, Jaxon.'

After a moment, Jaxon did.

'I did not give you everything to have you hurl it back at me,' he warned. 'You can be my mollisher, or you can be fair game. After all, if you are not the Pale Dreamer, who are you?'

As soon as he was gone, I kicked over my chest of trinkets, then sank on to the edge of my bed. Nick crouched beside me.

'Paige?'

Jaxon had left red fingermarks on my arm. I lifted a hand to cover them.

'It could strengthen the syndicate,' I said. 'It could bring us together, like it did in Oxford.'

'Only if you had proof of the Rephs. Even then, the truth would end the syndicate as we know it,' Nick said. 'You want to turn it into a force for good. Jaxon isn't interested in that. He wants to sit on his throne and gather spirits and be king of the underworld until he dies, and that is all he cares about. But a mollisher supreme has power, too.'

'A mollisher supreme isn't an Underlord. Look at Cutmouth,' I said. 'Only an Underlord could change everything.'

'Or an Underqueen,' Nick said. 'We haven't had an Underqueen in a long time.'

Slowly, I met his gaze. The smile slid from his lips.

'I couldn't,' I murmured. 'Could I?'

After a pause, Nick said, 'A disloyal mollisher threatens the pecking order.'

'Is it against the rules?'

'Probably. It's never happened, not in the whole history of the syndicate. Would you follow a backstabber?'

'I'd rather follow one than walk in front of one.'

'Don't be smart. This is serious.'

'Fine. Yes, I'd follow a backstabber if she told me the truth about Scion. If she wanted to stop the systematic *murder* of clairvoyants—'

'Paige, you've seen Jaxon, getting us to do the dirty work while he smokes and drinks absinthe. You really think people like him will command an army for you? Put their lives at risk for you?'

'Maybe to save their own necks in the long run.' I breathed out. 'Say I *was* to apply. Would you be my mollisher?'

'I don't want you to do it, Paige. At best, you'll be known as a turncoat of an Underqueen. At worst, you'll lose and wind up getting killed.'

'We're weeks away from Senshield. The Rephs are on the cusp of having another city in France. Now could be our only chance to strike,' I said. 'Some risks are worth taking, Nick. This is one of them.'

'Then you'd better make sure you're prepared for the consequences.' Nick stood. 'I'll calm him down.'

He closed the door behind him.

If you are not the Pale Dreamer, who are you?

The Pale Dreamer had been there when I needed her. Now her time was ending. To transform the syndicate into an army that could stand against the Sargas, I would have to become not just a mollisher, not just a mime-queen, but the Underqueen of the Scion Citadel of London.

When you arrived in this city, I did not meet the Pale Dreamer. I met Paige Mahoney. The memory warmed me. *And I think that she is a force to be reckoned with.*

After a minute, I gathered up the things I had scattered across the floor. Old newspaper clippings, brooches, antique numa – and a third edition of *On the Merits of Unnaturalness*, confiscated from a busker who had been mocking it in Soho. I traced its title, an idea forming.

Words give wings even to those who have been stamped upon, broken beyond all hope of repair.

There were ways to raise my voice. I dug out a pen and a piece of paper and started to write a message to Camden.

II

URBAN LEGEND

4 October 2059

'**A** what?'

Nell looked almost impressed by my sudden display of insanity. Her hair had been cut so it fell to her chin, ironed straight and dyed at least ten shades of orange. With cinder glasses and glossy black lipstick, she was unrecognisable.

The five of us had gathered in a rooftop bar in Camden Market. Since it was open all night, we had agreed to meet at dawn, when fewer people were around and the night Vigiles had returned to their barracks. The music from the market was enough to ward off eavesdroppers.

'You heard me,' I said. 'A penny dreadful.'

Felix sat to my left. His disguise was one of the filtering masks people wore in the industrial citadels of the north, which left only his eyes uncovered.

'You want to tell a *story* about the Rephs?' His voice was muffled. 'Like it's not real?'

'Yes. *On the Merits of Unnaturalness* made the syndicate what it is today,' I said, keeping my voice low. 'It revolutionised the way we think about clairvoyance. Just by putting his thoughts on paper, one obscure writer changed everything. Why can't we?'

Felix held his mask away from his mouth. 'Okay,' he said, 'but that was a pamphlet. You're suggesting a penny dreadful. A cut-price horror story for people with too much time on their hands.'

'I used to read *Marvellous Songbirds for Sale*. You know, the one about the orthinomancer who's a gutterling and sells talking birds,' Jos said wistfully, 'but my kidsman found my stash and burned it.'

Scion hadn't mentioned Jos. Clearly even they knew that hunting a child would look tyrannical. Nell had still bundled him up in a scarf and hat.

'Good,' she said. 'That stuff will rot your brain.' There were rings under her eyes. 'And Grub Street pumps it out at a rate of knots.'

'I just don't know if we should make it a horror,' Felix said. 'What if people think it's fiction?'

'How do you kill a vampire?' I asked him. Felix struck me as the sort of voyant who pretended he read Nostradamus in the evenings, but devoured *The Vamps of Vauxhall* and *The Ealing Necromancer* on the sly.

'Garlic and sunlight,' Felix said, frowning.

'How do you ward off fairies?'

'Cold iron.'

'They don't exist. How do you know?'

'Because I read it in—' He flushed. 'Okay, fine. I might have read a couple of potboilers when I was Jos's age, but—'

'I'm thirteen,' Jos groused.

'—can't we just write a serious pamphlet? Or something like a handbook?'

'Oh, great,' Nell said, deadpan. 'The Rephs will be shaking in their boots over Felix Coombs and his *handbook*.'

'I'm not joking, Nell. The White Binder could help us, couldn't he, Paige?'

'No. He doesn't like rivals,' I said shortly. 'And the difference between a pamphlet and a penny dreadful is that pamphlets claim to tell the truth. Penny dreadfuls don't. We can't just shout about the Rephs in the street. A penny dreadful will turn them into an urban legend.'

'What good will that do?' Nell rubbed the skin between her eyebrows. 'If we never prove it—'

'We're not trying to prove anything. We're trying to *warn* the syndicate.' I looked around the table. 'This isn't just my story. It's yours, too. What do you think?'

Opposite me, Ivy was hunched over a cup of saloop, her breath steaming from below a pair of round, gold-framed sunglasses. Her bony fingers tapped the table. She hadn't said a word since my arrival.

'We should do it,' Jos said. 'Paige is right. Who's going to listen to us if we say it's real?'

Nell chewed the inside of her cheek. 'What about the tunnel to Oxford?'

'It's been sealed,' I said. 'Without that, we have no evidence. The Abbess might be more competent than Hector, but I don't think she'll just take us at our word. She's also got her hands full with the scrimmage.'

Jos gave Nell a beseeching look. She looked back at him and sighed.

'All right,' she said, defeated. 'I just got a job on the silks at Camden Theatre. I'll write on my break.' She took a sip of cola. 'I reckon I can knock a decent story together. Jos can help me smooth it out.'

His eyes brightened. 'Really?'

'Well, you're the expert.'

'Nell, the Rephs know you're an aerialist. It's risky to work at the theatre,' I said. 'With your gift, I'm sure you could find a job in the syndicate.'

Nell shook her head. 'The Bully-Rook would come after me if he got wind I was back. Besides, everyone in the troupe wears a mask,' she said. 'I'll be fine, Paige. We'll get to work on the story tomorrow.'

Some of the tension left my neck and shoulders. There was no way I could work on a penny dreadful for days without Jaxon picking up on it.

'It might be best to write two manuscripts, in case one gets lost. Make sure you include the poppy anemone – the windflower,' I said. 'Its pollen can hurt Rephs.'

Nell raised her eyebrows. 'Is that what you used to get Merope off me, that last night?' I nodded. 'Can you buy it on the black market?'

'It's illegal to grow or possess it in Scion, but we might be able to get seeds into London on the ley lines. I'll look into it,' I said. 'How soon do you think you can finish a draft?'

'Give us a week or two. Where should we send it when it's done?'

'The Minister's Cat. It's a gambling house in Soho,' I said. 'I know one of the croupiers there. Babs works from Tuesday to Friday. Make sure you seal the envelope.' I finished my drink. 'How's Agatha treating you?'

Jos pulled a face. 'I don't like her that much. She wants me to start singing in the market.'

'The food she gives us is terrible,' Felix added.

'Stop it,' Ivy snapped, making Jos flinch. 'She's feeding us with money from her own pocket, not to mention hiding us from the Rag and Bone Man. Whatever she's given us, it's all she can afford. And it's a damn sight better than what the Rephs made us eat, when they let us eat at all.'

There was a brief silence before Jos mumbled an apology. Felix turned pink at the ears.

'Agatha's all right,' Nell conceded. 'Staying with her is cheaper than a dosshouse.'

She raked a hand through her hair. A scar caught the light, sweeping from the corner of her left eye to her earlobe. It was too pale to be recent.

'Question for you, Paige,' she said. 'Who are you betting on in the scrimmage?'

'Oh, yes. Agatha says people are already placing wagers.' Felix leaned towards me. 'Is Binder going for it?'

'Naturally,' I said.

'If he wins, you'll be mollisher supreme,' Nell said, her gaze piercing. 'I think you'd do a decent job. You broke us out of Oxford, didn't you?'

'You all did a lot to help. So did Warden.'

'You got everyone on to the train. You got us all to keep fighting. Besides, you're the only survivor who might be able to get the Unnatural Assembly to do something.'

'You could force them to listen to us,' Felix agreed. 'Once we've got them ready with the penny dreadful, that is.' When someone passed our table, he quickly put his mask back on. 'Who do you think did it?'

'His mollisher,' Nell said with conviction. 'If Cutmouth didn't do it, why wasn't she there?'

'Because she knew people would judge her.' Ivy seemed to force the words out. 'If she did kill him, it's because he deserved it. He gave her that scar, you know. She hated his guts.'

It was hard to see her eyes through those lenses, but her fingers bunched into a fist.

'You knew her,' I said. 'I saw her the night Hector died. She asked where you were hiding.'

After a moment, Ivy spoke again: 'What did you say?'

'I told her I didn't know where you were.'

Nell eyed her. 'How did you know her, Ivy?'

Ivy shifted. 'We grew up in the same community.'

'Hector smacked his gang around,' I said, 'but I never heard that he was the one who sliced Cutmouth.'

'He did it to all of them. Took or maimed a part,' Ivy said, keeping her gaze on her drink. 'That's how they got their syndicate names. Slipfinger was missing a finger. Slabnose had her nose broken. Magtooth had some of his teeth pulled. It showed they could endure pain.'

'So you stayed friends with her after she became his mollisher, and she confided in you about how much she hated him,' I said, watching her face. 'That was dangerous information to share with a gutterling.'

'You know people are saying it was you who killed them, Paige?' she said, an edge to her voice. 'Agatha says it's all over Camden. The Abbess cleared you of any wrongdoing, but you were on the Devil's Acre that night. Why are you so interested in Cutmouth?'

I leaned back in my seat, trying not to notice the confused look Jos gave me.

Ivy was right to suspect me. I did want to find Cutmouth, though I had no intention of killing her. If the Unnatural Assembly took her into custody, it would clear my name once and for all.

'I'm going back to the shop.' Ivy stood, pulling her hood lower. 'See you.'

Without another word, she left. As I rose to go after her, Nell caught my arm.

'Leave her, Paige,' she said. 'She's confused. Agatha's been giving her sedatives to help her sleep.'

'She's not confused.'

I followed Ivy out of the bar. She was taking the walkway that joined several buildings in the Lock Market. I went after her at a brisk clip.

'Ivy.'

No reply.

'Ivy,' I said, 'I don't particularly care how or why you know Cutmouth, but I need to find her. She didn't show up to take her place as Underqueen. Do you have any idea where she could be hiding?'

Her shaved head was bowed, her hands shoved into her pockets. When she reached a small bridge, she turned round and thrust something towards me. A switchblade glinted in the blue light of a streetlamp.

'Drop it, Paige,' she said, with a coldness that stopped me in my tracks.

Her hand trembled a little, but her dark eyes were hard with resolve. She kept the knife pointed at my heart until I took a step back.

'Ivy, I'm not going to hurt her,' I said. 'She could be in danger. Whoever killed Hector will be looking for her, to finish what they started.'

'And you're going to help her, are you?'

'I need to know what happened that night. She might have information.'

'She and I haven't spoken in years. Even if I did have a clue where she was, I wouldn't tell you,' Ivy said quietly. 'How could you work for the White Binder, Paige?'

I clenched my jaw.

'You think Hector was cruel, but Binder is why so many of us wound up in the gutter. You might have got us out of Oxford, but you worked with Rephs.' She shook her head. 'I don't trust you one bit.'

'Ivy—'

'Just leave me alone, Pale Dreamer. Run back to your mime-lord.'

The knife snapped closed. She swung over the balustrade and vanished into the market.

It might be nothing. Perhaps Cutmouth and Ivy were old friends who had stayed close enough to share their secrets, and that was the end of it. Either way, Ivy was right – if she did know where Cutmouth was hiding, she had no reason whatsoever to trust me with that information. She didn't know me from the next person she had met in Oxford.

At least we had agreed on the penny dreadful. It could be a terrible idea, but so far, it was all I had. Jaxon had been nobody – a self-educated gutterling – yet his pamphlet had changed more than any Underlord.

Writing didn't carry the same risks as speaking. You couldn't be shouted down or stared at. The page was both a proxy and a shield. If people at least *knew* about the Rephs, I could work up to proving their existence.

The two Rephs I had sensed hadn't returned. I knew I hadn't imagined it, but they must have lost my scent. Still, it was only a matter of time. I had to get hold of some poppy anemone, and quickly.

Not wanting to take a rickshaw, I made for Seven Dials, taking a long way through the backstreets. One of our botanomancers lived in Berners Mews. He often traded at the Garden. I had time to drop by and ask him about the windflower.

As the sun rose over the citadel, the streets came alive with commuters. I took a detour to buy a coffee at a voyant-run establishment in Bedford Square, then crossed Tottenham Court Road.

I stopped dead when I saw the SVD vehicle.

'… miscreants, seditionists, and the vilest of unnaturals,' a day Vigile was bellowing through a loudhailer. 'These traitors work for Paige Mahoney. She plots to destroy the laws that protect you. If the fugitives are not found, they will spread the plague of unnaturalness all over our citadel!'

They had rounded up a group of nine voyants. One of them, a medium, had broken down in tears. I quickly retreated into Bayley Street.

The botanomancer would have to wait. I headed straight to Seven Dials.

Back in the relative safety of my room, I found a stack of chapbooks on my bed. I picked up the nearest and read the title: *A Concise History of Clairvoyance in London, in Three Volumes.* I leaned against my pillows and opened it.

Originally, the clairvoyants of London had only ever met in small groups. There had been a few large gangs with voyant members, like the Forty Elephants, but it was a 'mirror-reader' named Thomas Merritt who had stepped up and taken charge of it all in the early 1960s. Interesting that the first Underlord had been a soothsayer, the lowest of Jaxon's orders.

Along with his lover, the 'flower-caster' Madge Blevins, Merritt had divided the citadel into territories, created the black market, and offered shelter to destitute voyants. His loyalists were raised to positions of power, becoming the first mime-lords and mime-queens. By 1964, his work was done. Tom Merritt had declared himself Underlord, and Madge his faithful mollisher.

It was strange to see a record that didn't use Jaxon's classification system. *Mirror-reader* and *flower-caster* had long since been replaced by *catoptromancer* and *anthomancer.* There were other archaisms scattered through the text: *numina* instead of *numa,* *spirit-reel* instead of *spool.*

Twelve years after their crowning, Good Tom and Madge had been killed together by falling masonry, leaving the underworld without a leader. The resulting battle for the crown – the scrimmage – had been won by a summoner known as the Golden

Baroness, real name Rosamund Hart, the first Underqueen. She had ruled for another four years before being murdered by an 'axe-diviner' called the Filching Mort.

Upon the Underqueen's gruesome Demise, it was decreed by the Unnatural Assembly that her Mollisher, the Silver Baron, would inherit the Crown in the style of the deposed Monarchs of England, whose line was interrupted by the arrival of Scion – for as one wise Mime-Queen said, we are the Monarchy of those who have been crushed beneath the Anchor. From that point on, Mollishers would always inherit, except in the rare situation that both Underlord and Mollisher were killed at the same time, or the Mollisher refused or ignored their Claim.

That must be why Cutmouth had gone to ground. It was safe to assume that whoever killed Hector wanted her dead, too. She was clever enough to know that, and clearly prized her life above the crown. When I opened another volume, published in 2045, I clenched my jaw.

It is in this period of our History that the great Pamphleteer – known under the pseudonym 'An Obscure Writer' – stepped forth to reorganise the Syndicate with his Debut, On the Merits of Unnaturalness. *In 2031, this Work caused a minor spate of Disagreements (including the historic Imprisonment of the Vile Augurs) before its Implementation as the official System by which we understand Clairvoyance in the Syndicate. Grub Street is proud to have published this stupendous and groundbreaking Document. As of the present Time, the Obscure Writer, now formally known as the White Binder, is Mime-Lord of I Cohort, Section 4.*

I lifted an eyebrow. *A minor spate of disagreements* was certainly one way to describe the gang wars. Next, I turned to the section on syndicate customs.

The Scrimmage is based on the medieval Art of MÊLÉE. Mime-Lords, Mime-Queens and their Mollishers fight to the Death in the Rose Ring, an enduring symbol of the Plague of Unnaturalness. Each of the Combatants fights for themselves, but a Mollisher may assist their Mime-Lord or Mime-Queen at any given Time during the Battle. The last Candidate standing is declared Victor and presented with the ceremonial Rose Crown, so named because the Underlord or Underqueen rules 'beneath the Rose' – Roses being a Symbol not just of the Plague, but of Secrecy. It signifies Authority over both the Living and the Dead of London. From that Moment, the Victor rules the Syndicate, and bears the Title of Underlord or Underqueen, depending upon their Preference.

When there are only two Combatants left in the Rose Ring, and they are not a Mime-Lord- or Mime-Queen-and-Mollisher duo, they must do battle to the Death for a final Victor to be declared. Only by using a specific Declaration – 'in the sight of the Æther, I yield' – can a Combatant end the last Fight without Bloodshed. Once this Declaration is spoken, the other Party will be considered the Victor. This Rule was introduced by the Golden Baroness, first Underqueen of the Scion Citadel of London, our Ruler from 1976 to 1980.

A fight to the death. I had anticipated violence – we were criminals – but I hadn't necessarily expected to be taking my life in my hands. Then again, voyants lived alongside the dead. Perhaps it made sense for our leaders to have to face death themselves.

Jaxon knocked on the wall with his cane. I closed the chapbook and laid it on the nightstand.

In the study, the smell of flowers was overwhelming. There were fresh-cut blooms all over the desk, along with a pair of scissors and a length of orange ribbon. On the couch, Nadine was counting our latest earnings.

'There you are, Paige.' Jaxon waved me to a seat. 'Where did you go this morning?'

Our explosive argument was already forgotten. Jaxon had a knack for behaving like a monster, then pretending none of it had ever happened.

'I woke up early,' I said. 'Thought I'd get a coffee from the Grecian.'

'Don't wander off like that again. I need to know if you're leaving the den,' he said. 'You're far too precious to lose.' He sniffed, his eyes bloodshot. 'Wretched pollen. I'd like your opinion, if you would care to cast your eye over these blooms.'

I sat down in the opposite chair. 'I didn't have you down as a botanist, Jax.'

'Not botany, but custom. Any voyant who wishes to enter the scrimmage must send a posy to Grub Street,' Jaxon said. 'We use the language of flowers as a tribute to Madge Blevins, the first mollisher.' Each sprig had a small label. 'Here are my choices for both of us, darling. Forsythia, to let them how much I'm looking forward to the fight. Ragged-robin, of course, for wit. And lastly, monkshood.'

'Isn't monkshood poisonous?'

'It is. Historically, it either means *chivalry* or *beware*. Nadine doesn't think I should send that one.'

'No,' Nadine said, not looking up. 'I really don't.'

'Oh, come now. It will be fun,' Jaxon purred. 'Most mime-lords send begonia as a warning of their skill in combat, but monkshood is far more refined. One must take risks to stand out from the crowd.'

I looked down at the purple bloom. 'Do they only accept your application if you stand out?'

'That may be the case for the independent candidates. There is a limit to the number of combatants who can reasonably fit into the Rose Ring,' Jaxon said, 'but Minty would never reject mine.'

'Then you don't especially *need* to stand out. If I received a poisonous flower right after the Underlord was murdered, I might consider it a threat. I'd stick to your classic begonia, personally.'

'Thank you,' Nadine said.

'Damn you, dullards. So long as the Grub Street hystericals don't *eat* the monkshood, they'll recover.' Jaxon tied a length of ribbon around the flowers and held the posy out to me. 'Place these carefully in our dead drop. Minty is sending couriers to check for them over the next few weeks. The first collection is today.'

'Consider it done.' I took them. 'Fancy a quick walk, Nadine?'

'I am quite sure you can manage by yourself. Nadine and I have something to discuss.'

Nadine dropped her chin. I left them to it.

London was still deciding whether or not to let the sun out. Rain spat from a layer of cloud. I checked the street for Vigiles before I stepped out of the den, pulling a hood over my hair.

Why Jaxon ever bothered asking for our opinions, I had no idea. He didn't care. Still, it was a good thing he had asked me to do this particular errand. Now I knew how to apply for the scrimmage.

Our dead drop was just north of Seven Dials. It was only a stone's throw from the den, but even a short journey could get me killed at this rate. The Vigiles were stepping up their game.

At this time of the morning, there was no one in the backstreets. When I reached the alley, I reached up to the sign reading BOOK MEWS and opened it like a small door, revealing a hole in the brickwork. I tucked the posy into it and put the sign back in place.

No sooner had I turned around than two huge figures were in front of me.

I should have flung my spirit, but my body acted first. I knew no human weapons could hurt the Rephs, yet I still drew two knives, driven by adrenalin and instinct. Before I could let them fly, a gloved hand grabbed me by the collar.

'Put the blades down,' said a cold voice. 'They will not help you.'

'If you're thinking of taking me back to Oxford, you can kindly cut my throat first, Reph.'

'Oxford is behind us. No doubt Nashira would find somewhere else to imprison you, but fortunately, I am no friend to her.'

The iron grip released. I clung to my knives, reaching for the æther. I had almost forgotten that the Rephs could hide their dreamscapes.

The face above me was concealed by a blank mask. When the Reph removed it, a chill of recognition scampered along my spine.

'Terebell,' I said.

She was one of the scarred ones, the Rephs who had rebelled against Nashira. Warden called her his ally.

'Indeed,' she said. 'I do not believe I ever formally introduced myself, dreamwalker. I am Terebellum Sheratan, sovereign-elect of the Ranthen.'

'Paige.' I put my knives away. 'Paige Mahoney.'

'Otherwise known as the Pale Dreamer.'

'Yes.'

In Oxford, the Rephs were often half in shadow. Now I saw Terebell Sheratan clearly – the dark hair that hung to her shoulders, the elegant nose, and the yellow eyes, slightly upturned. Both her lips were spare, making her look disapproving. As with any Reph, it was impossible to tell how old or young she was.

Where Terebell had skin like rose gold, the other Reph was pure silver, with a lean build and large, wide-spaced eyes. He was also bald as a spoon, unlike every other Reph I had seen.

'You might have scared the hell out of me, but I'm happy to see you,' I said to Terebell. 'I was starting to think I'd hallucinated you all.'

'Why would you think something so patently absurd?'

'Long story.'

The light in her eyes was dim. She hadn't fed in a few days.

'Arcturus told us that you live in Seven Dials,' she said. 'You have done well to evade Scion. Nashira still has every intention of taking your gift for herself.'

'I could tell.' I held a hand to my pounding heart. 'You came here a few days ago.'

'Yes. We hoped you would come to us.'

'Of course not. I sensed two Rephs I didn't recognise in the moment,' I said. 'How are you able to conceal your dreamscapes from me?'

'That is for us to know.'

Both Rephs wore buttoned leather gloves and black overcoats. They didn't dress like monarchs any longer, but like ordinary denizens.

'I don't think I saw you in Oxford,' I said to the bald one. 'Who are you?'

'Errai Sarin,' he said curtly. 'You would not have encountered many of my kin, if any. They visited the city, but none of us volunteered as keepers for your Bone Season.' His jaw tightened. 'So you are the one who helped Arcturus and Terebell. You are not what I expected.'

'Errai is one of the Ranthen,' Terebell said. 'We are those who stand against the Sargas. In Oxford, you knew us as the scarred ones.'

'Warden told me there were at least six of you. I know of you, him, Alsafi and Pleione,' I said, thinking back. 'Who were the others?'

'Rigel Chertan and Merga Sargas,' Terebell said. I didn't think either of them had been keepers. 'Merga was captured in Oxford, but Rigel escaped. Alsafi remains our double agent in the Archon.'

'Is that where Nashira is living now?'

'Yes. All of her loyalists have been relocated to London or France.'

They had been here the whole time.

'We ought to speak inside,' Errai said. 'Where can you take us, dreamwalker?'

'With all due respect, I don't know either of you from a slice of lemon,' I said. 'I'd rather not be in an enclosed space with you until I find out what you want.'

'We will speak inside,' Terebell said, eyes heating. 'You are beholden to me for shielding you from Thuban Sargas. I do not forget when I am owed a debt.'

There was a short silence, during which I fought down my pride. These two might have news of Warden.

'Fine,' I said.

It would be a risky walk. The Rephs might look human from a distance, but their height and bearing pulled in looks, setting me on edge. One busker dropped her tin of money when she saw them.

'Morning,' I said briskly.

'Um, good morning to you, Pale Dreamer.'

I led the Rephs to Catherine Street, where I used an old key to open a door. The homeless sometimes used this derelict building in the winter, but I sensed no one inside today. Terebell and Errai followed me in.

The Old Lyre had once been a popular music hall. Now it was rotting away, waiting for Scion to work out what to do with its carcass. Inquisitor Mayfield had shut down many such establishments, believing that art propagated dissent. *Give them paint, and they will paint over the anchor. Give them a stage, and they will shout out treason. Give them a pen, and they will rewrite the natural order.*

This place had a resident shade called the Man in Grey, who occasionally required soothing. Otherwise, the gang rarely came here. All was still and dark. I led Errai and Terebell between the many seats.

On the stage, tables and chairs had been left abandoned, either overturned or modestly dressed in sheets. The red curtains sighed with years of dust. An old flyer clung to the threadbare carpet.

On Wednesday, 15th May 2047
witness THE MADNESS OF MAYFIELD
A new comedy on recent happenings in Ireland

My jaw set. While we fought for our freedom from Dublin to Dungarvan, the denizens of Scion had been laughing in their music halls. I picked the flyer up, thinking of Finn and Kay for the first time in weeks. To my cousin and the woman he loved, nothing in the world had been more important than keeping the anchor out of Ireland.

Twelve years this piece of paper had been here. I looked up slowly, seeing the scars of retribution: scorches on the stage curtains, rusty stains on the carpet, chips in the walls. Only fools had dared to mock Mayfield.

'This will suffice,' Terebell said. 'It seems a great deal of this citadel is derelict.'

I dropped the flyer. 'You look a bit tired yourself, Terebell.'

'We had no train to take us under Gallows Wood.' She held my gaze without blinking, a disconcerting mannerism. 'Nashira is aware that you live in this section. I am surprised to still find you here, dreamwalker.'

'I've nowhere else to go,' I said. 'Seven Dials is where I have the most power.'

'To do what?'

'Nashira fears the syndicate. I want to use it against her.' I sat on the edge of the stage. 'Could you tell me what happened after the Bicentenary?'

'Nashira and Gomeisa barred themselves inside the Residence of the Suzerain, along with their loyalists – Rephaite and human – to wait out the destruction. We fought alongside your rebels, but there were too few of us to take the city. Arcturus entrusted the surviving humans to Rigel, who agreed to lead them through Gallows Wood. Fazal Osman was certainly among them.'

'What about Julian and Gail?'

'Gail Fisher is dead. The Overseer shot her before Arcturus could reach Magdalen,' Terebell said. 'As for Julian Amesbury, I do not know.'

'How can you not know?'

'Arcturus could not find him.'

I wished Gail had left Magdalen sooner. At least Fazal might have survived.

It was difficult to accept that I might never know what had happened to Julian. If Rigel had left without him, he would have had no way out of Oxford. He was either imprisoned or dead. I closed my eyes and breathed out, willing myself not to kick something in frustration.

'You wish to destroy Nashira. We share this goal,' Terebell said. 'Arcturus believed we should form an alliance. That is why I sought you out, as little as I care for humans. We require a human associate in London.'

'How many of you are there?'

'There are not many Ranthen,' Errai said. 'Against the thousands of Sargas supporters, we are but a small army.'

'Thousands.' I huffed. 'Please tell me you're joking.'

'Jokes are the declarations of fools.'

The mere thought of thousands of Rephs made me want to lie down and never get up again.

'I don't understand,' I said quietly. 'I didn't even see a hundred Rephs in Oxford.'

'Many of the others are stationed in the free world, learning human weaknesses. Some dwell elsewhere in Scion. As to the rest, they cling to a diminished life in the Netherworld, though they must cross the veil to feed.'

'The Netherworld is rotting, and they'd still rather live there?'

'Earth is rotting. So are you, human.' Errai dealt me a cold look. 'Do you not see your charnel houses, or feel the life leaving you with each breath?'

I smiled thinly. 'I forgot how charming you Rephs are.'

Errai turned his nose up. I could tell we were going to get on famously.

'Though we are few, only the Ranthen stand against the Sargas,' Terebell told me. 'If we are ever to gain the upper hand, we must find Arcturus.'

I grasped the edge of the stage.

'Warden,' I said, softer. 'He's alive?'

'After the train returned for the emissaries, Arcturus left us, intending to find you. He followed the tunnel from Oxford to London.'

'You didn't go with him?'

'Pleione and I remained in Oxford for a week, discreetly searching for survivors. After that, we left through Gallows Wood and sought our nearest allies, including Errai,' she said. 'We had agreed to rendezvous with Arcturus in London. I assume you have not seen him.'

'No.'

'But you can find out where he is.' Terebell stepped towards me. 'Arcturus told us about your golden cord with him. Breathe a word of it to anyone but the two of us, dreamwalker, and I will cut out your tongue.'

'I'll thank you not to threaten me. You're on my turf now.'
I stared her down. 'If Warden told you about the cord, why can't I
tell anyone else?'

'That can be discussed later,' Terebell said. 'The cord is undesir-
able, and a complication. However, since it exists, it behoves us to
use it.'

'Arcturus has been missing for weeks,' Errai said. 'He is an
upholder of our movement. If he is not found, we have lost a great
warrior.'

'I haven't felt the cord. Not once,' I said. 'He didn't teach me
much about it.'

'You do not need to be taught. You are not dull-witted, and
you know at least a little of how the æther works,' Terebell said.
'Despite *his* lack of expertise, Arcturus was able to use the cord to
save you from Kraz Sargas. For his sake, you must discover how to
follow it to him.'

'When did you last hear from him?'

'When he arrived on the fifth of September. It was agreed that he
would inform us as soon as he located you, but we never received
word.'

On the fifth of September, I had still been in the dosshouse in
Soho. I couldn't work out why Warden hadn't been able to find me
there.

Wherever you are, I will know where to seek you.

'Are you *sure* Nashira hasn't got him?' I asked them. 'Could
someone have tailed him from Oxford?'

'If she had captured Arcturus, we would know,' Terebell said.
'More likely he has fallen prey to opportunistic humans. He told
me you are a criminal. You know well that some humans will do
anything for coin.'

My thoughts raced. I knew every sort of criminal imaginable,
but no one jumped out at me.

'Check your backpack,' Terebell said. 'It may help.'

'How?'

She chose not to dignify this question with an answer.

Agreeing to this would be madness. Scion was hunting me, I
hadn't felt so much as a quiver from the golden cord, and London

was far too big to search alone – but if anyone had a chance, it was me.

And I wanted to see Warden again. Too much had been left unsaid; too many questions unanswered. I needed to know that he was all right.

'Fine,' I said. 'I'll do it.'

Errai said nothing, but I glimpsed doubt in the way he looked at Terebell. She reached into her coat and handed me two large silk pouches.

'To protect yourself,' she said. 'The white contains salt of the mountains; the red, pollen of the poppy anemone. Use the red pouch frugally.'

'Thanks.' I fastened them into my inner pocket. 'How do I contact you?'

'When you find Arcturus, he will send word to us. In the meantime, dreamwalker, see to it that you stay hidden. If there is one thing we Rephaim excel in, it is biding our time. Nashira has plenty. She will not stop hunting you until your face is fixed in plaster in her halls.'

The death masks in her residence. I could never forget those sleeping faces, taken from victims of her reign.

As Terebell covered her face and turned to leave the music hall, Errai stopped her.

'We must feed.'

'Don't even think about it,' I said.

They looked at each other once more and left. By the time I reached the door, they were nowhere to be seen.

Trying to find one man in the Scion Citadel of London would be no mean feat, even if he was a Reph. It was a sprawling labyrinth of streets, radiating out for miles in all directions, and there was almost as much of it underground as there was above.

Late that afternoon, I sat on the roof of the den, watching the sun go down. This was the most beautiful time of the day, when soft light shone between the buildings and turned the skyscrapers to blades of gold.

Jaxon and the others were all in the study, feasting on real wine and smoked cheese to celebrate his application. I couldn't bring myself to join them. It would be too obvious that my mind was elsewhere. I had dislocated my spirit, searching for any trace of Warden, but his dreamscape was nowhere to be found. That either meant he was more than a mile away, or his dreamscape was cloaked.

Warden would have been well dressed and travelling alone. That might have made him tempting to certain strains of criminal – the sort that even Jaxon found unpalatable. If a trafficker or burker had spotted him, they might well have scented a rich source of income, even if they didn't understand what he was.

Then again, Warden wasn't exactly an easy target. He was nearly seven foot tall and muscled to match; he would have been difficult to restrain. If he *had* been captured, the perpetrators must have used the windflower, which meant they likely worked for Scion.

So far, this wasn't looking good.

I briefly considered the possibility that one of the other survivors was involved, then dismissed it. I also wondered if Warden was hiding of his own free will, but I couldn't think of any reason he would do that. He had come to London specifically to find me.

Wherever you are, I will know where to seek you.

'Paige?'

I surfaced from my thoughts. Nick had come to join me on the roof.

'Party food.' He passed me a striped paper bag and sat down at my side. 'He notices when you're not there, you know.'

I knew all too well.

'Nick, I want you to cover for me tonight.' I turned the package over in my hands. 'Just for a few hours.'

'Why would you go out at night?'

'It's hard to explain.'

It wasn't. If I found Warden, I would need the cover of darkness to get him through the citadel.

'At least let me know where you're going,' Nick said.

'I'm not sure yet.'

Nick waited for me to elaborate. I picked at the butterscotch sweets he had brought.

'I don't like it,' he said, 'but I'll cover for you. Just be careful.' He paused. 'I've been meaning to tell you, but there never seemed to be a good time.'

'Tell me what?'

'I told Zeke how I felt.'

I looked up. 'When?'

'Not long after Trafalgar Square. After I let Warden take you, I ran to Vauxhall, like he said. I got back to the den at sunrise,' Nick murmured. 'I was distraught. I thought I'd just lost you again. Zeke comforted me, and—' He drew a breath. 'Well, it just came out.'

'And?'

'He said he felt the same.'

A strange feeling came over me, like the air was a little too heavy to breathe. Nick watched me with a knitted brow.

'Of course he did,' I said softly. 'You're a catch, Nick Nygård.' I leaned over to kiss his cheek. 'And you deserve it more than anyone.'

A wide smile answered mine. He wrapped both arms around me and held me close, allowing himself a chuckle that warmed me through.

'I'm happy, sötnos,' he said. 'For the first time in years, I feel like it could be all right.'

His heart was beating fast against my ear, as if he had been running for years to reach this state of mind. I listened to it, remembering when this news would have broken me. When I had thought his love for Zeke would take him away from me for good.

I knew better now. He had loved Zeke when he went to Oxford, risking everything to save me. He had loved Zeke when he listened to my story. He loved Zeke now, while he held me close.

It hadn't changed a thing.

'We can't tell Jaxon,' Nick said quietly. 'You'll keep it secret, won't you?'

'You know I will.'

Jaxon had always forbidden us from having *liaisons* – said with a suitable measure of disgust – that lasted more than a night. He would blow a gasket at the thought of a relationship within his own gang. Given his unpredictability of late, he might even turf them both out.

We slipped back through the window and stepped over a few scattered palettes. The outline of a horse had been sketched on the canvas.

'Jax got Eliza a new muse,' Nick said. 'George Frederic Watts, the Victorian painter.'

'Do you feel like she's not been herself lately?'

'Yes. I asked her about it, and she said one of her friends is ill.'

'*The Seven Seals do not have friends. Only those who would break us, and those who can't,*' I said, quoting Jaxon.

'Exactly. I think she's seeing someone, too.'

'She never has any time to herself. How could she?'

'Good point.' He glanced at the canvas. 'It could be exhaustion. Jax is overworking her.'

'He's overworking us all.'

'I can't decide if he'll be better or worse as Underlord.' Nick turned to face me, lowering his voice. 'If you insist on going out, take a burner. I'll stay awake and warm the car up, just in case. Call if you need me.'

'Thank you. I wouldn't go if it wasn't important.'

'I believe you.'

We parted ways on the landing. As he went downstairs, I noticed a gentle spring in his step, as if a weight had been lifted.

The others were still talking and laughing in the study. I had never felt less like joining them. Nick went in and shut the door.

Jaxon would make me pay for my absence. The others might have got away with missing his party, but as his mollisher, I was expected to be at his side whenever he desired my presence. To soothe his wounds, to boost his ego; to follow his orders to the letter.

Frankly, I had better things to do.

Other than my red dress, which I had buried in a drawer, I had only brought one thing from Oxford. I crouched beside the bed, where my backpack was hidden, and drew it out. For the first time, I took a close look at it. There was a clip on the side, meant for holding a water canteen. It had snapped in January, and I had never replaced it.

That broken clip had saved my life, the night of my arrest. It was the only part of the backpack that could have caught on a wire, stopping my fall.

There were a few supplies inside, which Michael must have packed. I emptied them on to the floor, then delved into the pockets.

I soon found two vials, wrapped in thick cloth. One of them was full of molten light, though its glow was fading. When I gave it a shake, it brightened again, just for a moment. This was ectoplasm.

Reph blood.

When I held the other vial up, I knew exactly what it was. My breath caught in my throat. Hardly daring to hope, I pushed up my right sleeve and tipped a few precious drops of amaranth on to the scar. The wound cracked open like old paint. As I circled my finger over it, it washed away, leaving my inner arm as smooth as buttermilk.

And just like that, Jaxon could no longer tarnish my name before the Unnatural Assembly.

He had no power over me.

I slumped against the nearest wall, my smile hurting my cheeks. When I had calmed down, I looked back at the vials. A scroll hung from the one that held the ectoplasm. I opened it to find a note, written in a familiar hand.

Until next time, Paige Mahoney.

I had shoved the backpack out of sight, not even thinking to search it. The key to finding Warden had been right under my bed. He had told me the golden cord might reveal itself more slowly to me than to him, because I was mortal, while he carried the æther in his blood.

It made sense that his blood would help me.

Warden had needed that vial of amaranth. Wherever he was, he would be suffering for his sacrifice, racked by the pain in his scars. I picked up the vial of ectoplasm.

Until next time, Paige Mahoney.

Next time would be now.

12

THE INTERCHANGE

London – beautiful, immortal London – has never been a city in the simplest sense of the word. It was, and is, a living, breathing thing, a stone leviathan that harbours secrets underneath its scales. It guards them covetously, hiding them deep within its body; only the mad or the worthy can find them. It was into these ageless places that I might yet have to venture to find Warden.

While Jaxon and the others drank themselves senseless next door, I lay on my bed and hooked myself up to my life support. With my eyes closed, I reached as far into the æther as I could without leaving my body.

The dislocation wasn't smooth; more like trying to tear a thick piece of fabric. When I finally felt the æther, it was singing with dreamscapes and spirits, as it always was in London. There was still no trace of Warden. Returning to myself, I opened the vial of ectoplasm.

'All right,' I said softly. 'Let's see if this works.'

I took off the stopper and drank. The ectoplasm shocked my teeth like a mouthful of iced water, leaving an aftertaste of metal.

It hit me in a few heartbeats. My sixth sense heightened painfully, overwhelming the other five. Every move the muses made upstairs was like a physical touch. As for the others, their dreamscapes and auras were almost shining. Suddenly I was a lightning rod, conducting the æther in a way I never usually could.

On impulse, I entered my dreamscape. I ran through my poppy anemones, searching for any clue, any difference. Each flower was dripping light.

It was only when I looked down that I saw. A golden thread trailed from my dream-form. It led through my flowers, into the æther.

I had seen the golden cord in his dreamscape. Now I could see it in mine.

His blood had made it visible.

When I emerged, I sat up at once. He was closer than I had thought. I put on a jacket and gloves, then swung on my backpack and opened the window, careful not to make a sound. Leaving it ajar, I climbed down to the courtyard.

Going out at night was madness, but my gift had always helped me avoid Vigiles. With ectoplasm and amaranth coursing through me, I could use it with ease, without so much as a twinge of a head-ache. With no idea how I was doing it, I followed the cord out of Seven Dials.

It was as easy as reading an internal compass – as if this was a path I had taken before, and now I was remembering it. I had a feeling that if I were sighted, I would be able to see the cord with the naked eye.

As night fell over London, I found myself heading north. I ran along busy streets, through winding and sinister alleys, across the rooftops when I could.

By the time I reached Euston Road – the boundary between cohorts – Warden was less than a mile away, within the usual range of my perception. I could almost see the beacon in the æther, beck-oning me even farther north. The realisation almost stopped my breath.

Warden was in Camden.

If that was a coincidence, then I was Queen Victoria.

Camden Town was known for its nightlife. It was easy to blend in. I still wrapped on my red silk and walked with my head down, so my hood shadowed my face.

Fortunately, there were no Vigiles. I still had to get this done before the ectoplasm wore off.

I strode down Camden High Street. To my surprise, I spotted Jos, wearing a peaked cap over his cornrows, perched like a bird on a statue of Lord Palmerston. I had been so focused on the cord, I hadn't noticed his dreamscape. A young whisperer stood beside him, playing a slow tune on her piccolo while Jos sang in a delicate voice.

A large crowd watched in reverent silence. Polyglots sang best in Glossolalia – the language of spirits and Rephs – but they could make the grisliest street ballad sound beautiful.

Five ravens feasted on a winter's day,
On the White Keep's highest tower, so they say,
When the coffin carried the queen.

Not one raven chose to leave the fray
While the queen turned cold down Frogmore-way,
And the widow wore snow-white on the day
That London was in mourning.

Five ravens feasted on a summer's day
On the White Keep's highest tower, so they say,
When the king fled from his throne.

Every raven turned and flew away
While the blood turned cold down Whitechapel-way,
'He was stained,' they claimed, 'by the Ripper's blade;
He is our king no more.'

At the end of the song, the crowd clapped and tossed coins at them both. Jos collected them in his cap, and the girl took a bow as the audience dispersed. Seeing me approach, she ran off. Jos waved me over.

'Hello, you,' I said. He smiled. 'Who was that?'

'Rin. We busk together,' he said. 'How come you're here?'

'I'm looking for someone.' I pushed my hands into my pockets. 'Where are the others?'

'Ivy is asleep at the shop. Felix got a job with a costermonger. Nell said she'd meet me for supper – she gets wages for doing the silks now,' he added, 'but she didn't show up. I was about to look for her.'

I frowned. 'Is Agatha not feeding you?'

'She gives us bread and bloaters.' Jos looked queasy. 'I sneak the bloaters to her cat. I know it's better than what the Rephs gave us, like Ivy said, but I'm sure Agatha could afford something else. She has a huge slice of pie and a whole spice cake every night.'

Quite a few costermongers sold bloaters – salted herrings, cheap and gamey. I had the distinct feeling that Agatha was making a point.

'Come on,' I said. 'I'll get you something.'

Jos walked with me towards the Lock Market, tipping his hat to the odd gutterling. All the while, I looked around, trying to fix my perception on Warden. My gaze caught on the beggars of the district, huddled in doorways with threadbare blankets and half-empty tins.

Jaxon must have been like that once, lingering around the costermongers, hoping for a bite of hot food. I could almost see him – a thin, pale boy, angry and bitter, loathing what circumstance had done to him. A boy who begged for books and pens as often as he did for coin. A boy with his arms torn to ribbons, plotting his escape from poverty.

'Aside from the food,' I said to Jos, 'how is Agatha treating you?'

'She's kind to Ivy, but she's quite strict with the rest of us. We have to give her most of our wages,' Jos said. 'Nell thinks we should leave, but it's really expensive to rent here. We could never save enough.'

If only I had more money. I could find them somewhere to sleep in my district, but I wasn't sure how long or well I could support them with my income. I was certain Jaxon had been skimming my pay.

'We'll work on it,' I said. 'How's the writing going?'

'We're nearly finished. Nell is brilliant,' Jos said. 'She could be a psychographer.'

'What's the story about?'

'It's our story. The story of the Bone Season. We have all the humans escaping to London and the Rephs coming to hunt them, but a few of them helping us, too.' His dark eyes peeked up at me. 'We made Liss the main character, as a tribute. Do you think that's okay?'

A knot filled my throat. Liss, who had suffered every wrong with dignity, never losing her compassion; Liss, whose life had been cut short before she could break free. If anyone deserved to be the hero, it was her.

'Yes,' I said. 'I think it's okay.'

Jos looked better for the reassurance. When we got to the Lock Market, I bought him a cup of saloop, a hot penny pie, and a wedge of spice cake. We sat on a bench while he ate in silence, clearly famished.

The detour had broken my concentration, but now I grasped the cord again. It was pointing to the building that loomed over the Lock Market – a derelict warehouse, from the looks of it, though the red brick was in good condition.

'You said you were looking for someone,' Jos said. 'Is it one of the other survivors?'

'In a manner of speaking.' I nodded to the building. 'What's that?'

'Camden Interchange. Nobody's allowed in there.'

'Why not?'

'It's the Rag Dolls' den. You won't try and break in there, will you?' Jos said, looking worried. 'The Rag and Bone Man would be really angry.'

'Have you ever seen this famous Rag and Bone Man?'

'No. Agatha says his mollisher runs things – Chiffon, short for La Chiffonnière. She tells the Rag Dolls what he wants, and they tell other voyants.'

'I might have a polite word with this Chiffon,' I said. 'Is there a front door?'

'The entrance is just behind these buildings. If you want to see the Rag Dolls, you go through and knock on the black door. Will Chiffon actually see you?'

'Maybe. I'm a mollisher, too.' I stood. 'I'd better head off, Jos. You should try to find Nell.'

Jos looked doubtful. 'You *are* going to break in, aren't you?'

'Only if necessary.'

'I'll come with you, then. I can help.'

'No,' I said. 'It's too dangerous, Jos.'

'I helped in Oxford,' he said earnestly. 'The Rag Dolls can't be much worse than the Rephs.' He got up. 'You need someone to keep a lookout while you're searching. What if the Rag and Bone Man comes?'

My instinct told me to say no, but he made a sound point.

'You have to do exactly as I say,' I told him. 'If I tell you to go – even if you have to leave me behind – then you run straight to Agatha. Promise me, Jos.'

'I promise.'

'All right.'

The brick archway was just behind the Lock Market. Rusted steel letters must once have spelled the name of the building, but the years had picked the words apart. Instead of CAMDEN INTER-CHANGE, the sign now read CAN IT CHANGE. A graffito of an inverted anchor had been daubed on a nearby wall, then crossed out with one slash.

A few lamps flickered around the Interchange, but no light came from inside. Planks had been hammered over the windows; every door was chained. Even if I could worm my way inside, it might be fitted with alarms. Scion often put them on valuable derelicts, to prevent squatters. The Rag Dolls might have turned that to their advantage.

'Most people don't go any farther than here,' Jos told me. 'The gutterlings once dared someone to knock on the black door. He never came back.'

'Great,' I said.

Warden, what have you got yourself into?

I did a quick sweep in the æther, scouring the building for dreamscapes. 'I sense a few people,' I said, counting. 'Not too many to avoid.'

Jos glanced up at me. 'You can tell how many people are in there?'

'I can. It's part of my gift.'

'You must be really good at stealing.' Jos considered. 'Two of them are probably the door guard and her dog. I reckon the others are Rag Dolls.'

'It's okay. I can sneak around them.'

'You never told me who you were looking for,' Jos said. 'Is it Warden?' At my nod, he grinned. 'I knew he would come. What took him so long?'

'That's what I'd like to know.'

I had no idea what to make of this. As far as I was aware, Warden had no contacts in the syndicate but me.

'Jos,' I said, 'I need you to climb up as high as you can and keep an eye out while I look for a way into this place. If you see anyone coming, make a noise.'

'I can use this.' Jos went into his pocket and held up a tiny silver crescent. 'Bird whistle. It's loud.'

'Good idea. Just don't be seen.'

We went under the archway and started to walk along the eastern wall of the building. A cold wind teased a few dark curls from under my hood.

'Up there. That's a good lookout.' I nodded to a nearby roof, which afforded a view of two sides of the Interchange. 'Can you reach it?'

'Yes.'

Jos ran towards the building and started to climb, using window-sills and protruding bricks.

Warden was close. I stopped, confused by what I was feeling. I was almost on top of his dreamscape, but I couldn't physically see him.

A few old cars were parked behind the Interchange. I spotted the black door. Two dreamscapes lurked behind it – one animal, one human. When I narrowed my focus to the human one, I swore under my breath.

The guard was unreadable. Not even a dreamwalker could affect her mind. The Rag and Bone Man clearly knew what he was doing. I could try possessing the dog and making a fuss, but the door must be locked from the inside. I hooked my thumbs into my belt loops and took a few steps away from the Interchange, looking up at the windows.

The heel of my boot struck metal. I glanced down to see an iron grille.

If you can't go over something, go under it.

Nick had told me that once, long ago. I crouched beside the grille and dropped a stone through the gap. A moment later, I heard it *ping* against a solid floor.

This was no drain. It was a vent. There was an open space under the Interchange. Many sewers and passages coursed beneath London, but I had never heard of underground tunnels in Camden. Then again, keeping them secret would only have served to bene-fit the Rag and Bone Man. Especially if he was holding prisoners down there.

I still had no idea how to use the golden cord to communi-cate, but I could guess. Closing my eyes, I called up an image, the way I imagined an oracle would. I pictured the grille, down to the very smallest details: the metalwork, the paving, the seams that ran between iron and stone. As I held the image in my mind's eye, I pulled on the cord.

And Warden answered. This time, his dreamscape flared, as if he had woken from a deep sleep. It only lasted a moment, but I felt his sudden awareness of me.

Against all odds, I had found him.

Jos descended from the roof. 'Do you see a way in?'

'Maybe.' I patted the vent. 'This grille here. Have you seen any others?'

He nodded. 'In the market.'

That bolstered my theory, but even if I had been able to pull this thing up, the opening was too narrow for me to fit through. 'Okay.' I stood. 'Jos, what's on the other side of the Interchange?'

'The Inquisitors' Canal.'

'Can you show me?'

Jos led me around the building to the towpath. A footbridge arched over the dirty water, almost flush against the Interchange building.

'Dead Dog Hole is under here.' Jos peered over the balustrade. 'You can only see it from across the water.'

'Dead Dog Hole?'

'The old canal basin under the Interchange. Ivy says dead animals and stuff used to wash up here, back in the monarch days. That's how it got its name.' His eyes brightened. 'Maybe this is a secret entrance.'

A smile pulled at the corners of my mouth.

'Only one way to find out,' I said. 'Help me get something to use as a raft.'

'What if you fall in?'

'I'll survive.'

Between us, we scrounged a piece of wood and fed it into the water. It looked like part of a crate, just large enough for one person to kneel on. Unless Warden was in any state to swim in filthy water, I would have to find us a better exit. Jos kept an eye on our surroundings, checking for passers-by as he handed me a plank to serve as a paddle.

'Should I be the lookout again?' He clung to the railings with one hand. 'What if the Rag and Bone Man is in there?'

'I can deal with him.' I found my balance. 'Whistle if you see the Rag Dolls, okay?'

'Okay.'

'I might not be able to come back this way. Give me half an hour at most, then go back to Agatha. Any sign of trouble, you leave. Got it?'

'Got it,' Jos said. 'Be careful.'

'Of course.'

I pushed the raft away from the towpath, on to the Inquisitors' Canal. When I looked at the bridge from this new angle, a chill laced straight along my spine. Beneath it was a yawning space, like the mouth of a cave, where the water disappeared under the Interchange.

This had to be it.

Jos watched from the towpath. I sculled into the absolute darkness of Dead Dog Hole.

The silence was broken only by echoing drips. I switched on my torch, holding it between my knees so I could use my hands to row.

Riveted columns ran from the ceiling and vanished into the black water. The walls on either side of me were the same red brick as the warehouse, slick with algae and old dirt. Between two archways, I spied a passage.

I tossed my backpack towards it first. As I shifted my weight, the raft capsized. My hands reached the ledge, but most of my body plunged into freezing water. I hauled myself into the passage, my arms shaking with the effort, my wet clothes like a second skin. The toes of my boots pushed at the wall, lifting my legs clear of the canal.

I crawled and grasped two iron bars. There was just enough space for me to slip between them, into the passage beyond. I peeled off my jacket and tied the sleeves around my waist. My fingers were already stiffening, and my clothes reeked of whatever grime was in the water.

When I checked the æther, I tensed. Warden *was* down here, but so was one of the humans. They must have left a guard with him. I reached into my boot for a knife.

I might be allowed on other voyants' turf, but infiltrating their den was another matter. If I was discovered here, the Rag and Bone Man would be well within his rights to drag me before the Unnatural Assembly.

Then again, he might just find it more convenient to kill me.

My boots hardly made a sound as I stole along the arched brick tunnel. Naked bulbs hung in cages from loose wires. Graffiti and chicken wire covered the walls. A few shades brushed past, but none of them bothered me.

The tunnel soon branched into a maze of vaults. It must once have been a basement, but it stretched beyond the Interchange. I continued through the darkness, stopping when I found a vent. I could see people in the market above; their shadows flickered over me.

This was a perfect spot to eavesdrop. Each time I was here, the Rag Dolls could have been watching.

The vents gave some light, filtered down from the streetlamps. I switched off my torch and dug a bag of climbing chalk from my backpack. If I was going to go deeper, I had to make sure I wouldn't get lost.

The Rag Dolls used these vaults for storage: barrels of alcohol, rubble and junk. A few mattresses were laid out here and there. As I explored the passages, I marked each one with chalk. One unventilated room was enormous – a great underground chamber, not unlike the Garden. The ceiling was low, with sweeping arches. A spotlight cart stood in the far corner, casting a harsh electric glare, and tables and chairs were stacked in one corner. I checked the æther and darted across the stone floor, heading for a passage on the other side of the vault.

A thin, filthy cat streaked past with a yowl. I sprang back, knife raised. The cat vanished into another tunnel.

My heart clobbered my ribs. I drew a fist to my breastbone, breathing hard. If a stray had found its way down here, there must be another way out.

As I got closer to Warden, I slowed down, listening for footsteps. Instead, I heard the fuzzy crackle of a radio, tuned to the evening news. Readying a second knife, I chanced a look around the corner. An old signal lantern sat on the floor in the next tunnel, illuminating a closed door.

The guard was skinny as a match, with orange hair down to his waist. He slouched against the wall, smoking as he listened to the flagging radio. A few days' worth of stubble had crawled down his neck.

A summoner. They could pull spirits across vast distances just by calling their names. I would have a brutal fight on my hands if I faced him.

Fortunately, the cocktail of amaranth and ectoplasm was still fizzing through my veins. Like an arrow, my spirit streaked through the wall and struck his dreamscape. When I snapped back, I heard the satisfying *thud* of a limp body collapsing on stone. I found him on the floor and stepped right over him.

There was no padlock on the door. Nobody had expected a break-in. I took hold of the handle and walked into the cell beyond.

'Warden,' I whispered.

13

THIEF

Manacled to a wall in the dark, Arcturus Mesarthim looked nothing like he had in Oxford. There, he had dressed in Tudoresque finery, knowing he was a sight to behold. There, he had slept on silk pillows, lulled by forbidden music.

Now his clothes were filthy, and as far as I could tell, he was out cold. I stowed my knives and went straight to his side.

'Warden?'

No answer. His aura was like a candle in a draught, weaker than I had ever sensed it. The sight of the manacles turned my stomach.

'Warden,' I said again, 'wake up. Come on.' I lifted his leaden head. 'Arcturus.'

His lids cracked at the sound of that name, and he slowly came around. I framed his face as he regarded mine, his eyes dim and flickering.

'Paige Mahoney.' His voice was almost too soft to hear. 'Good of you to come to my rescue.'

My breath left me in a rush.

'You can thank me later.' I let go of him. 'Warden, who did this to you?'

'That is not important.' He lifted his own head. 'Paige, you must leave.'

I was already going back to the guard, rummaging through his pockets. Finding a bunch of keys, I returned to Warden and dealt with the first manacle, freeing his arm. When I went to spring the other, he caught my elbow.

'No. I have not fed in days,' he rasped. 'The hunger is taking me.'

'It isn't taking you anywhere. I am,' I said. 'Terebell and Errai sent me.'

'I will not … remember you, Paige.'

'Warden, stay with me. You're fine.' I unlocked the other manacle. 'I'm breaking you out of here, but you have to get up. I can't lift you.'

Warden watched me dully, as if accepting a defeat. He must be delirious.

'If we are to escape,' he said, 'you must remove the flowers.'

'What?'

He lifted his chin. I shone my torch. There were poppy anemones around his neck, laced together like the daisy chains I had made as a child.

Incredible that a small red bloom could do so much damage to Rephs. He must not even be able to break the chain himself. I got the flowers off him, then leaned in to look at the mottled grey stain on his skin.

'Do you need salt?'

'No. Only aura,' he said, sitting up. 'But I will not take yours, Paige.'

'Good thing there's an alternative, then.'

The guard really was having a bad night. I took him by the wrists and hauled him into the cell on his back. Dry groans punctuated each pull on his arms. I locked him into the manacles and held a knife to his throat.

The guard woke with watering eyes. He squinted at me, blood under his nose.

'Who are you?'

I raised my eyebrows. 'I was going to ask you the same thing, summoner.'

'Fuck.' His breath smelled of stale coffee. 'My head—'

'I'd be more concerned about your other body parts right now.' I brought my knife up to his face. 'You must work for the Rag and Bone Man. Who is he, and what the fresh hell are you plotting down here?'

He stared at the blade, then looked up. Seeing the manacles, he thrashed so hard I thought he would dislocate his own shoulders. When he realised it was a lost cause, he glowered at me and Warden, panting.

'The others will be back soon.'

'You'd better hope I don't get bored of you before then,' I said. 'Start talking.'

'I don't know shit,' he said. 'You can do what you want.' He took in a deep breath and bellowed, 'Sarah Whitehead, I summon—'

I slapped a hand over his mouth.

'Now, that's just showing off,' I said. 'The resident poltergeist of the Bank of Scion England. Very impressive catch.' He glared at me. 'Try another summoning and my friend here will drain you *very* slowly of your aura. You can be helpful, or you can be amaurotic. Got that?'

The summoner glared again, then nodded. As soon as I removed my hand, he spat at me, catching me full in the face. I reeled back in disgust.

Warden played his part beautifully. He moved towards the guard with the silent intent of a predator, his yellow eyes still just alight. The man yanked against the manacles, his boots scuffing the floor.

'Call him off,' he yelped. 'Call him off, brogue!'

'I'm afraid he's not a dog.' I sleeved his spit off my cheek. 'Let's try again. Tell me who the Rag and Bone Man is. Tell me his real name.'

'I don't *know* his real name!'

'What do you know about Rephs?' I stepped towards him, giving my knife a pointed spin. 'How many people have you chained up down here?'

'You'll get nothing out of me. Whatever you do, Rags can do worse.'

'Who told you that?'

Still fuelled by ectoplasm, I pushed my spirit against his dreamscape. He cringed against the wall. 'What—' The cords in his neck stood out. 'What are you doing to me?'

'The Rag and Bone Man,' I said, louder.

'I've never even seen him! We take orders from his mollisher,' he gritted out. 'Chiffon told me to stand guard. I'm no one. Just stop—' When Warden closed in on him, he cracked. 'You said you'd call him off!'

'I didn't, actually.'

Warden fixed his gaze on the summoner. I watched as the man convulsed, overwhelmed by our attack. His eyes bled and rolled back as he passed out, still held up by the manacles.

'Sleep tight.' I tucked my knife back into my boot. 'Can you walk now, Warden?'

'Not for long.'

His eyes had turned the orange of embers, but he still looked weary. I needed a car.

I took out my burner phone and dashed off a message with the address. As I had expected, it refused to send. There was no vent in here, but there was one in the tunnel. I hauled a crate under it, stood on the top, and held the phone up as high as I could, pushing it through the bars.

'What are you doing?'

Warden had managed to leave the cell. As soon as I was down from the crate, I checked my phone again. Nick had received the message.

'Calling our getaway car,' I said. 'Did they bring you in through the black door?'

'Yes,' Warden said. 'How did you enter?'

'Through the canal basin. Unless you want to swim, we're not going that way.'

'These tunnels are connected to the warehouse. I can lead you out.'

'There's an unreadable guard and a dog up there.' I pocketed my phone, along with the stolen keys. 'We'll have to hope we can get around them.'

'Very well.'

He seemed lucid now, but he was leaning hard on to the wall. Before I could think better of it, I went to him and wrapped my arm around his waist.

'I've got you,' I said quietly. 'Come on.'

Warden looked down at me. When I returned his gaze, he draped his lower arm across my shoulders. I doubted it would help, but I couldn't just let him stand there.

We made slow progress. His movements were stiff. I held the torch; he guided me with small nods in the right direction. All the while, I tried not to notice his warmth, or the reassuring weight of his arm.

'The people who captured you,' I said. 'How did they do it?'

'With poppy anemone,' Warden said. 'They came for me during the day, when I was resting. They blindfolded and bound me, then transported me to this place in a car. I heard them call it the Camden Catacombs.'

My heart rate was climbing. The Rag Dolls shouldn't know a thing about the Rephs, let alone how to capture them.

We kept going, turning into yet another passage that looked identical to the last. When his hold on my shoulder loosened a little, I gripped his hand to keep it in place. Both of us were wearing gloves.

'Nick is on his way,' I said. 'He won't be long.'

'Neither will my captors. They left to take their supper in the Market Hall.'

Before I could ask more, he stopped dead. In the silence that followed, I heard birdsong, coming down to the vaults through a grille. I checked the æther, realising that Jos had moved back to his first lookout.

'Jos,' I murmured. 'I told him to warn me if someone was coming.' I steeled myself for a fight. 'Are any of the guards full-sighted?'

'No. They are half-sighted.'

'Good. Less chance they'll see our auras. If we can just—'

A *clang* rang elsewhere in the vaults. Warden steered me into an alcove, where I switched off my torch and stood with my back to his chest, aware of both my breathing and his silence. My revolver pressed against my waist, fastened into its holster. I had to save it for the unreadable.

'… feed him again at some point.' A voice and loud footsteps. 'Last time he almost sapped Cambric.'

'Cambric got too close.'

'Why can't we just drag someone else in here to feed him?'

'Surely I don't need to impress the need for secrecy on you again, Hodden.'

'You sure none of ours have already squealed about him?'

'No. That would risk my displeasure, and that of the Rag and Bone Man.'

Warden drew me a little closer as they passed. I wondered if he could hear my heart almost leaping out of my chest. Within a minute, a shout came from behind us.

'Dowlas, where's the creature?' one of the voyants demanded. 'Have you lost our leverage?'

'Chiffon,' the summoner rasped (I strained my ears to hear them all), 'some … Irish woman came and took him. I think she was an … oracle.'

La Chiffonnière, mollisher and mouthpiece of the Rag and Bone Man. I was itching to confront her, but I couldn't abandon Warden.

'Oh, Dowlas. Poor you,' she said. 'What did she look like, this Irish oracle?'

'Short black hair and a red scarf over her face. She … did something to my dreamscape.'

'And where is your brogue now?' Footsteps. 'Tell me, Dowlas.'

'She's gone.'

'Is she, now?' Her voice was flat. 'Then consider yourself unemployed.'

A single gunshot echoed through the tunnels. One of the dreamscapes faded from my perception.

'That's one way of fixing his dreamscape,' Hodden said. 'Any idea about the oracle?'

'Not an oracle,' La Chiffonnière said. 'His nose was bleeding, and we're looking for a brogue with a red aura. That sounds like the Pale Dreamer.'

Shit.

'The Pale Dreamer,' Hodden echoed. 'I thought she'd left London?'

'She's back.'

'Rags won't be happy. We've just lost our bargaining chip.'

'Dowlas was the one who lost him. The Rag and Bone Man will understand.' A brief silence. 'The blood on his nose is fresh. They're still here.'

I pulled Warden out of the alcove at once. We pressed on, not letting go of each other. A single misstep could betray us, but the Rag Dolls were loud.

Warden was taking me back to the large vault. The Rag Dolls seemed to be heading in the same direction, already too close for comfort. As soon as we made it there, I pulled out the power cord on the spotlight, and the room went black. I let Warden lead me, hoping Rephs could see in the dark.

The vault was too large to cross quickly. By the time the two strangers caught up, we had concealed ourselves behind what felt like a velvet curtain.

'Great, the light's janxed.'

'Shh. Even dreamwalkers breathe.'

I risked a glance. The pair circled with torches, searching behind pillars and under tables.

'Now, where to hide a wounded giant?' La Chiffonnière passed right by our hiding place, but her senses were duller than mine. 'In the largest room, I'd say.'

Warden was still as stone. Beside him, I felt deafeningly human, each breath like a gale.

'There's nowhere to run, Reph.' Hodden was getting too close. 'All the exits are blocked. If you don't come out, I'll take my sweet time killing your friend. You can keep her corpse in your cell, if you like.'

Sweat slithered down my back. My hand slid into my jacket, finding my revolver. The last thing a murder suspect should be doing was shooting a voyant from another gang, but I might not have a choice.

Beside me, Warden touched my arm and nodded towards something I had thought was a table. In fact, it was a jukebox, concealed behind the curtain with us.

The footsteps were getting closer. I dug around in my pocket, coming up with one precious coin. Warden slotted it into the machine.

An old recording erupted from inside it. My ears rang in protest as a woman sang out in jubilant French, accompanied by what sounded like an entire orchestra. Warden and I moved away from the jukebox, inching along the wall behind the curtains. The vault was sepulchral, blending and overlapping the music, making it echo. It was difficult to tell where it was all coming from.

'Find it,' La Chiffonnière snapped.

We were nearing the back of the vault. I saw the gate to the passage we needed. Warden stepped out first, keeping to the deepest shadows. I could just see Hodden – a great mop of a man, with purple hair that gave way to a bald patch. We had almost reached the tunnel when the spotlight cart blazed back to life, and I froze, almost blinded.

'Pale Dreamer,' La Chiffonnière said. 'Does Binder know you're here?'

They both wore masks. The mouths looked as if they had been slashed open, then stitched from corner to corner, while the eyeholes were as round as buttons. I moved in front of Warden.

'Binder doesn't know everything,' I said. 'Though he'd tell you otherwise.'

'Trespassing alone doesn't go down well in this syndicate,' she said. 'What do you think happens to mollishers who steal a mimelord's property?'

'I wouldn't know.' I smiled. 'I'm a very good thief.'

Hodden suddenly pointed a horse pistol. I bowled my spirit at him, snapping back so quickly that I saw him fall. His scream raised every hair on my nape. Warden scooped me up and went for the gate.

La Chiffonnière sent a spool after us. I deflected it before Warden ushered me down a tunnel that forced us into single file.

'There's no way out.' La Chiffonnière laughed. 'You're rats in a maze down here!'

I rounded a corner into a wider passage, which split in two. Warden was faster now, keeping pace with me. He led me down the left tunnel, then under a low brick arch, his fingers interlocked with mine.

Nick was almost here. I could sense his dreamscape, moving towards the Interchange.

Now every tunnel looked the same. I could only trust that Warden remembered the way. The Rag Dolls' voices chased us as we fled through the darkness, our footfalls unsettling dead leaves and rubbish.

A grimy light sputtered ahead. On either side of us, crates were piled up in precarious stacks. Warden pulled one out from the bottom, toppling the whole thing in our wake. The din was deafening – glass shattering, wood breaking apart, metal rattling on stone. Meanwhile, I ran up a flight of steps and crashed headlong into another gate. I rifled through the keys, my fingers shaking.

'Warden, which key is it?'

Spools came flying past me, catching the edges of my dreamscape. As Warden took the keys from me, I threw a spool of my own at Hodden, who was climbing over the crates. He was already bleary-eyed, confused by the shock to his dreamscape. The spool knocked him flat.

The right key was the newest. Warden let me through and locked the gate behind us.

Now we were back on ground level, inside the Interchange. I could sense the unreadable hunting us. At this point, I would have been doomed by myself.

Before I could ask, Warden went to one of the boarded windows and wrenched two planks out of the way. Even in a weakened state, he was so much stronger than a human. I used a chunk of rubble to smash the glass, and he gave me a leg up, allowing me to clamber outside.

'Come on.' I beckoned him. 'Just a bit farther.'

A loud bark wrenched at my stomach. I grabbed Warden by the wrists, as if I could bodily drag him to safety. The guard dog came loping towards us, teeth bared, then stopped with a low growl, sniffing.

Warden glanced over his shoulder. The dog cocked its head and sat, tongue out. I helped Warden over, just as the unreadable appeared.

'Teddy,' she called to the dog, fuming. 'What the fuck?'

Jos had left the area. I hooked my arm back around Warden, urging him towards a petrol car I recognised, parked in the rain. The headlights flashed as we made towards it. Nick got out and opened the back door.

'Is anyone following you?'

'Yes.' I was heaving for breath. 'Right behind us.'

'Paige, what—' He stared. 'Warden?'

'Just drive, Nick!'

I guided Warden in and joined him. Nick rushed to the front and locked the doors.

A figure sprinted around the warehouse. Nick shoved down the handbrake and slammed on the accelerator. With a jolt that snapped my teeth together, the car jolted forward. The Rag Doll fired a shotgun, missing us. A stream of Swedish escaped Nick as he grappled with the steering wheel, sending us careening across the cobblestones, and put his foot down. The car roared away from the warehouse.

'Who are they?' Nick shouted at me. 'Paige!'

'Rag Dolls.'

'Did you just trespass in their den?'

'Nick, can we have this conversation when we're not being shot at, please?'

Sweat beaded on his brow. Our car was in no state for a chase.

The Rag Dolls had vehicles outside their den. They would be straight on our tail. Nick drove on to Oval Road, his eyes darting between the mirrors. I watched him harden, becoming the Red Vision.

'We need to get back to our turf,' he said. 'Do they know it was you?'

'Yes.'

'Then we—'

A bullet hit the rear windshield, cracking the glass. I risked a look, hiding behind the headrest. A black van was already screaming after us.

'Shit.' I drew my revolver. 'Nick, do you know the cameras in this area?'

'Yes. We can't go far without attracting Scion,' Nick said. 'I'll break their line of sight and double back on them. Stay down, both of you.'

Another few shots came from the black van. I cranked the window down. As our car veered left, I took aim at their wheels and fired one shot.

'Stay *down*, Paige,' Nick barked. 'Get your seatbelts on.'

The car swerved on to the high street. Ahead, a set of traffic lights shone red. A line of cars waited in front of it, blocking our way. Nick clenched his jaw and mounted the pavement. The car hit a stall and almost a streetlamp, sending people scattering in panic, throwing me against Warden.

A cacophony of horns went off as Nick cut between two cars. One braked to avoid us. Nick continued down the high street. I turned in my seat, straining to see. The Rag Dolls were falling behind, trapped behind the pocket of chaos Nick had created.

'Seatbelts,' he repeated loudly. I reached for the middle one without argument.

Nick spun us into Plender Street, tyres screeching. He drove in silence for several minutes. When he did speak, his voice was hoarse.

'Are they still following?'

Now the ectoplasm had worn off, it was harder to focus on the æther. 'No,' I said. 'They're looking.' I nodded to the right. 'Go that way.'

He did it without question, joining the nearest traffic as if nothing had happened. Only when he switched on the heating did I remember my wet clothes. Now the danger had passed, I was shivering. Instinct made me shift towards Warden, who had closed his eyes. I did his seatbelt for him, then removed the battery from my phone.

'He can't go to Seven Dials,' Nick said. 'Jax won't stand for it.'

'We're taking him to a dosshouse,' I said. 'Can you cover him for a few nights, at least?'

Nick let out a long breath.

'Yes,' he said. 'I can do that.'

Blossoms' Inn was a modest dosshouse, tucked away in an alley called Little Turnstile. In a small room on its second floor, Arcturus Mesarthim was dead to the world. No sooner had I got him through the door than he had gone to sleep on the bed, boots and all.

Nick sipped a coffee, dark circles under his eyes. He had left me here while he got rid of the car, then walked back to Holborn. I had told him what happened, from Terebell finding me to fleeing the Rag Dolls.

The only thing I hadn't mentioned was the golden cord. Until I understood why it existed, I wanted to continue keeping that to myself. Instead, I told him the fugitives had tipped me off about Camden.

'I don't know what to think of this,' Nick said, 'but he can't stay here for ever.' He nodded to Warden. 'Neither of us can pay his rent.'

'I'll find him somewhere.'

'He isn't your responsibility, Paige.'

'I know.'

My curls were dusty and tangled, my clothes damp. It was hard to remember a time when I hadn't been regularly caked in dirt and sweat.

'Thanks for coming,' I said. 'I would never have got him away without you.'

'I wish you'd told me what you were doing. I would have helped you.'

'I'll bear that in mind for my next big heist.'

'Good.'

Warden lay on the bedding in silence. I still couldn't quite believe he was here.

'There's a link between the syndicate and the Rephs,' I said. 'There has to be, or the Rag Dolls wouldn't have been able to capture him. I need to find out how much they know. And get the fugitives out of that district.'

'You're not going back to Camden.'

'The Rag Dolls can't touch me. Whatever they've been doing in those tunnels, I doubt they want to broadcast it. They wouldn't go to the Unnatural Assembly.'

'That doesn't mean they can't take matters into their own hands.'

'Fair point.' I scraped my hair back. 'What do you know about the Rag and Bone Man?'

'He's ruled II-4 for as long as I've been in the syndicate. He and the Abbess have bad blood between them, though nobody seems to know why.'

He rubbed a spot just above his eye in a soothing, circular motion I recognised. Whenever the æther sent him a vision, a migraine came on a few days before. Jaxon always dismissed it, claiming that a *trifling headache* was nothing to gripe about, but Nick was in agony on those days.

'The thing I'm trying to understand,' he said, 'is how a mime-lord could know about the Rephs. Has anyone ever escaped from a Bone Season?'

My pulse quickened.

'Twenty years ago,' I said. 'Remember I mentioned the failed rebellion?'

Nick nodded. 'Was the traitor allowed to leave Oxford?'

'Yes. This is why I need some time with Warden,' I said. 'He might know something.' When Nick gave me a wary look, I raised my eyebrows. 'I lived with him for six months, Nick. Another night won't kill me.'

'He needs some rest. So do you,' Nick said. 'Walk back to the den with me. Jaxon drank so much absinthe tonight, I doubt he'll even be awake. And I don't think he'll remember that you avoided the party.'

I did need a shower and something to eat. I glanced once more at Warden.

'Give me a second,' I said.

'All right,' Nick said. 'I'll wait outside.'

When he was gone, I moved to sit on the edge of the bed. Warden slept on, his face turned into the pillow. Against my better judgement, I ran a gloved hand over his hair.

He stirred a little at my touch. I moved away, not wanting to wake him.

I hadn't allowed myself to think of what could happen when he came back into my life, or how he would fit into it. Arcturus Mesarthim belonged to the ancient halls of Magdalen – to candle-light and libraries and music from a century ago. I couldn't imagine him on the streets of London, facing down the lords and queens of misrule at my side.

Twenty years ago, a human had betrayed him. Now I was wondering if Nick was on to something – if that human could have returned to London and concealed himself deep in the tunnels of Camden, where Scion could never catch him again, and named himself the Rag and Bone Man.

I had the sense that I was only scratching the surface of these machinations.

Whoever he was and whatever he was plotting in his dungeons, he didn't have Warden any more. Finding a pen and paper on the table, I thought about what to write, then remembered one of the notes he had left me in Oxford. With a faint smile, I scribbled a message.

I'll see you tomorrow. Don't open the door.

Oh, and do me this honour: survive the night. I'm sure you'd rather not be rescued twice.

– Paige

14

NEUTRAL GROUND

When Warden woke the next day, he did not find himself shackled to a wall in an underground cell. He did not find himself at the mercy of the Rag Dolls, starved and beaten at their pleasure. Instead, he found himself on a mattress that wasn't long enough for him, with his head on a limp pillow, staring down a dusty vase of sad plastic geraniums.

'Well,' I said. 'How the tables have turned.'

Warden observed the peeling walls, the water stains, the daylight. Then his gaze settled on me.

'Yes,' he said. 'Hello, Paige.'

His voice was exactly as I remembered it now – dark and slow, rising up from the depths of his chest. A voice that was felt as well as heard.

'Hi,' I said.

We took the measure of each other. I looked very different from the last time he had seen me: black hair, outlined eyes, a shoulder holster for my gun and blades. My sleeveless blouse and high-waisted trousers revealed some of the shape and tone I was regaining.

So much had happened in the weeks since our rebellion. Now we met on neutral ground for the first time. If anything, I had more power now.

'You could have mentioned the ectoplasm,' I said. 'I would have found you a lot sooner.'

'Perhaps I was distracted.' His gaze darted over my face. 'London suits you.'

'Regular meals do wonders.' I nodded to the nightstand. 'I brought you some clothes. They won't fit perfectly, but I assume Terebell can get you better ones.'

'Thank you.' He propped himself on his elbows. 'May I ask what time it is?'

'Nearly four. I checked on you this morning, but you were still asleep.'

'I did wake for long enough to read your note. Touché,' he said. 'Where have you been staying, Paige?'

'Seven Dials.'

Warden regarded me. I looked straight back at him, daring him to say anything.

'I see,' was his soft reply.

'You're in Holborn, if you were wondering.' I stayed by the window. 'Not exactly Magdalen, but you're safest on my turf, for now.'

'I am grateful for your hospitality.'

'No bother,' I said. 'Warden, where did the Rag Dolls capture you?'

'Seven Dials. I hoped that I would see you, or find some clue as to your whereabouts.'

'Why couldn't you find me with the golden cord?'

'You and I were seldom apart after it formed. I suspect the sudden distance between us may have strained it. Now we are together, I trust it will strengthen again.'

'I wasn't in Seven Dials when I first came back. I was in Soho.' I tucked my hair behind my ear. 'If you want to take a shower, I'll wait.'

'Very well.'

He rose. I looked out of the window while he went into the bathroom.

Even after we had struck our alliance, I had rarely been able to let my guard down around Warden. There had been too much danger in Oxford. He had been my ally, but never my friend. Now we had to work out what our marriage of convenience should become in London.

Except it wasn't just a marriage of convenience. The Guildhall had seen to that.

By the time Warden returned, I was sharpening one of my knives to distract myself. I smiled when I saw his dark shirt and trousers.

'Those aren't too bad, actually.'

'No.' The shirt pulled tight across his broad chest and his shoulders, and the sleeves were too short, but it could have been worse. 'Where did you find them?'

'Farringdon Market. Nick gave their fastest tailor your measurements, as far as we could guess them. I'll get your other ones laundered.'

'You need not trouble yourself any further on my account, Paige.'

'It's fine. I assume the Ranthen don't have many contacts in London.'

'Alsafi has a small network of human associates here, but the rest of us do not know their names,' he said. 'I also doubt that any of them would have been able to rescue me from the Camden Catacombs.'

'The cord helped,' I said. 'You told Terebell about it.'

'I sought her counsel on the matter.'

'Right. Speaking of which, we've a lot to talk about. Are you able for it?'

'Yes. I will need to take more aura, but it can wait.' Warden sat down on the bed. 'You mentioned Joseph yesterday. How many other survivors are there?'

I looked away.

'We had to go through the Tower of London. The Guard Extraordinary saw us,' I said, with difficulty. 'I don't know how many people made it. Five are left that I know about, including me and Jos.'

'Five.' His eyes darkened a little. 'I had better abandon the business of sedition.'

'You did your best, Warden.'

'Is Michael one of them?'

I hadn't wanted to break this news to him. He had entrusted them all to my care.

'We got separated,' I finally said. 'Scion has named him as a fugitive, so he could still be alive. I've had a few people on the lookout, but they've found no trace so far.' I paused. 'I'm sorry about Gail.'

'She cared for Magdalen for twelve years. I should have known she would want to protect it. Fazal is safe,' Warden said. 'I am glad that you survived, Paige.'

'I'm glad you did.' I studied him. 'I have so much to ask you.'

'We have time.'

'I can't stay long. Jax will be expecting me. I don't want him asking questions.'

'Perhaps I should ask one first,' Warden said, his tone measured. 'Why risk your life to escape Nashira, only to give yourself back to Jaxon?'

That got my hackles up. I had almost forgotten how good he was at getting under my skin.

'I haven't given myself to anyone,' I said, bristling. 'I did try to leave him, but he started poisoning the syndicate against me. He has the power here. Standing up to him once was never going to change that.'

Warden listened in silence.

'You told me I could wield the syndicate against Nashira,' I went on, 'but I need to be on the inside to change it, and I need to be high up. Without Jax, I have no authority, no income. I'm just Paige Mahoney, a fugitive from Scion. For now, I need to be the Pale Dreamer.'

'If you have returned to Jaxon only out of necessity,' Warden said, 'I take it you are thinking of some way to win your independence.'

'I have one idea. The Underlord was murdered. We're holding a ... competition to choose our next leader. I was thinking of entering.'

'Hm. I suppose you do not know the identity of the murderer.'

'His mollisher is the prime suspect, but I have my doubts. She's gone to ground.'

'How was the Underlord killed?'

'Beheaded in his own parlour. His gang had their throats cut and their faces disfigured,' I said. 'It wasn't just a random attack or a burglary. Hector had a solid gold pocket watch. That was still on his body.'

'A statement, then.' Warden seemed to think. 'The Sargas favour decapitation as a punishment – the severance of the dreamscape from the body. It is quite possible that a Rephaite did it. Perhaps Nashira learned the identity of the Underlord and chose to be rid of him.'

He made a sound point. Suddenly I recalled what Nadine had said to me, the night Hector was killed. *Your friends in Oxford looked quite strong.*

Some of the more callous Rephs had thrown humans around with ease. I had been at the receiving end of their brute force myself. It would have been easy for just one of them to murder eight armed voyants.

'She'll have shot herself in the foot, if so. Hector would never have threatened her,' I said. 'He was too lazy and corrupt.' I took a deep breath. 'I'm a suspect on the streets. If I'm going to rule as Underqueen, I need to clear my name. It would help if I found the killer.'

'Why would you be a suspect?'

'I discovered the bodies. Hector was about to expose one of our best sources of income – ethereal forgery,' I said. 'Jax sent me to pacify him.'

'Could Jaxon himself be involved?'

The thought had crossed my mind, but I had always tamped it down, not wanting to face it. Now I was forced to confront the possibility.

'Anyone could be involved,' I said, 'but Jax doesn't do that kind of dirty work. If he *is* part of it, I seriously doubt he got his hands bloody.'

And yet the Abbess had implied that someone could have framed me. Jaxon wanted me on a short leash, and he also wanted to be Underlord. By killing Hector and sending me to the scene of the crime, knowing I would be implicated, he would have achieved both ends.

'Maybe it doesn't matter,' I said. 'Maybe someone killed Hector out of spite, and that's it. But now I'm wondering if there's some connection to the Rag and Bone Man. Did his gang ever mention Hector?'

'Not that I heard, but I was not often awake.'

'Were they torturing you?'

'In a manner of speaking, by withholding aura. They did not seem to want information.'

'They called you a bartering tool.' I sheathed my knife. 'I'll look into it.'

Warden nodded. His hair, usually walnut brown, was dark and dripping from the shower.

'In Oxford, you were a stranger in my territory. Now I find myself in yours,' he said. 'If I am to help you, I should learn more about the syndicate.'

I quirked an eyebrow. 'You still want to help me?'

'Your courage allowed me to break free of the Sargas, Paige. If I can assist you in breaking free of Jaxon, you need only say the word.'

'You don't have other things to do?'

'Terebell will bring you abreast of our plans. She is the leader of the Ranthen.'

'She told me. I'd assumed it was you.'

'No. I was simply best placed to train you.' Warden held my gaze. 'You were a force of nature in Oxford. I believe you can be Underqueen.'

He still looked at me as if he could see into the heart of my dreamscape.

'Well,' I said, 'thanks for the vote of confidence.' I cleared my throat, my face warming. 'What do you want to know about the syndicate?'

'Tell me how it operates, and what role your gang plays in its running.'

'I'm not sure you'll like me if I tell you.'

'It would be hard to shake my good opinion of you.'

My gaze dropped. He had seen a few things in my memories, but not all.

'The syndicate is a protection racket,' I said. 'The mime-queens and mime-lords take a cut of members' income in the form of syndicate rent and tax. In exchange, they vow to shield their voyants from Scion.'

'And do they?'

'Some of the time. Maybe if a Vigile cornered someone in a dark alley,' I said, 'but Jaxon would only sanction that sort of assistance if it didn't endanger him personally, or threaten his interests in any way.'

'What if they fail to pay their tax or rent?'

'They'd forfeit our protection. Jaxon would also … create problems for them. The sort of problems that might encourage them to cough up.'

Warden narrowed his eyes a little.

'We have various other operations,' I said. 'Our section has a dedicated network of pickpockets, footpads, burglars, tomb looters – every sort of thief you can imagine. Our fences handle the goods and get them to the black market. The hub is on our turf, so we have a significant presence there – drug and alcohol trafficking, smuggled goods from the free world, that sort of thing. The aster trade is very lucrative.'

'Including white and purple?'

'Yes.'

The two addictive sorts of aster. I really was covering myself in glory here.

'Jax has a whole host of other criminals in his pocket. Card sharps, underground fighters, jarkers and rufflers, couriers and kidsmen,' I said. 'We also invest in the spirit trade. There's an auction house where we can bid on them, and we hunt them ourselves. Most sections have a few binders and summoners to handle their acquisitions.'

Warden appeared to digest all of this. I could only imagine what he was thinking.

'There are seven members of your gang,' he said. 'What are your roles?'

'I told you what I do as mollisher. I enforce the rules and assist Jaxon,' I said. 'My presence keeps people in line. He's spent three years hamming up my gift, so the whole section thinks I can walk in their heads.'

'That is true.'

'It's true *now*,' I said. 'Eliza grew up in the syndicate – the aster trade, specifically – so she has a lot of contacts, and the general charm to exploit them. She's also our breadwinner, through her ethereal forgery.'

'Your memories of her were very bright.'

'She's like an older sister to me.'

'What of the others?'

'Dani is our gunsmith and inventor, and she tends to be the muscle. Jax wanted Zeke to do that, since he's unreadable, but Zeke hasn't a violent bone in him, so he takes charge of looking after our spirits. Nadine monitors the citadel for opportunities and supervises our buskers.'

'And Nick?'

'Nick is the eldest, so he tends to wrangle the rest of us. He's the fixer and the cleaner, who deals with anything we can't. He also punishes any insult to Jaxon, as you'll remember.' I patted the scar on my side. 'And patches us up when we get into scrapes, which is often.'

'His position as a violent enforcer does not seem to be in accord with his nature. He struck me as selfless and compassionate in your memories.'

'He does it to spare me. I *should* be doing all of that, but Nick didn't want Jax to use me as a weapon, so he became the weapon himself.'

'Has he killed for Jaxon?'

'I've never asked.'

Warden just looked at me.

'I did tell you.' I offered a thin smile. 'We're not nice people, Warden.'

'Paige, I lived in Oxford for one hundred and eighty years before I rebelled against Nashira. I am no bastion of moral goodness, either.'

I nodded slowly.

'Well,' I said. 'Maybe we *can* extend our understanding, then.'

A knock on the door interrupted us. Sensing a familiar dreamscape, I opened the door.

'Nick?'

Sweat coated his brow. He was in his work uniform, so pale he looked ill. 'Jag kunde inte stanna,' he muttered. 'Jag kan inte göra det här—'

'Nick, what's wrong?' I ushered him towards the chair. 'What's happened?'

'They got one of the Bone Season prisoners.'

My skin prickled. 'Who?'

'Ella Giddings.' He swallowed. 'Did you know her?'

'No. Julian and Felix did,' I said. 'She was with them in Trinity.' I took my flask of water from my backpack and unscrewed it. 'How did you find out?'

'They brought her to my department.'

'Why?'

'To watch them test Fluxion 18. They've been using her as a lab rat, Paige.'

Often, my anger burned hot. The rage that gathered now felt like ice, hardening me.

'I didn't know they'd finished the new version of flux,' I said.

'Just in time for the red zone. They gave Ella a massive dose,' he said. 'I've never seen anyone react to flux the way she did. She was vomiting blood, ripping at her hair—' He closed his eyes. 'The two senior developers started asking her questions. About you and the others.'

'Did she recognise you?'

Nick hung his head. 'She reached out to me. Just before she had a seizure.'

He had removed his mask on the train. Ella had been sitting in the same carriage as us.

'They asked if I knew her. I said I'd never seen her before. We were sent back to our labs, but I left early,' Nick rasped. 'They'll put it all together.'

'You can't go back there.' I passed him the flask. 'You've been playing with fire for too long, Nick.'

'I worked for years to get that position.'

'How much use are you going to be to anyone when you're on the waterboard, or—' I tensed. 'That wasn't what your vision was about, was it?'

'No. I would have felt it coming.' He drank. 'There's more. They're not just going to put Senshield on the Underground. They're going for essential services, too. Doctors' surgeries, hospitals, homeless shelters, banks – all of them will be equipped with the scanners.'

'How do you know this?'

'Oh, they told us.' He let out a hollow laugh. 'We gave them a round of applause.'

Using homeless shelters had always been risky for voyants, but this was a new level of danger. Come the New Year, many would lose their jobs. Employers didn't usually check people for unnaturalness, but with Senshield, it would be much easier. Most voyants would have no choice but to give up their double lives, gather what they could, and flee the capital. The syndicate would only be able to take so many of them.

Nick finally calmed down enough to focus on Warden. He rose to his feet, his face tight, and drew me to his side.

'I don't think I ever introduced you two,' I said.

'You didn't,' Nick said.

They had met twice. On one of those occasions, Warden had taken me away from him.

'Nick, this is Arcturus Mesarthim,' I said. 'Warden, this is Nick Nygård.'

'Dr Nygård.' Warden inclined his head. 'I have heard a great deal about you.'

'All good, I hope,' Nick said.

'Very.'

There was a loaded silence. I had a feeling Nick wouldn't be too happy if he learned how much Warden knew about him, thanks to the memories he had seen.

'Give me a minute,' I said. 'I need to put my contacts in.'

Nick nodded, but didn't take his eyes off Warden. I went into the bathroom and pulled the light cord, leaving the door ajar so I could eavesdrop.

'I'll just come out and say it, Warden,' Nick said. 'I know you had an understanding with Paige, but that doesn't mean I have to like or trust you. From what she's told me, you trained her to get back at Nashira for some conflict Paige doesn't even know about. You used her.'

At least he cut to the chase.

'I do not deny it,' Warden said. 'The humans of Oxford would not have followed a Rephaite, with good reason. Paige has an iron will and great strength of character. I would have been a fool to overlook it.'

'She's brilliant,' Nick agreed, 'but if you cared about her, you could have let her go. Instead, you made her learn possession, which she never wanted. I spent years trying to stop Jaxon bullying her into it.'

'If I had let Paige go, I would have been forced to use another human as a cat's paw,' Warden said. 'Would that have been more ethical?'

Nick huffed out a laugh. 'No. But I don't think you Rephs are too good with ethics.'

'All ethics come in grey, Dr Nygård. In your profession, you should know.'

'Meaning?'

This wasn't going well, and I wasn't sure I liked being talked about. I went back into the room before Warden could answer, silencing them both.

'You should talk to Jaxon,' I said to Nick. 'He can help you disappear.'

'That's where I'm heading,' he said. 'I wanted you to come back with me.'

I looked at Warden, hesitating.

'Just for a few hours,' Nick said quietly. 'Zeke said he made a pointed remark about you being distracted. We don't want him to get wind that Warden is here.' He buttoned up his coat. 'I'll wait outside.'

'All right.'

Nick shut the door behind him. I blew out a long breath.

'Go,' Warden said, very softly. 'You have a life to lead. I understand.'

'I wanted to stay longer.' I pulled on my jersey. 'I'll show my face to Jaxon and come back when I can. I still have a few questions for you.'

'I look forward to it.'

There was a light in his eyes that I might have thought playful if he hadn't been a Reph. I couldn't help but smile as I picked up my jacket and left him to his own devices.

15

THE MINISTER'S CAT

The minute I walked away from the dosshouse, I wanted to go back. Jaxon was now keeping me from doing what I wanted, and that made him feel too much like Nashira. I resented having to slink back to the den just to keep him from cutting my pay. I was nothing but a dog on his leash, and I was sick to the back teeth of it.

The scrimmage was my only chance to break his grip on me. Until then, I would have to stomach him.

Nick had walked from work. We made our slow way back to Seven Dials, keeping our heads down. He lowered the brim of his hat.

'Paige,' he said, 'I don't trust him.'

'I could tell.'

'Maybe he does want to help you,' he said, 'but he kept you prisoner for half a year, all to use you as his puppet. He threw you into the woods with one of those monsters. He watched them *brand* you—'

'I know. I remember.'

'But you don't hate him.'

'I'll never forget those things, but no, I don't,' I said. 'If not for him, I wouldn't be alive. Nashira will be hunting him for what he did in Oxford.'

'How is he going to sustain himself?' Nick pressed. 'Oxford was my first experience of being fast food, Paige. I don't want to repeat it.'

'He's not going to feed on us.'

'He has to feed on someone.'

'That's his concern. Like you said, he isn't my responsibility,' I said. 'I'll look after him for a couple of days, then send him to Terebell.'

'You do what you like, but I'm not helping you see him. If anything happened, I'd never forgive myself.'

His face was drawn. Instead of replying, I linked his arm.

Nick had lost his younger sister to Scion. He could never have stopped what happened to Ella, but I knew he would always wonder, in the dark hours.

She was almost certainly dead. From what Julian had told me, she had been too afraid of the Rephs to rebel, but she had still found the courage to reach the train. Now she would die in the cold labs of Scion.

As I thought of Ella, Liss Rymore and Sebastian Pearce came to the front of my mind for the first time in days. I hadn't had a proper chance to mourn the dead of Oxford. Voyants didn't hold funeral services – it wasn't in our culture to grieve over an empty corpse – but it might have been a comfort. Given me a chance to say *sorry* and *goodbye*.

When Nick glanced at me, I schooled my expression. I needed to be strong for him today.

As we passed the sundial pillar, a whistle caught our attention. A lanky medium was sitting at the base.

'Hearts,' Nick said. 'What is it?'

'Got a message for the Pale Dreamer.'

I turned out my empty pockets. With pursed lips, Nick handed Hearts a few coins from his wallet.

'Thank you kindly, Red Vision.' Hearts stowed the money in his coat. 'One of your friends has left you a package. It's at the location you agreed on.'

'Thanks,' I said. 'When did you get this?'

'Just now. The courier came from Camden,' he said. 'The Rag Dolls are checking every voyant who leaves II-4. Took her some time to get the envelope out of the section without them noticing, apparently.'

Hearts doffed his hat before he slunk away. Nick looked down at me.

'Have you ever heard of couriers being searched?'

'No, but we just rustled a Reph out of their section. They must be feeling paranoid,' I said. 'I'm worried they're going to find the others. Agatha knows I'm involved with them. Ivy trusts her, but I'm not sure I do.'

'Maybe you can move them to a derelict. We could make them comfortable.'

I nodded, thinking of the music hall. Nick unlocked the den.

At least Jos had got away from the Rag Dolls. I had already sent a message to Camden Lockets and received a note from Felix in return, confirming everyone was fine. I'd check in on them again soon.

Jaxon was in his study, his fingers steepled, wearing shirtsleeves and a stiff expression. As soon as Nick and I entered, he narrowed his eyes.

'Another stroll, darling?'

'Just a quick one.' I folded my arms. 'Is that all right with you, Jaxon?'

'Don't be pert. I told you not to leave the den without informing me.' He turned his attention to Nick. 'Why are you in that ghastly uniform?'

'I came from work,' Nick said. 'Jax, I think my position has been compromised.'

As Nick explained the situation, Jaxon twirled a fountain pen. Once again, his face was impassive.

'Much as I despise your moonlighting with Scion, I'm afraid we need your income, Dr Nygård,' he concluded. 'Hold your nerve, as you always have. It would only incriminate you further if you were to abandon your post.'

We couldn't need money that much. Even after what had happened at the black market, the section had been running normally.

'Jax, he's in danger,' I said. 'What if they arrest him?'

'They won't, honeybee.'

'You're raking in a fortune from syndicate rent alone. You can't possibly—'

'You may be my heir, Paige,' Jaxon cut in, 'but unless I am mistaken, I am mime-lord here.' He didn't deign to look at me. 'I can shelter one fugitive under my roof, but two would be tempting the noose. One glance from a voyant is not enough to implicate our oracle.'

'So you're happy to risk Nick for a few more pennies in your coffers?'

'Leave me with my mollisher, Dr Nygård,' Jaxon said coldly. 'Take a well-deserved break.'

Nick clenched his jaw. He gave my shoulder a gentle squeeze as he passed.

A distorted recording of 'The Boy I Love is up in the Gallery' was warbling from the turntable. An empty reservoir glass stood on the desk. I sat in my usual armchair and crossed one leg over the other, giving Jaxon what I hoped was an innocent and expectant look.

'The scrimmage,' Jaxon said, dangerously soft, 'is less than a month away. I have seen no evidence whatsoever that you are attempting to prepare for it.'

'Of course I am.'

'How so?'

'I've been working on my gift. I can drift without life support for a while now.'

'And what of possession?'

I said nothing.

'You disappoint me, Paige. I would have thought you wanted to be mollisher supreme.' Jaxon scrutinised me. 'If your gift had been stronger, Scion would never have been able to detain you. I know you have some … moral qualms, but true dreamwalking would all but assure our success in the Rose Ring. Come, darling. Do this for me.'

I forced a smile. It was embarrassing that I had fallen for this act for so long.

'Fine,' I said.

'Good.' He placed a small glass bottle in front of me, full of greenish oil. 'You have also neglected to use the bay laurel I purchased for you. I can't have you distracted by your wound in the Rose Ring.'

I had worn long sleeves around him for days. He had no idea the mark was gone.

'It hasn't hurt since you bound the Monster,' I said.

'Irrelevant. Until I see some evidence that you are addressing your weaknesses,' Jaxon said, 'I will be withholding your wages.'

I stared at him, fuming.

'I've done everything you've asked of me,' I said, trying to keep the bitterness out of my voice. 'Delivered the messages, gone to the auctions—'

'—and through it all, paid not one iota of attention!' Jaxon swept the glass off his desk, along with reams of paperwork. 'I suggest you manage your time a little better. I shall ask Nick to train you up for the fight.'

My heart hammered. Jaxon collected another glass from the cabinet.

'Off with you, now,' he said. 'Have an early night. You need your rest.'

I left without a word.

Now the bastard was sending me to bed, like I was some wayward child. I stomped up to the kitchen to make something to eat, only to find Eliza on the landing, gazing blankly at the wall, her mouth ajar.

'Eliza,' I said, wary.

Oil paint sleeved her arms from fingertip to elbow. Her hair hung in greasy coils down her back, reeking of old sweat, and her eyelids were heavy. She was humming an obscure tune from the seventeenth century.

When Pieter had Eliza, we could usually only stop the possession by shouting at him, preferably in Dutch. Unable to shout back, he would find other ways to express his annoyance, and the last thing I needed was another palette to the face.

'Eliza.' I stood in front of her. 'Is that you?'

'Yes,' Eliza murmured. 'Where have you been, Paige?'

'Holborn.' I looked into her dull eyes. 'When was the last time you slept?'

'I'm not sure.' She reached for my shoulder. 'Do you know when Jax is paying us?'

'Friday. Why do you ask?'

'He wants to see progress. Need to make progress.'

'You've made plenty of progress.'

'No. I have to carry on.' She shook her head. 'I have to finish it, Paige.'

'Eliza, I want you to take the night off. I want you to eat a square meal, have a shower, and get some sleep,' I said. 'Can you do that for me?'

A heavy nod. I steered her into the bathroom with a towel and a clean nightshirt.

Danica was on her side of the garret. I knocked on her door, entering when I didn't get an answer. The room overflowed with scraps, bought from mudlarks on the Thames or scavenged from the Stone Hall.

'I hate it when you knock,' Danica groused. 'You come in either way.'

'You never open the door,' I pointed out. 'Sorry, but I need a favour.'

'I don't do favours.'

'It's nothing strenuous.'

'Not the point. That seat isn't for people,' she added as I sat down.

I scanned the scraps of paper on the floor, all covered in neat Cyrillic script. 'What are you working on?'

'The jamming device.'

'How's it going?'

'I'll let my face speak for itself.' She wore a loupe over her eye. 'You heard me tell Jaxon I need a prototype, but he never listens.'

'If you get bored, do you think you could modify my oxygen mask for me?'

She glanced up. 'Modify how?'

'I need it to be more discreet.'

'Jaxon won't pay me for that. This is the job he gave me, inane though it is.'

'It's for the scrimmage. Besides, you haven't bought so much as a sock since last year.'

'This may come as a shock to you, but I need the money to pay for parts, not to mention the rent at my registered address, which is in Shoreditch. That aside, what I do with my coin is none of your business.' She took off the loupe. 'If I agree to do this, will you go away?'

'If you also make sure Eliza eats a full meal before she gets back to work.'

'Yes.'

That was the best I would get out of her. I went back to the landing to wait for Eliza.

After a while, she tottered out. I dried and plaited her hair, then tucked her into bed. When the muses drew in, I forced them into a spool and knocked them unceremoniously to the other side of the room.

'She needs to rest. Bother someone else.'

George brooded in the corner, while Rachel and Philippe hung sadly above the door.

'Don't give me those looks,' I muttered. 'You might not have eyes, but I can sense them.'

Pieter shot off in a huff.

Eliza was already sound asleep. I pulled a thick blanket over her shoulders.

Jaxon didn't want me to rest. If he was interested in our welfare, Eliza wouldn't be wandering around like an automaton in week-old clothes. When I returned to the second floor, he was smoking outside his study, watching. I went into my room and slammed the door in his face.

Straight away, I unpicked my pillow and counted my savings. I sewed them back inside, then lay down and closed my eyes, coursing with frustration.

Warden was waiting in the dosshouse. The penny dreadful was waiting in Soho. If I couldn't reach either of them tonight, I might as well sleep.

I was still awake by the time the streetlamps bathed the streets in blue. Not having his own room, Nick was in the study. The others fell asleep.

At some point, I must have dozed off. When I woke again, it was almost midnight, and the stairs were creaking. When my door swung open, I sat up, my knife in my hand.

'Shh. It's me.' Nick crouched beside my bed. 'You're sleeping with a knife?'

'You sleep with a gun,' I said. 'What's the matter?'

'Go back to Warden.' He nodded to the window. 'Jaxon has filled every hour of your day tomorrow. I'll cover for you if he wakes up.'

'You said you wouldn't help me see Warden.'

'I trust that you know what you're doing. And I might need you to do the same for me if I sneak out with Zeke,' he added. 'Be careful, sötnos. And if you can't be careful—'

'—be quick.' I kissed his cheek. 'I know. Thank you.'

A thick fog had descended on London. It would help conceal me from the Vigiles. Bundled up in a hooded jacket, I left the den and headed for Soho.

The district was heaving with amaurotics. They came for the gambling houses and theatres, the coffee and music joints, the oxygen bars that glowed along Dean Street. This was where Eliza had grown up.

I dropped Warden's clothes at the penny wash, which was open all night. When I reached Soho Square, I slipped into the Minister's Cat, a gambling house tailored to voyants, with stringent rules on which of us could bet and how. There was a lottery held here every month, with the winner entitled to a modest sum of money from Jaxon. It was also a neutral stop, where members of other gangs were allowed to linger without his express permission. Most districts had a handful of them, where turf disputes and grudges were ignored.

Troggu and Call the King were popular games, along with amaurotic staples, like whist. My fingers itched – I loved cards, and a few wins could fill my pockets – but I couldn't waste my time away from Jaxon.

As always, the Minister's Cat was full. Certain places were considered safe after dark, since the night Vigiles didn't want them shut down. I moved between people and tables, leaving whispers in my wake. This particular establishment was a breeding ground for gossip.

Babs was presiding over a game of minchiate in the corner. I would have to wait. I leaned against the bar, meeting the gaze of anyone who looked my way.

A soothsayer in her late twenties sat nearby, drinking mecks in a booth. Her skin was dark brown, and a band of violet silk held back her cloud of tiny corkscrew curls. I didn't think I had seen her before.

Before Oxford, I would never have asked another voyant for a reading, but Liss had changed my perspective on soothsaying. Perhaps I should use the æther to my advantage, the way the Rephs did.

'Hey,' I said. 'Got time for a reading?'

She looked up from beneath heavy lids. While her right eye was deep brown, the left was green, with a loop of yellow around the pupil. It was the second time in my life that I had seen a pair of eyes like that.

'If you've got coin for it.' The woman rubbed the bridge of her broad nose. 'I assume you know I can't comment on any gambling you're to do.'

'I'm not here to gamble.' I dug out some money. 'Is this enough?'

She unravelled the notes. It would buy her another few glasses of mecks.

'Well,' she said, 'I suppose it's better than nothing.'

Her deep voice held a trace of an accent. I sat down in the booth and took off my gloves.

'You're an astragalomancer,' I said.

'Very good.'

Her fingernails were painted white, dotted with black. There were flecks of white above her eyes, too. She took two small knucklebones from her sleeve. Both were inscribed with tiny numbers.

'Not all astragalomancers work the same way I do,' she said. 'I keep it very simple. You ask five questions; I'll give you five answers. They might be vague, but you'll have to deal with it. Give me your hand.'

I offered my left one. She grasped it, then dropped it like it was a frayed wire.

'It's freezing,' she said. 'Did a breacher touch you?'

When I realised, I closed my fingers over my palm. The scars had always been colder than the rest of me. I had got used to not covering them in Oxford.

'Yes.' I put my left glove back on. 'Sorry. I had a run-in with a poltergeist.'

'It's like shaking hands with a corpse.' She accepted my right hand instead, holding the dice in her free palm. 'All right. Ask your questions.'

'Who killed the Underlord?'

The soothsayer smiled. 'You haven't had many readings, have you?' she said. 'If that was going to work, someone else would have done it by now. The æther can't just deliver a name like a vending machine.'

'Right.' I paused, mulling it over. 'Did Cutmouth kill the Underlord?'

'Babs has been taking bets on that sort of thing. Are you sure you're not gambling?'

'No,' I said. 'I'm mollisher of this section. You won't get into any trouble.'

'You're the Pale Dreamer?'

I nodded once. The soothsayer narrowed her eyes before she cast the knucklebones.

A two and a two.

'I see a set of scales,' she said, in the same monotone Liss had used when she read my cards. 'One bowl is full of blood, weighing it down. Four figures stand around the scales – two on one side, two on the other.'

My forehead creased. 'Does that answer the question?'

'I did say it could be vague.'

'You're the expert,' I said. 'Does my coin include your interpretation?'

'I could stretch to that.' She pondered. 'In my experience, scales usually point towards justice or truth. In this case, you have two people on the right side of justice and two who aren't. That's my feeling, but remember, you're the querent. The æther is replying to you, so you should have the tools to understand the meaning. I'm just the conduit.'

Either I was thick as a plank, or the æther enjoyed bewildering people. Possibly both.

'Next question, then.' I sat back. 'Did Cutmouth kill the Underlord?'

'You just asked that.'

'I'm asking it again.'

'Are you testing my abilities, jumper?'

She seemed more amused than insulted. 'I might be,' I said. 'I've seen a few charlatans in here.'

'It's your coin.'

She did it again. A two and a two. I repeated the question once more and got the same answer.

'Please.' The soothsayer sighed. 'Get on with it. Two more questions.'

There were so many I wanted to ask, but I had to be careful. Everyone was curious about the murder, but I didn't want my interest in the Rag Dolls to be known.

'Say I wanted to know about a group of people,' I said carefully, 'but I didn't want to say who they were.'

'So long as *you* know who you're talking about, that should work. Again, you're the querent.'

I tapped my fingers on the table, thinking of how to phrase it.

'The one who lives by the water,' I said. 'How does he know about the giants?'

It was clumsy, but it had to be indecipherable. From her expression, the soothsayer had heard stranger things. Her knucklebones rolled across the table and stopped next to my hand, both showing a single dot.

'A hand without living flesh, its fingers pointing to the sky. Red silk surrounds its wrist like a manacle,' she said. 'The hand snatches crushed petals from the ground. Two fingers break away, but it keeps snatching.'

She shook her head, took another gulp of her drink.

'I need some help with that one,' I said.

'No idea about the hand. Red silk is likely blood or death. Or neither,' she added. 'Fallen petals could represent ... lost parts of a whole.' A vein stood out in her forehead. 'Last question. I'm getting tired.'

I was silent for a while, trying to think of something that could point me in the right direction.

'Who is the King of Wands?'

'Ah.' Her smile was knowing. 'You *have* had a reading before. Just the one?'

I didn't answer. Talking about Liss would only bring back the pain of her death. The soothsayer flicked the two dice up with her thumb and caught them in the same hand. A three and a four.

'Seven,' she said.

'No vision?'

'No. I don't get them often,' she said. 'Having more than one is unusual.'

My gaze dropped to the knucklebones again.

'Remember the way the number is divided. A three and a four,' she said. 'That division will be significant.' She returned the knucklebones to her inner pocket. 'The White Binder doesn't think much of soothsayers. I know we often speak in riddles. But no matter how much like nonsense they sound, there is meaning, Pale Dreamer.'

'I believe you,' I said.

And I did. No matter how confusing her cards, I sensed Liss would be right about everything.

'Don't worry about it too much,' the soothsayer advised me. 'Nothing you can do about your future, I'm afraid.'

'We'll see about that.' I stood. 'Thank you.'

The soothsayer nodded, kneading her forehead with one hand. I left the booth and returned to the bar, my stomach a cradle of snakes.

Now the card game had finished, Barbara Bryant – a freckled, cheerful polyglot – was on her break from dealing, pouring drinks instead. Some said the monarchy was still alive and well in Babs – she was a self-declared queen of chin music. She raised a hand when she saw me.

'Pale Dreamer,' she exclaimed. 'Haven't seen you in a while. How are you?'

'Could be better, Babs.' I sat on one of the wooden stools. 'I'm told you have a package for me.'

'Oh, yes, I do.' She rummaged under the counter. 'Something from an admirer?'

I shook my head, smiling. 'You know Binder wouldn't allow that.'

'Oh, he is cruel to you all, that man. You know he's stopped the lottery, don't you?'

'Since when?'

'August. Nobody was happy, but I suppose he was generous to do it in the first place.'

Jaxon really was counting his coppers. I still didn't understand his insistence that we were running out of money.

'You're busy tonight,' I said.

'We've been taking bets on the outcome of the scrimmage. Bless old Hector for dying – we were struggling for a while,' she said. 'Vigiles used to come, but Scion has them too scared to sneak out of their barracks.'

'How do you mean?'

'Beatings and worse, I hear. Hock is losing patience with this fugitive situation, saying the night Vigiles must be hiding their own kind.' She glanced up at me. 'Speaking of fugitives, you've been the talk of the house.'

I sighed. 'Does *everyone* know who I am now?'

'Pretty much, and odds are high that you're the one who killed Hector.'

'So I heard. What do you think?'

'Dreamer, I've known you for two years. I can't imagine you beheading anyone. No, I reckon it was Cutmouth. I mean, if it wasn't, why hasn't she come forward to claim the crown?'

'Because she knows she's a suspect. Or a target.'

'She wouldn't care a jot, that girl. She wasn't too bad without Hector pulling her strings,' she added. 'Came in here quite often for a game with one of her girlfriends.'

'Cutmouth had girlfriends?'

'On the sly, I think.' Babs handed me a thick envelope. 'Here, love. I haven't laid a lamp on it, sure as I'm a sensor.'

'Thank you.' I still checked the wax seal before I tucked it into my jacket. 'I'm a bit short, Babs. I'll pay you when I get my wages.'

'Instead of money, humour me with a game. There's some peacocks in here that need a good thrashing.'

'Who?'

'The corner table. They're in most nights.'

I looked over my shoulder, seeing a tall woman in a diamond necklace and earrings, among others. 'Your one in the sparks, you mean?'

'Aye.' Babs lit a roll of blue aster. 'I ask you, who has that kind of coin?'

'Where are they from?'

'Kensington. They're no trouble, but they win a little too often for my liking.' She grinned. 'Ah, I'm just remembering when you took Magtooth down a peg. I've never laughed so hard as when he skulked in the next day, just to cough up all the money he'd bet on himself.'

That had been a good week. It seemed a hollow victory now Magtooth was dead.

The voyants in the corner were fashionably dressed. I recognised the elegant redhead from the auction, lounging in a tea dress with cap sleeves, looking over her fan of cards. These players answered to the Abbess. That explained why they were flashing such expensive jewellery in the middle of Soho – no one would dare rob them while their boss was Underqueen.

'Maybe next time,' I started to say.

Then I saw him.

One of the players at that table sat apart from the others, his face overcast. His short hair was dark blue, and he wore a pinstriped waist-coat without a shirt, allowing me to see the tattoo on his right arm – a tattoo of a skeletal hand, outlined in black, its fingers reaching for his shoulder.

A hand without living flesh, its fingers pointing to the sky.

'That's a Rag Doll,' I said quietly.

Babs opened a bottle of mecks. 'Hm?'

'Playing with the Nightingales.'

She looked. 'Oh, so it is,' she remarked. 'The Nightingales are always playing friendly games with other sections.' She started to fill a row of glasses. 'Mind you, I'm surprised they'd stoop to playing with a Rag Doll. He must have paid good money to enter their tournament. Binder *is* still all right with other gangs stopping here, isn't he?'

'They're fine.' My heart drummed. 'Do you know why the Abbess hates their mime-lord so much?'

'This might surprise you, but I've never heard.'

It did surprise me. Babs knew everything there was to know in London.

'That symbol on his arm,' I said. 'Any idea?'

'Declares their loyalty to the Rag and Bone Man,' Babs said. 'Looks shit, doesn't it?'

I cracked another smile at that. 'I've got to go,' I said. 'Thanks again for the package, Babs.'

'All right.' She reached over the bar to embrace me. 'You be careful, Dreamer. The streets aren't very kind these days.'

'You, too.'

Before I left, I shut myself into another booth, where I took out the pages of the manuscript and smoothed them out. Nell had done well to get two copies to me so quickly.

They had called it *The Rephaite Revelation*. I opened it and started to read.

CHAPTER I

LISS IS SNATCHED FROM LONDON

The writing was sparse, but gripping from the first sentence. Nell had nailed the style. The story followed Liss, a poor and kind-hearted cartomancer, trying to make ends meet. The sketches didn't show her face; only her long black hair. In a noble attempt to save a friend, she was detained. In the next chapter, she woke up in an unfamiliar room.

The story explained the trafficking of voyants to a nameless city. Finding herself alive but imprisoned, Liss learned about the origin of Scion.

The ensuing chapters described her ordeal at the hands of the Rephaim, giants from a fallen realm called the Netherworld. She endured many trials, slowly learning the truth about the Rephs and their ancient enemies, the Buzzers. Nell had mentioned that some Rephs had good in them, while others despised humans.

I raced through it. I knew this story, but I still wanted to know what happened next, and I was by no means a prolific reader. If *The Rephaite Revelation* was published, it would tell the syndicate everything it needed to know – most importantly, how to identify and fend off a Reph. When I had got the gist, I flicked to the last pages. At the end, this Liss broke free of the city and rallied London to overthrow Scion. She did what the real Liss had never had the chance to do.

Here, on these pages, she was alive. This story would make her immortal. I returned the manuscript to its envelope and fastened it into my satchel.

I would take it to the Spiritus Club in the morning. First, I wanted to see Warden.

When I emerged, Babs was still behind the bar with another croupier, roaring with laughter, while the Rag Doll had disappeared. I rapped on the Nightingales' table, making them start. The redhead stubbed out her aster.

'Pale Dreamer.' Half of her face was concealed by a mask. 'Can we help you?'

'The Abbess said she was sending your gang here to help us track Cutmouth down,' I said. 'Did you follow up on the lead Binder gave her?'

'Oh, yes,' one of the men said, not taking his eyes off his hand of cards. 'Unfortunately, we found nothing of use. A few people do remember Cutmouth visiting Soho, but alas, no one has seen her since.'

'Any reason you're playing with Dolls?'

'He challenged us and insulted our lady. We told him to put his money where his mouth was.' One of the other women, an augur, blew a curl of smoke at me. 'Do you want to do the same, Pale Dreamer?'

'Stop it,' the redhead warned her. 'This isn't our turf.' She placed a fine-boned hand on my arm. 'The Abbess is very grateful for your hospitality and cooperation. We do hope Cutmouth will be found soon.'

'Don't we all.' I turned away. 'Enjoy your game.'

'You're too kind.'

As soon as I was outside, I checked my watch. I had five hours before I needed to be back at the den, which gave me plenty of time to see Warden. Keeping my satchel close, I headed to the penny wash to finish laundering his clothes, then made my way towards Holborn.

The fog worked in my favour, as did the new moon. I slipped into the narrow Flitcroft Street, where there were no streetlamps. This stretch was an alley in all but name, leading to Book Mews.

About halfway down it, the back of my neck prickled. I kept walking. There were no alarm bells in the æther, but every human instinct told me something was wrong.

Away from the safe establishments in Soho and Piccadilly, there were few voyants on the street at this hour. If I called for help, not many would hear.

I picked up my pace without meaning to do it. I had almost reached the dead drop when two figures closed in on me, and a punch to the jaw knocked me clean to the ground.

16

DANGEROUS KNOWLEDGE

A bag descended over my head. My arms were wrenched behind my back. I arched and kicked with a scream of anger, but a strong hand clapped over my mouth, almost choking me.

Something hard struck the back of my skull, setting off an explosion behind my eyes. My ears rang as the agony leaked deep into my jaw and cheekbones.

The bag had blinded me. I became aware of hands grasping me under my arms, the asphalt carving up my knees, rough breathing somewhere overhead.

'Sorry, Pale Dreamer,' a strained voice said, 'but I'm afraid you know too much.'

They bundled me around a corner. My thoughts clotted like blood. As I fought to stay conscious, I tried to keep track of where I was going. Either they were taking me to a car, or they planned to kill me in Book Mews. I tried to shout – some of our thieves lived nearby – but the hand on my mouth only pressed harder, smothering me.

I had let my guard down on my own turf. That had been my first mistake.

It might just be my last.

Suddenly I was dumped on the ground. The bag came off my head again. My ragged breathing was all I could hear. When I saw the sign reading BOOK MEWS, I turned so cold that I could no longer feel my body.

Jaxon had chosen this place as our dead drop because no one had any reason to go there.

'Scream again and I'll cut you, moll.' A knife bit into the side of my neck. 'If you want to live, you'll tell us where you took the creature.'

'What—' I could hardly speak. 'What creature?'

'The one you stole. Pretty eyes,' another voice said. 'Shall we jog your memory?'

A fist collided with my face. This time, the shock didn't paralyse me. Something in me leapt awake, rearing in panic and fury. I slashed at the nearest dreamscape – not with a blade, but with my entire being.

My vision shorted out again. One of the attackers gave a shout, and his knife clattered to the ground. I snatched it up and thrust it out, lurching back to my feet. I strained to feel the æther, my head swimming from the blow. One of my attackers was an augur, the other a medium. They were blocking my way out of the alley. As they approached, I made out those unsettling masks from the Interchange.

'Kill me and you'll never get the Reph,' I warned, taking a step away from them. 'It's the Rag and Bone Man who wants me dead, I take it.'

'Clever of you to have found his sanctuary.' The augur pointed a silenced pistol at my face. 'Too clever for your own good, Pale Dreamer.'

Before I could even consider the risk, I had rushed her. I grabbed the pistol with one hand and twisted out of the line of fire, just as it went off with a *snap*. The woman tried to wrest it back, but I kept a firm hold, the way Nick had taught me. Trying my utmost to break her grip, I stomped on her foot and kicked her in the knee.

I was outnumbered. As we fought over the gun, the second attacker came at me. I caught the augur in the cheek with my fist, sending the pistol clattering to the ground, and whirled to face the medium. My world narrowed down to the knife he had drawn.

Before he could even try to stab me, the augur seized my jacket and pulled me to the ground. As she held me down, I grappled with her, stripped to raw survival instinct. I tried once more to shout, but all I could do was gasp for breath as she managed to pin my wrist with her boot.

When those Underguards detected you, you must have believed your life hung in the balance. I could almost hear Warden. *Your spirit responds to danger.*

A familiar pressure rose behind my eyes. I felt myself being sucked from my body, bone and spirit cleaving as I jumped. My spirit tore straight through her mind, taking her spirit with it. Now I was back in the æther, and her spirit was tumbling with me. Her silver cord snapped.

A heartbeat later, the corpse slumped on top of me. I blinked, my lashes wet.

'Moreen—'

I struggled out from under the augur. The other attacker was rooted to the spot, no doubt trying to understand why his accomplice had just died.

All at once, he charged me. He bunched his fists in my jacket, hauled me upright, and smashed me against the wall. When the knife swung down, I caught his wrist and held it back with all my strength. My arms shook as his fingers dug into my shoulder. In desperation, I tried dreamwalking again, forcing him to let go of me.

He was on me again in moments, his knife like a waltzer at a fairground, swinging at me from every angle. My hands flew up to block him. The point missed my neck by an inch.

I had survived knife attacks before, but the blow to my head was draining me, all my knowledge vanishing as darkness threatened to close in. My arm and fingers seared. When the medium was near enough, I trapped his elbow and rammed my knee between his thighs. A huff of breath came through the mask, past my ear. I drove my fist into his stomach, then used my weight to throw his balance, rolling him to the ground.

I could not have fought tooth and nail to escape Oxford, only to die alone in an alley.

The medium was bigger than me. Before I knew it, he was gaining the upper hand, and I was the one pinned. I writhed until I could bite him, clamping down until the roots of my teeth ached. A muffled roar escaped him, but he kept a rigid hold on me, even when my teeth sank deep and my mouth filled with the taste of pennies.

I knew myself too well to risk jumping again. Instead, I groped for my boot knife, my fingertips just closing on it. He screamed when I drove it into his side. I scrambled away, and we both lunged back to our feet.

His blade came at me from every angle. As I ducked and circled to avoid him, I realised his movements were slowing. Even if I had only been able to glance off his dreamscape, it must have shocked him. The mask had to be restricting his vision.

With the inch of clear thought that remained, I remembered the beginning of this ambush. I sprinted past the medium, back on to Flitcroft Street. I picked up the brick on the ground. Just as the medium reached me, I turned and struck him across the face, cracking his mask. He crumpled.

I gripped my knees. When I could draw a steady breath, I limped back to the dead woman and took off her mask. I didn't recognise her face. Trying not to look at it, I searched her.

When I got to her inner pocket, my fingers brushed against smooth fabric. I drew out a length of silk. A red handkerchief, stained with blood.

The calling card from the Devil's Acre.

I looked back when the man gave a short groan. His mask was next to come off. Aside from a scar near his temple and a smattering of stubble, he had no distinguishing features whatsoever. I stuffed the handkerchief into my pocket and lifted his chin, making him look at me.

'Remember this,' I said quietly, 'the next time you think about attacking the Seven Seals.' I showed him the handkerchief. 'You were going to plant this on me. Why does your boss want me framed?'

'I'll never tell.' His nose was bleeding. 'Are you going to kill me, dreamwalker?'

'You want me to, so you can join your friend back there?'

'No. I enjoy … the spoils of living.'

'So you're willing to kill for the Rag and Bone Man, but not to die for him. That's the mark of a real coward.' I tightened my grip. 'Tell him I'm going to find out what he's doing. Tell him he can send every pathetic lackey and cutthroat he wants, but he will *never* get the Reph back.'

The medium wheezed with laughter. 'We're all puppets, mollisher,' he rasped. 'Make sure you know … who's holding your strings.'

His eyes closed, and he fell unconscious. Breaking into my deepest reserves of strength, I pulled him back into Book Mews, where I used my belt to fasten his wrists behind his back. I left him beside the corpse.

I should have gone back to Seven Dials. Instead, I continued towards Holborn.

By sheer dumb luck, I didn't pass any night Vigiles as I stumbled along the backstreets, my hand clamped over my upper arm, where my sleeve was damp. I veered off course at least twice, cold and disoriented. I was on Wild Street when gloved hands cupped my elbows.

'Paige.'

I looked up. A long way.

'Warden,' I said faintly.

My knees buckled. Warden caught me before I could fall on my face.

'I have you,' I heard him say, just as the darkness thickened around me. Not pausing to ask questions, he took me the rest of the way back to Holborn.

I didn't quite remember getting to Blossoms' Inn. Next I was fully aware, I was sitting on the edge of the bed, and Warden was crouched in front of me, studying my face with blazing eyes. I blinked a few times.

'Paige.'

I swallowed, tasting copper. 'Did we come in through the front door?'

'I used the window. What happened?'

Slowly, I looked down at my slashed gloves. My hands were shaking. 'The Rag and Bone Man,' I said. 'He sent two voyants to kill me.'

'They attacked you on your turf?'

'Yes.' I reached for the back of my head. 'They hit me with something.'

'May I see?'

When I nodded, Warden rose and moved around my seat to look. I held still as he gently parted my hair, sending a prickle along my scalp.

'The wound is not deep, but it has bled a great deal,' he said. 'Do you have medical supplies?'

'Yes.'

'Very well. Let me know if you need me.'

'Thanks.'

As soon as I was in the bathroom, I leaned over the sink, my head throbbing. When I was confident I wasn't going to throw up, I stripped to my underwear. I rinsed the blood away, cleaned the cuts, washed the grit from my knees, and carefully dressed all of the injuries.

'Warden,' I called hoarsely, 'I laundered your shirt. Do you mind if I wear it?'

'By all means.'

I buttoned it on and pushed up the long sleeves. It came down almost to my knees.

By the time I emerged from the bathroom, gauze pressed to the back of my head, the television was on. Warden looked from it to me.

'I believe the shirt may need some adjustments.'

'A few.' I sat on the bed. 'You know, since I came back to London, I've been chased, punched, spat on – three fucking times – and now there are people trying to stab me. I'm almost starting to miss Oxford.'

'You do not mean that.'

'Possibly not.' I nodded to the television. 'Anything on ScionEye?'

'Scion has announced the creation of an elite subdivision of night Vigiles called Punishers. Their primary function is to hunt down the preternatural fugitives.'

'An even more unnatural sort of unnatural, I take it.'

'Yes. A new classification of criminal.'

'I'm flattered.'

'I suspect these Punishers are red-jackets,' Warden said. 'Now Oxford is compromised, they must have been put to work in the citadel. Nashira will spare no expense to find you.'

'Naturally.' I sank against the pillows. 'Did you get in touch with Terebell?'

'Not yet.' Warden drummed his fingers on the arm of the chair, a habit he had brought from Magdalen. 'I take it Jaxon has sanctioned this visit.'

'No, actually. He has no idea where I am,' I said. 'I'm letting him think I'm under his thumb, but I wasn't going to let him stop me seeing you.'

'Does he know I am here?'

'No, and he's not going to find out. He wants me to pretend I never went to Oxford.'

'Does he not fear Senshield?'

'Don't even get me started.' I sighed. 'I don't want to talk about Jaxon tonight.'

'What would you like to talk about?'

'I'll start by asking you for the truth.'

'A grand request,' Warden said. 'Whose truth do you seek, Paige?'

'Nashira forced you to be her consort. You confirmed that in Oxford. You also told me the conflict between you went deeper than how the city was managed,' I said. 'I'd like to know more about that.'

'At the time, you told me you would prefer not to involve yourself in my grudges. What changed?'

'I didn't think it would be my problem after Oxford, but here we are.' I sought his gaze. 'I know why you had to keep things from me. But if we're going to continue this ... understanding, I need to know everything.'

'To explain, I must take you back a long way.'

'All right.'

Warden leaned back in his chair, not taking his eyes off me. It was a relaxed posture, reminding me of the way he had sat by the fire in Magdalen.

'The Netherworld was once an intermedial realm. It stood between the æther and Earth,' he told me. 'Nothing grew or perished there, and those that dwelled there did not age, for they were not made of mortal flesh. We were the highest and strongest of these beings.'

'What *are* you made of?'

'We call it *sarx*. When we are speaking English, we use this word to distinguish our immortal bodies from the corporeal substance of yours.'

'I assume you also have bones.'

'Yes, but they are far stronger than yours, reinforced with adamant.' Warden clasped his hands. 'The names I will use in this story will not be our true names, but those we use now.'

'Okay.'

My head felt heavy. I nestled into the pillows and turned my body towards Warden.

'Go on,' I said. 'I'm listening.'

'Hm.'

The Rephaim had always been in the Netherworld. They were not born, like humans, nor had they evolved (to their knowledge); instead, they simply emerged, fully formed and conscious. The Netherworld itself was the cradle of immortal life, the womb in which they were created. There were no parents or children. More Rephs would surface now and then, though unpredictable waves of creation.

They had not been called Rephaim then. That was a name that humans had given them, since Glossolalia was impossible for most of us to articulate.

Once, they had been responsible for preserving the delicate balance between worlds. Their overriding duty was to ensure that humans accepted death, so their spirits moved on to the end of the æther.

In the early days of humankind, the Rephs had relied on their messengers, the psychopomps. In the Netherworld, these fragile spirits took the form of birds. They had been able to fly across the veil and guide the recent dead into the Netherworld, where the Rephs would help them to let go of their old lives and prepare for their unmaking.

'So the Netherworld was a halfway house,' I said. 'A waystop.'

'Yes.'

But as time went on – and Rephaim, he told me, still had trouble grasping the concept of *time*, a force which had no effect on the Netherworld or its inhabitants – humans had grown more and more violent. Full of hatred, they had fought over everything imaginable, killing without remorse. More and more had lingered after death, refusing to move on, clinging to Earth. Eventually, their number had risen so high that the psychopomps had been overwhelmed.

'The ethereal threshold,' I recalled. 'That's what you're talking about.'

'Precisely.'

At that time, the Rephs had been ruled by a different family, the Mothallath. Ettanin Mothallath – their leader and sovereign – had decreed that they must help the psychopomps. They would have to cross the veil themselves and deal with the ethereal unrest at the source.

As he recounted all of this, Warden would pause from time to time. His eyes would narrow, and his mouth would thin. Finally, he would settle on a word and press on – still with a faint look of dissatisfaction, as though the English language had failed him in some way.

I knew the feeling, but he needn't have worried. His voice held my attention as well as music. In that dosshouse, I could see the Netherworld.

A proud and respected family of scholars had disagreed with the Mothallath. They had believed that crossing the veil would be an act of inconceivable desecration, and that their immortal bodies would perish on Earth.

'Let me guess,' I said. 'The Sargas.'

'Very good.'

Procyon, Warden of the Sargas, had swayed many Rephs to his way of thinking. Still, the number of spirits was climbing, and the Mothallath rejected their counsel. Since they had made the decision, they agreed to bear the risk. They would send one of their own across the veil.

The Reph they had chosen was Azha Mothallath, who had successfully crossed the veil and communed with as many spirits as she could. She had returned safe and sound, and the threshold had lowered. It seemed the Sargas had been wrong. There was no harm in the crossing.

'That must have pissed them off,' I said.

'Immensely,' Warden confirmed. 'Procyon did not like to be wrong.'

Azha had soon been needed. A war had broken out on Earth, sending the psychopomps into disarray.

'The Sargas protested again,' Warden said. 'My family, the Mesarthim, were sworn guardians to the Mothallath. We wanted to accompany Azha, as did the Sargas, to protect and assist her – but we soon discovered that only the Mothallath could step between the worlds.'

'Why?'

'That remains a mystery. To pacify the Sargas, Azha and her watchers – those Mothallath who travelled with her – swore that they would never cross the veil without our blessing. They would wear armour made of adamant to protect themselves from corruption. Most importantly, they would never reveal themselves to the living. They would always maintain their distance from humans.'

He stopped.

'Someone … didn't,' I said.

'We do not know exactly what happened,' he said, 'but the Netherworld began to deteriorate. The signs were very small at first, but soon the change had touched us, too. We were growing weak and slow.'

'Doesn't sound like you.'

'No,' Warden granted. 'Procyon Sargas gathered us together. He accused the Mothallath of crossing the veil without our knowledge or permission. In our culture, breaking an oath is a serious matter. My family stood with the Mothallath, but many others condemned them.'

Azha had gone back to Earth, resolved to clear the family name and work out what had happened. No sooner had she left than the ailing Rephs came under attack from creatures they had never seen before.

'The Buzzers,' I said. 'This is starting to sound like the story Nashira told.'

'Not quite,' Warden said. 'Nashira neglected to mention the civil war.'

The first and only war in their history. Procyon had declared his intention to overthrow the Mothallath. The Mesarthim had sprung to their defence. The Rephs had split down the middle, their families declaring for either the Mothallath or the Sargas. The Sarin had initially remained neutral, but even they had finally been drawn into the fray.

'Let me get this straight,' I said. 'You were fighting a war against both yourselves *and* the Emim, all while you were slowly wasting away?'

'Our strength took some time to fade,' Warden said, 'but you have it right. We call this period the Waning of the Veils.'

'Did Azha ever come back?'

'Yes. She returned with the news that some humans had shown the ability to connect with the æther. The living could now converse with the dead.'

'Clairvoyants,' I said softly. 'You mean we hadn't always been there?'

'Not to our knowledge,' Warden said. 'It was the death knell for our side of the war. Few believed this happenstance was a coincidence. Ettanin was overthrown, and the Mothallath were usurped and destroyed.'

'All of them?'

'Yes, along with most of my family.'

Rephs rarely expressed their emotions, but I thought I could see grief, in that moment. The dimness of his eyes, the slight downward tilt of his head.

'I'm sorry,' I said.

Warden nodded.

'Procyon Sargas had been the loudest voice of dissent against the Mothallath,' he said, 'but by the time they fell from power, he was incapable of leadership. Two members of his family rose to take his place.'

'Nashira and Gomeisa.'

'Yes. By then, only a few of us were still loyal to the Mothallath,' Warden said. 'Nashira declared that she would take one of us as her consort, ostensibly to knit our people back together. In truth, it was to prove that even her enemies would submit. As ill luck would have it, she chose me.'

He stood and went slowly to the window, placing both hands on the sill.

Now I understood why the other Rephs had mocked him. He had been a war trophy.

'Nashira is the most ambitious of us,' he said. 'With the Ranthen subdued, she declared that we would have to abandon the Netherworld to the Emim and cross the veil to Earth.'

'You said only the Mothallath could cross.'

'That was no longer the case. Nashira had also discovered that we could use human auras to sustain ourselves,' he said. 'By the end of the war, we were exceptionally weak. She believed that we would be able to recover our strength on Earth, so long as we never allowed humans – violent, cruel, foolish mortals – to hold dominion over us.'

I could see his eyes burning, reflected by the window.

'To that end,' he said, 'we revealed ourselves to Lord Palmerston, telling him that the Emim were demons and we, angels. Almost without question, he surrendered control of the government to Nashira.'

The wings struck off the statues. All religious texts destroyed. Every place of worship gutted or reduced to rubble, making way for the new gods.

England itself had become their house.

'Queen Victoria was allowed to maintain an appearance of power, but she had no more sway over England than a pauper. The death of Prince Albert hastened her departure,' Warden said. 'On the day their son was crowned, he was accused of bringing unnaturalness into the world. And the inquisition into clairvoyance began.'

'Scion,' I murmured.

Warden let me sit with this trove of knowledge for a while. I went over it all in my head. It was strange and unsettling to think that his realm had always existed alongside this one, out of humans' reach. That my life had been shaped by events that had taken place in another world.

'The Ranthen were the ones who supported the Mothallath,' I said. 'You're all that's left, aren't you?'

'Yes.'

'And you still hold a grudge against the Sargas.' I nodded slowly. 'Okay. I get it now.'

'Knowing all of this, would you be willing to continue our alliance?'

'Depends what you want.'

'To overthrow the usurpers and forge an open and cordial relationship with humans,' Warden said. 'The Sargas have become precisely what they criticise in mortals. They wish to conquer Earth. We do not.'

'But you can't live in the Netherworld.'

'We hope the Netherworld can one day be restored,' he said, 'but until then, we would be content to dwell among humans without ruling over you. Ideally, we would have an advisory role in your world, to keep the number of spirits in check and establish a fair balance of power. If we cannot do this, we fear there will be chaos.'

'What sort of chaos?'

'If the Netherworld can fall, so can Earth.'

A chill darted through me.

'When you first came here,' I said, 'did you agree that humans should be subjugated?'

'Yes and no. In the early days of living on Earth, I formed the opinion that many of you were reckless and selfish, destined to destroy both yourselves and the æther with your endless, petty wars. Over and over, you ignored your own history, repeating the mistakes of the past. I thought – perhaps naïvely – that you would benefit from our leadership.'

'Of course. The witless moths, drawn to the flame of your wisdom.'

'I took no pleasure in the degradation and misery of Oxford.'

'No. You just went along with it.'

'For a time.' Warden returned to his seat. 'You are right to question our intentions, Paige. I will be honest with you. Even among the Ranthen, there is a profound contempt for humans and Earth.'

'What's wrong with Earth?'

'Everything here is dying. Nothing in this world escapes the ravages of time,' he said. 'To deathless beings, that is a disturbing thought. They see it as the reason why humans are so bloodthirsty. Even many of your fuels are made of decomposed matter. Most Rephaim would leave if they had the choice. Unlike the Sargas, the Ranthen do not categorically blame humans for what happened to the Netherworld – but they do not see you as their equals, either.'

'Do you?'

'Yes.'

'What makes you so different from the others?'

'I fell in love with human music,' Warden said. 'With all your arts, in fact.'

I didn't question it, remembering his gramophone.

'Our original plan was to destroy Nashira and Gomeisa,' he went on, 'but Oxford proved that we are not yet strong enough to do this. For now, we must devote ourselves to weakening Scion, their source of power on Earth. We need human allies. Your numbers are far greater.'

'So they are,' I said.

'For more than a century, we looked for a human who could help us. We found you,' he said. 'A woman with intimate knowledge of both the syndicate and the Rephaim, with a powerful gift and a taste for rebellion.' His voice softened. 'I do not ask this of you lightly, Paige.'

'As you've pointed out, there *are* a lot of humans.' I met his gaze. 'I'm sure you could find someone more useful than a criminal.'

'If I could choose anyone on Earth, it would still be you, Paige Mahoney.'

I brushed my hair behind my ear and crossed my arms, prickling with goosebumps.

'I like you. You know I do,' I said. 'But—'

Warden watched me as I sat there, torn.

'I understand that you must have complicated feelings towards me,' he said quietly. 'Nick is right. I used you as a weapon, just as Jaxon does. I know that you can never truly forgive me for that – nor for using my gift to see your memories, regardless of my reasons.'

'I might be able to forgive you. Provided you never do it again,' I said. 'I can't forget.'

'As an oneiromancer, I have infinite respect for memory. I would not expect you to forget.'

'Did you tell Scion about Bill Bunbury?' I asked him. 'When you tested my claim that I wasn't in the syndicate, you noticed he was still paying me. Bill was detained and hanged. Oxidate has been shut down.'

'No,' Warden said, 'but Scion would have detected the financial discrepancy, as Alsafi did. He was the one who informed me about it.'

I studied his face, finding I believed him.

'Let's say I do become your associate,' I said. 'What will I get in return?'

'You mentioned your lack of access to money.'

'Yes.' I paused. 'How much do you have?'

'Enough.' His eyes glowed. 'Did you think we had planned to go against the Sargas without a penny to our names?'

My heart pounded.

'We have a human ally in the Westminster Archon, who manages the money on our behalf,' Warden said. 'If you can persuade Terebell that you are capable of handling it, and if you promise her your support, she will be your patron.'

It took me a moment to breathe again. For nearly a month, I had relied on Jaxon for bed and board. That could be a thing of the past.

'If I become Underqueen,' I said, 'we *might* be able to rally the syndicate. But I'll be up against half the mime-lords and mime-queens of this citadel, including Jaxon.'

'I take it they are all like him.'

'What, bloodthirsty peacocks? Almost uniformly.'

'Then you must win. They are feasting on their own corpses, Paige.'

'It will still be an organisation of criminals. And I'll still be one of them.'

'You are not bloodthirsty,' Warden said. 'In Oxford, you had every opportunity to prey on those weaker than you. Yet as a red-jacket, you protected the performers. If the syndicate is properly governed, it could pose a great threat to Scion – but not with a leader like Jaxon.'

'I know,' I said. 'I'm going to stop him.'

He looked at me for a long time.

'I do not expect you to pay for me to stay here any longer,' he said. 'I will contact Terebell. Do you have a candle?'

I reached into my satchel and passed one to him, along with a lighter. Most voyants kept them handy for séances. Once it was lit, he murmured in Gloss.

When a spirit entered the room, I flattened myself against the wall, staring in amazement. A psychopomp. Jaxon had been trying to get close to one for years – to no avail – so he could finish his next pamphlet. They were skittish and retiring, rarely seen outside burial grounds.

Warden made a glassy sound in his throat. The psychopomp circled him and took off, leaving a thin layer of frost on the window.

'That was a psychopomp,' I breathed.

'Yes,' Warden said. 'Their original duty became defunct when the Netherworld fell. Now they serve as our messengers on this side of the veil.'

'I've never seen one so close.'

'They are nervous around the living.' He snuffed the candle. 'Terebell will collect me. I assume it would be sensible for us to stay on your turf.'

'Until I've dealt with the Rag and Bone Man, I think that's for the best. You're welcome to use the Old Lyre,' I said. 'It's a derelict, but it's in decent condition. Terebell knows where it is.' I stood and dug the key from my coat. 'Here.'

'Thank you.'

As he took it, our hands almost touched. Against my will, I remembered his embrace around me. The warm lilt of his lips on mine.

Warden looked up at me. In Magdalen, I had grown used to his appearance. Now I tried to see him as if for the first time. The blunt yet elegant strength of his jaw; the tousled hair that grazed his nape and fell over his forehead. My fingers tingled with the urge to brush it back.

Most of his features passed as human, but his eyes were unearthly. His pupils reflected no light. His irises were flame behind stained glass, still tinged with orange, their glow as warm as fire through amber. You could burn in those eyes if you looked for too long.

A hollow ache filled my stomach as the silence grew. I had to break it now, or I might do something I regretted.

'I should get back to Seven Dials,' I said.

'The night Vigiles will be on duty for some time yet,' Warden said. 'If you would prefer to stay here until sunrise, you are welcome.'

'I don't want to put you out of your bed.'

'You came to my rescue. Allow me to start repaying that debt.'

It was a short walk back to Seven Dials. If I left early, I would make it there before Jaxon woke up. I was too exhausted to go before dawn.

'Well,' I said, 'if you insist.' I smiled. 'You can keep watching the news, if you want. I'm a deep sleeper. Do you mind waking me at dawn?'

'As you wish.'

Warden lowered the volume. Still wearing his shirt, I sent a short message to Nick, then got into bed. As I closed my eyes, I thought about mentioning the kiss. Asking Warden if he still thought about it. If he might ever want to kiss me again, given the right circumstances.

Instead, a more pressing question occurred.

'Warden,' I murmured. 'Why did the amaranth bloom in Oxford?'

It was some time before he answered.

'If I knew,' was his soft reply, 'I would tell you.'

17

PENNY DREADFUL

6 October 2059

I slept for the rest of that night. Just after dawn, I walked back to Seven Dials and climbed through my own window, wondering how the hell I was going to hide all this from Jaxon.

In my room, I changed into a black turtleneck and tweed cigarette trousers. As I was lacing my boots, Nick knocked. When he saw the state of me, he came in and leaned down to look at my face, his eyes wide.

'What happened?'

'Rag Dolls,' I said in a low voice. 'The Rag and Bone Man must have put a hit on me.'

'They came to *our* turf?'

'I've clearly rattled them. They ambushed me in Flitcroft Street,' I said. 'I killed one and trussed up the other. They should be in Book Mews.'

'You killed one of them?'

'With my spirit.'

He took a moment to absorb the news. 'I'll check Book Mews on my way to work,' he eventually said. 'Are you hurt anywhere else, sötnos?'

I sat on my bed to show him. He inspected the wounds on my head and hands.

'I don't think it will need stitches,' he concluded. 'Put some fibrin gel on it. I'll come back to check on you later.'

'You can't do anything suspicious. Stay at your registered address tonight. I'll be fine.'

'Send me a message if you feel worse.' He touched my cheek. 'How are you going to explain this to Jax?'

'I'll think of something,' I said. 'I always do.'

Nick sent me a message at half past seven, just one word: *nothing*. Somebody must have come to collect the Rag Dolls, leaving no trace of their presence.

As luck would have it, Jaxon slept in, leaving me to do as I pleased. I raced through my tasks – collected his order of cigars, emptied the dead drop, checked that Eliza had showered and slept – before I hailed one of our rickshaws and asked the driver to take me to Grub Street.

Considering its distinguished position as the only voyant publishing house in London, the Spiritus Club was a shabby affair. Tall and narrow, crammed between a poetry lounge and a printing press, it boasted half-timbering and a beak of a roof, along with a green door and dirty bow windows. You would never think it was the stronghold of voyant creativity, the beating heart of polite mime-crime.

I checked that I hadn't been followed before I rang the doorbell. Even with gloves, my hands were cold. After two more rings and a knock on the door, a mellifluent voice fluted from a speaker on my right.

'*Go away, please. We've enough poetry collections to paper every house in London.*'

'Minty,' I said, 'it's the Pale Dreamer.'

'*Oh, not you. I've had enough trouble with booklice without a fugitive on my doorstep.*'

'I'm looking for Alfred. The agent?'

279

'*Yes, I know who he is. We are not hiding multiple Alfreds in here, I assure you.*'

'He knows me. I just want a quick word.' I rattled the handle. 'It's freezing out here, Minty. Will you just let me in?'

'*Wipe your feet. Don't touch anything.*'

The door swung open. I stamped my boots on the doormat and waited in the hallway. Inside, the décor was predictably quaint: floral wallpaper, sconces, a pedestal desk, a scuffed oak floor. A mug read WE PUT THE DEAD IN DEADLINE.

The emblem of the Spiritus Club – a pocket watch with two crossed fountain pens instead of hands – was carved on to a shield above the mantelpiece. That emblem was stamped on every illegal novel, pamphlet and chapbook in the citadel. I had never asked what it was supposed to represent.

'Alfred,' Minty Wolfson shouted from somewhere above me. 'Visitor for you!'

'Yes, yes, Minty, wait a tick—'

'Now, Alfred.'

I sat on the edge of the desk to wait, keeping a tight grip on my satchel.

'Ah, the Pale Dreamer returns to Grub Street,' Alfred called as he came down the staircase. When he saw me, his smile fell. 'Oh, dear. What happened?'

I had dabbed my bruised cheek with greasepaint, but apparently not enough. 'Just training,' I said. 'For the scrimmage.'

'You ought to be more careful, dear heart. To what do I owe the pleasure?'

'I wondered if you might be free for a chat.'

'But of course.' He beckoned me up to the first landing, stepping over gold stair rods with decorative brackets. 'I say, you could almost be Jaxon's daughter with that hair. Clever of you to dye it.'

A woman I didn't recognise came flying down the stairs from the next floor, wild-haired and bespectacled. She looked as if she was still in her nightclothes.

'Who on *Earth* are you?' she demanded, as if I had some nerve to be on Earth at all.

'Why, Ethel, this is the Pale Dreamer.' Alfred placed his hands on my shoulders. 'Mollisher to our most successful writer, and herself the most wanted person in London, which makes her very welcome among us.'

'Bloody troublemaker, from what I've heard,' Ethel said, squinting at me. 'I hope you know where you are, young lady. The Spiritus Club is the finest voyant publishing house in London.'

I raised an eyebrow. 'It's the only one, isn't it?'

'Ergo, the finest. We were built on the glorious foundations of the Scriblerus Club.'

'Indeed we were,' Alfred said. 'All great satirists, the Scriblerians. Passionate in their pursuit of dullards.' He ushered me through a door. 'Be a dear and make us some tea, Ethel. My poor guest is thirsty.'

I could have sworn the ruffles of her dress quivered with outrage. 'I am not a waitron, Alfred. I have work to do – *work*, Alfred. Definition: *exertion* or *effort* directed to produce or *accomplish* something—'

Alfred shut the door before she could continue, sweating.

'I do apologise for Ethel,' he said. 'The north will seem peaceful after this lunacy.'

I lowered myself into a chair. 'Just a holiday, is it?'

'Certainly not. I've heard of a first-rate psychographer in Manchester, and I have every intention of poaching him.' He pushed a tier stand of biscuits towards me. 'I'm very glad to see you after our escapade. Close shave, wasn't it? I usually have better luck bribing them.'

'I'm a preternatural fugitive. A numen was never going to help.' As he sat, I noticed a monochrome photograph in an elaborate brass frame, propped up on a tallboy behind his desk. 'Friend of yours?'

Alfred looked over his shoulder. The woman in the photograph was about thirty, with thick, straight hair that fell just past her shoulders.

'Ah, that's Floy. My first and only love,' he said. 'She was a good woman. Distant, perhaps, but kind and talented.'

'Was she voyant?'

'Amaurotic, as a matter of fact. An odd match, I know. She died very young. I'm trying to find her in the æther, but she never seems to hear.'

'I'm sorry.'

'Oh, dear heart, it's hardly your fault.' For the first time I noticed the ring on his finger, a thick gold band with no adornments. 'Now, how can I help you?'

'I hope you won't think I'm being presumptuous, but I have a proposal for you.'

'I confess myself intrigued.'

'You said nothing has ever made you as much coin as *On the Merits of Unnaturalness*.' I reached into my satchel. 'I have some acquaintances who've written a penny dreadful together. I think it has some potential, but I'm no expert. Would you mind taking a look?'

'I would be delighted. What a treat.'

I fanned the pages across the desk. Alfred reached for his pince-nez and peered at the title.

THE REPHAITE REVELATION
Being a true and faithful Account of the Creators of Scion, and their Reaping of Clairvoyants

'My word.' He chuckled. 'Who are these imaginists?'

'They want to remain anonymous.'

'Of course. Most voyant writers do.'

As Alfred leafed through, a shiver trailed along my spine. If Jaxon found out I was doing this, he would boot me out of Seven Dials and leave me to my fate. Then again, he wasn't exactly thrilled with me now.

Alfred occasionally murmured words like *fascinating* or *eccentric*. I could see the story working its enchantment on him. When he reached the final sentence, he looked up at me slowly and released his breath.

'It could use some work,' he said, 'but the idea *does* have potential, Paige. Great potential. Even in voyant circles, you rarely see literature that openly criticises Scion.' He stroked his small chin.

'Jaxon would be furious if he found out that I was involved in this, but I always was a gambler.'

'You took a gamble with *On the Merits*. That paid off for you,' I said. 'There is one catch. The writers want it to be out within the next couple of weeks.'

'Gracious. I'm not sure publishing can move that fast. Why the rush?'

'They have their reasons.'

'No doubt, but it isn't just me they have to convince. It's Minty, who allocates the money to pay the Penny Post. They are the bookshop – a living, itinerant bookshop, made up of thirty messengers,' Alfred explained. 'It's how Grub Street has evaded Scion for all these years. It would be far too dangerous to sell forbidden stories in one place.'

There was a knock on the door before a thin, trembling man tottered in with a tray. His aura almost shouted what he was: psychographer.

'Tea, Alfred,' he said.

'Thank you, Scrawl.'

Scrawl put the tray down and stumbled back out, muttering to himself. Seeing my expression, Alfred shook his head.

'Not to worry. Poor fellow got himself possessed by Madeleine de Scudéry,' he said. 'A prolific novelist, to put it lightly.' He chortled into his teacup. 'He's been scribbling away for a month.'

'Our medium sometimes paints for days without sleeping,' I said.

'Ah, yes, the famous Martyred Muse. Mediums do get the short end of the stick in this business, don't they?' Alfred sighed. 'Speaking of which, I must ask – are your friends psychographers?'

'I'm not sure.' I stirred my tea. 'Will that affect the Club's decision?'

'I shan't lie to you, dear heart. It may well do. Traditionally, they believe that unless a story is written by someone whose link to the æther is *sustained* by writing, it's a story not worth telling. Elitist claptrap, if you ask me, but my opinion only goes so far around here.'

'They made an exception for Jaxon.'

'So they did.' He twirled his pipe between his fingers. 'I will certainly put this to Minty. I hope she will see its potential, but publishing this would be a dangerous affair. If the Ministry for Arts caught wind of it, it could bring Scion down on us like so many bricks.'

'The Club kept *On the Merits* secret.'

'For a while. Scion knows about it now. We can only be thankful that they never located this building, thanks to the Penny Post.' He looked down at the pages again. 'There's enough material here for a novel, though that would be harder to distribute. A penny dreadful may be the right choice. May I take these pages for Minty to peruse?'

'You may.'

'Thank you. I shall call you with her verdict. How should I contact you?'

'By note, if you wouldn't mind. You can leave it with Babs at the Minister's Cat in Soho.'

'Very good.' His rheumy eyes gazed into mine. 'Tell me, Paige – truthfully, now. Is there even a slither of fact in here?'

I smiled.

'No,' I said. 'It's just fiction, Alfred.'

'All right, then. I'll be in touch.' Without getting up, Alfred took my hand between his larger ones and shook it. 'Thank you for bringing this to me, Paige. I hope to see you again soon.'

'I'll let the writers know you're vouching for them.'

'Very well. Not a word to Binder, or we'll all be in for the high jump.' He slid the pages into a drawer. 'I shall give these to Minty as soon as she's finished writing. Stay safe, won't you?'

'Of course,' I said, knowing I wouldn't.

The sun burned a deep autumn gold. My next destination was Raconteur Street in Mayfair, where Jaxon had heard of amaurotic pickpockets targeting passers-by ('They're stealing from *our* hapless victims, and I don't like it one bit'). None of the others were available to deal with it, and if I wanted my next pay packet, I would have to keep doing as I was told. I didn't have the Ranthen's patronage just yet.

Alfred called himself a gambler. Perhaps I was, too, though I hadn't made a penny from the risks I was taking. If Jaxon found out I had been seeing Warden – in any capacity – his rage would be unspeakable.

There was no sign of the pickpockets, though I could see a few of ours at work. It was the perfect day for it. Across the inner citadel, amaurotics were flooding into the vast department stores on Raconteur Street, buying stacks upon stacks of gifts for Novembertide. It was the most important festival on the Scion calendar, celebrating the formal opening of the Scion Citadel of London.

Red glass lanterns had been strung between the streets, while tiny white lights, smaller than snowflakes, cascaded from window-sills and snaked in perfect spirals around lampposts. Vast painted banners of previous Grand Inquisitors hung from the largest build-ings. Beneath them, students from the University handed out posies of red and white flowers.

Even if he was allowed to go home for Novembertide, my father would spend the festival alone. I pictured him at the kitchen table, reading his newspaper, my face staring back at him from the front page.

I had asked Witcher Cully to inform me if Scion let him return to the Barbican. So far, she hadn't sent word. I hoped that was because her couriers had missed it, not because my father was locked in the Steel.

'I don't know what you're talking about.' A nervous voice reached my ears. 'Please, Commandant—'

'Nobody wants to hear your lies, Ms Mahoney.'

I froze.

A black armoured vehicle was parked on the other side of the street, marked with SUNLIGHT VIGILANCE DIVISION. I stepped behind a lamppost and pulled down the peak of my cap.

It was rare to see military vehicles on the streets. They had patrolled every major citadel during the Molly Riots, but never since, to my knowledge. Next to its back doors, a pregnant woman stood with her hands cuffed in front of her. She had the wary look of someone who knew they were in danger.

'You claim to have arrived in 2058,' a Vigile commandant was saying. One of his subordinates was writing on a data pad. 'Can you prove that?'

'Yes. I have my papers,' the woman said, keeping her composure. She had a firmer spine than most. 'If you'd just let me collect them from—'

'You're not going anywhere, boglander.'

The woman lowered her gaze in a way I recognised, though her mouth thinned, her chin pinching. She was about my height, but her wavy hair was a darker blonde than mine, and she wore the crisp uniform of a paramedic. I could tell from here that she was amaurotic.

'I'm from Scion Belfast,' she said, her voice wavering. 'I work for ScionAID.'

'You brought your unnaturalness to my shores. If I had it my way,' the Vigile said, 'we wouldn't employ brogues at all. Especially not unnatural farm girls.'

'My name is Niamh Tully,' the woman said. 'I don't know Paige Mahoney.'

'Where do you live?'

'Kensington. I have permission to—'

'Who's the father?' The Vigile aimed his pistol at her rounded stomach, eliciting gasps from the crowd. 'Felix Coombs? Julian Amesbury?'

Julian.

At once, I looked to the nearest screen. A new face had been added to the cycle of preternatural fugitives. A bald man with deep brown eyes and skin, a rigid set to his jaw. Julian Amesbury, guilty of high treason, sedition and arson. If Scion didn't have him, he must be alive.

'Please—' Niamh hunched over her stomach, trying to shield it with her cuffed hands. 'I've no idea who you're talking about. Can't you *see* I'm not Paige Mahoney?'

'Where are you hiding her, then?'

'I am not hiding *anything*,' Niamh burst out. 'Why can't you just leave us alone?'

The Vigile struck her.

The impact radiated through the crowd. I flinched as Niamh fell hard on her side. When she saw the blood, she let out a faint sound of disbelief, staring at the Vigile.

Murmurs passed through the crowd. I caught words like *inconsiderate*. The denizens of Scion wanted unnaturals gone, but not while they were doing their shopping. To them, we were just litter being taken to the landfill.

'You brogues are all the same,' the Vigile sneered. 'Take her to the Steel.'

My heart was racing. It wasn't like day Vigiles to so much as raise their voices to the general public, let alone to use this degree of violence.

Niamh was hauled to her feet by three Vigiles. Her cheek was already an enraged red, her eyes brimming with tears. She started to sob as they bundled her into the armoured vehicle. The sound tightened my throat.

I could take out one or two Vigiles with my spirit, but I couldn't summon the syndicate to help an amaurotic in broad daylight. I could do no more for Niamh Tully than I had been able to do for my own father.

'Move along,' the commandant roared, startling the onlookers, who expected courtesy from day Vigiles. 'Any of you know any brogues, you can tell them to get ready for questioning. When I find out where they've been hiding Mahoney, they'll go to the gallows with her.'

He climbed into a second vehicle.

'This is wrong,' someone called out. A young amaurotic man, bright-eyed with outrage. 'She wasn't doing anything. You can't just arrest an innocent woman in broad—'

Another Vigile struck him with her truncheon, right at the front of his skull. He crashed into the pavement. A stunned silence fell over the crowd.

When there were no more voices of dissent, the Vigile beckoned to her squad. As the young man pushed himself up, the other amaurotics surged away from him. I could only watch as the armoured vehicle and its escort drove away, feeling as if the world and all its walls were crashing down on top of me. Before anyone could notice the real Paige Mahoney standing in their midst, I slipped into Carnaby Street.

Black hair and a pair of contacts wouldn't hide me for much longer. I forced myself to walk slowly, even though I wanted to break into a sprint. I forced myself to be silent, even as a scream built in me.

Seven Dials was less than a mile away. When I reached the den, it took three tries to get my key into the lock. Nadine sat on the lower stairs in the hallway, polishing her violin. She looked up when I came in.

'What is it?'

'Vigiles,' I said thickly.

Nadine stood at once. 'Where?'

'Mayfair.'

'Paige, that's nowhere near us. Was it the Punishers, or something?' When she saw my tearstained face, she stared. 'What happened?'

My chest heaved. 'They just arrested an Irish woman. Sent her to the Steel,' I forced out. 'The Vigiles think my fellow brogues are hiding me.'

Nadine gripped the newel, her gaze darting.

'They might be asking people for their papers,' she said. 'I need to get Zeke.'

She grabbed her jacket and rushed out, closing the door behind her. I went to my room and sank down on my bed, my stomach wrenching.

During the Molly Riots, anyone with an Irish name, or who Scion had even *suspected* of being Irish, had been subjected to endless spot checks and interrogations. Now history was repeating itself, all because of me. Niamh Tully, whose only mistake was to be in the wrong place and from the wrong country, might well be dead by morning, tortured for information about someone she had never met. Even if I gave myself up, there was nothing I could do to save her.

The snake of guilt tightened its coils, but my fury was growing. Nashira had done this in Oxford, using innocent people to manipulate me. If she meant to force me out that way, I couldn't allow her to succeed.

I sat there for a long while, breathing slowly until I was calm. A rapping on the wall undid my efforts. Jaxon Hall demanded an audience. The bruises on my face were already purple – he would know something was wrong at once – but I had to face the music at some point. I composed myself and crossed the landing.

Jaxon lay on the chaise longue like a statue, his face warmed by the golden sunlight. Empty wine bottles crowded the coffee table, and both ashtrays were overflowing. I stood in the doorway, wondering how long it had been since he had last bothered going outside.

'Afternoon,' I said, arms folded.

'Indeed it is. A rather cold afternoon,' Jaxon said. 'Would that be because the winter steals ever closer, and with it, the scrimmage?' He took a sip of absinthe from a swirl glass. 'Where have you been, Paige?'

'In Mayfair, checking for those pickpockets. I couldn't see them.'

'What were you doing for the rest of this morning?'

'All the things I usually do to keep this section running, Jax.'

'Such as?'

'Picking up your cigars, for one thing. I also started collecting the rent from Mayfair,' I said, voicing the lie as it entered my head. 'And I thought I'd check on William Terriss.'

'Oh, don't think, darling, it's a dreary habit. Zeke looks after our locals, doesn't he?'

'Zeke doesn't like poltergeists.'

'I don't need him to like my orders. I need him to obey them. Tell him that from me, won't you?' He wafted a hand. 'Do leave the money on my desk.'

Of course he wanted to see the money straight away. I went back into my room and removed a wad of my savings from my pillow. When I handed it to Jaxon, lips pursed tight, he counted it in front of me. Now I really *would* have to go back to Mayfair, so I could pocket the rent myself.

'Good.' With a clumsy flourish, Jaxon presented me with a measly two notes. 'For your troubles.' Bloodshot eyes peered at me. 'What the devil happened to your face?'

'Two voyants tried to kill me.'

That woke him up.

'Whose voyants?' He stood, almost knocking a glass off the table. 'In *my* territory?'

'Rag Dolls.'

'An attempt on your life is a serious matter. The fact that they were bold enough to do it within earshot of Seven Dials only serves to add insult to injury. Why did you not inform me straight away, you fool?'

'You were asleep. I did try to wake you.'

'When did this happen?'

'Early this morning,' I said. 'I dealt with them, but someone already came to pick them up. You won't find any evidence they were ever there.'

If he realised I had gone out at night, in blatant disregard of his orders, he would lock me in the nearest cupboard. His nostrils flared as he picked up a matchbox and opened the new case of cigars.

'I will speak to the Abbess.' He stuck a cigar between his teeth. 'Do you have any idea why the Rag and Bone Man would target you, Paige?'

'No.'

'Then he must be trying to eliminate his competition.' He struck a match and lit up. 'I never thought he would care to enter the scrimmage, but I can't imagine another explanation. Every suburbanite and sloven will crawl out of the woodwork for the Rose Crown.'

'Do you know much about the Rag and Bone Man?'

'Next to nothing. Not even what sort of voyant he is, though his name implies osteomancy.' His expression was pensive. 'In all my years as a mime-lord, I have never seen him. From what I hear, he lives a miserable subterranean existence, speaking only through his mollishers.'

'He has more than one?'

'No, but he informs the Unnatural Assembly of changes to his chain of command. So far, he's had four mollishers,' Jaxon said. 'The first was the Silken, then the Wild Hunter, then the Jacobite, and the most recent is La Chiffonnière. She became mollisher this year, in April.'

'What would make him have four different mollishers?'

'Perhaps the first three annoyed him.' He pulled a glass ashtray across the desk. 'Tell me, Paige – have you heard from the local ventriloquists?'

I frowned. 'Who?'

'The Rephaim, darling.'

'Oh, now you're interested.'

'Answer the question.'

'I haven't heard from them,' I said. 'I must have been imagining things when I thought I sensed them.'

'Excellent. Then we have no distractions.'

'Depends what you mean by *distractions*. The Vigiles are going to start interrogating Irish settlers. They think all the brogues are conspiring to hide me.'

Jaxon tutted. 'The Chief of Vigilance must be *aching* for new ways to waste time.'

'Any chance of you helping them, Jax?'

It had shot out before I could think better of it.

'I am quite sure the Underqueen will extend her assistance to the voyants among them,' Jaxon said. 'Many of them live on her turf, in the Jennings Lodgings. The amaurotics will have to sink or swim.' He opened the door before I could speak again. 'Now, on to more important matters. Come out to the courtyard with me, Paige.'

Of course Jaxon wouldn't lift a finger himself. I followed him down the stairs in icy silence, wondering why I had even bothered asking.

When I was thirteen, my father had found me writing in Gaeilge. It was one of the few times he ever lost his temper with me. He had ordered me to never so much as think in my first language again. If so much as a word slipped out in public, we could lose our apartment and end up in a rookery like the Jennings. That could have been where Niamh had lived.

The thought gave me fresh determination. The only way to change things was to defeat Scion, and the next step was the scrimmage.

Ching Court was among my favourite places in London – a triangle of tranquillity at the back of our den, paved with smooth white stone. Two small blossom trees grew there, and Nadine kept the wrought-iron planters overflowing with flowers, even at this time of year.

Jaxon sat down on the bench. 'Do you know the rules of the scrimmage, Paige?'

'I know it's close combat,' I said.

'You did read the histories.' He regarded me. 'The two of us will find ourselves engaged in a series of small battles in the Rose Ring. At close quarters, you must be wary of those whose numa can be wielded as weapons – axinomancers and macharomancers, for example.'

The slashes on my fingers ached. I had concealed them with my gloves.

'You may recall this from *A Concise History of Clairvoyance*,' Jaxon said, 'but using amaurotic tactics to end any of your individual battles – stabbing a voyant to death with an ordinary blade, for example – is called a *rotten ploy*. It used to be forbidden, but nowadays it is allowed, so long as it's carried out with sufficient flair.'

I raised an eyebrow. 'Is that what the syndicate wants from its Underlord?'

'Would you follow someone with no hint of panache, darling?' he asked. 'Besides, the scrimmage would be bland without a little bloodletting, and amaurotic weapons are perfectly adequate for that.'

'*A Concise History* didn't mention if guns were allowed.'

'No. It would all be over too quickly.' He tapped his cane. 'I remind you of this rule because I don't want you using too many rotten ploys if you can help it. The scrimmage is not just a competition, but a display of power. We must show the spectators the strength of our gifts, so that when we rule this citadel, none will rise against us.'

I clenched a fist behind my back, making one of the cuts bleed.

'You and I have a vital advantage,' Jaxon said. 'At any time, we can fight together. Only a mime-lord and mollisher may do this.'

'Do most participants fight in pairs?'

'All but the independent candidates, who have more to prove.'

'Is it really a fight to the death?'

'Oh, yes. Grub Street will tell us to stun where possible – they don't want to lose the entire Unnatural Assembly – but there are always deaths during a scrimmage. To ensure we both survive, we must know each other's gifts as well as we both know our own. That way, we will be able to anticipate each other's movements as we fight.'

He couldn't leave it alone. Jaxon still had no idea that my gift had matured as much as it had, and I wanted to keep it that way – but if I refused to reveal my new skills, he would think I was slacking off.

Perhaps there was a middle ground.

'All right,' I said. 'I wanted to surprise you, but you're like a dog with a bone.'

Jaxon tilted his head. I went back inside for my mask and attached a fresh can of oxygen.

In Oxford, I had possessed a butterfly. I had told Warden that I would never jump into an animal again, but I had to try, if only to get Jaxon off my back.

When I returned to the courtyard, I lay flat on the ground and strapped the mask on. Taking a deep breath, I fine-tuned my sixth sense, allowing myself to feel the dreamscapes of the nearest animals. As a bird flew overhead, I steeled myself and made the jump.

It was easy to seize control of this body. Four steps and I had moved its frail spirit; a heartbeat more, and I was seeing through its eyes.

Not so easy to *keep* control. I was soaring on the whims of the wind, with nothing to stop me plummeting. This couldn't be like it was with the butterfly.

This time, I would spread my wings.

My vision flickered once before the world spread out below me, the streets and rooftops painted with a brighter palette than before. When I possessed the butterfly, I had been terrified I would forget myself – but my human spirit was piloting the bird, still connected to my body, carrying my human memories and awareness. My silver cord held strong. With fresh confidence, I nestled into my new bones. It felt like squeezing into clothes that had shrunk in the wash. I slammed my wings downward, lifting my host, and rose into the vivid sky, where there were no anchors.

Just as joy of it kicked in, my silver cord pulled at my spirit. I was going too far. I followed that lifeline back to the courtyard, managing to land right on Jaxon. Clumsily, I flapped to his shoulder, opened my beak, and chirruped in his ear. He was still laughing in delight when I snapped into my own body and took in a gasp of air.

'Wonderful!'

I sat up and dabbed the sweat from my forehead. My heart was palpitating.

'I *knew* you could do it,' Jaxon burst out. 'My brilliant mollisher. Three years of work, and you finally soared. Didn't I always say you could?'

For a sweet and heady moment, I was seventeen again. His praise washed over me, hot and lovely as sunlight, and all I wanted was to soak it up.

'I can't do it for long.' I grinned in spite of myself. 'Just a few seconds.'

'A few seconds longer than you could do it before. You've made *progress*, my Pale Dreamer.' His eyes were glittering with triumph. 'Coy of you to keep it from me, but what a fine surprise. Oh, if only I could send the other five to Oxford to improve *their* gifts. The place sounds like a veritable whetstone for the spirit. Send them all, I say.'

My smile tightened. He came to my side and helped me up, holding me like a partner in a dance.

'Quite brilliant,' he told me again. 'You will rule as mollisher supreme – and one day, you will make an extraordinary Underqueen.'

His façade could be so convincing. My throat ached with longing for a time when I had still believed this kind man was the real Jaxon.

I *wanted* to believe it. It frightened me that even now, I craved his approval.

'Of course, you can't possibly wear that mask in the Rose Ring,' Jaxon said, eyeing the can of oxygen. 'If you leave your body vulnerable on the ground, a rival will cut your throat and be done with it, and then you will be of no use to anyone. That aside, a bird is not a human, so we must not be complacent, darling. For the rest of this month, we should devote our efforts to refining you.'

A headache bloomed above my eye. I couldn't keep the smile up any more.

For more than three years, Jaxon had coaxed and pestered and threatened me, determined to turn me into his weapon. All that time, I had somehow resisted him. Now I had given him what he wanted, and it had satisfied his ambitions for all of half a minute.

Being enough had been nice while it lasted.

'Of course.' I gently extricated myself from his grasp. 'Your turn, Jax.'

'Mm?'

'You said we had to get to know each other's gifts. I'd like to hear more about yours.'

'Ah, mine is nowhere near as fascinating. Still,' he said, 'it will help you to learn.'

Jaxon took a seat again, beckoning me on to the bench. The bird I had possessed was still beside him, blinking slowly, stunned and silent.

'My boundlings are usually free to wander within the confines I set for them,' Jaxon said, once I had joined him. 'When I need them, however, I can use them in spirit combat. You saw that in Trafalgar Square.'

'Yes.' I looked from the bird to his face. 'When a spirit becomes a boundling, does it change its nature?'

'That depends. A ghost will no longer seek out a haunt; a revenant will stop being drawn to its bones. My will overrides those base instincts,' he told me. 'But breachers always remain breachers.'

My hand almost strayed towards the pendant, cool between my collarbones.

'When a voyant spools the average group of spirits, they can only aim the spool at their opponent and hope for the best,' Jaxon said. 'You know spirits retain some memories from their old lives. They can push these remnant memories into a dreamscape, causing the affected voyant to hallucinate.'

'Apparitions,' I said.

'Precisely,' he said. 'Most spirits are rather easy to deflect. My boundlings are superior, for they carry my strength with them – the will and awareness of the living, giving them a power I imagine is akin to yours, when you take spirit form. This fortification means they can inflict damage on the dreamscape – even manipulate its appearance.'

Nashira had used her fallen angels – a form of boundling – against me. It had been nothing like being hit with a spool.

'If they're like me,' I said, 'can they kill, even if they're not breachers?'

Jaxon looked at the bird, the expression sliding off his face. The æther shifted as one of his boundlings came prowling from the den. The bird gave a horrible jerk as the spirit cut through its dreamscape, shattering its silver cord. I watched it flop on to its side and die with a last twitch.

'Apparently,' Jaxon said. 'Life, for all its wonders, is rather flimsy in the end.'

He gave the little corpse a flick, and it rolled off the bench. Its glassy eye stared into nothing.

'We will win,' he said. 'We will triumph, darling. This citadel will be ours to command.' He leaned across the bench and gave me a peck on the cheek. 'And all will be right with the world. Just you wait.'

I had to leave the den before I suffocated. My drug of choice had been dangled before me, and now I was shaking from the withdrawal. That aside, the possession had drained me. As soon as Jaxon had retired to his boudoir, I walked the short way to Chateline's and brooded at my favourite table, away from the windows.

So much for keeping my secret from Jaxon. At least he didn't know I could already walk in human dreamscapes.

I tried to imagine facing him in the scrimmage. He had at least thirteen boundlings, including three poltergeists: Weeping Sukie, Jean the Skinner, and now the London Monster.

At least I had the pendant. I wrapped my hand around it, releasing my breath.

Most of the other patrons were looking at the small transmission screen, which showed the great stone arch of the Lychgate. There had been hangings almost every week since my return. Nitrogen asphyxiation – the official method of execution – must be falling out of favour. Perhaps the amaurotic elite didn't want painless punishment for unnaturals after all.

I watched as the Grand Executioner led two prisoners on to the flat roof of the Lychgate. One of them made a last plea for clemency, even as the noose came down. His shift was stained, his face swollen and bruised. The second man stood in absolute silence, waiting for the plunge.

Before they could die, the broadcast was replaced by an illegal silent film, *The Essex Haunting*. The patrons cheered and went back to their suppers.

A silver tray was deposited in front of me. Chat folded his arms with a satisfied nod, tucking the smooth end of his wrist into the crook of his elbow.

'That Grand Executioner is a piece of work,' he said. 'Always leaves it as long as possible. None of us need to see that tonight, do we?'

'I could do without it,' I admitted.

He looked down at me. His right pupil was cloudy – one of his souvenirs from the Bucket of Blood, the old fighting pit in Covent Garden.

'Quite a shiner you've got there,' he said. 'Thought I'd take the liberty of bringing your usual.'

'Thank you.' I touched my bruised cheek. 'It's been a long few weeks.'

Chat glanced at the screen. 'That won't happen to you. You've got the syndicate,' he said gruffly. 'We protect our own. Always have.'

'And what about everyone else?'

'You can only take so many punches at once. One fight at a time,' he said. 'Take it from an old boxer.' He nodded to the tray. 'On the house. I'll be rooting for you at the scrimmage, Pale Dreamer.'

He returned to the bar, leaving me with a bowl of chestnut soup, fresh bread, and a slice of treacle tart, as well as a cream coffee. As I picked up the spoon, I caught sight of my reflection in the tray. My skin looked pasty against my black hair, making both the bruises and my dark circles more obvious. No wonder he had brought me food.

I took my time eating, needing to be on my own. By the time one of our couriers approached me, it was dusk.

'Pale Dreamer.' She offered me a green envelope. 'Babs asked me to find you right away. The Spiritus Club dropped this at the Cat.'

'Thanks.' I took it. 'I'll leave your money with Babs in the morning.'

When she was gone, I turned the envelope over. The wax seal was gold and bore the emblem of the Spiritus Club. Cracking it open, I took out the note inside.

So long as the authors contribute a modest amount to the cost of ink and short-notice distribution, the Spiritus Club would be honoured to publish The Rephaite Revelation. *Minty can get it to press in a fortnight, and the Penny Post will distribute. I shall be far from London by morning, but if you could deliver the money by Monday, the Club would be most obliged.*

My warmest thanks for this unexpected and delightful opportunity.

When I read the amount of money Alfred was expecting me to cough up, I closed my eyes. All the scrimping and saving on Earth wouldn't get me a thousand pounds in a week, but I knew someone who could.

'Chat,' I called. He came back to my table. 'I think I need something stronger than coffee.'

18

THE OLD LYRE

The two fingers of brandywine gave me a decent sleep, but didn't take away my problems. Until the Ranthen returned, I had no way to pay the Spiritus Club. My plan, in all its brilliance, had already ground to a halt. I gave the golden cord a tug, but Warden seemed to have vanished again.

I trusted that he would come back. In the meantime, I threw myself into training. The scrimmage was less than a month away, and no matter what happened with the pamphlet, I had to be ready to fight to the death.

Nick and I practised in the courtyard, focusing on physical combat. I was a decent fighter, quick and limber, but the scrimmage would be an attack from all sides. Pleased by my show of commitment, Jaxon invited Chat to the den to share his wisdom from the Bucket of Blood. He took over my training when Nick was at work.

With each lesson, my form improved. Still, I couldn't punch and kick my way to victory. If I was going to win, it would be with my spirit, not my fists.

Jaxon was right about my weakness. When I dreamwalked, my body crumpled to the ground, and he wouldn't be able to guard it for long. Warden might be able to help me with that, whenever he decided to return. I hoped it was within the next few days, or *The Rephaite Revelation* would languish unpublished, and I needed it to go out.

A week after the ambush, I balanced a tray on my hip and knocked on the door to the boudoir. When there was no answer, I pursed my lips.

'Jax, I've got your supper.'

A grunt came from somewhere inside. I threw caution to the wind and went in.

The room was dark and stifling. It smelled of cigarettes and unwashed skin, shot with a faint, cloying sweetness. Jaxon was sprawled on his back on the floor, clasping a small bottle with a cork stopper.

'Fucking hell, Jax,' was all I could say.

'Go away.'

'Jaxon.' I put the tray down and grasped him under the arms. 'Come on. At least get on the couch.'

He was a dead weight. When I gave up and dropped him, his only reaction was a dull groan. I should have left it at that, but I was his mollisher. My job was to clean up for him, even when he was the mess.

'Jaxon.' I tried once more to prop him up. 'Look, you lazy sot, if you just—'

His hand came flying up, shoving me into the desk. An inkwell toppled off the edge and rolled across the floor. I took a deep, calming breath.

'Fine.' I straightened my blouse. 'By all means, stay there.'

He muttered something incoherent. Out of absurd pity, I shoved a cushion under his head and threw the mantle from the couch over his back.

'Thank you, Nadine.' His words weren't quite as crisp as usual, but he stopped just short of slurring. 'Do leave my supper on the desk.'

'It's Paige,' I said curtly. 'Did you speak to the Abbess about the Rag Dolls?'

'Looking into it.' His arm curled around the cushion. 'Goodnight, sweet Dreamer.'

I shook my head and left.

Jaxon had always liked a drink. He smoked white aster now and again – tiny doses, not enough to be addictive – but I had never seen him like this. I had a sinking feeling it was laudanum in that bottle.

A melancholy tune drifted from downstairs. Nadine, playing her violin. Zeke was in the study, researching a possible haunting in Suffolk, while Danica read a novel. In the garret, Eliza had fallen asleep.

To prevent any more ambushes in the run-up to the scrimmage, Jaxon had decided to impose a curfew on the gang. Since Nick and Danica worked late, they were exempt, but the rest of us had to be in the den by seven, when Jaxon would ceremonially lock both the front door and the gates to Ching Court.

Every day, the leash tightened.

I ached from a long day of training. Not quite tired enough to sleep, I went out to the courtyard and lay down on the stone bench, just to breathe fresh air. The den felt too much like a birdcage.

London was a terrible place for stargazing. There was too much light pollution. Still, a few shone bright enough to be seen through the cold blue haze. The night sky reminded me of the æther – myriad lights in unknowable darkness, promising both wonder and death.

The golden cord rang.

I sat bolt upright, my breath escaping me in a cloud of fog. Warden was very close. I rushed through the access passage and found him standing behind the gate.

'Finally.' I grasped one of the bars. 'You took your time.'

'Forgive me. The Ranthen had matters to discuss,' Warden said. 'Terebell wishes to speak to you. We have gathered at the derelict music hall.'

'Jaxon has given us a curfew.' I pushed the gate to show him. 'We're locked in.'

'He has no right to hold you against your will.'

'Try telling him that.'

His eyes burned. 'Is there any other way out?'

'I'd climb, but I don't want to risk breaking my ankle this close to the scrimmage.' I glanced over my shoulder. 'Jaxon *is* drunk out of his mind. I'll try getting the key. If I don't come back, he's caught me.'

'Very well. I will wait by the sundial pillar.'

He left.

I slipped back into the den, considering a quick change of clothes. Terebell had always dressed plainly in Oxford, shunning the cloaks and gems that some of the other Rephs had worn. Better not look as if I had expensive tastes. I chose a simple black top with long sleeves, paired with grey woollen trousers, which I belted at the waist and tucked into heeled boots.

In the bathroom, I glanced into the mirror. Hoping I looked shrewd and sensible enough to handle large amounts of coin, I buttoned my coat and slung on a scarf. When I emerged, I almost walked into Nadine.

'Paige.' She kept her voice down. 'How are you?'

'Fine. It's good to hear you playing,' I said frankly. 'It sounded great.'

'I've had enough practice in recent weeks.' Her eyes narrowed. 'Are you leaving?'

'I thought I might. Jax has passed out.'

'Where are you going?'

I stepped towards the stairs. 'That's my business.'

'Right. It *is* your business,' she said. 'So why don't you let someone else look after *his* business?'

I stopped and turned to face her.

'I hear you did a good job in my absence.' I pocketed my hands. 'You want to be mollisher.'

'You're distracted. I don't blame you,' Nadine said, 'but you only just started training for the scrimmage. You're jumping at shadows. You clearly have your own aims now. If you stepped down, you'd have more time to look for the Rephs, or whatever it is you're doing tonight.'

Before I had been detained, Nadine had never shown any interest in going above and beyond for Jaxon. I didn't understand it.

'In the unlikely event that he would *let* me step down,' I said, 'he wouldn't make you his mollisher, Nadine. You're forgetting who he is.'

'He relied on me when you were gone. I've proven myself,' Nadine said under her breath. 'You're only his mollisher because you're a dreamwalker.'

'Exactly.' I moved closer. 'Think about it. He never officially made you his mollisher, even when he thought I was dead. It's not about loyalty or talent. It's about our gifts, and the worth he ascribes to them. He's dangling a carrot for you. Don't chase it, Nadine.'

She crossed her arms, mouth tightly shut.

The door to my left cracked open. Eliza peered out, rubbing her eyes.

'Can you two please stop whispering?'

'Sorry,' I said.

I left before she could ask questions.

Jaxon was still out cold on the floor. I secured my scarf over the lower half of my face, then stole in and took the right key from his pocket. I closed the door behind me and unlocked the gate.

Warden waited for me at the base of the sundial pillar. His new black coat had clearly been tailored.

'We should move swiftly,' he said. 'There are night Vigiles on Shaftesbury Avenue.'

'Okay. You say you went to the Old Lyre?'

'Yes.'

He shadowed me down Earlham Street. This early in the evening, there were more than enough people and cars to keep us from standing out too much, even with Warden being so tall. There were no Vigiles that I could see, but any of them could be in plain clothes.

I stopped at the end of Floral Street and looked around the corner. Sensing a voyant, I held Warden back.

Bow Street was brightly lit, the streetlamps glowing vivid blue from one end to the other. The voyant patrolling it was not dressed like a night Vigile. Instead, they wore a black leather gilet over a red doublet with paned sleeves. A more elaborate take on a familiar uniform.

'That's a Punisher,' I said quietly. 'Isn't it?'

Warden looked over my head. 'Yes.'

The voyant wore a closed helmet, like most Vigiles. When I recognised the dreamscape, I clenched my jaw. It was Oliver, one of three red-jackets who had ambushed me in Oxford.

There must be other Punishers nearby. The entrance to the theatre was on nearby Catherine Street; there wasn't much of a way around Oliver.

I glanced back down Floral Street. There was a night parlour at the end – Adkins Coffee house, better known to voyants as the Lusty Gallant. All its permanent residents stood ready to get rid of Vigiles who got too close to the Garden. Their duty was to protect and distract from the entrance, but I could use them to my advantage tonight.

'Stick with me,' I said to Warden.

When I reached the right window, I knocked on it, tapping out the beats of a ballad. Rose, one of the nightwalkers, slid the window open.

'How are you, Pale Dreamer?'

'There's a Punisher on Bow Street,' I said. 'Can you get rid of him, Rosie?'

Rose leaned out a little, looking. 'We haven't dealt with Punishers yet.'

'The usual tricks should do.'

'As you like.' Her lips curved up when she caught sight of Warden. 'Hello there, handsome. What brings you to Covent Garden?'

'Rose.' I arched an eyebrow. 'Punisher.'

'Right you are.'

She closed the window. Warden gave me a questioning look, which I studiously ignored.

Three voyants soon emerged from the parlour, pink scarves wrapped over their faces, and ran towards Bow Street. I tracked them in the æther, sensing them rush past Oliver, probably swiping his truncheon.

Once he had gone after them, I quickly led Warden across the thoroughfare into Catherine Street. There were four dreamscapes in the theatre, with distinctive armour.

'The key I gave you,' I said. 'Do you still have it?'

'Yes.'

He took it from his coat. Just as I accepted it, he clasped my gloved hand in his own.

A tiny shock flew down my arm. I looked up at him, the rest of me stilling.

'In Oxford, you concealed the truth for my sake,' he said, his voice low. 'I ask you to do this once more, because it is for your sake, Paige.'

I waited, too aware of his fingers wrapped around mine, the thin layers of silk and leather that kept him from touching me.

'Nashira saw us in the Guildhall,' he said, as if I could have forgotten. 'She means to use our alliance to stain my reputation – and, by extension, to discredit the Ranthen. Three days ago, she sent her messengers far and wide, spreading word that I am a flesh-traitor.'

He had acknowledged the Guildhall. It came as such a surprise by itself that it took me a moment to process what he was saying.

'Flesh-traitor,' I echoed. 'What does that mean?'

'That I consort with humans, profaning my own sarx.' He held my gaze. 'In our culture, any direct contact with a human – any manner of physical congress – is the gravest of transgressions, punished with permanent ostracisation. A blood-traitor betrays the ruling family. A flesh-traitor betrays all Rephaim.'

I stared at him.

'We do not know precisely what caused the Netherworld to fall. Only that a boundary was crossed, and that it might have involved humans. In that ignorance, fear grew,' Warden said. 'A fear of any intimacy between the inhabitants of the Netherworld and those of Earth.'

Slowly, I looked down at our hands.

'That's why,' I whispered. 'Why you wear gloves.'

My body had already been cold. Now it might as well have turned to stone.

'What happened between us is already common knowledge on both sides. Nashira has seen to that,' Warden said quietly. 'But you must deny it – repeatedly and forcefully, if need be – to the Ranthen.'

'I thought Terebell and Errai would know. You told them about the cord.'

'Not the rest.' His gaze flicked over my face. 'Not the trap room.'

'Did you say Nashira was lying?'

'Yes,' Warden said. I tensed. 'My fellow Ranthen are not the same as the Sargas. They do not seek to harm or subjugate humans – but they do adhere to the doctrine of distance. If you confirmed what happened in the Guildhall, any chance of an alliance would be scotched. They would also go to any lengths to keep us away from each other.'

'You want me to keep it a secret,' I said. 'That's what you're asking me.'

'Yes.'

A tingling heat spread over neckline and cheeks. When it reached my eyes, I set my jaw against it, pulling my hand out of his gentle hold.

'Paige,' Warden said, very softly.

Not trusting myself to speak, I gave him a single nod in return. His touch had left goosebumps under my sleeves. I unlocked the door, wondering how I was going to keep the sudden disquiet off my face.

I kept my distance from him as we entered the music hall. A few candles had been lit near the stage, where Terebell stood with three other Rephs. When we reached them, Warden stopped at my side. I couldn't look at him.

'Dreamwalker,' Terebell said. 'We are pleased you could join us. I assume you remember Pleione Sualocin.'

'Vividly,' I said.

The first Reph I had ever seen. She was reclining on the theatre seats, her eyes a sinister green in the gloom. Her thick black curls were shorter now.

'Good evening, 40,' she said.

'I have a name.' I folded my arms. 'I'll thank you to use it, Pleione.'

Pleione tilted her head. 'What was it, again?'

'Paige. It's just the one syllable,' I said. 'I'm sure you can remember it.'

'Perhaps.' She motioned to the stranger. 'This is Lucida Sargas. One of the few with Ranthen sympathies.'

I tensed, reaching into my jacket. 'Sargas?'

'Indeed,' Lucida said. 'I have heard a great deal about you, Paige Mahoney.'

She had the classic Sargas look – hooded eyes; pale sarx, hovering between silver and gold (more on the silver side); thick hair that gleamed like new brass, an impossible shade of blonde. Like Pleione, she wore it to her collarbone, while Terebell had cropped hers even shorter.

'Yes,' I said. 'I imagine you have.' I released the pouch of pollen in my pocket. 'Does your family know you're Ranthen?'

'Oh, yes. I deserted my residence at Oxford before the first rebellion,' Lucida said. 'Consequently, Gomeisa declared me a blood-traitor, though his blood is mine. I have lived as a renegade ever since.'

'Good for you. It's nice that some people have the courage of their convictions.'

Warden glanced at me.

The Rephs still favoured black clothing, albeit more practical and discreet than their old finery. All five of them wore buttoned gloves.

'As requested, Paige has come here to discuss a potential alliance between her syndicate and the Ranthen,' Warden said. 'We owe her a great debt for challenging Nashira in Oxford, proving the Sargas regime is not unassailable.'

Errai and Pleione said nothing, while Terebell slashed her gaze over me again.

'There was a Punisher just outside,' I said, to break the silence. 'Did he catch wind of you?'

'No,' Terebell said. 'We can evade detection, just as you can, dreamwalker.'

I leaned against one of the folded red seats. Warden remained standing in the aisle.

'Oxford was a devastating loss to the Sargas. It was their strong-hold on Earth,' Terebell said. 'Your confrontation with Nashira struck a crucial blow. She has spent two centuries denigrating humans. Your possession – fleeting though it was – made her appear weaker than you.'

'Glad I could help,' I said. 'I think.'

'Many of the emissaries at the Bicentenary had never seen us before,' she said. 'Nashira meant for the Bicentenary to establish our power and authority. Instead, she was humiliated by a human, and her city was compromised. The Westminster Archon has silenced its own emissaries, but those from other countries will report what they witnessed. This may yet sow the first seeds of internal conflict in Scion.'

'Just to confirm,' I said, 'only Frank Weaver and his inner circle knew about you before Oxford, didn't they?'

'You have it right,' Lucida said.

'After failing to depose Nashira twenty years ago, we have now taken our first step towards ensuring her eventual downfall,' Terebell said, 'but it will not be an easy battle. The Sargas have powerful gifts, and their grip on Earth will only strengthen as their empire grows. Before we can overthrow them, we must dismantle Scion.'

'Fine by me,' I said. 'Now Oxford is gone, what do you think is their next move?'

'You will have noticed that the red-jackets have been put to work in London,' Terebell said. 'As we speak, Vindemiatrix Sargas is indoctrinating humans in the free world, training them as sleeper agents. Meanwhile, Sheol II will soon be established, providing a new home for loyalists. Tuonela III will follow.'

'Any idea where they'll be?'

'Not yet,' Lucida said. 'We know only that Sheol II will be in France.'

'Right.'

'Once their hold on Europe is secure,' Terebell said, 'there is a possibility that the Sargas will choose to reveal their presence on Earth.'

I looked between them all, finding the usual gallery of straight faces.

'That sounds insane,' I said. 'I don't know a lot about global politics, but if the whole of humankind found out about you at once, it would cause absolute chaos. The free world might even declare war on Scion.'

'On the whole, the free world tolerates Scion,' Terebell said. 'Its governments appear to practise a policy of non-intervention. Scion also has a vast and brutal army, of which I believe you have some experience.'

Warden must have told her that I had survived the Dublin Incursion, to reassure her that I was the right human for the job.

When I was young, I had dreamed of the free world rising to voyants' defence. I had believed an army would one day liberate Ireland. I had thought that if I only waited long enough, justice would come.

It had never been that simple. Through whispers at the black market and talking to Nadine and Zeke, I had learned that the free world had its own problems – too many for them to care about voyants, whose existence many governments apparently doubted. Nadine was convinced they would only fight Scion to defend their own interests, or if they anticipated a reward, like resources or influence.

For now, we were on our own.

'There will be more invasions before the Sargas announce their presence,' Terebell said. 'We may be able to avert them – if we can gain a swift foothold in London. If the capital falls into chaos, other citadels will follow. You work in its criminal underworld. Arcturus tells me that your syndicate leader was murdered.'

'Yes,' I said.

'Evidently,' Errai said, 'this was the work of a Rephaite mercenary, eliminating a threat to the Sargas. Situla Mesarthim may be the killer.'

'It seems likely,' Pleione agreed.

Lucida looked from them to me. 'What do you think, dreamwalker?'

They really didn't want to use my name, but at least they had dropped the number. *One fight at a time*, Chat had told me. Good advice.

'It's possible,' I conceded, 'but I think it's more likely it was a voyant with an axe to grind, literally. Hector wasn't popular.'

Terebell considered me. 'Who could have done it?'

'Most people suspect his mollisher. We're all trying to find her,' I said. 'So far, the only other suspect on my list is a mime-lord called the Rag and Bone Man. He's the one who captured Warden. I've no idea if he's involved in the murder, but he's clearly up to something.'

'With the Underlord gone, I understand there will be a competition to establish his successor,' Terebell said. 'You intend to enter.'

'Yes. It's the only way I can tell the syndicate what happened in Oxford. And I've thought of a way to prepare them for it.' I took out my spare manuscript of *The Rephaite Revelation* and offered it to Errai, the nearest. 'I'm trying to get this published before the scrimmage. If it goes out, every voyant in London will know about you.'

Errai looked as if I had just presented him with a dead rat. 'What is this, dreamwalker?'

'A penny dreadful. Well, a manuscript, at least.'

Terebell snatched it from me. Her eyes heated as she read the front page.

'I have heard of these. Cheap, sordid entertainment,' she said. 'How dare you belittle our cause with this mockery?'

'Terebell, with all due respect, I wanted to warn the syndicate about you as soon as possible. I didn't have time to write an epic poem.'

Errai hissed at me, a sound like water being thrown on a fire. 'Do not speak to our sovereign with that tone. You had no right to expose us without permission. You should have waited for us to advise you.'

'I didn't realise I needed your advice, Reph.'

'Do you think yourself all-knowing, mortal?'

'Hiss and sneer at me all you like. None of you frighten me any more.'

He spat something at Warden in Gloss, causing a ghost to flee the hall. Warden said nothing. Instead, he took the pages from Terebell and showed them to Lucida and Pleione, who leaned in to look.

'How … unusual,' Pleione concluded.

'I do not think this such a crass idea,' Lucida said, 'though it could make it more difficult for us to traverse the citadel without drawing attention. If humans read this, they may begin to notice us moving among them.'

'That may not matter,' Warden said. 'Scion denizens fear the onset of unnaturalness. They have no wish to see visions of giants, and if they did, they would certainly not report them to a Vigile.' His gaze darted across the pages. 'I do not believe this will restrict our movements.'

'But it does tell humans how to harm us.' Pleione looked up. 'Does your syndicate have access to pollen of the poppy anemone, Paige?'

'There is a supply line somewhere,' I said, 'but I don't think it's widely known. I certainly can't find it.'

'This Rag and Bone Man captured Arcturus with the windflower. If you send out this … tale, others could also take an interest in hunting us.'

'The idea was that they'd be able to defend themselves from Sargas loyalists.'

'You forget that we require aura to survive.'

'She is sabotaging our ability to feed,' Errai said to Terebell. 'Why should we allow this human to expose our weaknesses?'

'Well, Errai, you'll be pleased to know I can't do it without you,' I said. 'If *The Rephaite Revelation* is going to be read before the scrimmage, I need a thousand pounds by Monday.'

'I should have guessed that you wanted money,' Terebell said, looking towards the ornate ceiling. 'The eternal obsession of the human race.'

'Material possessions cannot last, yet they fight over them like vultures.' Errai turned up his nose. 'Disgusting greed.'

'*Fruitless* greed,' Pleione chimed in.

'All right,' I bit out. 'If I'd wanted lectures, I would have gone to the University. I'd love to help you out of the kindness of my heart, but my heart can't pay for anything – unless I scoop it out and sell it on the black market, which would still only get me so much.'

'You cannot survive without a heart.' Lucida looked to Arcturus. 'Can she?'

'For the love of—' I took a calming breath. 'Look, Warden seemed to think you might be willing to back me. If not, I can't do anything.'

'If you became Underqueen,' Terebell said, 'would you not have your own money?'

'A certain amount. I'd receive a regular tribute from the Unnatural Assembly,' I said, 'but it wouldn't be enough to transform the syndicate into an army equipped to fight Scion. I also don't want to be an Underqueen who exploits her voyants. The more I take, the less they have for themselves. That won't help anyone.'

'If we gave you money, how would you spend it?'

'I'd start by publishing the penny dreadful,' I said. 'If I do win the scrimmage, I'll have to give the mime-lords and mime-queens a financial incentive to fight Scion. If we *can* get some kind of revolt off the ground, I'll need plenty of coin to keep it going. Buying weapons, feeding voyants, patching them up when Scion hits back – all of that will cost a fortune. More than a bunch of misfits could ever scrape together by ourselves.'

The Rephs exchanged glances.

'You'll have to decide if you trust me to do this,' I said. 'I'll remind you of what I told Warden in Oxford, which is that I'm not a strategist. I'm a criminal, and so is every member of the underworld. All the violence and greed you hate in humans is written through the syndicate like a stick of rock. I can try to change it, but if you can't fund me, you'll have to find a human associate with fuller pockets than mine. But as a mollisher, I'm probably your best chance of gaining a voyant army.'

I had to assert myself as their equal, not their lackey. The syndicate voyants wouldn't be their red-jackets, with me as their Overseer.

'Tell me,' Terebell said, 'what was your plan if you did not have our support?'

'To help voyants survive Scion,' I said. 'You're asking for revolution.'

Terebell looked to Warden, who met her gaze in silence.

'Our reserves are not infinite,' Terebell eventually said. 'At any given moment, our human contact in Scion could be detained. We do not have the resources to fund an extravagant lifestyle for an Underqueen.'

'I understand,' I said.

'Then we will consider supporting your reign, both financially and in an advisory capacity,' she said. 'In recognition of what you did in Oxford, I will also give you one thousand pounds for *The Rephaite Revelation*. In return, you will make an oath. First, that you will do your utmost to protect the Ranthen from any adverse consequences.'

'Fine.'

'Second,' she said, 'that if you win the scrimmage, you will unite your forces with mine. A joint enterprise to resist Scion and the Sargas.'

'It isn't quite that simple,' I said. 'I can promise that if I win, I'll do my utmost to persuade the syndicate that taking down Scion is a good idea, but it won't be easy to turn thieves and smugglers into soldiers.'

'The Ranthen are warriors,' Pleione said. 'We may be able to assist you, just as we trained humans to use their gifts in Oxford.' (*Preferably not in the same way*, I thought.) 'We can also provide natural resources from the Netherworld – alysoplasm and amaranth.'

'What's alysoplasm?'

'Emite blood,' Warden said. 'A single drop will corrupt the aura for a time, so its nature cannot be known. A larger dose conceals the dreamscape.'

That explained a few things. More than once, I had failed to notice Rephs approaching, even with my heightened ability to sense the æther.

'Naturally, harvesting it is a perilous venture, as is consuming it,' Warden continued. 'Once you drink alysoplasm, you will not be able to use your gift until it wears off. You will be hidden, but defenceless.'

That was a significant downside, but it sounded priceless.

'Senshield will be able to detect our auras,' I said. 'Could alyso-plasm block it from doing that?'

'Perhaps.'

It could be the missing ingredient in creating a jamming device. If I could get some for Danica, she might actually crack a smile for once.

'We will train your criminals,' Terebell said. 'Once word of the sign has spread, we will be able to contribute our own warriors to the cause.'

I shook my head, lost. 'The sign?'

'The amaranth in bloom,' Errai said, looking as irritated as Rephs could. 'It is our call to arms. Do you know nothing of our history?'

'The night of the Bicentenary, the amaranth – our sacred flower – was restored to life in Oxford,' Terebell said, before I could think of a sharp retort. 'Nashira will take pains to destroy or hide it, but we have already borne witness. No amaranth has ever bloomed on Earth.'

'I hear you don't know why that happened,' I said.

'No,' Pleione said. 'It is a mystery.'

'One that we intend to solve,' Terebell said. 'I accept that you cannot guarantee your thieves' cooperation, but I also expect you to strive for it. Can you guarantee that you will win the scrimmage?'

'No. More likely I'll be killed in the Rose Ring,' I said, 'but I've been working on my strategy. I just need to resolve some … issues.'

Terebell glanced at Warden again. He gave her a small nod. After a long moment, she reached into her coat and handed me a thick envelope.

'For *The Rephaite Revelation*,' she said. 'And for your courage in Oxford.'

'Thank you.' I tucked it into my jacket, out of reach of pick-pockets. 'The scrimmage is on the first of November. How should I contact you?'

'Arcturus can send word to me. He will stay in this district to protect you.'

'Protect me?'

'From any further attempts on your life.' She fastened her coat. 'You are our investment now, dreamwalker. I protect my investments.'

My jaw clenched. She and Jaxon might be cut from the same cloth.

Terebell spoke in Gloss. The other four Rephs walked out of the music hall, leaving us alone.

'Arcturus can train you for the scrimmage,' Terebell said. 'His style of instruction clearly helped you in Oxford. I trust that he can raise your chances of survival. But first, you will answer a question.'

Even knowing what she was about to ask, I felt my hands go clammy in their gloves. I pushed them into my pockets, the warmth returning to my cheeks.

'Nashira claims that Arcturus degrades himself with humans. That she discovered him *in flagrante delicto* with you in the Guildhall,' Terebell said, her face even harder than usual. (I had no idea what that meant, but I could guess.) 'Thuban Sargas and Situla Mesarthim have upheld this attack on his integrity. What say you to this, dreamwalker?'

I considered telling her the truth, just to see the look on her face. To get back at Warden for the small, burning hurt he had left in my pride.

Then the haze cleared, and I came to my senses.

'I was in the trap room with Warden,' I said. 'He asked me there to make sure I was all right. That I wasn't too afraid to fight Nashira.'

Terebell listened, searching my face.

'She found us alone together and drew her own conclusions. That, or she saw an opportunity to spin a lie,' I said. 'I never touched him.'

'You deny her claim.'

'I deny it.'

'What is your opinion of Arcturus?'

'I like him,' I said. 'I would call him an ally. That's as far as it goes.'

'Good.' Terebell straightened to her full height. 'I may have agreed to fund your army. You may no longer be our subordinate – but you were forged of flesh, not sarx. Do not forget your station, Paige Mahoney.'

She walked out of the theatre without another word. I watched her leave, thanking the æther I was a good liar.

———

Outside, the sky had opened. Fortunately for the Punisher, he hadn't returned – at that moment, I probably would have killed him. With my hands balled into my pockets, I strode away from the music hall, trying to shake off the chagrin.

I had been naïve to hope the Ranthen would be kind. When it came down to it, even Warden could apparently live with his own friends' disdain for humans. At the end of the day, he was still a Reph. He would always be a Reph.

'Paige.'

He had waited for me. I slowed, trying my level best to tamp down my frustration.

'I don't think we should talk now,' I said. 'I might need a few days, Warden.'

'May I ask why?'

'I can think of several reasons.'

'I have plenty of time to hear them. Eternity, in fact.'

'Fine.' I kept walking. 'Some of your so-called allies are treating me like dirt on their boots, and I don't appreciate it.'

'Bluster and empty threats. Do not allow them to rattle you, Paige.'

'Let's see how rattled *you* get when I start mouthing off about what a bunch of tyrannical, self-important bastards you Rephs can be.'

'By all means,' Warden said. 'They would benefit from a lesson in humility.'

I rounded on him, stopping us both. The rain was picking up, damp hair clinging to my cheekbones – and for once, he looked as human as I did, standing in this downpour in the dim blue glow of Martlett Court.

'Don't act like you're different,' I said. 'You couldn't put those gloves back on fast enough, could you?'

He watched me.

'Don't get me wrong. I wasn't planning to shout from the roof-tops about the Guildhall,' I said coolly, 'but I never imagined that even your allies would think I'm beneath you. Or that you would expect me to stomach it.'

'Your anger is justified.'

'You told me freedom was my right, yet here you are, sacrific-ing yours again. Would it have killed you to admit what really happened?'

'Think me a recreant if you wish,' Warden said, 'but I do not intend to rest on my laurels. The Ranthen respect me, as the Sargas did not. I believe I can change their perspective on humans, but it will take time, just as it will take you time to change the syndicate. We may have escaped Oxford, but you and I hold power in flawed institutions, Paige.'

'Yes. Thanks for reminding me.' I folded my arms. 'I covered for you, even if I didn't like doing it. I just thought you had more of a spine on you, Warden.'

Warden took this in silence, assessing my features. Rephs must have to work hard to understand human expressions, since they had so little expression themselves.

'You wish for me to tell them about the Guildhall,' he finally said.

'No. You're missing the point.'

'Tell me.'

'You claim the Ranthen aren't the Sargas, but they still don't like or respect humans, and you've clearly decided that's not a deal-breaker. If this alliance is going to work, I need to know how far you plan to go to stay in their good books.'

'That decision should be yours.' He held my gaze. 'I did not only arrange this meeting to allow Terebell to take the measure of you. It was so that you could judge the Ranthen. Now I have told you their beliefs, and the price of ensuring their cooperation. If you would sooner walk away, I would not blame you, Paige.'

'And what if I would prefer the Ranthen to know the truth?' I asked. 'What if I didn't want to hide it?'

'Then I would accept the consequences. And do all I could to prevent them from touching you.'

I considered his face, weighing his sincerity. After seven months, I should be able to read him.

'No,' I said. 'I want us to make this alliance. I need that money. I also don't want you to suffer because of some ridiculous … doctrine, but I won't have you standing by while Terebell rides roughshod over me, Warden. This can't be a repeat of Oxford.'

'I intend to use my influence to be your advocate. That is the very reason I asked you conceal the truth.'

'Fine.'

Warden stayed where he was, watching me as I paced in the rain. I maintained a frigid silence.

'There is not long until the scrimmage,' he said. 'What trouble have you had with your gift?'

'Nothing you won't have noticed before,' I said. 'I just need to get better.'

'I told you I was willing to help you gain the Rose Crown. If you wish to train with me, we can return to the music hall.'

'Are you even allowed to be alone with me?'

'What I do in my own time is my prerogative, Paige Mahoney. Thanks to you, I am my own master.'

'Doesn't sound like it.'

A furnace roared to life behind his eyes.

'Jaxon did not want you to come here,' he said. 'Yet here you stand.'

I raised my chin.

'I'll train with you,' I said, 'if only because Jaxon is completely buckled tonight. I don't know when I'll be able to leave after dark again.'

'I hoped you would say that.' Warden turned back towards the music hall. 'Terebell has allowed us to train, but she did not specify the manner in which I should train you. I have had an idea.'

As he walked away from me, my anger cooled, replaced by curiosity. I breathed out and went after him.

19

CIULEANDRA

The music hall was deserted when we returned, though I still checked for dreamscapes. Warden closed the doors behind us, and we made our way back towards the stage.

'Do you trust Lucida?' I asked him.

He looked down at me. 'Why do you ask?'

'She's a Sargas.'

'Did you agree with your father on everything, Paige?'

'I wouldn't know,' I said. 'We didn't talk much. Not about important things.'

'What has become of him?'

'They let him out for a while. Now he's apparently in Coldbath Fields.'

'Coldbath Fields is a humane prison, in comparison to those built to hold voyants. He is unlikely to be executed, given his value to Scion.'

I nodded once, hoping he was right. When we reached the stage, I hitched myself on to the edge and brought one knee up to my chest.

'Lucida broke away from her kin more than twenty years ago,' Warden said. 'I believe she is committed to the Ranthen.'

'What about the others?'

'I trust them all, even if the alliance will not be easy. Their tolerance for humans waxes and wanes. Terebell has always been a harsh judge of mortals.'

'I noticed,' I said. 'Any specific reason, other than general prejudice?'

'I have studied many books on your history. If there is one thing I have learned from them, it is that it is not always possible to find reason in tradition.'

I made a noncommittal sound.

Warden took a seat on the stage beside me, not quite close enough to touch. 'Before we begin, I wonder if you would indulge a question, to continue my education in syndicate politics,' he said. 'What was the establishment on Floral Street?'

Of course he was asking that. I grasped the stage, shifting my hips.

'A night parlour,' I said. 'They sell pink aster at a premium. As far as I understand it, they also … partake in it with their patrons, if you catch my drift.' I avoided his gaze. 'The voyants who work there are called nightwalkers. You pay them in secrets or coin.'

'It seems there are many secrets in London. Including this music hall.'

'Yes.'

We both looked at the carved pillars, the high and extravagant ceiling. Unlike the others, he saw the violence that had been wrought on this building. His gaze found the scorched curtains, the bullet holes.

'I thought the penny dreadful was an enterprising idea,' he said. 'As ever, you defy conventional means of achieving your aims, Paige.'

'I'll take that as a compliment.'

'That was my intention.'

I tried to release the tight knot of tension below my breastbone, where my breath seemed to be trapped.

Warden had made me no promises. I had known that kiss was stolen; that nothing could ever come of it. I had told him so in the moment.

I know this can't mean anything.

320

We sat together for some time. The strain lingered, but it was slipping away by the moment. For better or worse, I liked his company.

'Tell me about the scrimmage,' Warden said, breaking the silence. 'How is a victor chosen?'

'It's close combat. A fight to the death.'

His eyes darkened a little.

'If I'm going to survive, I need to use my gift,' I said. 'It's the only way I'm going to get the upper hand over the bruisers – but the second I jump, my body falls. It will be a fatal flaw in the Rose Ring.'

One stab through the heart, and my silver cord would snap, casting me out of my body for good. I would be like every other drifting spirit.

'I can't see a way around it,' I said. 'If you have any bright ideas, I'm listening.'

'I may.' Warden clasped his gloved hands. 'Have you possessed anyone since coming here?'

'A bird and a Vigile.'

'I am impressed that you attempted to possess an animal again.'

'I managed to stay calm this time,' I said. 'Other than that, I haven't dreamwalked since Oxford. I've been trying to keep a low profile.'

'Good. Nashira will have very little means by which to trace you. On the other hand, your lack of practice may have thwarted your progress.'

'It has. My dreamscape has recovered, but I'm finding it hard to switch from flesh to spirit.'

'You are not a novice any longer. I am confident you can return to making well-oiled jumps before the scrimmage.' He moved to stand on the stage. 'Before we address the vulnerability of your body, I want to see fluidity from you. I want you to jump into the æther as if you belonged there. I want you to fly between dreamscapes.'

He went behind the curtains. When he returned, he had an armful of large red cushions, which must have been taken from the seats. I gave him a quizzical look.

'What *are* you doing?'

'Wait and see,' he said.

My brow creased as he placed the cushions around the stage. Next, he brought out a record player in a wooden case. Against my will, I smiled.

'Where did you get that?'

'Somewhere or other,' he said. 'Like most of my belongings.'

He set it down and took off his gloves, laying them beside the record player.

'Oh, off they come again.' I sighed. 'Make your mind up.'

'I will for ever be known as a flesh-traitor. I may as well embrace a life of sedition.'

'How daring of you. What's next – your coat?'

A quick fire in his eyes. 'Is it wise to torment your mentor before he begins your training?'

'Why break the habit of a lifetime?'

'Hm.'

He proceeded to remove his coat. Beneath it, he wore a collared white shirt and a black waistcoat, which must be as close as he could get to a jerkin. I watched him place a record on the player.

'Is this ... related to training, or did you just want some music on?'

'I would have trained you like this in Oxford, had I been allowed to choose.' He set the needle over the record, then rose and bowed to me, keeping his eyes on my face. 'Let us see if dreamwalkers can dance.'

'Are you serious?'

'Quite serious.'

A rich, soulful voice began to sing in Romanian, a language I often heard in London. I stood and unbuttoned my coat. 'I'm not exactly dressed for dancing,' I said, taking it off. 'But I'll give it a shot.'

'This is no ordinary dance,' he warned. 'I am no longer your keeper, but I still consider your training a grave matter. I will not go easy on you, Paige.'

'I'd be disappointed if you did.'

My body slid with ease into its training stance. In the early days of Oxford, I had been shivering in my white tunic, barely understanding my gift.

I was ready for him now.

'Let us try a little combat first,' Warden said. 'Evade me.'

'With pleasure.'

We circled each other. When he aimed a mock punch at me, I ducked.

'No ducking in a dance, Paige,' he said. 'Try to move in your body as you would in the æther. Or in a waltz.' When he tried it a second time, I whirled neatly to the left, avoiding his gentle feint. 'Good.'

I kept moving, keeping my steps in time with the music. 'Who's this singer?'

'Maria Tănase. A Romanian actress from the twentieth century.'

'Her voice is so powerful.'

'Indeed. A great talent.' He clasped his hands behind his back. 'I hope to find other records in this citadel. I could not save many from Magdalen.'

'There are plenty in the Garden. I could get some for you, if you'd try to be less of a bastard.'

'I will endeavour to reform.' He swung at me again, and I swept to the right, out of the way. 'Very good. Now anticipate my next move.'

'How?'

'You may have noticed that sighted voyants often make especially quick fighters. You are unsighted, but you can learn to sense what they see. Concentrate on my aura. Watch it carefully as I move.'

'Hold on.'

I thought of an old trick Jaxon had taught me when I had started learning to dislocate my spirit. I imagined six vials, one for each sense, each filled with a little wine. In my head, I decanted five of those vials into the one marked ÆTHER, winding down my other senses one by one. I tuned out the slight chill in the room, the smell of must, the sound of the music and our footsteps, the sight of Warden.

When I opened my eyes, I breathed out, feeling lighter. I still couldn't see auras or spirits, but now I had drilled into my sixth sense as much as I could, I made out the slightest flickering around Warden.

He kept pacing. I mirrored him. Out of nowhere, he came towards me. I retreated, and he stopped, just as the song paused for a beat.

'Did you notice?'

'I don't think so,' I said.

'Try again.'

Maria Tănase continued to sing, and our boots were still keeping time with the music. I looked harder at the disturbance around Warden.

It had his aura. This time, I caught the change as it happened. A split second before he moved, his aura seemed to lean to the right, betraying his intention. My muffled senses came rushing back. I slid out of his path, and he followed. I spun to face him again. When his aura went left, I skirted around him in the opposite direction.

'Now I know how it feels to predict the future,' I said. 'That *is* a clever trick.'

'A subtle one,' Warden said. 'It may not serve you in the heat of the fray, but if you practise, it will be a useful tactic for your arsenal.'

The song was getting faster, verse by verse, beat by beat. Even with my senses back in balance, I could no longer feel the cold in the music hall.

'When you see a window of opportunity, attack me with your spirit,' Warden said. 'Leave your body, as if you mean to possess me.'

'A quick-fire jump, you mean?'

'Yes.'

I nodded, and our dance went on. A dance in which we never touched, but orbited each other.

In Oxford, he had sometimes asked me to dreamwalk several times in a row, with only brief pauses between. As our paths wound in tighter and tighter circles, I waited for the right moment. His eyes narrowed a little. I smiled at him.

I lined myself up with one of the cushions, realising why they were there. Just as his lips parted – probably to ask if I was ever going to jump – I did it. In moments, I withdrew into my dreamscape, fought through each ring, and hurled myself headlong into the æther.

Spirit and flesh strained at the seams. My silver cord turned rigid, like metallic wire. Before I knew it, it had wrenched me back into my body. I woke with a sharp intake of breath, my head on the cushion.

'Your first try will never be your finest,' Warden said.

'You always know what to say.' I climbed back to my feet, clutching my chest. 'Well, that was shite.'

'Your emotions are not strong enough. You are no longer afraid of me.'

'No, but I am fuming with you.'

'Even still.' His eyes flamed. 'We know that fear and anger spur your spirit. In the scrimmage, the danger should work in your favour – but in the long term, you will be able to control your gift, regardless of your emotions. It should be as easy to dreamwalk for pleasure' – he stepped around me – 'as it is instinctive when you are in peril.'

'I can't imagine dreamwalking for pleasure.'

'Do not deny yourself the possibility. This power belongs to you, not your fear.'

We drifted away from each other again. I jumped at him twice more, and twice more I crashed to the floor, almost missing the cushion the second time.

'That was close.' I got back up, light-headed. 'I need to invest in a helmet.'

'Or you could remain standing.'

'Go on.'

'When you leave your body, I think you could leave some awareness behind,' he said. 'Enough for you to keep control of your own body, even as you inhabit another.' The look on my face must have shouted disbelief. 'Even when you jump, your spirit remains connected to your dreamscape through your silver cord. This allows you to retain your free will and memories, even when you leave.'

'I realised that when I possessed the bird,' I said. 'It's how I don't forget who I am, even when I have a different brain and dreamscape.'

'Precisely,' Warden said. 'I am no dreamwalker. You must decide how to remain aware of the body you leave behind when you jump.'

'I've no idea. Even when I see my dreamscape, it feels like falling asleep.'

'Even when you sleep, your body knows to keep breathing,' he pointed out. 'When you look into your dreamscape, you do not sleep, but enter a state of low consciousness. You can remain standing in that state. I have seen voyants do it.'

'Really?'

'Yes. Since the silver cord roots you to your dreamscape – and your body, by extension – the same is theoretically possible when you dreamwalk.' He continued to pace around the stage. 'Let us start with a middle ground. Try to make your jumps faster. If you can, touch my dreamscape and return to your body before you hit the floor.'

'That sounds a little optimistic.' I caught his eye as I passed. 'I assume you were born knowing everything there is to know about your gift.'

'Never assume.'

As I wove around him, I tore free of my body again. As always, the jump demanded every inch of my awareness, collapsing my physical form in my wake. I got back up and kept moving.

'Try again,' Warden said. 'A light throw and a quick return. When you are back in your body, try to keep your footing. Dance as you fall.'

'How can I do both?'

'Remember Liss. Her act – her life, at times – depended on dancing as she fell.'

Her name hit me hard, but he had a point. I thought of how Liss would climb up her purple silks, then untangle herself as she fell towards the stage.

'Now, feel the æther.' Warden gave me a gentle push away from him. 'Come to me.'

The invitation sent a long shiver across my skin. Our gazes met, and I cast off my body. I flew across the space between us, glanced off his dreamscape, and woke on the floor, sprawled like a dropped marionette.

'At least you have the falling down to a fine art,' Warden observed.

I blew a curl out of my eyes. 'Have you ever paused to reflect on how annoying you can be?'

'Once or twice. Try again.'

The song was becoming frantic. A film of sweat covered my collarbones. I leapt out again, then back to myself. As our dance became faster, taking us all the way across the stage, I kept trying. The sixth time, I sprang up as soon as I bit the dust, only faltering a little.

'I've almost got it.' I caught my breath. 'I woke up just before I hit the floor.'

'Very good. You have mastered and improved upon the techniques we developed in Oxford,' he said. 'Now your spirit is used to jumping again, we can endeavour to keep your body standing.'

I stood. 'How?'

As I asked the question, the song came to an end.

'By your leave,' Warden said.

He offered me a hand. My stubborn pride told me to deny him, but the rest of me only wanted to dance.

So I let him take my hand. He lifted it high and spun me himself. I glided under his raised arm, and my hair brushed against his waistcoat.

'Your body is your anchor to the earth.' His voice was soft. 'The more it preoccupies your thoughts, the heavier it will feel, and the more difficult it will be to lift yourself free of it. I told you this in Oxford.'

'Yes.'

'But you must strike a fine balance if you are to remain standing. You must acknowledge both your spirit and the house you leave behind.' He spun me again. 'Dance into the æther, but do not forget your mortal form.'

With his hand around mine and his aura beside me, I was already starting to find that balance. I savoured the rising warmth of my skin, the drumming of my heart. The swoop in my stomach when his fingers pressed mine through my glove. The awareness of him. My breath caught when his other hand brushed my waist.

I remembered his hands in my hair. The feelings his embrace had woken.

I let my spirit reach for him.

My weight tilted. The muscles in my core pulled tight. My spine straightened and my ribcage lifted. I circled him again before I took three long steps back. I was hanging on to the earth by my fingertips.

'On my count,' Warden said. 'One, two, three—'

I soared to him.

This time, my flight to his dreamscape was painless, my spirit light as a pennyweight. Following the golden cord, I caught a glimpse of a glimmer of light, tempting me to find his dream-form. Instead, I grasped the silver cord and followed it back to myself. I hurtled into my own dreamscape, sheathing my spirit in flesh—

—and woke to my palms slamming into the floor.

The shock jarred my arms, right to the shoulders. I took a huge breath, staring at my hands. My legs shook, but my boots were still planted in place.

The song ended just as my knees gave way. And even though my head was in pain and my heart protested, I was laughing. I hadn't fallen.

I could win.

Warden cupped his hands under my elbows and helped me rise. 'That is the music I wanted to hear,' he said. 'When was the last time you laughed?'

I smiled up at him. 'Have you *ever* laughed, Warden?'

'There is very little to laugh about when one is the blood-consort of Nashira Sargas.'

'You're not her consort any more.'

'No.'

If another song was playing, I didn't hear it. We stood too close to one another, my elbows still cradled by his palms, holding me against him.

'Thank you,' I said. 'I might survive now.'

'It is your victory. Only you have ever held the keys to unlocking your gift.'

'I might not have found this one without you.'

'Just as I might never have escaped Oxford without you.'

The candles were nearing the end of their wicks. A few of them had blown out as we danced, and the vast dark of the hall was closing in.

'I have one more thing to share with you. For *The Rephaite Revelation*, if you have time to include it,' he said. 'We are most vulnerable where our bodies are closest to touching the physical world. Stab a Rephaite in the heel or hand, and you are more likely to cause them pain than you are by striking the head, or the heart.'

'I'll keep that in mind,' I said.

'Hm.'

Our gazes held. In those moments, nothing in the world could have persuaded me to dreamwalk. I was aware of the way he felt against me; of every point our bodies touched, every inch of space between us.

I didn't know who I was trying to fool. I wanted to be close to him.

'You call a former lover an *old flame*.' His golden eyes were chilling, his face carved out of nothing earthly. 'For Rephaim, it can take a long time for a flame to catch. But once it burns, it does not go out.'

It didn't take long to understand what he meant.

'But I will,' I said. 'I'll go out.'

There was a long silence.

'Yes,' he said. 'You will go out.'

He slowly released my arms.

'I know you're trying to spare my feelings,' I said quietly, 'but you don't need to make excuses, Warden.' I turned away. 'I needed you in that moment, but I never expected anything more. Even if you were human—'

I stopped, holding myself.

Now our dance had ended, I could feel the cold again. There was a painful silence, during which I wondered if I should stay or go.

'Paige,' Warden said, 'I did not tell you this to … let you down gently. Quite the opposite.'

Now I stood very still, listening.

'Not all secrets are kept out of shame. Some are kept to guard a truth, or to protect a life,' he said. 'Others are kept for selfish reasons, for those who know them fear that sunlight will burn them away.' He came to join me. 'And some secrets are kept for their sanctity.'

I glanced at him. He kept a respectful distance, but I was too aware of him.

'Know that I may not always understand you,' Warden said, 'but I will always try. Know that there are things I cannot give you, and that the road walked at my side is not an easy one. Know that if we were to be discovered, it would not only imperil the alliance, but your life.'

My voice came out in a whisper: 'Why are you telling me this, Warden?'

'In the Guildhall, you said that you knew that moment could not mean anything.' His gaze burned against the darkness. 'What if it could?'

I searched his face again.

'The night I first saw you, I feared you,' Warden said. 'By the time you left, I could not imagine never seeing you again. It defied my expectations – just as you did, at every turn.'

All I could do was stare at him, feeling as if I had just slipped out of my body.

He reached for my fingers and cupped them to his chest, just like when we had struck our truce. I looked at his naked hand, clasping my gloved one. Beneath them both, I felt the steady cadence of his heart.

'It must remain a secret until this conflict ends. It cannot be for ever, because we do not have that long.' His voice was soft as shadow. 'You are not beholden to the Guildhall. But if you still want me with you – if you will have me, despite the danger – then I want the same.'

I just know I want you with me.

It was one of the last things I had said to him in Oxford. My heart pounded. I needed to answer, but for once, I was at a complete loss for words.

'Take as long as you wish to decide.' Warden let go of my hand. 'If you need me before the scrimmage, use the golden cord. I will come.'

'I still need to apply.' I managed to speak. 'Tomorrow is the deadline.'

'Alsafi once learned that the syndicate uses the language of flowers. Is that still the case?'

'Yes. It's our way of keeping secrets from Scion.'

'Then I have something for you.'

Warden retrieved his gloves. I stiffened a little, and he glanced at me.

'There are always reasons.'

With the gloves on, he reached into his case. When he returned to me, he was holding a red flower. The flower that would hurt him if he touched it.

'To send a message.' He offered it to me. 'If you so desire.'

I took it.

'Do you have any doubts about this?' I asked. 'Or are you as sure as you seem?'

Warden cupped my cheek. Even with his glove, his touch warmed my skin. 'If I fear anything, it is not that I want you,' he said quietly. 'Only that I might want you too much. And for too long.'

He lingered on my jaw.

'You can never want too much. That's how they silence us,' I said. 'They told us we were lucky to be in a prison instead of the æther. Lucky to be murdered with nitrogen and not the noose. Lucky to be alive, even if we weren't free. They told us to stop wanting more than what they gave us, because what they gave us was more than we deserved.' I picked up my coat. 'You're not a prisoner any more, Arcturus.'

Warden looked at me in silence. I left him in that ruined hall with one last candle burning.

By the time I got back to the den, the gate to the courtyard had a chain on it. I climbed up the front of the building and down on the other side. Once I was indoors, I filled a jar with cold water for the poppy anemone.

In my room, I took off my boots and gloves. As I removed my coat, I spotted the note on the nightstand, written in sleek black ink.

I trust you enjoyed your stroll. Tell me, are you a dreamwalker or a flâneuse, sauntering about the town by night?

Fortunately for you, I have been called to a gathering, but we will discuss your disobedience in the morning. I am losing my patience.

Jaxon could take his patience and shove it down the neck of a bottle. I scrunched the note and threw it away. Still in my shirt, I lay down and gazed at the painted stars on my ceiling, thinking of Warden.

I had never felt anything like this. Not for anyone. Sometimes I had wondered if I ever would. Either way, I had been content with it.

For most of my time in Oxford, the idea that I could be attracted to Warden had never entered my head. Rephs were untouchable, passionless, distant. I wouldn't have so much as entertained the possibility.

And then his lips had touched mine and changed everything. That act had cleared my eyes, allowing me to see his appeal. I liked his forbearance and strength, his maverick approach to things, the way he raised my confidence without laying it on too thick. He had a quiet and gentle manner that I found endearing.

I didn't quite know how to hold this feeling, or what to do with it. I also didn't want to let it go. In those last moments in Oxford, I had wanted us to have another chance. Now we did. All I had to do was take it.

Our connection had been founded on fear – my fear of his control, and his fear of my betrayal. Now it had been severed from those roots, to grow on different ground. Perhaps it could give rise to something new. If I was going to explore the idea of having a relationship, I thought I would feel safe with him, despite the risk it would invite.

I was human. He was a Reph. It might take us years to understand each other, if we ever did.

But fear and understanding were kindred things. Both involved the loss of the familiar, the need for knowledge, the danger of uncharted waters. If we could survive that first step, perhaps we could survive the next.

This path would be more perilous than any I had ever taken. Warden hadn't tried to hide that.

Then again, I was used to danger.

Perhaps I even thrived on it.

I imagined what Nick would say if I confessed. He would tell me that the strain of captivity had forced me to develop an irrational degree of empathy towards Warden. That by lowering my guard around him, I risked granting him power over me again. That I should leave the feeling well alone.

I imagined how Jaxon would sneer if he knew. He would tell me this feeling – whatever its name – was a weakness in a mollisher; a tragic flaw in an Underqueen. *Hearts are frivolous things, good for nothing but pickling.*

But Warden cared if I laughed. He could have trained me however he liked, but of all things in the world, he had chosen to dance with me, to remind me there was more to life than fighting to survive. And that meant something.

Some secrets are kept for their sanctity.

I breathed in. If no one knew about Warden, no one could use him against me.

I was getting ahead of myself. He hadn't even told me if he was looking for a fling or a committed relationship. But the space he was taking up in my head, the tingle of exhilaration – no matter which path I took, I did want him.

Sudden resolve pushed through me. Barefoot, I stole into the boudoir, where 'Danse Macabre' was playing, and took a pen and paper from the desk. Jaxon would be gone for a while. In the gloom, I sat in his chair and bent my head to write my application for the scrimmage.

Just before dawn, I descended to the Garden and headed for the flower carts. The black market was usually deserted at this hour, but a few people were admiring the display on this final day of applications. Each kind had a label to describe its meaning in the language of flowers.

I walked past the popular ones, the ones the others would have chosen. Gladiolus, the warriors' flower. Cedar for strength. Begonia – a warning of a fierce fight in the ring. Instead, I took Bells of Ireland – for luck – and purple bittersweet.

TRUTH, the label said.

I threaded them all together with black ribbon: luck, truth and Rephaite's bane, the flower that could bring down giants. Under the rising sun, I walked to the dead drop.

Whatever happened next, I was not going to be the Pale Dreamer for much longer.

PART THREE

POMEGRANATE

And now tell me how he rapt you away to the realm of darkness and gloom, and by what trick did the Host of Many beguile you?

– HOMERIC HYMN TO DEMETER

INTERLUDE

Ode to the Underworld

The monarchy had long since been dismantled, severed at the root by blood and blade. Under cover of night, the lords and queens of death were masked, dancing in the shadow of the anchor.

The oracle sensed a change in the world. The threads of the future tangled around him.

The cuckoo clock is ticking in the room.

These days end with red flowers on a tomb.

The violinist played a sweet sonata, lonely on a street bejewelled by rain. The voices of the dead were in her bow.

A man without words looked up at the moon. He sang in a language he should never have known.

The hand without flesh lifted the crimson silk, laying it down on the woman with two smiles and a fractured heart.

The gods dwelt between the bones of the citadel, exiled from their fallen realm, their fates bound to the dreamwalker and her ring of roses. A golden thread encircled her, joining her to the lord of hindsight.

All across the citadel, lights stirred. Fingers skimmed a crystal ball, and wings beat deep within it. Wings, dark wings on the horizon, putting out the stars.

For the sole attention of

THE PALE DREAMER,

ESTEEMED MOLLISHER OF I COHORT, SECTION 4

The precise location of the fourth Scrimmage
will be delivered personally to your Mime-Lord in
two days' time by a Courier from II Cohort, Section 4.
A Rickshaw will be sent to your designated Meeting Point
at ten o'clock on the Night of November the first.

PLEASE FIND THE CHOSEN NAMES OF ALL TWENTY-FIVE CONFIRMED COMBATANTS BELOW:

VI COHORT: *The Hare and the Green Man* * *Jenny Greenteeth and the May Fool*

V COHORT: *The Wretched Sylph and Bramble Briar*

IV COHORT: *Redcap and the Faerie Queene* * *Faceless and the Swan Knight*

III COHORT: *The Bully-Rook and Jack Hickathrift* * *The Glym Lord and the London Particular*

II COHORT: *Bloody Knuckles and Halfpenny* * *The Wicked Lady and the Highwayman*
* *Ark Ruffian and the Knife Grinder*

I COHORT: *Mary Bourne and Falcon Brook* * *The White Binder and the Pale Dreamer*

INDEPENDENTS: *The Maverick Medium* * *The Bleeding Heart* * *Nicnevin* * *Black Moth*

Minty Wolfson.

Secretary of the Spiritus Club, Mistress of Ceremonies

On behalf of the Abbess
Mime-Queen of I-2
Interim Underqueen of the
Scion Citadel of London

20

MISPRINTS

On Thursday the thirtieth of October, *The Rephaite Revelation* – the first anonymous piece of fiction to be released by Grub Street in a year and half – hit the streets of London like a firework. The Penny Post was all over the citadel, selling the tale of the Bone Season in every corner of the underworld.

I was in Seven Dials when I saw a finished copy for the first time. A bell rang as I stepped into Chateline's and folded my arms on the bar.

'Morning, Chat.'

No answer. For once, Chat hadn't even looked up. When I saw what he was reading, a shiver trickled down my back.

'Chat,' I said.

'Oh.' Chat took off his reading glasses, clearing his throat. 'Sorry. What was that, Dreamer?'

Chat never looked anything less than stone-faced. Now he was almost feverish.

'It's payment day,' I reminded him.

'Right. Course it is.' He showed me the penny dreadful. 'Have you read this?'

I took it, trying not to look too interested. Grub Street usually printed in black and white, but they had added red ink to this one, as they had for *On the Merits of Unnaturalness*.

'No,' I said. 'What's it about?'

'Scion.'

'Wow.' I smiled. 'You've the money now, or will I come back another day?'

'No,' Chat said. 'I've got it.'

He went to the back of the cookshop, a deep ruck in his brow. I ran my fingers over *The Rephaite Revelation*, my smile widening. The thousand pounds from Terebell had clearly been put to good use.

Grub Street had paid an illustrator – probably a medium – to bring the words to life. Beneath the dramatic title, a Reph and a Buzzer were locked in mortal combat. The Buzzer had been drawn as a melting corpse, with stretched limbs and white orbs of eyes. Beside it, the androgynous Reph was a work of art, all sinew and divine strength. It wielded a great sword and a shield bearing the anchor.

'Here.' Chat returned with an envelope. 'Send Binder my regards.'

'Of course.' I took a small cut of the notes from inside and offered them straight back to him. 'For training me. We appreciate it, Chat.'

'Not a problem.' He tucked the notes into his shirt pocket before he picked up *The Rephaite Revelation* again. 'You should get one of these, give it a butcher's. I don't usually read these rags, but this is good stuff, proper stuff.'

'It does look interesting.'

'I don't know how the writers came up with it. It says there are these beings that came to London for voyants, because they need us so much, and Scion was built to help them find us.' Chat flipped a page, shaking his head. 'Imagine that.'

'Imagine,' I said.

'It's not *real*, mind. That's just how they're selling it. You'd have to be barking mad to believe giants are running Scion. Still, it's a cracking good read.'

'Some people think voyants aren't real, in the free world. We don't know what's out there.' I lifted my silk back over my face. 'Have a good day, Chat.'

Chat grunted.

Nell had a promising career ahead of her. Now this was out, I imagined Grub Street would be happy to offer her a permanent contract.

I walked out of the cookshop, into the watery sunlight. The breeze had a sharp chill in it, reminding me it was almost November. Just two days left until the scrimmage.

For a week, I had kept training with Chat and Nick. I had also worked on my dreamwalking, armed with new techniques. At first, Nick had volunteered as my target, but ruefully stepped down after his tenth nosebleed. Jaxon had bribed Danica next. I had barely touched her dreamscape before she trudged away to give Jaxon his coin back.

And so I danced alone, taking my record player to the courtyard. I fell constantly, but now and then, I could keep my footing. With each session, my jumps got faster, and I left more of my awareness behind.

Nick waited for me on a bench, his face tipped into the luke-warm rays. He looked up at me.

'Got it?'

I nodded. 'Let's head back.'

'I need a coffee first.'

'You'll get no argument from me.'

There was a coffeehouse under the den, but it was a front, selling glorified dishwater. Our local was Sugar Tin, tucked away in Tower Court. Inside, a few voyants were sipping coffee, hidden from the eyes of Scion.

No less than six of them were holding copies of *The Rephaite Revelation*.

'Grub Street just published a penny dreadful,' I said casually to Nick, once he had ordered our usual. 'I hear the writers are new to the scene.'

'Oh, really?' he said, smiling. 'I might take a look. What's it called?'

'*The Rephaite Revelation.*'

He stared at me.

'Paige,' he said. 'Please tell me you didn't.'

I tilted my head. 'Didn't what?'

'Jax will go *spare* if he thinks you're muscling in on his pamphle-teering,' he hissed. 'He's going to guess right away that it's you.' His eyes were round as bottle tops. 'What were you trying to achieve?'

'It tells voyants what they're up against,' I said under my breath. 'Nashira was counting on the Rephs being a secret until they *choose* to announce themselves. I want to hear their name on the street and know that we've undermined her, even if it's just through gossip.'

'Jaxon is going to kill you.'

'I'm his shiny dreamwalker,' I reminded him. 'He needs me to win the scrimmage.'

Nick pinched the bridge of his nose and made a low sound of frustration.

'It'll be fine, Nick,' I said. 'It's done, anyway.'

'It's done,' he agreed wearily.

The waitron brought our drinks and pastries, refusing payment, as always. It was a short walk back to the den, but we moved at a brisk pace.

Three days before, a squadron of Vigiles had come through Seven Dials, knocking on random doors to ask questions. Jaxon had rushed us into the bolthole. By a stroke of luck, the Vigiles had left the den alone, and the whole district had kept its silence, but it had shaken everyone.

Nick took his courtyard key from his pocket. 'I don't want to witness what happens next,' he said grimly. 'Let's do your training first.'

'If you insist.'

'Have you heard from Warden?'

'He's gone off somewhere with Terebell. I'm sure he'll come back soon.'

'At least he's making his own way.'

Thinking of him sent an odd, warm feeling through my bones. He had been gone for days. Even if I hadn't yet decided on my answer, I wanted to finish the conversation we had started in the music hall.

In the courtyard, Nick dropped his coat on the bench and stretched his arms above his head. His smooth blond hair glinted in the sun.

'How are you feeling about the scrimmage?'

I drank my coffee. 'As good as you *can* feel, knowing you're about to fight to the death.'

'You're going to be fine. Remember, be quick. That's your advantage,' he said. 'And keep eating.'

'Fine by me.' I took a bite of my pastry. 'Where's Zeke?'

'Coram Street. He's checking on Harriet.'

One of our quieter poltergeists. 'We haven't solved her murder yet, have we?'

'No. Zeke feels sorry for her, so he goes there to talk to her sometimes.'

'That's sweet of him. You should take him for dinner when he gets back.'

He shot me a smile. 'I want to, but he's always busy when I'm off work, and there aren't too many places we can go discreetly around here. Jaxon's boundlings are never too far away.'

I considered his tired face. 'Don't you ever find it hard to stomach?'

'Of course,' he said. 'But being with him quietly is better than not being with him at all.' With that, he stood and took a defensive stance. 'That's enough wallowing. Come on. You have a scrimmage to win.'

'So I do.'

He kept me in the courtyard for an hour – punching and dodging, feinting and ducking, doing pull-ups on the tree. At one point he pulled a wisp out of nowhere and flung it in my face, throwing me off my feet and sending both of us into fits of laughter.

By the time he let me off for the day, I was aching all over, but pleased with my progress. I sat down on the bench to catch my breath.

'Okay, sötnos?'

'Fine.' I flexed my hand. 'Any chance you could get me a brace for my wrist?'

'How is it?'

'It's holding up.'

'I'll take a look at it later. And yes, I can get you a brace.' He glanced at the windows. 'Go on. You should give Jax that money.'

'All right. If I don't come back, assume he's killed me.'

'Don't even joke.'

I went upstairs to shower before changing into fresh clothes. Leaving my hair wet, I knocked on Jaxon's door.

'What?'

'It's Paige,' I said.

A daunting silence followed. I went in.

He sat on the couch, hunched over, hands clasped like a bridge between his knees. For once, he wasn't drunk, but in his lounging robe and striped trousers, he looked small and exhausted in a way I had never thought possible.

'Chat's tax,' I said.

'You know where it goes.'

He watched me, his gaze unnerving. I tucked the money into his bejewelled coffer.

'Take half for yourself,' Jaxon said.

I paused. 'That's a lot.'

'Yes, Paige.' He lit a cigarillo. 'Don't you deserve it?'

This was definitely some kind of trick. Usually he made a big show of our pay packets, and I couldn't remember the last time I'd had that much money from my work. After a moment, I took half the notes and stowed them in my jacket before he could change his mind.

'Well,' I said, 'thanks, Jax.'

'Anything for you, O my lovely.' He held up the cigarillo, studying it. 'You know I *would* do anything for you, don't you, darling?'

I tensed.

'Yes,' I said. 'Of course.'

'Of course. And when I have risked my neck, my section and my Seven Seals to come to your rescue, I do not expect outright

344

mutiny.' He reached for his reading material. 'Something was delivered to me this morning, while I was enjoying my breakfast.'

I tried to look interested. 'Oh?'

'Oh, yes. Oh, dear.' He shook out the penny dreadful, his face stiff with disgust. '*The Rephaite Revelation,*' he read out in a mocking tone. '*Being a true and faithful Account of the Creators of Scion, and their Reaping of Clairvoyants.*' With a flick of his wrist, he tossed it away. 'From the quality of the writing, I might think this was Didion, but Didion Waite is about as inventive as a sack of potatoes. And however offensively this hack forms their words, it certainly stretches the imagination to breaking point.'

Suddenly he was inches from my face, his hands gripping my arms. His fingers bit deep enough to bruise.

'When did you write it?'

I stood my ground. 'I didn't write it.'

His nostrils flared. 'Do you take me for a fool, Paige?'

'It was one of the other fugitives,' I said firmly. 'She was talking about writing a pamphlet. I warned her not to do it, but she must have—'

'—asked *you* to write it?'

'Jax, I couldn't write something like that to save my life. You're the pamphleteer.'

He eyed me.

'True.' Smoke curled from his mouth. 'You are still in contact with these fugitives, then.'

'I've lost track of them now. Not all of them have wealthy mime-lords, Jax,' I said. 'They needed some way to support themselves.'

'Of course.' The anger seeped out of him. 'Well, there's nothing to be done about it. It will all be dismissed as fanciful nonsense, mark my words.'

'Could I see it?'

Jaxon cast me a withering look.

'Next I'll be catching you reading Didion's poetry on the sly.' He waved me away. 'Off with you.'

I fished the penny dreadful from the floor and left.

He would find out about my involvement. He was probably calling Grub Street whenever he had a spare minute (which seemed to be every minute), demanding to know the identity of the author. I wanted to trust Alfred, but he and Jaxon had been friends for a very long time – longer than I had been alive. In the end, the secret would come out.

The first thing I noticed in my room was that several things were out of place. The magic lantern. My chest of trinkets. Even my backpack and my red dress had been moved. I checked my pillow and found the stitches untouched. Jaxon really was overstepping the mark.

I took *The Rephaite Revelation* to my bed. Lying on my front, I flicked through to the chapter where Lord Palmerston was faced with his terrible choice.

When in the morning Palmerston rose and made his way to the Octagon Hall, there the creature stood again, decked in her finery, a perfect queen in all but name. 'Bright one,' he said, 'I fear your request will not be granted. Though I have tried to persuade the high lords of your good nature, they think my brain addled by laudanum and absinthe.'

And the creature smiled, as beautiful as she was strange.

'My dear Henry,' she said, 'you must assure the lords that I do not come to harm your people, you who are blind to the spirit world. I come only to liberate the clairvoyants of London.'

My brow furrowed.

That hadn't been in the original. The word had been *incarcerate*, not *liberate*, and I was sure Nashira hadn't been described as *beautiful*. Had she?

I read further. If it was just one misprint, it would be fine. But no, there were more and more of them, accumulating like a growth of mould on the heart of the story.

Then the lady's shadow fell across the street, and with trembling hands the seer beheld her, and at once, her kindness soothed his wounded spirit.

'Come with me, poor lost soul,' said she, 'and I shall take you to the place beyond despair.'

And the seer rose, and he was overjoyed.

Goosebumps broke out all over me.

This was wrong. Nothing had been written about Nashira's kindness, or its soothing of anyone's wounded spirit. And no, not *overjoyed* – the right word was *terrified*. I remembered it clearly from the manuscript.

In moments, I was down the stairs and racing out of the front door. I ran to Long Acre, where I shut myself into a call box and dialled.

When I had dropped the money to the Spiritus Club, Minty Wolfson had given me some contact numbers, just in case I needed to make last-minute revisions. When Minty didn't pick up – probably in a meeting – I tried Alfred. The phone rang and rang.

'Come on,' I hissed.

Finally, someone picked up: 'Yes, what is it?'

'I need to speak to Alfred.'

'One moment.'

I glanced over my shoulder, checking for Vigiles. Finally, a familiar voice piped down the line: 'Hello, dear heart! How fares publication day?'

'The story has been edited extensively.' I fought to keep control of my voice. 'Who did this?'

'The writers, of course. Did they not tell you?'

The bottom dropped out of my stomach. 'The writers,' I repeated. 'Did they come to Grub Street?'

'Indeed they did. They felt that, on reflection, one of the two factions ought to be firmly on voyants' side. Minty and I happened to agree. The moral ambiguity of the Rephaim might have worked in a novel or play – which Minty would be delighted to publish – but a penny dreadful needs to be punchy. As the Rephs are the less repulsive figures, they were chosen as the *good guys*, to use a colloquial phrase.'

'When was this?'

'Oh, just before it went to press.' Pause. 'I had assumed you knew. Is something wrong?'

My heart was pounding.

'No,' I said. 'Never mind.'

I hung up.

The Rephs in this story didn't feed on humans. There was no sign of the poppy anemone, or the vulnerability of their heels and hands, which I had added to the text before it went to press. They were shown fighting the wicked Buzzers, protecting feeble clairvoyants. It was the beautiful myth, the lie they had told for two hundred years – an epic tale of gods on Earth, defending us from monsters.

Terebell was going to be raging. Her money had been used to glorify the Sargas.

I couldn't blame Minty or Alfred. They had only been doing their jobs – and even if I went to Minty now and pleaded with her to stop the Penny Post, she wouldn't be able to do it. The money was already spent. Besides, neither of them would have any idea why I was upset. It was only a story, after all. Only someone else's story.

Whoever had visited Grub Street, it hadn't been Jos or Nell. Someone must have got wind of our plan – someone who wanted to both extol and protect the Sargas, ensuring they had a spotless reputation. It had to be the Rag and Bone Man. He knew about the Rephs.

And all the writers – the survivors – had been living on his turf.

The Rephaite Revelation couldn't be stopped. What mattered was making sure the fugitives were all right. I refused to lose one more survivor.

Back in the den, I disguised myself properly, bundling my hair into a peaked cap. As I pushed the window up, Eliza walked into my bedroom.

'Paige—'

She stopped when she saw me. 'I have to go,' I said, already halfway out. 'If Jaxon asks, tell him I've had to help Zeke. If Nick asks, tell him I've gone to see the other fugitives.'

'I assume that one is the truth,' she said drily. 'Where are they staying?'

'Camden Market.'

'Oh, I haven't been to Camden in ages. I'll come with you,' Eliza offered. 'Jax needs some more white aster. They sell it cheap on the canal.'

That gave me pause. 'He's out already?'

Eliza glanced at his door. 'Just between you and me, I think he's slipping it into his absinthe. I don't want to get it for him, but you know what he's like,' she said. 'I can't work out what's wrong with him lately. He's going to drink himself to death before he's Underlord.'

If Jaxon was upping his doses, it meant he wanted to forget something. Whatever it was, he would never tell us. I had no room to think about it.

'We won't be shopping. Camden is in lockdown,' I said, 'but I could use your help, if you're free.'

'What are we doing?'

'No time. I'll tell you when we get there.' Just before I vaulted down, I looked back at her. 'If you want to come, bring a knife. And a gun.'

I got a local driver to drop us off at the northern end of Hawley Street, as near as she could get to the Stables Market.

'The Rag Dolls won't let us get any closer to the markets, – couriers, bob cabs, any syndies who operate from outside the district. Don't know what's got into them,' she said. 'You'll have some trouble accessing it.' She held out a hand. 'Fifteen pounds, please.'

I crushed two notes into her grasp and opened the car door. 'Keep the change.'

As she drove away, I shinned up some nearby scaffolding. Eliza followed, looking none too happy.

'Dreamer,' she said, exasperated, 'what is going on?'

'I have to see the other fugitives,' I called back. 'Something's wrong.'

'And you know this how?'

'I just know.'

'Oh, come on.' She let me pull her on to the roof. 'Even voyants don't get to say that sort of shit, Paige.'

'Just keep up with me.'

I took off at a run across a row of lodgings. When I reached the last one, I jumped over a gap and landed in a crouch on the coffee-house at the end of Hawley Street. I continued to its highest point to survey the scene below.

Chalk Farm Road was busy, the pavement thronged by amaurot-ics and voyants. A short way down the street, to our right, was the entrance to the Stables Market. For the time being, it didn't look guarded.

I looked to my left. Under the railway bridge, a Rag Doll slouched against the wall, blue-haired and armed with two pistols, but she was too far away to pick up on our auras. Eliza appeared behind me.

'Paige, I'm not Nick,' she said. 'I only run if someone is chasing me.'

'Pretend someone is chasing you. They might be, if we're not careful.'

She noticed the Rag Doll. 'We can't sneak in there.'

'Yes, we can. We just need to be quick.'

When no one seemed to be looking, I climbed down the build-ing, using its awning to slide to the ground. As soon as Eliza had made it, we dashed across the street, under the archway reading STABLES MARKET. I pulled Eliza straight under a stall so I could get my bearings.

'Are you off the cot?' she hissed. 'You heard what the cabbie said!'

'I heard,' I said. 'I want to see what the Rag Dolls have to hide from the rest of us.'

'Who cares what the other sections do?' Eliza despaired. 'Your shoulders aren't big enough for the whole of London's problems, Paige.'

'If Jaxon wants to be Underlord, his shoulders need to get a little wider. So do mine, if I'm to be his mollisher supreme.' I took a deep breath. 'Okay. We're heading for a shop called Camden Lockets.'

'I've been there,' Eliza said darkly. 'I treated myself to a necklace, but it was fake.'

I looked at her. 'Did they ever sell aster?'

'Not that I knew about.'

Agatha had claimed she had once stored it in the cellar. I nudged Eliza out from under the table.

'There are grilles on the ground here and there,' I told her. 'Avoid them. The Rag Dolls will be able to spot us from the tunnels.'

'What tunnels?'

'I'll tell you later.'

The Stables Market was busy at this time of the morning. We made our way between stalls and through shops and under dusty chandeliers, keeping a constant lookout for Rag Dolls. Anyone here could be working for them. The moment I sensed an aura, I moved out of sight, towing Eliza with me. By the time we got close to Camden Lockets, I had spotted five voyants in blazers, armed with spools, not seeming to care who they intimidated as they stalked around the place.

I wished I had asked Warden for alysoplasm. If my gift was concealed, I would tempt less attention. Still, Eliza and I managed, finding holes in their defences. Between us, we reached the right place.

Camden Lockets was boarded up. A sign on the door read CLOSED FOR RENOVATION, and another group of Rag Dolls stood outside. One of them – a bearded medium with wiry green hair – had a carton of food balanced on his knee. The others were on high alert.

I switched my focus to the æther. There were multiple dreams-capes underneath the market, patrolling the Camden Catacombs. The survivors' were not among them.

There were four possibilities, and none I liked. Either they had been murdered, dosed with alysoplasm (that one was unlikely), taken out of the district, or captured by Scion.

Cold sweat covered my skin. I needed to find out what had happened, and if the Rag and Bone Man had posted six guards around Camden Lockets, there must be something in there. If they were just waiting here to ambush me, they would be hiding, not strutting about with spools.

One of the survivors might have been able to leave me a message, a clue as to what had befallen them. The only way to find out was to look inside.

'Paige.' Eliza grasped my arm. 'Were the fugitives in there?'

I nodded. 'I need to get in. Think you can distract the Dolls for me?'

'You *can't* go in there, Paige. Imagine if someone tried to sneak into one of our buildings. Jaxon would—'

'—beat them senseless, I know.' I wouldn't need to worry about that; if this lot caught me, I was dead. 'Once you've led them away, I want you to get back to Seven Dials.'

'You'd better pay me for this, Paige. You owe me two weeks' wages. Two *years'* wages.' When I just looked at her, she sighed. 'All right. Give me your hat.'

I took it off and passed it to her. 'Remember,' I said, 'don't wait for me.'

'Nick will kill me if I leave you here.'

'He'll understand.'

'Have you *met* Nick?'

'Please, Eliza.'

With a last glare, she crawled from our hiding place. I waited, watching the shop.

Eliza was a master of distraction and quick getaways, even if she hadn't done much legwork since Jaxon had employed me. After a couple of minutes, I saw her emerge from a haberdashery, wearing a stolen pair of cinder glasses and my hat, clearly trying to look as shifty as possible. As soon as the Rag Dolls caught sight of her, they stiffened.

'Hey.'

Eliza made towards the nearest passage. A Rag Doll with lavender hair picked up his rifle.

'Charvet, stay here,' he said. 'I don't like the look of her.'

'Yeah, all right.' The man in question looked up from his food for long enough to roll his eyes. 'It's not like there's anything to steal in here.'

'Well, if there is, and it goes missing, you'll be the one explaining things to Chiffon. And she's not in the best mood these days.'

Eliza broke into a run, and the Rag Dolls shot after her. As soon as they were gone, I circled around to the back of the shop, avoiding the remaining guard.

There had been a small window in the cellar, which had been left slightly ajar, presumably for ventilation. It was a tight squeeze, but I just about got myself through the gap.

The cellar was empty. The mattresses had been removed, but everything else was the same. To the untrained eye, there was nothing out of the ordinary.

Broken glass glistened in the light from outside. As my eyes adjusted to the gloom, I searched the floor and walls.

That was when I noticed. One of the bookcases around the room was now empty. I crouched beside it and traced a smear of dry blood across the floorboards. It disappeared under the bookcase.

Agatha claimed to have stored aster here once. I was starting to wonder if the Rag and Bone Man had given her another role. If Camden Lockets sat on top of a bolthole – not just a hiding spot, but a way out of the district in case of raids. If someone had been trying to discreetly move the fugitives, they had been in the perfect place.

I dug my fingers in behind the bookcase and pulled. It swung open on well-oiled hinges. Beyond it was a narrow stone passage, too low for me to stand up straight. Cold, musty air drifted out, unsettling my hair.

A sensible part of me told me to wait until I had backup, but listening to that voice had never got me anywhere in life. I took out my torch and walked inside, leaving the bookcase ajar behind me.

It was a long walk. The passageway started off small and nondescript, with barely enough space for me to extend my elbows beyond my ribcage, before it widened again. I had to keep my head down and my shoulders hunched to keep from knocking myself out on the ceiling.

As I walked, I tried to sense Eliza, but her dreamscape had already disappeared into the moil. I hoped on hope that she had got away from the Rag Dolls, or she would be the next person to vanish without a trace.

I shook myself. Eliza had cut her teeth on burglary and high-risk pickpocketing. She would be able to elude the Rag Dolls. I forged on.

Soon I was peering into the Camden Catacombs through a grille in the side of the tunnel. It was too dark to make out much, but I could see enough to unnerve me. The whole market seemed built for spying and surveillance.

I was starting to suspect that Ivy's trust in her old kidsman had been misplaced. Agatha had been the gatekeeper of the Rag and Bone Man's lair – and something else, from the looks of it. Our bolthole only took us a short distance away from the den. This one seemed to leave Camden.

Nerving myself, I continued down the tunnel. At some point, my torch gave a flicker and went out, leaving me in absolute darkness. I tapped my watch to make it glow. At least if I got lost down here, Warden might be able to follow the golden cord to me. Using my hands to navigate, I kept going, bumping my head every few paces, until I emerged into a passage with the distinctive arched ceiling of the London Underground.

I drew back at once, one hand on my revolver.

The tunnel was deserted. A lost station, but not part of the Pentad Line.

A small train waited. It only came up as high as my waist. The ends were painted red, the central parts in rusted black. REPUBLIC OF ENGLAND POSTAL SERVICE was stamped in faded gold paint along the side.

Nick had told me about this. In the early twentieth century – after the fall of the monarchy, but before Scion had been formally named – a postal railway had been established to carry secret messages across the new Republic of England. It had long since been abandoned, but Scion must have left its skeleton to rot, along with that of the London Necropolis Railway, which had once transported corpses to Surrey.

Finding this reminded me so much of the Pentad Line that my body started to race with chills. I grasped my knees, breathing hard, as I remembered the Tower of London, and how close we had all come to dying.

My heart knocked against my ribs like a fist. The last thing I wanted to do was climb aboard another train to the unknown, but I couldn't abandon the other survivors. I refused to let them be transported again.

From what I could tell, most of the line was now closed, leaving only one route open. I walked towards the train, wishing I had Danica with me. She would be able to work out how to operate this. Then again, I doubted the Rag Dolls were engineers. It might be as easy as riding a bike.

I found a manual in the train and shone my light on it. Once I thought I knew what I was doing, I slid into the tiny driver's compartment, swearing under my breath. I was starting to hate trains. With a low rumble, the train moved forward, into the dark. Nick was going to kill me when I told him about this.

The darkness pressed on me. This train was nothing like the one that had taken me to Oxford and back – too small, travelling too slowly – but it didn't stop me breaking a cold sweat again. I kept an eye on my watch.

As the train ground along, I stayed aware of the æther, searching for the others. By the time I sensed them, my body ached from my awkward, scrunched position. I stopped the train at the next platform, as nondescript and narrow as the last, and climbed out, my legs numb.

By now I had to be a good few miles away from Camden. The journey had taken a while, but given the size of London, I was probably still in I Cohort.

I walked through another passage and up a winding flight of steps. Next, I climbed up a short ladder, into a tunnel that was so low I had to hunker down. Finally, I spotted a sliver of light on the floor – warm, indoor light. There were fifteen dreamscapes nearby. Ivy, Jos, Felix and Nell were all here, still alive.

Now to find out why.

I slid on to my hands and knees to stop my boots squeaking. When I reached the end of the passage, I found myself looking through a series of slats, the sort one would find on a wardrobe door. I could see the back of an upholstered seat, and a head with short green hair.

Agatha Lamb.

She was facing away from me, staring into a fire. I took in as much of her surroundings as I could, trying to work out where I was. High-backed velvet armchairs, a coffee table and a cheval mirror decorated the area around the fireplace, all positioned on a wooden floor. On the other side of the room was a canopy bed, made up with a dusky pink coverlet, white sheets, and sleek cerise bolsters.

Beside it, a polished nightstand held up a glass vase of pink aster flowers. Now I recognised the scent in the room.

When a door creaked open, I withdrew into the shadows. Agatha turned in her seat.

'There you are,' she rasped. 'Been waiting long enough.'

'May I ask what you're doing here, Agatha?'

My gut tightened.

I knew that voice, low and smoky. I knew the dreamscape, too. When I looked through the slats, even the memory of warmth drained from my body.

It was the Abbess.

21

SYMBIOSIS

A large Community of Vile Augurs is known to thrive
near Jacob's Island, the great Slum of II Cohort. It is my
strong Advice to the Reader to avoid this Sector of the Citadel.
— AN OBSCURE WRITER,
ON THE MERITS OF UNNATURALNESS

'I've come for my payment,' Agatha said. 'You said half of what they've promised you.'

'Once they are delivered, yes.' The light shifted. 'I suppose this is about the shop. You do understand why we had to close it, don't you?'

This had to be the Chanting Lay, the night parlour where the Abbess lived. My hands were sweating in their gloves, my breaths coming shorter.

'The entrance to the tunnel is behind two hidden doors. Nobody would ever have found it,' Agatha said. 'I made good money in that shop.'

'A necessary precaution.'

The Abbess appeared in my line of sight, dressed in a green silk peignoir. Her hair cascaded down her back, thick and glossy, curled into delicate spirals at the ends. Framed by firelight, she took a seat in the armchair opposite Agatha.

'Did the Jacobite wake?'

That name rang a distant bell.

'She did.' The Abbess poured two glasses of sparkling rose mecks. 'It seems her punishment has strengthened her will, rather than broken it. We have the information we require, but it took some … coaxing.'

Agatha grunted. 'Serves her right for leaving my service. I plucked her out of the gutter, and she repays me by running off to work with your master.'

'Be assured, I serve no master.'

'Then why does he never emerge to help you, Underqueen?' Agatha asked. 'Why does he skulk in tunnels while the little people do his dirty work?'

'Those *little people* are leaders of this syndicate. He and I have many friends,' the Abbess said. 'In the days to come, we shall have many more.'

'Many pawns, more like.' A dry chuckle. 'Well, I won't be one. I might be losing my voice, but I haven't lost my wits just yet. If your little endeavour is making enough to keep you in fine jewels and dresses, you can put some coin in my pocket now, Hortensia Smythe. Remember that we speakers can't always control our tongues.'

Agatha held out a hand. The Abbess took a sip of her mecks, not taking her eyes off the other medium.

Endeavour. Leaders of this syndicate. I needed to commit the words to memory, so I could fit them together. *Dirty work. Jacobite.* Whatever was going on here, it went deeper than I had ever imagined.

Another dreamscape was drawing closer to the room, approaching from a lower floor.

'The Rag and Bone Man did have a question for you,' the Abbess said lightly. 'Why did you not inform him about the fugitives immediately?'

'Because I didn't want the Pale Dreamer sticking her haughty nose any further into my business,' Agatha said. (I was almost flattered.) 'You've heard the things a dreamwalker can do. If her friends had gone missing on my watch, she would have been on me like a rat on a corpse, as well you know. I was protecting our enterprise.'

'The Pale Dreamer has proven difficult to manage,' the Abbess said. 'She has an unfortunate habit of worming into places she ought not to be.'

You have no idea, I thought.

'But she will be managed.' She took a sip of mecks. 'Like all the rest.'

'I spent good coin feeding those fugitives before I even found out how much they were worth,' Agatha said. 'I could have let them die, like the other two, and you wouldn't be getting your nice little payment.'

The Abbess tilted her head. 'The other two?'

'The rottie got shot at the Tower. Couldn't do a thing for him. But the seer recognised me.' Agatha huffed. 'A fine memory. She must have only glimpsed me once, and many years ago. Even the Jacobite never knew I was involved, but Maya Carnell did. I had to get rid of her.'

I turned cold.

'A single mistake *can* be dangerous in this business,' the Abbess said.

'I've been in it for a long time. It's time you paid me like it.' Agatha stood. 'I want the money now. You make enough off your Nightingales.'

'Of course,' the Abbess said, her gaze cold. 'Here is your reward, Agatha.'

'Good.' Agatha turned around. 'There you are. It's about—'

A gun went off.

The noise was so close to my hiding place that I only just stopped myself from gasping. Agatha hit the floor, and her spirit came loose from its cord.

'Agatha Lamb, be gone into the æther,' the Abbess commanded. 'All is settled. All debts are paid. You need not dwell among the living now.'

The spirit evaporated. A clipped voice said, 'You didn't want to keep her?'

'Her part in this is over.' The Abbess swirled her mecks. 'Is everything ready, Eustace?'

'Yes.'

'Good. I must … prepare myself.'

The Monk walked across the room, stepping over the body. He wore a grey cowl. 'Hortensia,' he said. 'Are you still taking the lithium?'

'Yes.' The Abbess breathed in deep, holding the arms of her chair. 'You needn't worry about me, Eustace. Our symbiosis is much stronger now.'

'Your body isn't getting any stronger. The last time exhausted you,' the Monk said gruffly. 'They must be able to find someone else with your gift.'

'No one who would keep the secret,' she said. 'Last time it was eight armed thugs – strong, albeit drunk. This time it's a single mollisher. By tonight, Chelsea Neves will no longer stand in our way.'

'What about the Pale Dreamer?'

I breathed as softly as I could. The Abbess rose, emptying the rest of her mecks on to the corpse.

'I want more Rag Dolls around Camden Lockets until the exchange has been made. It will take place on the second of November,' she said. 'Find someone else to take over those premises.'

'It will be done.'

The Abbess drew her hair back and fixed it in place with a clasp. 'I will need some time to … engage him,' she said, her voice flattening. 'Knock on the door and wait for my answer before you come in, Eustace.'

'Are you sure you'll be all right?'

'Yes.' She took his arm. 'Soon this will be over. Our hold will be secure.'

The light shifted again as they left. I waited until their dreamscapes had retreated, then crawled forward and pushed at the wardrobe door, finding it locked from the other side. If I broke it down, the Abbess would realise someone had discovered the tunnel. She would move the fugitives elsewhere, and I might never find them again.

Even with my gift, I couldn't take out everyone in this building on my own. I was going to have to leave the survivors here and return with backup. If the *exchange* the Abbess had mentioned was

360

palming them off to another party, I had a few days to hatch a plan and come back.

I didn't have a few days to save Cutmouth.

The Abbess was going to kill her, just as she had killed Hector. Everyone had thought they were close, but that would have made a perfect cover when he was murdered. I couldn't even picture it – the elegant Hortensia Smythe, rubbing elbows with a slattern like Hector Grinslathe.

My brain was overheating, sifting through the broken clues: *lithium, symbiosis, endeavour.* I had to slot the pieces of this puzzle together, and fast. I could get to the bottom of why the Abbess had killed Hector, but it had to wait. What mattered now was beating her to Cutmouth.

To do that, I had to work out exactly where Cutmouth had gone to ground. I had to crack the mystery no one had yet been able to solve.

Warden had the wisdom of immortality. Jaxon threw fancy words like knives. Nick had been a child prodigy, while Danica could solve complex equations. I might not have any of that on my side, but I had enough wits to have lasted this long. Surely to fuck I could reason this out.

I thought of Ivy, trapped in this building. She claimed to have grown up in the same community as Cutmouth. Ivy had ended up as a gutterling, while Cutmouth had impressed Hector. To be a gutterling, Ivy must have been quite young. If they had left their community as children, they had to have been running from something.

It was a strange word for Ivy to have used, *community.* Not a district or a gang. That word tapped into a memory of reading *On the Merits of Unnaturalness.*

Wait.

There was one vital link between Cutmouth and Ivy. Both of them were vile augurs – Cutmouth a haematomancer, Ivy a palmist.

Tell me where Ivy Jacob is hiding.

That surname. The clue had been sitting in plain sight, and I had missed it.

Twenty-eight years ago, *On the Merits of Unnaturalness* had condemned all voyants who used the substance of the human body in their work. Many had been imprisoned, to ensure they could never harm other voyants. And where had the syndicate seen fit to put them?

Where might they still be taken if they didn't have influence or protection, even now?

Where were their children born?

There was only one place that Ivy and Cutmouth could have grown up together. One place where Chelsea Neves could hide, because no one in their right mind would expect her to return there, if they even knew she had been there at all. I launched back down the tunnel.

Cutmouth was in Jacob's Island.

When I got back into the train, I shoved the lever up as far as it would go. It took fifteen minutes to reach Camden – it went much faster at a push – and ten minutes at a dead sprint to get back to Camden Lockets. When I was outside, I gulped down the fresh air like it was water.

No time to stop. Avoiding the Rag Dolls, I ran from the Stables Market and rushed up Chalk Farm Road, looking for a bob cab. As soon as I saw one, I ran out and slammed my hands down on the bonnet, stopping it. The driver leaned out of the window, glaring at me.

'Hey!'

'Bermondsey.' I climbed in, drenched in sweat and breathless. 'Now.'

'You must be joking,' the driver said, red-faced with anger. 'I'm on my way to pick up a passenger. Who do you think you are?'

'Just get me to Bermondsey,' I barked. 'The White Binder will pay you for your haste.'

That got him driving. 'Where in Bermondsey?'

'Savory Dock.'

He huffed. 'You really are trying to get yourself killed.'

'I know what I'm doing.' I took out my phone. 'It's syndicate business.'

The driver shook his head before turning the car around. I sent messages to Nick and Eliza, using the last of my phone battery, then clung to the door as the cab swung around a corner.

If I was wrong, it would be too late.

It might already be too late.

―――――――

The cab raced across the citadel, crossing the Thames at Southwark Bridge. I willed the driver to go faster. The Abbess had needed to prepare herself – whatever that meant – but she would soon be on her way. When the cab stopped, I threw some money at the driver and ran north.

The fog was thicker on this side of the Thames. I knew my way only from maps. If there was one place in the citadel I shouldn't be going, it was here.

Jacob's Island, a cluster of streets in a crook of the Thames, was among the worst slums in London. Written off as a dreg of the monarch days, it had been decaying since before the Rephs had even come.

After *On the Merits*, several vile augurs had been murdered. Most of those who hadn't fled the citadel had found themselves imprisoned here, separated from the world by the reeking waters of Folly Ditch.

Jaxon had claimed that vile augurs were dangerous and cruel. He had eventually retracted the worst of his remarks, but a terrible mistrust had lingered. Even though vile augurs were no longer officially sent here, the existing prisoners had been quietly kept where they were, to stop them from taking revenge on the syndicate. They would have had children since their imprison-ment – children who had never seen the world beyond this corner of Bermondsey.

Ivy had no surname on the screens. A birth here would never have been registered. She had broken out of her cell on our first day in Oxford. She was clever enough to escape.

So was Cutmouth.

Folly Ditch surrounded most of the slum. Once, its waters had been red, stained by tanners' dyes. Now they were greasy brown and stagnant.

Across a short wooden bridge, a grizzled binder stood guard with a rifle. As well as the flooded ditch and a fence, thirty-six powerful spirits surrounded the slum, one from each section of the citadel. Jaxon had contributed a sinister old poltergeist named Herne the Hunter.

A rusted plaque had been nailed to the fence. I read it, jaw clenched.

JACOB'S ISLAND

II COHORT, SECTION 6

TYPE D RESTRICTED SECTOR

Type D was for condemned sites. That was how the syndicate must stop amaurotics from coming too close.

My cheeks were already raw from the cold. The light rain dewed my hair. My curls tightened and frizzed as I stepped on to the bridge, which creaked.

'You,' the binder called. 'What do you want?'

'To enter the Island.' I called up my cold mollisher voice, one that invited no argument. 'I need to speak to one of its residents urgently.'

'No entry without permission from the Wicked Lady or the Underqueen.'

'The Abbess doesn't wear the Rose Crown just yet,' I said coolly. 'I'm the Pale Dreamer, mollisher to the White Binder. Tell the Wicked Lady and the Abbess what you like, but I'm going in there.'

When I tried to get past him, he shoved me back so hard I almost went into the mud.

'I don't answer to the White Binder,' he said, sneering. 'Don't think you can sneak in, either. These spirits will destroy your dreamscape.'

I dug into my jacket and thrust out the money Jaxon had let me take. 'Here,' I said. 'Is that enough for you to let me in and keep your trap shut about it?'

The binder took the roll of money and made a point of counting it. His bushy eyebrow drifted up before he pocketed the lot.

'Take this.' He lifted a chain from around his neck, revealing a small pouch. 'A rare sage from the free world. You won't find it in the Garden.'

'What good will that do me?'

'It wards off spirits. Not for long, but it will get you past the guard.'

I tucked the fragrant pouch under my jersey. It sat below the pendant, soft against my breastbone. The binder undid the padlock on the gate.

'You're on your own in there,' he warned. 'I won't be coming in to get you out.'

'No,' I said. 'You won't.'

With a flick of my spirit, I knocked him unconscious, leaving him crumpled by the gate. Not even the barest hint of a headache followed. I took the bundle of notes from his pocket, returned it to my own jacket, then rose. The spirit guard parted like a set of curtains.

I hadn't known that any sort of sage repelled spirits. A lifetime of clairvoyance, and I still had things to learn.

The gate led into a tight passage. As I walked, *On the Merits* rattled through my thoughts. Extispicists and haruspices used animal entrails, while splanchomancers preferred human ones. Osteomancers burned or handled bones. Haematomancers scried with blood, and drymimancers with tears. The oculomancers favoured eyes, whether they were in a head or not. There might be others.

Despite the chill, sweat was pouring down my face, and my cheeks were burning hot. My heart was pounding out of my chest. Tamping down a surge of foreboding, I thought back to the story Jaxon had told me.

My kidsman worked with two others. All three were osteomancers.

I had never understood his contempt for the vile augurs, even if I had never plucked up the courage to question it to his face. After all, binders used blood in their work, even if the art was different from haematomancy.

Now I wondered. I wondered if Jaxon was vengeful enough to imprison a whole swathe of voyants just to get back at the ones who had wronged him.

On the other side of the passage, smoke coughed from the remains of a pit fire. A stench hit me, turning my stomach – mildew and burning, mingled with sewage.

The streets here were unpaved, trickling with thin streams of water. My boots sank into deep mud. I walked past cramped and rotten dwellings, under the precarious wooden galleries that overhung the narrow paths, dripping with grimy laundry. They were built with billy-sweet, a cheap mortar that never quite dried; I had seen it in another slum, the Old Nichol. There were few doors and fewer windows.

When one of those doors swung open, I hid behind a fence. A small woman emerged. She was thin and pale as bone, with lank blonde hair. I committed her aura to memory. More than three years in the syndicate, and I had never sensed this particular kind of augur. Holding a bucket in one hand, she walked to an old water pump, shoulders hunched. As soon as her back was turned, I darted into a crooked alley.

This was worse than I could ever have imagined. The Rookery had been a palace in comparison. Scion should have razed this place a century ago.

I was too exposed here, even with the fog. Despite everything *On the Merits* had claimed, I doubted the vile augurs would hurt me, but they wouldn't take kindly to my presence, either. Especially not if they worked out who I was. Stopping in a doorway, I reached for the æther.

Cutmouth was here.

I wasn't too late.

She was close. Using her dreamscape as my compass, I emerged from the alley, into the widest street I had come across so far. There was a break in the clouds, and the mist seemed to thin around me, showing more of the decay. A crow took off from a nearby rooftop.

Pain erupted in my shoulder.

A gasp wrenched through me before I could stop it. I reached for the root of the agony. There was something wedged in the meat of my shoulder, cold and curved, with a sharp point. It had carved straight through my jacket and jersey. The next thing I knew, I was yanked off my feet.

I landed hard in the mud and swill. The pain was excruciating. At once, footsteps splashed towards me. With gritted teeth, I reached for my knives, but there were already several hands on me, hauling me up.

A young man swung down from a gallery, holding a crossbow, which seemed to be made of wood and scrap iron. A thin rope trailed from my left shoulder to him.

'Looks like we've caught a trespasser.' Freckles peppered his sunburned cheeks, and auburn curls hung into his eyes. 'How did you get in here?'

'First in a while,' a barbed voice said. 'Is the syndicate doing tours now?'

'Perhaps so,' the young man said, his smile thin. There were shadows under his hollow grey eyes. 'And is it just as you thought, oracle?'

One of the others loosened their grip on me. I made a quick grab for my revolver, but the redhead gave the line such a yank that the hook tore clean out of my shoulder, taking a chunk of me with it. A searing curse slammed against my teeth, but I swallowed it, even as I bled.

'Look,' I heaved out, 'I'm not here to cause trouble.'

'Your weapons say otherwise,' a woman said, her dark eyes flashing.

'I always carry them, for Vigiles.' I took a slow breath. 'Nice crossbow you have there, by the way.'

'We should take her to the Ship,' someone else said. 'Wynn will know what to do.'

The redhead seemed to consider, then nodded. 'Disarm her, if you please.'

I clenched my jaw as they found my holster. My revolver and blades were taken, followed by the knife in my boot, before I was frogmarched towards a boardwalk. Blood pulsed from the tear in my shoulder.

This was a fine state of affairs. Nick and Eliza knew I was here, but if the vile augurs decided to get their own back, nobody could reach me in time.

After a minute of walking in silence, the ringleader pushed me ahead of him, towards a low fence. I could hear the swash of the Thames now.

'What's this?'

I looked up, eyes watering. They had brought me to an old public house, a drinking establishment from the days before Scion. A pale man stood on its steps, barrel-chested and bald, with light blue eyes and a grim set to his mouth. A discordantly beautiful sign hung from a gable above him, spelling out THE SHIP AGROUND in bold silver paint. When I didn't speak, he folded his arms.

'Caught a raider, have you, Lan?'

His accent was Irish. I thought he might be from the south, like me.

'Aleks did. She was sneaking around.' The woman shoved me towards him. 'Look at this aura.'

Blood soaked my shirt and jersey. I clamped my hand over the wound, my brow clammy. Nick would be able to stitch me up later, once Cutmouth was safe. The bald man came down the steps and crouched in front of me.

'Who are you?'

Invoking the White Binder would usually get me out of a situation like this. In this case, it might be a death sentence.

'I'm here to speak to one of your people,' I said. 'She's in serious danger.'

'I take it you don't work for the Wicked Lady, or you wouldn't be creeping around like a rat. Does the gatekeeper know you're here, or did you break in?'

'He knows.'

'Are you a member of the syndicate?'

'Yes.'

'We should ransom her,' Lan declared, to shouts of approval from the others. 'The Unnatural Assembly would have to let some of us out.'

'Vern?'

The voice was high-pitched and curious. A young woman in a pinafore had stepped outside, a bucket in one hand. 'Go back inside, Róisín – it's cold,' the bald man said gruffly. 'Nothing to worry about.'

'Is she an outsider?'

The wind blew strands of brown hair from the left side of her face. A shiver flickered through me when I saw the blue welts on her pallid cheek.

During the later years of the Molly Riots, Scion had unleashed an experimental nerve agent, with devastating results. I had never learned its English name, but the Irish had called it *an lámh ghorm* – the blue hand – after the distinctive marks it left on those who survived it.

Doors and shutters were creaking open, footsteps slapping through damp mud. My throat tightened as the vile augurs emerged from their shacks and surrounded me. A dull thump echoed through my ears.

Their clothes were faded and thinning. Most went barefoot or walked on cardboard fastened to their soles with string. The younger ones were staring at me as if I were something gleaming and bizarre that had jumped out of the river. Two elderly augurs stayed in their doorways.

I was back in the Rookery. I could see the performers, huddled in their shacks. Liss behind the frayed curtain that had served as her front door, guarding the few things in the world that were still hers.

Another woman stepped out of the public house, wiping her hands on a dishcloth. She was in her late thirties or early forties, with dark eyes and freckled brown skin. Her thick black hair was drawn into a fishtail braid.

'What is it, Vern?'

'Aleks caught an intruder,' the bald man told her.

'We *are* busy this afternoon.' She folded her arms, looking me over. 'You were clever to get in here, girl. If only it were as easy to get out.'

Her accent reminded me of my father. Either she was from Dublin, or she had lived there for a long time.

'I don't mean you any harm,' I said. 'Are you the leader here?'

'No. This is a family, not one of your gangs,' she said curtly. 'I'm Wynn Ní Luain Jacob. I'm the healer in this community. Who are you?'

'A friend of Ivy,' I said, hoping on hope that someone knew the name. 'I've looking for someone who grew up here. She sometimes goes by Cutmouth.'

'She's talking about Chelsea,' an older woman shouted. 'Tell her to leave us alone!'

'Enough, now.' Wynn looked back at me. 'Chelsea left us years ago. She isn't here.'

'Yes, she is,' I said. 'I can sense her.'

A few murmurs followed.

'Wait.' Róisín had produced a newspaper, so damp and wrinkled it had to be almost illegible. She held up the front page. 'You're Paige Mahoney.'

My own face looked back at me. The vile augurs fell silent, looking between the photograph and me, matching features to features.

Another hand pulled up my chin, and a man came to stand in front of me, showing rotten teeth as he squinted into my eyes. 'Her hair's different,' he said hoarsely, 'but I think you might be right, Róisín.'

'We could sell her.' A woman grasped my nape. 'She's *preternatural*, this one. Scion would show us clemency. They might let us be Vigiles.'

The dark-haired Irish woman said nothing. My spirit was about to rupture its thin bonds, but I suppressed the instinctive jump, tasting blood.

'Chelsea said the syndicate would be looking for her.' Róisín looked terrified. 'Please, don't hurt her.'

'I just want to speak to her.' I pulled my chin free. 'When did you meet the blue hand, Róisín?'

Recognition jumped into her eyes. 'I was ten.'

'Where?'

'Bray.' Róisín glanced at Wynn. 'Were you there when Scion came?'

The Sack of Bray had been one of the most shattering defeats of the Molly Riots. After a moment, I nodded.

'Éire go brách,' I said.

My first language slid off my tongue. Wynn looked between us, her brow creasing.

'Put her down,' she ordered. The augurs holding my arms let them go. 'You say you can sense Chelsea here. What is it you want to say to her?'

'Someone is coming here to kill her,' I said, raising concerned mutters. 'Wynn, I swear to you, I'm not going to hurt anyone. I just need to ask her what happened on the night the Underlord was murdered.'

'She had nothing to do with that.' Wynn scrutinised me. 'Is Ivy still alive?'

'Yes. But if I can't speak to Chelsea, she'll be in danger, too.'

Wynn breathed in, a muscle feathering in her cheek.

'Vern,' she said, 'take her to Reeds Wharf.'

Lan stared at her. 'You're going to let her see Chelsea?'

'Briefly, and with Vern beside her.' She took the newspaper from Róisín. 'This young woman and Ivy are both fugitives. If we're ever going to see her again, I feel we should help one of her friends.'

'Ivy would never be friends with an oracle.'

'I'm not an oracle,' I said. 'I *am* someone who wants her weapons back.'

'Collect them on your way out.' Wynn folded her sinewy arms. 'Vern.'

He grasped my elbow with a nod, leading me away. 'Go on, Vern. Take out the rubbish,' a grey-haired man shouted from a gallery. 'Don't come back, syndie!'

Vern walked with enormous strides, not looking at me. The stink of sewage lifted as he escorted me away from the public house, replaced by the smell of fish and briny water. A man with aching eyes watched from a shack, wrapped in clothes so filthy they were all one shade.

'I'm taking you to Reeds Wharf. That's where Chelsea is hiding,' Vern told me. 'I'll be coming in with you.' He kept a tight hold on my arm. 'There's already an enforcer here. You mustn't let her see you.'

I looked at him. 'What?'

'The Wicked Lady sends her thugs from time to time. They're meant to check on us,' Vern said, his voice dripping contempt, 'but they only ever come for sport. At least this one has gone about her business.'

'When was this?'

'Not a quarter of an hour before you showed up. First visit we've had since the last time the—' Before he could finish his sentence, I pulled free and broke into a run. 'Oi! You don't know where you're going!'

The Abbess was already here. She had been here before I even arrived. I couldn't feel her dreamscape, but now I knew there was a way to hide in the æther. I sprinted towards Cutmouth, ducking under washing lines and loose slats of wood, my boots splashing through puddles.

She was still alive. The Abbess had to be stalking through the streets, trying to find her. I crossed a rickety bridge, to a stretch of the slum that must be sandwiched between Folly Ditch and the Thames.

A group of children mudlarked in the flooded trench. Seeing me, they fled like a startled flock of birds.

'Hey,' I shouted at one of them. 'Which building is Chelsea in?'

She pointed at the one straight ahead of me. I ran towards it and slammed through a rusty gate, stepping into water that came up to my shins.

'Cutmouth.' I waded to a decayed staircase. 'Chelsea!'

No answer.

Her dreamscape was up there. I started to pick my way between the steps. Most of them were missing, like teeth punched from a mouth. Vern barged in, huffing for breath.

'Not that way!'

A splintering crack underfoot. My boot plunged as the damp wood gave. I lunged for the stairs above me, only for another one to collapse under my weight. I made a grab for the banister and clung.

My shoulder burned where the hook had torn it. As water dropped on to my face from above, I pulled myself up, on to a firmer step. This house was falling apart.

'Chelsea hid up there to avoid the enforcers,' Vern said, frustrated. 'She can lower the rope ladder if we call her from outside.'

'I don't think she can hear us.' I caught my breath. 'I'll find her.'

'Don't you try anything. I'll meet you up there.'

Vern left. At the top of the stairs, I readied my spirit. A wrong step could cause the floor to cave in. I found more stairs, less rotten, leading up to the next floor.

A door was ajar at the end of the corridor. I pushed it open. The room beyond was dim, the broken shutters letting in only hairlines of daylight. It had been turned into a den, with a mattress and a paraffin stove.

And there, lying on the floor, was Chelsea Neves.

I knelt and gathered her into my lap, the rightful Underqueen of London. Her clothes and hair were soaked in blood, her shirt awash with it. Her cheeks had the same precise cuts as those I had found on the rest of her gang, and her fingers were curled around a red handkerchief.

'Chelsea.' I gave her the gentlest of shakes. 'Chelsea, can you hear me?'

Her eyes flickered open. 'Dreamer.'

I searched the æther again, looking for the Abbess. There was a dreamscape, faint and strange, moving quickly. The urge to run after it whipped through my limbs. When I looked down at that scarred face, damp with blood and tears, I stayed exactly where I was.

'I won't leave you,' I said quietly. 'Chelsea, did the Abbess do this?'

'Not alone.'

'Who else?'

Her skin was already freezing, as if death were breathing over her. When her left hand twitched towards mine, I took it. She was still wearing her blouse and dark trousers from the night Hector had died.

'Sorry,' she murmured. 'For all of it.'

'It doesn't matter now.'

Cutmouth managed a tiny nod.

Footsteps thumped on the landing, so hard I thought the whole building would collapse. Vern almost fell into the room.

'Chelsea.'

His fists clenched on the doorframe, his face contorting with anger. Her gaze drifted towards him, but her hand was still gripping mine. 'Wasn't her,' she murmured. Vern clamped his mouth shut, white-faced. 'Dreamer. Paige, they—' I leaned closer. 'They killed Hector.'

'I know,' I said. 'Why?'

A tear seeped down her cheek, smearing blood. 'Tell Ivy. She was—' Her throat shifted. 'Everything. So sorry. She has to … make it right.'

I had watched Liss Rymore die like this, bleeding on a cold, hard floor.

'Chelsea, why did they kill Hector?' I spoke as softly as I could. 'What did he do or know?'

'About Rags. About *them*.'

'The Rephs?'

'Got too greedy. I told him,' she whispered. 'I told him.'

Tears flooded her face, and now they were in my eyes, too. I clenched my jaw.

'Did so much wrong,' Cutmouth whispered.

'The æther takes us all. No matter what we've done.' I stroked her soaked hair. 'Tell me what they're doing. Tell me how to stop them, Chelsea.'

A rattling breath.

'The grey—' Her chest fell and rose again. 'Grey market. Her and Rags, selling us to—' The æther strained. 'The rawhand. She still has it.'

Then she grew limp. Her silver cord broke with a gentle snap, releasing her from her body, and the weight of her grew heavy in my arms.

Vern sank to the floor. I stayed where I was, kneeling in the blood, too shocked to think straight.

'I suppose you think we deserve this,' Vern said. 'That *she* deserved this.'

My voice was hoarse. 'What?'

'What was it the White Binder wrote about us? *Base Practices, primitive and clumsy.* And the best one: *should properly have died out by this era.*' Vern looked into my eyes, his own glinting. 'Why do you hate us so much?'

I couldn't think of a single excuse.

'You think there are really killers in this place – that we oculomancers rip out eyes, or drymimancers torture people for their tears?' he asked roughly. 'You think Binder was right to put out bitter guesswork and call it research?' He hunched over, one hand on Chelsea. 'If the syndicate gets even a whiff she was killed here, it will be the end of us.'

'Binder won't hear it from me.'

'He sees everything. He knows this whole citadel down to its bones.'

Chelsea hung above us. I wished I could ask her more about Hector, but new drifters were usually too bewildered to help the living. No psychopomp would come to guide her to the Netherworld.

The door swung open, and Wynn stumbled into the room. She sagged against the doorframe and closed her eyes, her mouth pinched.

'Is nothing enough?'

'I'll do everything I can to find out why this happened,' I said. 'I'm sorry.'

'Give her to me,' Vern said coldly. I eased her body into his arms. 'Get out.'

He covered her face with the red silk. I stood, covered in blood again, and turned away from their shared grief. Wynn approached the spirit.

'Chelsea Neves,' she said quietly, 'fly into the æther, now. All suffering is past. All deeds are done. You need not linger among the living.'

A different threnody to ours. The spirit evaporated from the room, sent far away to the outer darkness. Vern buried his face in one hand. I looked at the body once more – looked until every detail had burned itself into my memory – before I went back to the corridor and leaned against the wall.

Cutmouth had been cruel and violent. I had used my fists and gift to serve a mime-lord, too. I had obeyed without question, no matter what he asked. All those years we had been enemies, we had been more similar than our pride would ever have allowed us to admit.

Chelsea Neves must have fought her way up the ladder. As a vile augur, she had needed Hector for protection and authority. She must have loathed me for working for Jaxon, just as I had never understood how she could work for Hector.

The door shut behind me. Wynn wiped the blood from her hands on a cloth, looking tired.

'She wasn't a bad woman,' she told me. 'Even after your syndicate took her from her mother and locked her in here, she was kind, even if she was angry.'

'She wasn't born here?'

'No. Until she was twelve, she lived in Lambeth.' She regarded me. 'You look a little younger than Róisín. Did you see much of the Molly Riots?'

'Enough to remember. I was in Dublin.'

'I was there, too.' She unfastened a few buttons on her shirt, opening the top. There was a gunshot scar between her neck and chest, pressed into her skin like a fingertip into soft clay. 'I was the librarian at Trinity College.'

'My cousin went to Trinity,' I said. 'Finn Mac Cárthaigh.'

A thread of dry laughter escaped her. 'Oh, I remember Finn Mac Cárthaigh. He was always disturbing the quiet in my library. I suppose he was killed, along with the others.' I gave her a small nod. 'And now we survivors find ourselves here, in the enemy stronghold.'

'When did you get here?'

'Vern and I went to Wexford straight after the massacre. We joined a group of rebels on a boat to England, hoping to end the invasion at the root,' she said. 'We hadn't been in London for a month before the Wicked Lady put us here. She picked on the vulnerable augurs, those with no one to speak for them. Every day I wish we hadn't crossed the sea.'

I had never spoken to another survivor of the Imbolc Massacre. I wished I could ask her more about Finn, but this wasn't the time.

'The enforcer,' I said. 'Did you see her, Wynn?'

'From a distance. She wore a mask,' Wynn said. 'I didn't think anything of it. When the enforcers come knocking, we try not to be seen or heard.'

'Did Cutmou—' I caught myself. 'Did Chelsea tell you about Hector?'

'Only that he was dead, and that his killers would come after her.' Wynn stepped towards me. 'Tell me you weren't lying, and that Ivy is all right. I loved both those girls as my own. Ivy was only ten when we arrived here, orphaned as a baby. Her parents died here. I looked after her.'

'She's alive, but she's in trouble,' I said. 'I know you have no reason to help me, Wynn.'

'But you'd like my help.'

'The interim Underqueen killed Hector and Chelsea. The Abbess clearly has a vested interest in who rules the syndicate,' I said. 'I'm entering the scrimmage. If I win, I can put her on trial, but I'll need witnesses.'

'The Unnatural Assembly would never accept testimony from an augur from Jacob's Island,' Wynn said. 'Not while the White Binder holds power.'

'If there was a new leader, he might not.'

'If that were the case, perhaps certain other rules could be changed. Perhaps the vile augurs of Jacob's Island would no longer be forced to stay in this small corner of Bermondsey,' Wynn said. 'And we are very happy to help those who help us.'

I returned her gaze and nodded. She took off her oilskin and held it out to me.

'Wear this,' she said. 'You're covered in blood.'

It smeared my hands and chest. My trousers were plastered with mud, to say nothing of my boots.

'If you take this.' I lifted the silk pouch from around my neck. 'It will get you through the spirit guard.'

'Ah. The mysterious sage.' She rubbed it between her fingertips. 'This amount won't get more than one or two people through the guard.'

'I only need one or two,' I said. 'The scrimmage is being held on the first of November. I don't know where yet, but I'll leave you a note in the call box on Long Acre.'

'Will they let us in?'

'I'll make sure they do.'

'Then I accept your invitation.' Wynn hung the pouch around her own neck. 'Your weapons are waiting at the gate. I hope to see you again soon, Paige Mahoney. For now, leave us to mourn. And please, help Ivy, wherever she is. This will break her heart.'

22

HIGHGATE

There was poison in the blood of London. Cutmouth had been weak and afraid, but her last words had been chosen with care.

I picked up my weapons and left the slum, passing the unconscious gatekeeper. The spirits attacked at once, but my pendant deflected them, and they left me alone.

In just a few hours, I had witnessed two deaths and uncovered a conspiracy. I couldn't see the depths of it, but Chelsea Neves had brought me one step closer.

At first glance, it looked simple. The Abbess had murdered Hector and Chelsea. Her friendship with Hector had been a ruse, designed to lower his guard. She had done it to gain power, and that was the end of it.

Except the Abbess wasn't trying to make her position as Underqueen permanent. Her name hadn't been on the list of candidates.

The Rag and Bone Man was involved. That much, at least, was clear. Their public enmity must be a smokescreen to conceal their alliance. But *he* wasn't entering the scrimmage, either. I couldn't work out how his knowledge of the Rephs might connect to the murders, but it must.

Ivy was the only person left who might possess the missing link that tied all this together. Now the Abbess had her, and I had days to save her life.

I should have pried it out of her, that morning in Camden, when she had admitted to knowing Cutmouth. Now she and her knowledge were under lock and key.

The fog still hung over Savory Dock. When I reached the Thames, I washed the blood from my hands and the mud from my boots. The oilskin came down to my shins, hiding most of the other stains.

'Paige?'

I turned on my heel as I rose, drawing my knife. Nick raised his hands.

'It's me,' he said, staying calm. 'It's just me.'

'Sorry.' I sheathed the knife. 'Sorry, Nick.'

'It's okay. We brought the car.' He took a step towards me. 'Are you all right?'

I nodded, then shook my head. He ushered me towards the car, which had its headlamps on. I clambered into the back, and he joined me.

'Sorry we didn't come sooner.' He closed the door, and Zeke started driving. 'Jax is in the silent phase of anger, Paige. Where have you been?'

'How did you get to Bermondsey?' Eliza demanded. 'I left you in Camden, about to sneak past the Rag Dolls. We've been worried sick.'

Her hair was beautifully curled, red tint shining on her lips. I rasped, 'Why are you so dolled up?'

'We're on our way to Old Spitalfields.'

My thoughts were slow.

'Right,' I said. 'To see Maria.'

'Yes. Jax thinks we should give the Garden a break until he's Underlord. He told you this yesterday,' Eliza said, her voice thin with impatience. 'Paige, will you please just explain what's going on?'

'I need—' I gripped the door. 'I need a minute. Zeke, can you pull over?'

'We really have to get over there,' Zeke said ruefully. 'We're already going to be late.'

'I found Cutmouth,' I forced out. 'I found her in Jacob's Island.'

Zeke slammed on the brakes, jolting us all forward. 'She was here?'

'You went to Jacob's Island, of all places?' Eliza stared at me. 'Paige, you're the White Binder's mollisher. Are you *trying* to get yourself beaten to a pulp?'

'The Abbess killed Cutmouth there,' I said. 'Turns out she also killed Hector.' They looked at each other. 'She's also imprisoned the Bone Season survivors, and I think she's in league with the Rag and Bone Man.'

After a silence, Nick released his breath. 'You found the body?'

'She was still just alive.' I opened the oilskin, showing them. 'I ... stayed with her.'

When Eliza saw the rusty bloodstains on my jersey, she lifted a hand to her mouth. Nick closed his eyes for a moment. 'How was she killed?'

'Same as the Underbodies.'

'Zeke, keep driving.'

Eliza raised her eyebrows. 'Are you serious, Nick?'

'Paige found both Cutmouth and Hector. If that gets out, no one is going to think it's a coincidence. We should keep our appointments, to help establish an alibi.' He looked at me. 'That oilskin doesn't fit you. Zeke will lend you his jacket. Can you do this, Paige?'

He was the Red Vision now, cleaning up our messes. I nodded once.

Zeke got the car moving. Seeing me shiver in my damp clothes, he turned up the heating.

'Paige, I'm going to need you to keep talking,' Eliza said. 'How did you find out about the Abbess?'

'I'll tell you. Hold on.'

I shucked the oilskin. My trousers must have blood on them, but they were dark enough to hide it. As I reached up to remove my jersey, Nick stiffened.

'Paige, your shoulder. That's your blood.'

'Yeah.' I winced at the pain. 'One of the augurs shot a hook at me.'

'Let me see.'

I got the jersey off, then peeled my damp blouse away from my shoulder, tensing at the flare of pain. Nick leaned across to examine it.

'Eliza,' he said, 'my kit is under your seat.'

As Zeke drove us back across the Thames, Nick cleaned and dressed the wound. I told them how I had taken the secret train to a building I thought was the Chanting Lay, where I had seen Agatha die. How I had raced to find Cutmouth, just in time to hear her last words.

'The rawhand,' Eliza murmured. 'That's the mark of the Rag Dolls, isn't it?'

I looked at her. 'That's what it's called?'

'Yeah. They have it inked here when they join.' She patted the top of her right arm. 'If they leave the gang, they're not allowed to visit a removal clinic. The Rag and Bone Man burns it off with a blowtorch.'

'How do you know?'

'I spent the night with a Doll a few years ago. Dowling, or something?' Eliza said. 'I saw the tattoo, obviously. He told me about it.'

'Dowlas,' I said slowly, wondering if I should mention that he was dead.

'That's it.'

'So if the Abbess still has this rawhand, it means she's working for the Rag and Bone Man?' Zeke stopped at a red light. 'The guy she's supposed to hate?'

'I can't imagine otherwise, or he would have burned it off her.' Eliza glanced at me. 'Do we really think she could have killed the Underbodies?'

Not alone, Cutmouth had whispered.

The car passed a squadron of night Vigiles. Zeke locked the doors and looked straight ahead. One had his gun pointed at a kneeling amaurotic; another man seemed to be pleading with him. As the car rounded the corner, I glimpsed the Vigile raising his truncheon, and the two men crouching on the pavement with their hands over their heads.

'Paige,' Nick said, 'the Abbess could have killed you at the end of that tunnel. You should never have gone in. If you'd had some backup—'

'I did take Eliza as far as the shop,' I said.

'I would have gone all the way,' Eliza pointed out.

'You got used to fighting on your own in Oxford,' Nick said. 'You need to remember we're here for you now. No matter what you do.'

I nodded and leaned against him, tired to my bones. He drew me to his side.

Zeke parked on Commercial Street, where he unfastened his jacket and handed it over. He was broader and slightly taller than me, but it was a decent fit. I turned up the sleeves and waited for Eliza, who took a large rectangular package, wrapped in paper, from the back of the car.

'Act natural,' Nick told us.

Eliza shut the door. 'Don't we always?'

'No.'

The Garden was our black market, but pitches there were both expensive and competitive. Many voyant traders operated within amaurotic markets, the richest of which lay in one section of the citadel. Collectively named the Splendid Four, they were Leadenhall, Petticoat Lane, Farringdon Market, and the largest, Old Spitalfields.

Ognena Maria ran the voyant side, assisted by her mollisher, Witcher Cully. Between them, they selected voyants to infiltrate the Splendid Four and taught them how to hide their goods in plain sight. Old Spitalfields served as the main amaurotic foil to the Garden, selling every sort of product under its roof, which was made of cast iron and glass. I kept my head down, hiding behind my scarf.

Zeke stopped at a stall displaying chatelaines and other antiques. 'I'll catch up,' he said to Nick, who nodded.

I kept pace with the other two. 'I hope Maria likes this,' Eliza said, gathering the painting close. 'You know her, don't you, Dreamer?'

'We're on good terms,' I said.

'She wanted Dreamer for her section,' Nick said. 'It's a sore spot.'

'Really?'

Nick smiled. 'Dreamer used to live in the Barbican, which is in her territory. Maria and Jaxon argued over it, but she dropped it, in the end.'

Maria had made that observation the first time we had met. My initiatory assignment for the Seven Seals had been on her turf, in Farringdon. If I hadn't worked for Jaxon, this was probably the section I would have picked – busy, interesting, and smoothly managed.

Still, I had chosen Jaxon over Maria. That was one rod I had made for my own back.

I trailed behind the others. Stalls that sold forbidden items were easy to clock, if you knew the signs. They tended to be tucked into the darkest corners of the market, close to the exits. When we passed one, I broke away to see its wares. Noticing my aura, the seller indicated four items.

'Special offer on these today.'

'Thanks,' I said.

Some numa were easy to hawk in the open. Scion knew certain voyants used objects to reach the æther, but even they couldn't exactly ban cups or mirrors. The voyant traders had to hide other items with more care. The locket might conceal a tiny packet of aster.

As I looked at those products, laid out for sale, a phrase Chelsea had used rang through my head.

Grey market.

I shook myself, realising I had lost the others. Giving the trader a nod, I left.

Old Spitalfields had quickly swallowed Nick and Eliza. By the time I caught up with them, Eliza was already deep in conversation with Maria, who was holding court behind a stall of scented candles.

'... exquisite brushwork,' she was saying, 'and the paints have clearly been selected with care, to match what Pieter used in life. You must have extraordinary symbiosis with your muses to produce this sort of work.'

Our symbiosis is much stronger now.

'Thank you,' Eliza said. 'Pieter is my favourite, but I'll bond with any muse.'

'Does it affect you physically?'

'Oh, I'm fine. Binder looks after me,' Eliza said. 'I've been doing this for a few years.'

I had never seen anyone lie through their teeth with such a lovely smile.

'It is remarkable. I can see why Binder has kept you to himself for all these years,' Maria said. 'But if you were to—' She caught sight of me. 'Ah, Pale Dreamer. I was just admiring this magnificent painting.'

I nodded. 'You know she makes dresses, too?'

'I believe you. I was originally going to offer you a stall here in Old Spitalfields,' Maria said, 'but that was before I saw the quality of the work. And ethereal forgeries require careful placement.' She looked between us. 'How would you feel about selling in Leadenhall?'

Eliza was thunderstruck. 'Are you serious?'

'Absolutely. My dear friend Pam has retired to Marseille, and I've been looking for someone talented enough to take over her vacant gallery.'

'Pamela Atwan?'

'The very same.'

'I love her sculptures.' Her eyes lit up. 'You want me to move into her shop?'

'That's what I'm saying, sweet.'

I had to smile. Leadenhall was the most exclusive and beautiful of the Splendid Four, with tiny shops tucked into an ornate medieval building. If anyone deserved to sell her paintings there, it was Eliza.

'That's ... immensely kind of you, Maria, but we'll have to discuss the price of the rent,' Nick said, though Eliza was already trying to hold back tears of joy. 'I take it you charge a premium for Leadenhall.'

'Of course, but the paintings will go for a fortune,' Maria said. 'Eliza can't produce too many of them, for her wellbeing, so you won't be there all month. It will take me a while to find the talent, but I'll get another two artists to share the space with her. They can rotate.'

'Leadenhall.' Eliza turned to Nick, her gaze beseeching. 'Can we make it work?'

'If you're concerned about her safety, I'm happy to say that we've nearly taken the whole of Leadenhall for voyants,' Maria told him. 'I just need to scare off a watchmaker who I'm sure has been there for over a century. Once he's gone, this will be our answer to the Garden.'

'That's remarkable,' Nick admitted. 'I'll talk to Binder, but I'm sure he'll agree.'

'You won't regret it. Muse is the best medium in London,' I said to Maria. 'I'm happy to sell with her, if you still don't mind fugitives on your turf.'

'Oh, it's an honour to have you,' Maria said. 'I'm impressed you risked coming with Eliza today.' She shook hands with all three of us. 'I'll send Cully to Seven Dials to hammer out the fine details in November. Do watch out for Vigiles as you leave. They sometimes come through here on their way to the Guild of Vigilance.'

'Thank you, Maria.' Nick nodded. 'We should get Paige out of here.'

'You go ahead,' I said. 'I'll catch up.'

Seeing my expression, Nick took Eliza by the arm, and they headed back towards the entrance, Eliza glowing with pleasure. I followed Maria to the front of the stall, where she leaned against the table.

'What can I do for you, Dreamer?'

'Just checking on something,' I said. 'You were supposed to investigate those red handkerchiefs on the Underbodies, weren't you?'

'I was, and I did. They were bought on Petticoat Lane,' Maria said. 'The haberdasher puts a hallmark on them, but she sells too many for that information to be of much use.'

The next decision I made could be foolish, but I needed to be sure. I drew the red handkerchief from my boot and showed it to her.

'Is this one of them?'

Maria took it discreetly and ran it between her ring-laden fingers, searching for something. 'It is.' She looked at me. 'Did you take this from the scene?'

'No. From a Rag Doll who tried to kill me.'

'A Rag Doll?' Maria raised her eyebrows. 'Have you told the Unnatural Assembly?'

'No. I don't know if I trust the Abbess.'

'Oh, that makes two of us.' She returned the handkerchief, and I tucked it into my sleeve. 'You remember she wanted to speak to me, that day at the auction?'

'Yes.'

'Well, I met her at the Gilded Anchor. Turns out she was interested in employing twelve of my voyants, including Cully,' she said. 'She offered to pay me handsomely if I released them into her service.'

'What did you say?'

'I refused. Cully has been my mollisher for many years. I couldn't do without her,' Maria said. 'Besides, if the Abbess was coming to me personally, it meant she had already tried poaching the voyants herself, and they remained loyal to me. A few of us still have morals.'

'I see you're not going for Underqueen,' I said. 'Did you not think about it?'

'Oh, I wouldn't dare, sweet. I'm truly surprised there are so many combatants.'

'Why?'

'Hector weakened this syndicate terribly. It will collapse once Senshield comes,' Maria said. 'The last thing anyone wants is to put themselves at the prow of a sinking ship.'

'Then we need someone who won't let the ship sink.'

'Name me one person in the syndicate who could turn it all around at this stage.'

'I would have thought that you could.'

'You're very kind, but I'm content with the authority I have. Binder has always wanted more, and he's willing to kill for it,' Maria said, folding her arms. 'I'm only sorry he's forcing you into the Rose Ring, too.'

'I'll be fine.' Cold needles skittered up my sides. 'I sometimes wish I could go for the crown myself, but I'm told mollishers are ineligible.'

Even insinuating this to her was a risk. Maria had always seemed like a decent woman, but there was no guarantee that she wouldn't go straight to Jaxon with that sort of information.

Still, I had to see a reaction. To know how a member of the Unnatural Assembly would respond to the thought of a backstabbing mollisher as Underqueen.

Ognena Maria considered. 'There's no specific rule against it,' she said, 'at least to my knowledge. And I've been a mime-queen for a decade.'

'But people wouldn't like it.'

'Personally, I wouldn't raise any objections. Some mollishers outshine their superiors,' she said. 'Look at Jack Hickathrift and the Swan Knight. Both brilliant voyants – competent and relatively honest – and what do they do? Bow and scrape for lazy, corrupt leaders who probably maimed and swindled their way into those positions. If either of them went for the crown, I'd cheer their names.'

'Do you think all of the Assembly feel that way?'

'Oh, no. I'd say that most of them would declare you a traitor and an ingrate, but only because they're insecure in their own power. I'd give a chance to anyone who wants to give us hope,' Maria said. 'We're running low on hope in this citadel.' Her smile disappeared, and she snapped her fingers at one of her voyants. 'Poburzaĭ. The candles need restocking.'

The woman rolled her eyes.

'Thanks again for offering Eliza that spot,' I said. 'Send my regards to Cully.'

'I shall.' Maria regarded me once more, the candles flickering around her. 'Whatever you're thinking, be careful, Paige.'

The others were waiting for me in the car. Once I was safely inside, we sat in tense silence for a while, digesting everything we had learned.

'We need to tell Jaxon what Paige has seen,' Nick said, rubbing his eyes. 'I'm just trying to decide which news we should tell him first.'

'Knowing we've secured Leadenhall will put him in a good mood,' Eliza said. 'Then we can bring Paige in to tell him about the Abbess.'

'I don't know,' Zeke said. 'Might be better to leave Leadenhall until *after* the bad news, to put the good mood back in place, right?'

I was getting a headache. It was insane that we had to tiptoe around Jaxon like this.

'There's no point in telling Jaxon,' I said. 'He can't report the Abbess *to* the Abbess. If he lets on that he knows about it, she might just kill him, too.'

Nick tightened his grip on the wheel. Zeke was now beside him, in the passenger's seat.

'After he shot Agatha, the Monk asked if the Abbess had been taking lithium,' I said. 'She told him that her *symbiosis* with someone was strong.' I looked at Eliza. 'Maria used that word. Any ideas?'

'Lithium is a mood stabiliser. A lot of mediums take it,' Eliza said. 'Symbiosis is the relationship between a medium and the spirit that possesses them. I have good symbiosis with Rachel and Pieter now I've been working with them for a few years, but it takes me a while to get used to a new muse. I get unusually tired, or I'm sick, or I feel a lot of pain during the possession, when the spirit enters my dreamscape. Once the symbiosis improves, we reach an … understanding, if that makes sense. The spirit has more respect for my body.'

'The Abbess is a physical medium,' Nick said. 'Could she have used a spirit to kill Hector?'

Eliza hesitated. 'It's possible that she was possessed when she did it,' she said. 'If it was an angry spirit, it would have filled her with its rage – possibly given her some new skills, too. But she had to get through seven voyants to kill Hector, then cut off his head. Being possessed by a spirit doesn't make your body any physically stronger, and the Abbess doesn't look as if she could take down eight people, especially not the Underbodies. They were tough.'

After a moment, I asked her, 'What if the spirit was a poltergeist?'

'No sane medium would let a poltergeist use their body.'

'But let's say she theoretically did, or the possession was unsolicited.'

'I really don't know, Paige. It's a horrible thought.'

'We've all been wondering why the London Monster didn't drive the killer off. It only attacked Paige,' Nick said, clearly on the same train of thought. 'How would it have reacted to a possessed medium?'

'Again, I'm not sure. If it sensed murderous intent, it might have attacked.'

'But it wouldn't have attacked if it recognised the Abbess,' Zeke murmured. 'Maybe that's why she struck up a friendship with Hector.'

'Maybe,' Eliza conceded, 'but a poltergeist wouldn't *need* to possess a medium. They can kill on their own, without a host body. Why bother using a human, who could have been killed in the fray?'

'In all my research, I have never heard of a poltergeist killing more than three people at a time, and three is very rare. They can only use so much apport at once.'

'And poltergeists can only kill in certain ways,' Nick said. 'This murderer wanted to send a specific message.'

We all sat in silence for a few moments, thinking.

'Chelsea said the Abbess and the Rag and Bone Man were involved in something called the *grey market*,' I said. 'Anyone know what that means?'

Nick shook his head. 'If a black market is illegal, I suppose a grey market is … unauthorised. Or tolerated.'

Eliza pursed her lips. 'Are we really keeping this from Jax?'

'Paige is right. We might as well sit on this until he's Underlord, when he'll have the power to investigate the Abbess.'

As they debated, a distant tingle at my senses drew my attention. I hadn't sensed Warden for a few days, but now he was back at the end of the cord. For some reason, the moment I felt it, a sense of impending danger flooded me.

In Oxford, I had sometimes caught small drifts of his emotions. This felt the same.

As I sat there, a realisation unfolded. The Bone Season survivors were trapped in the Chanting Lay. Even if the gang helped me, I might not be able to break them out – but the Ranthen could. Rephs were strong and fast enough to storm the whole building in one fell swoop.

I had to get to them before they disappeared again.

'Nick,' I said, interrupting the discussion, 'you know you're my best friend?'

'Yes?'

'You know you said you'd all be there for me, no matter what I did?'

Nick nodded. 'What do you need?'

'I need you to drive.'

'Drive where?'

'Wherever I say.' I pointed at the windshield. 'Right now, that way.'

'Paige—' Eliza took a deep breath and released it. 'You've had a really long and upsetting day. Let's just get you home so you can lie down.'

'Nick,' I said, through gritted teeth.

'I did say.' Nick started the engine. 'Eliza, you could take a bob cab, if you want to get back.'

'No.' Eliza sighed. 'I'll only worry.'

'Zeke?'

'I'll stay,' Zeke said, sounding curious.

Nick pulled away from the pavement. I reached for the golden cord, focusing so hard it gave me a headache. 'Keep following Commercial Street,' I said. 'I'll tell you when you need to change direction.'

'This is just—' Eliza pressed her temples. 'I got the best news of the last few years, the Abbess is a murderer, and my friend is losing her marbles. All of these things can apparently be true in one day.'

'She isn't losing her marbles,' Nick said under his breath. 'We trust Paige.'

'Nick, she's obviously exhausted and shaken. We should just go back.'

I barely heard either of them. All I could think about was the cord, pulling me towards Warden.

Nick drove north along Commercial Street, glancing at me in the mirror every so often. I shook my head. When Old Street station came into sight, I pointed again. 'Turn right there. Keep going north.'

He did as I asked. We crossed the Inquisitors' Canal, entering II Cohort. By the time we passed Hampstead Heath, crossing the boundary of III Cohort, Eliza was clearly about to erupt with impatience.

'Paige, this is ridiculous.'

'Keep going,' I said firmly. 'We're getting close.'

'Close to what?'

'We can't go much farther,' Nick warned. 'Jaxon is friendly with the Fifth Sister, but his influence only extends so far.'

Still, he kept driving. When the golden cord had shortened enough, I stopped him. Across the street, a streetlamp glowed lavender, slowly cooling to a bright, clean blue. To our left was a gate set into a fence, etched with ornate letters.

HIGHGATE WOOD

'Highgate.' Eliza pressed her brow to the headrest in front of her. 'Why are we in Highgate?'

Zeke peered out of the window, looking nervous. 'Is this ... the suburbs?'

'It might as well be the bloody suburbs.'

'Jaxon is turning you into a snob, Eliza Renton,' I told her. 'Where do you think Ruislip is, if this is the suburbs?'

'I don't even know *what* Ruislip is, let alone—'

'Please, both of you.' Nick looked grim. 'Paige, I trust you, but Eliza is right to be concerned. It's almost dusk, we're in III Cohort, and we haven't asked the Fifth Sister for permission to be on her turf.'

'I'm sending Nadine a message,' Zeke said, already on his phone. 'Just so she doesn't think I'm dead.'

'You all just stay there.' I climbed out of the car. 'I need to find Warden.'

Before they could question me, I was running.

My heartbeat came in heavy thumps. Warden was somewhere in Highgate Wood, and I had no idea why. Now I was close, my awareness of him had widened, making it hard to pinpoint exactly where he was.

Even Scion didn't bother putting cameras in the woods. I lifted my chin free of my scarf and took off my hat as I ran, shaking my curls free. The urgent feeling was still there, tightening my chest. I couldn't breathe.

A twig snapped underfoot. As soon as I heard it, I froze. Suddenly I was back in my pink tunic, hunted by a monster, surrounded by Gallows Wood. I shoved the memory away, trying to keep my breathing steady.

'Paige, stop.' Nick arrived. 'Slow down.'

'Paige,' Eliza called, a short way behind him. 'Did you say Warden?'

'Yes,' I said.

'As in, your keeper?' Eliza reached us, letting out an angry sort of laugh. 'Are you saying he just got here, or have you been sitting on this secret?'

'Jax told me not to talk about it,' I told her. Zeke caught up. 'Warden has been back for almost a month. He's here, and I need to speak to him.'

Zeke raised his eyebrows. 'Warden is in these woods?'

'Yes. I just don't know where.'

'Should we ... shout for him, maybe?'

'No.' Eliza gripped his elbow. 'We can't draw attention to ourselves. If any of the Fifth Sister's people are here, they'll beat the snot out of us.'

'Would they be in the woods this late?'

'We are,' Nick pointed out.

Zeke shone his torch around, his brow furrowing. I had left mine in the car, but Nick and Eliza took out theirs, sweeping them in a circle. For the first time, I noticed the thick white clouds we were all breathing.

'It's cold.' Zeke paused. 'But that cold?'

I looked up, following his line of sight, to a tree. Glassy teardrops hung from the leaves, and ice draped the branches, making them creak. A spiderweb, strung among the foliage, had been transformed to a silver lacery.

We walked between tall oaks and hornbeams. The last glow of twilight had dimmed from the sky, casting the woods into darkness. My breath came short. I gave the golden cord a tug, hoping Warden could sense I was close.

'This is off the cot,' Eliza muttered. 'What are we doing here?'

'You had the choice to go,' I reminded her. 'Nick keeps saying he wants me to call you when I need you. Would you kindly stop complaining?'

'You are being so bloody difficult today.'

'Wait.' Nick slowed. 'Where's Zeke?'

I turned. Zeke was nowhere to be seen.

'Zeke,' Nick shouted. When there was no answer, he glanced at me. 'Can you sense him?'

I found his dreamscape and led the others straight towards it. 'Zeke,' I called as we closed in on him. 'Can you hear me?'

'Yeah,' came the reply. 'Sorry. I'm here.'

I ducked under a low branch, into a small clearing. When I saw Zeke, I stopped dead. He was crouching beside a patch of ice, wider than a maintenance shaft, with the faintest glow.

'Looks like a perfect circle.' He skirted his fingers around the edge. 'How likely is that?'

It didn't look like a perfect circle.

It *was* a perfect circle.

Nick and Eliza caught up with me, the latter slightly breathless. 'Wow.' Eliza walked towards the ice as if in one of her trances. 'What *is* that?'

'Incredible, isn't it?'

My sixth sense was ringing like a set of bells. The woods. The chill. The weight of the æther. My boots were rooted to the ground, my heart thudding.

'Get away from it.' I found my voice. 'It's a cold spot. Get *away* from it, now!'

Eliza tensed. Nick hooked his arms under hers and pulled her away from the ice, while Zeke scrambled to his feet, only to run into someone else – a complete stranger, almost hidden by the darkness. Zeke backed up at once, and we all drew our weapons, becoming one unit.

'We mean no harm,' Nick said, wary. 'Do you work for the Fifth Sister?'

The voyant didn't reply. He was gazing at the ice with something like reverence.

'I found it.' His eyes were unfocused. 'All these years of searching, and here it is.'

He was a rhabdomancer. Many of them lived itinerant lives, searching for a treasure they could sense, but never find. Jaxon thought so little of them that he could barely even muster any contempt.

394

'Get out of here,' I urged him. 'There's nothing but decay in there.'

The cold spot suddenly glowed brighter. I looked at my friends' stricken faces, thrown into sharp relief by its light. I saw the rhabdomancer step forward, tears glinting on his cheeks. He was smiling.

'A way home,' he told us. 'That's what it was, all those years. A way home.'

He took one more step, and the cold spot exploded. A million shards burst up from the ground, blinding us with splinters of stardust. With a scream that echoed through the woods, a Buzzer leapt from the gateway, into London.

23

THE WAX SEAL

With impossible speed, the creature was on top of us. It leapt on the rhabdomancer, clapped its jaws over his head, and ripped it clean off. The body crumpled.

None of us moved an inch, or made a sound. Cold fear held us all in place.

I watched the hulking silhouette. With the light from our torches and the cold spot, I could just make the Buzzer out. It was knotted with swollen muscle, and a spine pressed through its grey flesh like a knife edge. Everything about it was too long, as if it had been stretched: its arms, its legs, its neck. Its eyes were pure white orbs, like moons.

Sweat ran down my back and breastbone. This creature was far larger than the one I had faced in Gallows Wood.

'I can't see it.' Eliza spoke in the barest whisper. 'I just see darkness.'

I wrenched my gaze from the Buzzer to look at her. She was clinging to Zeke, who was holding her just as tightly, breathing out clouds.

'Nick,' I murmured, 'switch off your spirit sight.'

When I heard his quick inhalation, I knew he could now see exactly what I saw. The Buzzer must have some kind of corrupted aura, hiding it from Eliza and Zeke. They were full-sighted, unable to see past it.

Making no sudden movements, I shifted my backpack off my shoulder. Terebell had given me a pouch of salt, which I had decanted into a vessel and topped up, so I could use it for quick pouring. I drew the cellar out and showed it to the Buzzer. I didn't know how much it could understand, but it might sense what was inside.

The Buzzer stretched its neck with a hollow click, then shook its head so fast it almost blurred. It sank its blunt fingers into the earth, freezing it.

I tried to focus on the other three. Their dreamscapes registered like bad signals on my radar. Already the strength was leaving my knees. My vision shorted out for a moment.

The Emim cannot enter a salt circle.

I opened the cellar. The Buzzer looked straight at me. It opened its abyssal mouth, and a terrible scream emerged from inside it, making the others flinch away. I lost all feeling as I remembered that sound – not just one voice, but a thousand agonised moans and wails and sobs, merged into a tortured roar. It struck a primal chord in my body, racking me with sharp chills. My second test came rushing back.

'Run,' I barked.

The others needed no further invitation. We sprinted for our lives, back towards the car. Branches slashed at my face and snared in my hair.

'Paige,' Eliza gasped out, 'what is that?'

'Just run, Eliza!'

I pulled hard on the golden cord. Unless we could outrun the Buzzer, Warden was our only chance. Nick caught Eliza by the hand, rushing her along with him.

Our pursuer was faster than us, and I was growing weak. The ground seemed to cling to the soles of my boots; my limbs doubled in weight. The long day had exhausted me, but I hadn't been drained like this until now.

This feeling was familiar, though worse than it had been in Gallows Wood. This must be a more powerful Buzzer.

The æther was condensing. Thick clots were forming near the creature, like blobs of oil in water, merging into larger ones. Cold sweat poured off me as I groped for my throat, even though it wasn't air I needed. The Buzzer pushed closer, and those drops of oil became a spill, enveloping us all. And suddenly, I could barely feel the æther.

Zeke fell as if his bones had disappeared. Nick went next, taking Eliza with him. I ran back and grabbed him around the waist, trying to drag him up, but my arms were running water and I soon buckled as well.

Stop I need it stop it's like dying can't breathe stop—

My aura constricted, shortening my link to the tainted æther. Suddenly I couldn't sense Zeke, who was farthest away. With a blink, his dreamscape vanished from my perception.

'Zeke,' Nick rasped.

He was shaking hard. Eliza lay beside him, deathly pale, fainting away.

I tried to get up. My aura was a vital organ squeezed in a tight fist, hampering its function. My eyes watered with the effort of staying conscious. I could breathe, but I was drowning. I could see, but I was blind. One of my senses – the most important – was being ripped away.

Can't live stop can't think stop stop—

'Nick.' I had somehow kept hold of the salt. 'Make a circle.'

His breath came in a cloud. 'What?'

'Around us.' I could barely get the words out. 'A salt circle.'

'What about Zeke?'

'Get him to us.' I blinked, on the verge of blacking out. 'I'll cover you.'

I thrust the salt cellar at him, just as the chilling scream came again. Soaked in sweat, Nick cradled Eliza closer to his chest, cupping a protective hand around the back of her head. She was limp against him.

'He's not far,' he said, his voice barely there. 'Paige, can you do this?'

'Only chance,' I said.

The Buzzer loped towards Zeke, blurring with the darkness, white eyes and shadow and raw-boned rage. It opened that bottomless pit of a maw.

I threw my spirit across the clearing.

Most dreamscapes had barriers. Zeke had impenetrable ones, as an unreadable – no spirit could access his mind, even mine. But the Buzzer had no defences at all.

It didn't *want* to keep anyone out.

I hurled myself straight into the black hole. Until I crossed that event horizon, I hadn't known that my spirit could feel pain, as my body could.

Their dreamscapes are like flytraps, ensnaring the nearest spirits. Too late, I remembered that warning from Warden. *Yours included, I should think.*

I had just doomed myself.

A crushing darkness encompassed this dreamscape. There was no light at all. The only way I could see was by the glow of my own silver cord, which revealed that I was surrounded by strange, quaking sludge.

Within the confines of a dreamscape, its owner shaped the form my spirit took. I couldn't see myself in this one, and I was glad – I could feel that I was spindly and skinless, my flesh rotting off the bone. The harder I tried to retreat, the more the mud hauled me back down, and now I was almost consumed, fighting with no strength left.

The sludge was melted flesh and blood. As a scream of denial tore out of me, I thought of something Nick had said.

All those layers of history and death – they made me feel like a morsel, swallowed whole by something that had never even seen me.

A skeletal hand burst up from the sludge and snared me. I threw my weight backwards – trying to escape, to fly back to my body – but it was too late, I was already under.

Now I was the morsel, gone.

No air, no thought, no pain or name. The deeper I sank, the heavier the weight that towed me down, like an anchor. I was buried alive in the mind of a monster.

My silver cord was still attached, but this place would destroy it like acid. I tried to swim, but the dark bound my limbs. A withered hand brushed mine, its fingers limp and inert, the fight gone out of them.

Once, when I was very small, my grandfather had told me about bogs – the deep ones that kept hold of you, no matter how you fought. The ones that held on to corpses for centuries, keeping them whole in defiance of time. The strange lights that might lead you into them.

The Buzzer could be immortal. It would live for ever, with me trapped inside it. Perhaps it would feel my last desperate flutters. I was a moth inside a jar, unheard by the walls I could never escape. I was a body lost to the earth, and I would not have the mercy of death as I decayed. I wondered what would vanish first: memory, awareness, feeling.

As I gave up, one last thought in the void – that I could not have condemned myself to a worse fate than this.

A brilliant light seared into me, dazzling away the dark. At the same time, my silver cord – my harness – tightened around my spirit. It hauled me from the rot, bolstered by the golden cord. I surfaced in the hadal zone, striking away the desperate hands that grasped me. My two entwined cords flung me back across the æther, into my own body.

I took a desperate, heaving breath, the cold in it scraping me clean.

Nick collapsed so quickly he might have been shot, his arm falling across my waist. I looked up, eyes aching, to see the trail of salt around us.

The Buzzer stopped a foot away. It fixed its gaze on me, as if it knew how close it had come to devouring my spirit. I stared back at it, my face bathed in sweat and tears. With one last scream, it stalked away.

The four of us might as well have been corpses. I couldn't so much as lift my head. Eliza curled against my right side, out cold, while Nick was between me and Zeke, his arms wrapped around both of us.

'Paige.' He sounded distant. 'It was screaming in your voice. I heard it.'

As the words sank in, my stomach turned. I retched, my throat burning, agony flooding the front of my skull.

I must have blacked out. The next voice I heard was cool and familiar.

'Hearken to me, dreamwalker.'

My eyes snapped open. Pleione Sualocin surveyed me, her own eyes tawny.

'Are you injured?'

She was standing beside the circle, wearing dark leather, with her black curls swept to one side of her neck. They were secured there with a clasp.

'Buzzer,' I whispered.

'Yes. How did you find us here?'

I tried to get up, but couldn't. Even though I was back in my own body, I still felt detached from myself, like everything was too far away.

'Did you dreamwalk?'

Even my nod was agony. Pleione knelt beside me and reached into her coat, taking out a vial of amaranth. She placed a drop below my nose and dabbed my temples with two more. As I breathed deep, I sensed the æther returning to me and let out a weak laugh, tears welling.

'The Emite is gone, but it will return.' Pleione rose. 'Get up.'

The edges of my vision blurred, but I forced myself to stand, still nursing a headache. I hated how feeble the inhabitants of the Netherworld made us seem. My three years of scrapping paled in comparison to the devastating power of a Buzzer, or the cold strength of a Reph.

Eliza had crawled some way away. She was rocking back and forth beside a tree, grasping herself. With help from the amaranth, I made it to her side.

'I couldn't … feel the æther.' She was trembling. 'It was gone, Paige.'

'No.' I drew her into my arms. 'You'll feel better. I promise it will pass.'

Eliza buried her face in my neck and choked out a sob. 'Is that what it's like, being amaurotic?' she said, sounding wrecked. 'It's so … numb and still and empty. How do they live without a sixth sense?'

I tightened my embrace around her, guilt plucking at my chest. Eliza would never have known this feeling if I hadn't walked them straight into this.

Pleione came over. Eliza looked up at the sound of her footsteps. When she saw the towering woman, with her strange aura and fiery eyes, she let out a bloodcurdling scream. I clapped a hand over her mouth.

'Yeah. That's a Reph,' I said grimly. 'Still think I was hallucinating?'

She shook her head, eyes huge.

'Your friend is injured,' Pleione told me. 'You must bear him to a safer place.'

Eliza was breathing in short bursts, her lips quivering. I bolstered her up and led her back towards the salt circle, where Nick was on his knees, holding an unconscious Zeke in his lap. Seeing me, he swallowed.

'Paige, I can't wake him.'

Zeke had lent me his jacket. I took it back off and wrapped it around him. 'Did the Buzzer get him?'

'I don't know. As soon as you dreamwalked, I got him away from it, but it could have—' He stared up at me, his pallor ghastly. 'Will he die?'

The naked fear on his face disturbed me. I wasn't used to consoling Nick. He was the one who kept us calm, our capable Red Vision.

'No,' I said firmly. 'He's going to be fine. The Ranthen will be able to—'

'Paige?'

I turned, just as Warden stepped from a gap between the trees. The sight of him lifted a weight from my shoulders, filling me with pure relief. He took it all in – the salt circle, the wounded human, and me.

'Paige.' He came towards us. 'What are you doing here?'

'I needed to talk to you,' I said.

Pleione was in earshot. I couldn't explain how I had known he was here, or that he was in danger. Instead, I gave the cord a small tug.

Warden stopped in front of me. He looked as self-possessed as ever, except for his burning gaze.

'There is a corpse beside the cold spot,' he said. 'It is someone you knew?'

'No. It was a rhabdomancer.' A sharp pain in my side made it difficult to talk. Or breathe, for that matter. 'He was just ... standing there.'

'They are drawn towards cold spots.' He looked us over. 'You must be Eliza.'

'Yes,' Eliza said faintly.

'This is Warden,' I told her. 'The other one is Pleione.'

Warden nodded. 'Is either of you hurt?'

'Just shaken, I think.' I blotted my face. 'We can't wake Zeke. Can you help?'

'You should leave these woods first. The cold spot must be sealed, lest more Emim come through,' he said. 'Find somewhere to spend the night, where Ezekiel can rest and recover. I will come to you as soon as I can.'

'We shouldn't take him to Seven Dials.' I looked at Eliza. 'The Old Lyre?'

'No. It's too cold.' She dabbed her upper lip with her sleeve. 'I know somewhere better.'

'Nick, can you carry Zeke?'

'Not as far as the car,' Nick said.

Warden nodded to Pleione. She set her jaw, eyes simmering. Rephs rarely showed emotion, but they seemed to make an exception for annoyance.

'I will carry him.' She approached Nick. 'Give him over to me, oracle.'

Reluctantly, Nick released Zeke, and she scooped him up as if he were a child. I went after them, giving Warden a last glance.

Back at the car, Nick buckled Zeke into the back seat and covered him with his own coat. Pleione returned to the woods. I sat beside Zeke, while Nick and Eliza climbed into the front. Nick blasted the heating.

'Okay,' he said to Eliza. 'Where to?'

'Now it's my turn to direct as we go,' Eliza said. 'For now, just drive towards the Garden.'

Nick drove us away from Highgate Wood. He managed to keep to the speed limit, even as Zeke remained gaunt and silent, his head lolling. His brown skin had taken on a grey tint, deepest around his lips. I kept a sharp eye on him, trying to rub warmth into his stiff hands.

Jaxon was going to be furious, but I didn't care. I wasn't going back to Seven Dials tonight, scrimmage be damned.

Once we were back to our turf, Eliza seemed to recover from the shock of the evening. She directed Nick for a short way, and he parked the car on Bedfordbury, a narrow street to the south of Seven Dials.

We got out of the car. Between us, Nick and I propped Zeke up and followed Eliza towards the painted entrance to an alley I recognised.

Goodwin's Court was a hidden gem of the district, lined with black doors and quaint Georgian shopfronts. The entrance was well hidden, with good reason. This was the only gaslit street in London. The lanterns here burned gold, not blue, reminding me of Oxford.

Eliza went to one of the doors and took a key from her chatelaine. When I saw the tarnished plaque reading THE WAX SEAL, I raised an eyebrow.

'Leon Wax lives here.'

'Yes.' Eliza pushed the door open. 'I'll explain later.'

Nick followed her, supporting Zeke. I shut the door to the chandlery behind us.

Leon was one of the few amaurotics who made his living in the underworld. A jarker by trade, he specialised in forgery. I collected his syndicate tax every month. He didn't pay rent, but his tax was so high that it hardly mattered. Jaxon penalised the amaurotics for their dullness.

Still, Leon had earned his respect. Thanks to his skill and his network of contacts, he had been able to help Jaxon meet Antoinette Carter, as well as provide fake identity cards for the gang. I still had no recollection of Eliza ever meeting him in person. Why she had a key to his chandlery – the legal face of his business – I had no idea.

In the tiny parlour, we got Zeke on to a couch. I pushed at a light switch, to no avail.

'Eliza?'

'No electric lighting in this chandlery.' Eliza took a matchbox from an alcove. 'There's some wood in the hearth. Can you get a fire going?'

With a nod, I accepted the matches. I had watched Michael light enough fires in Magdalen.

The fire was soon crackling. Once there was enough light, I helped Nick ease Zeke back out of his jacket, leaving him in a white shirt and black knitted waistcoat. The firelight lent his skin a misleading warmth.

Nick unbuttoned the waistcoat. The dark wool had concealed a spreading bloodstain. He peeled the drenched shirt back, revealing a crescent of bite marks from his lower waist to his chest, made by a mouth like a bear trap. I had seen the same deep wounds on Warden.

Zeke made a low sound. The skin around the punctures had turned a milky grey, but the blood had already clotted. Nick examined them, sweat on his brow.

'What will happen, Paige?'

'Humans can survive Buzzer attacks. They carry some kind of … corruption, but it only affects Rephs,' I said. 'It must have been trying to take a chunk out of Zeke, or weaken him so it could eat him later.'

'It must have let him go when you dreamwalked. You saved his life, sötnos.' He breathed out. 'Is Warden coming?'

'He said he would. I believe him.'

Nick nodded slowly. He was better under pressure than anyone I knew.

'For now, I'll treat it like any bite,' he said. 'I need a few things from my apartment. Can you two clean him up and keep him warm for me?'

'We can do that,' I said. 'Be careful.'

'I will.'

He left the chandlery. Zeke turned his face towards the door, eyes moving beneath their lids.

'We should clean the wounds with salt water,' I said quietly. 'It will help.'

Eliza watched me. 'What else does he need?'

'I don't know.'

From there, I let her take the lead. Eliza had never been able to visit a hospital, or even a dentist. Instead, she had learned to care for herself and other voyants. So far, she had only lost two of her back teeth.

She fetched a pair of scissors and cut the shirt off Zeke. While she mopped up the blood, I tried to coax water past his lips, to no avail.

'Come on, Zeke,' I murmured.

Zeke shifted without rousing. He looked unwell, but not quite as bad as Warden had looked when the Buzzer had bitten deep into his arm.

Eliza patted the wounds dry. Leaving Zeke to rest, she bundled his bloodstained clothes into a bag. I felt his forehead, finding it clammy.

'Are you all right, Paige?'

I glanced at Eliza. 'It's been a long day.'

'Yeah. Let's just talk about everything in the morning,' she said. 'I could murder a bag of chips, but it probably isn't worth risking my neck.'

'Don't. One of my friends in Oxford was detained on his way to get milk.'

'Point taken. I'll make soup.' She paused. 'Paige, I'm sorry I didn't believe you.'

'It's fine,' I said. 'I wouldn't have believed me, either.'

She smiled and went into the kitchen.

After half an hour, Nick returned with a bag. By that point, Eliza and I were sitting by the fire with steaming bowls of soup. I hadn't eaten since the pastry.

'I avoided the Vigiles.' Nick closed the door. 'Any sign of Warden?'

'Not yet,' I said. 'He doesn't have a car, to my knowledge.'

'How *do* the Rephs get around?'

'No idea.'

'Nadine replied to Zeke,' Eliza said. 'She asked him when he's coming back.'

'You can't tell her.' Nick returned to his side. 'She'll lose her mind.'

'I didn't. I said we'd got stuck in traffic near Old Spitalfields, and Maria had let us spend the night at a neutral stop. Hopefully Jax buys it.'

'He won't.' I sipped my soup. 'But I do appreciate you covering for me.'

The golden cord tightened, just as a measured knock came at the door. I put my bowl straight down and went to open it. Warden stood outside.

'I apologise for the delay.'

'You're grand.' I stood aside. 'Come in.'

I closed the door behind him. Eliza shrank away from the huge, lamp-eyed stranger.

'The Buzzer bit Zeke,' I told him. 'Could you take a look?'

'Yes.'

Zeke was now shirtless on the couch, covered to his waist. Warden cast a steady gaze over him, while Nick grasped his fine-boned hand.

'We cleaned the wounds with salt water,' I said.

'Good,' Warden said. 'Does he use ethereal drugs?'

'No,' Nick said.

'Then he will recover.'

'But he looks—' His voice strained. 'He looks like he's about to die.'

'The Emim pollute the æther, which hinders voyants' ability to connect with it. Its bite has poisoned Ezekiel, weakening his aura,' Warden said. 'He will feel unwell for several days, and the wounds in his side will be slow to heal. Bind them, let him rest, and keep him warm.'

'This sounds like spirit shock,' I said. 'You can't treat him with amaranth or ectoplasm, like you did Liss?'

'Liss needed my help. Ezekiel does not,' Warden said. 'His condition is similar to spirit shock, but temporary. He will soon wake.'

Nick sank into an armchair, gazing at Zeke, whose breathing was deep and slow.

'I'll get you some fresh clothes and towels,' Eliza said. 'You can sleep here tonight. Leon is away.' She cleared her throat before looking a long way up at Warden. 'Do you … want to stay, too, Warden?'

'I would not wish to impose upon your hospitality, Eliza.'

'The garret is free. It's no trouble.'

'Stay,' I said.

After a moment, Warden nodded. His eyes were gold, bright as lamps.

'All right. I'm going to have a shower.' Eliza locked and chained the front door. 'See you in the morning.'

'Night,' I said.

She went upstairs. I pulled up a footstool beside Nick, while Warden took the seat by the fire, reminding me of Magdalen. 'You came some way to find me,' he said. 'It must have been a pressing matter.'

'You could say that.' I rubbed my eyes. 'I've had some long days, but this one takes the cake.'

'Tell me.'

While Nick tended to Zeke without speaking, I recounted everything to Warden. He listened in silence, never taking his eyes off my face.

'The reason I came to find you,' I said, 'is because I need you to rescue the survivors. The Abbess is holding them in her night parlour, but I don't see a way to get them out while they're under guard. You could storm the Chanting Lay once she leaves for the scrimmage.'

Warden narrowed his eyes in thought. I recognised that look from Oxford.

'I am willing,' he concluded. 'Terebell and the others could be prevailed upon to assist me, if this will strengthen your reign as Underqueen.'

'You have to convince them,' Nick said to him. 'Paige needs to remove any threats to her position as soon as possible. We can't let the Abbess leave the scrimmage unchallenged. Or the Rag and Bone Man.'

'If I win, I want to be able to expose them straight after the fight,' I said, 'but to do that, I need Ivy. I'm convinced she's the key to all this – that she has one last piece of information that unlocks the whole conspiracy – but I want all four survivors out of there, before the Abbess hands them off to someone else.'

'Very well,' Warden said. 'I will put this plan to Terebell and have word back to you by noon.'

'Thank you. You go up, if you want.'

He looked straight back at me. Giving me a small nod, he went upstairs.

'I've made a decision,' Nick said quietly. 'If you win, I'm going to leave my job. I'll clear out my bank account, steal as many supplies as possible, and give myself to the underworld. I'll embrace the Red Vision.'

I should have seen this coming. As soon as Ella Giddings had reached out to him, the fragile balance between his two selves had started to slip.

'It would be good to have you around more,' I said, 'but you've worked for so long to—'

'It's over, Paige. I'm still multiple promotions away from having the power to bring them down from the inside,' Nick said. 'I thought I had the patience to bide my time for a few more years, but I've seen enough. If I get any closer to the end of my rope, I'll be hanging from it.'

'What if I don't win?'

'I'll still leave,' Nick said. 'I didn't join Scion for Jaxon to spend all that money on absinthe.' It was rare to see his face so cold. 'No more.'

'What about your parents?'

'I've already warned them. They've always been ready to go into hiding.'

Bryndís and Rune were both voyant. He had probably sent them a vision.

'Okay,' I said. 'Maybe this is a good time to pop the question.' Nick tilted his head. 'If I win the scrimmage, will you be mollisher supreme?'

His face softened into a smile. 'It would be an honour.'

'You don't need a minute to think about it?'

'No. I did it for Jax once,' he reminded me. 'You'll be a much easier boss.'

I returned his weary smile.

'I'll spend the night down here with Zeke. I don't want to move him,' Nick said. 'Before you go, can I take another look at your shoulder?'

'Knock yourself out.'

I sat on the footstool. Nick carefully lifted the gauze. Falling silent as he concentrated, he stitched the wound, then dabbed it with gel. Once he had given me an injection, he nodded, apparently satisfied.

'I wish you hadn't got this just before the scrimmage.'

'I'll be fine.' I faced him. 'I was proud of you for working for Scion, and I'm proud of you for deciding to leave. I think Lina would be, too.'

'I hope so.' He touched my cheek. 'Get some rest. It's been a tiring day.'

I rose to leave. Just as I started climbing the stairs, Zeke said, 'Nick?'

Nick turned to him. Zeke gave him a weak smile. With a sigh of relief, Nick pressed their foreheads together, then kissed him on the lips. There was a final, clean snip inside me, as if a small thread had been cut.

Then it was gone.

A familiar painting hung on the wall. Eliza had worked on it without spirits over the course of a year, unbeknownst to Jaxon, to prove to herself that she could still make art without her muses. That she was more than just her gift.

I had never asked where it had gone, but here it was. It was her one and only self-portrait, showing her as a tarot card, the Queen of Cups. As it turned out, she was just as good without Pieter and Rachel.

A candle flickered in the bathroom. I peeled off my stained shirt and trousers.

Some believed augurs and soothsayers made their best predictions on their deathbeds. I wondered if Chelsea had glimpsed the future in her own spilled blood.

All at once, the whole day hit me. I grasped the sink, my legs shaking. Had it only been this morning that Nick and I had gone to Sugar Tin?

A deep chill held fast to my bones. I drew a long, steadying breath. The scrimmage was in two days' time. I didn't have room to fall apart now.

The mirror confirmed that I looked a state. The skin around my lips was smudged with grey, and my dark circles were starker than ever.

I looked closer, my brow creasing. One of my pupils was dilated, taking up most of my iris. Even when I looked at the candle, my left pupil refused to react. I would have to ask Nick about it in the morning. For now, I needed a hot shower. Once I had washed the blood and dirt off, I enfolded myself in a towel, steam curling off my skin.

Eliza was already asleep in the next room. On the second floor, I found a spare bed, where she had left a clean nightshirt, a comb and a toothbrush. I eased the shirt on and breathed in its delicate, floral scent. Once I was ready, I returned to the landing, trying to ignore the ache in my side where Nick had stabbed me. I would never tell him, but whenever I got cold, it still hurt. A bed-warmer might shake the chill.

As I headed for the stairs to the lower floors, Warden came down another flight, presumably from the garret. He stopped when he saw me.

'Paige.'

There was just enough firelight from downstairs for us to see one another. The sight of him sent a different sort of chill through my skin.

'Warden.' I kept my voice down. 'Has the cold spot been sealed?'

'For the time being.'

'What do you mean?'

'Oxford served as a beacon, drawing the Emim away from the citadels. Now it has been abandoned, London will tempt them next.' Warden studied my face. 'You tried to possess the Emite.'

'Maybe. Did you steal another memory?'

'I must profess my innocence on that front. Your pupils are unequally sized,' he said. 'It is a sign that your silver cord has been strained.'

He had good eyesight. I was standing far enough away that he should have had trouble seeing my pupils in the gloom.

'You helped me,' I said. 'My cord wasn't strong enough by itself.'

'I sensed your terror. I have never felt that much fear from you, Paige.'

I had tried to block out what I had experienced in that terrible dreamscape. Now the memory came flooding back, knotting my throat.

'You were right to warn me,' I said. 'Its dreamscape—' I took a few steps towards him, the floorboards creaking. 'There were other spirits in there, with no cords to save them. They're buried in that Buzzer.'

'It is possible to destroy an Emite, releasing the spirits it has devoured.' He laid his gloved hands on the balustrade. 'You should not risk dreamwalking into another.'

'I can't regret it. It saved Zeke,' I said. 'We didn't mean to hold up your hunt.'

'You were not wrong to seek me out, but you could have called me to your side. No matter how long it takes to find you, I will come.'

'I still don't know how. And I could feel that you were in danger.'

I stood at the balustrade next to him. The light from downstairs limned the strong lines of his face.

Our auras brushed, raising goosebumps. Even from here, I could feel his warmth. His chest might as well have been stacked with hot coals.

'I was afraid of you as well. The night we met,' I said. 'I couldn't imagine ever missing you, but as soon as I left you, I did. Leaving you behind was one of the hardest things I've ever had to do.' I glanced away, then back at him, working up the nerve to continue. 'I thought I was a chancer, but you risked your life for ... barely a moment with me.'

His eyes burned low. 'I would do it again.'

'You're mad.'

'Madness is a matter of perspective, little dreamer.'

I watched as he grasped the balustrade on either side of me, not quite touching my hips. Another chill worked its way up my inner thighs.

He hadn't even touched me, and I was on fire.

'I want this,' I said, 'but I don't know how much time we'll be able to spend together when I'm Underqueen.'

'I will take any stolen moment you offer.'

'And I still find you infuriating.' My fingers climbed his shirt. 'In several ways.'

'Hm. I would hate to bore you.'

My heart was hammering. When I lifted my chin, his nose listed against mine. I took his face between my fingertips, tracing his jaw, my breath coming faster. His grip on the balustrade tightened.

I had no name for what he made me feel. I had no real sense of what it was; only that it was blood-deep, like some forgotten instinct. Only that I wanted to let it take me over.

'Our lifelines will meet when the æther sees fit,' Warden said. 'That may not be often.'

'I can live with that.' I stroked his cheekbone. 'My whole life has been a secret. What's one more?'

Warden touched his lips to my temple. His hands moved from the balustrade, brushing up my hips and sides to encircle my waist.

413

As his fingers met at the small of my back, I reached down to grasp his wrists.

'Take the gloves off,' I said, very softly. 'Show me you're not afraid of this, Warden.'

His gaze found mine, and he nodded.

24

LIMINAL

As soon as I closed the door to the garret, Warden dropped the gloves and took my face between his callused hands. My fingers found the key and turned it, locking me into the dark with a Reph.

His veneer of humanity faded in darkness. His eyes were small eclipses, threatening to burn me if I looked too long. The same gold as the hidden lamps.

He lifted me against his chest, sweeping the floor from under my feet, and wrapped his arm around my hips. His other hand came back to my cheek. All I could hear was my own breathing, my own heartbeat. I turned my face into his palm, savouring the rough warmth of it.

In the Guildhall, time had been against us. Now we could let this unfold. He lowered his brow to mine, and a fire danced in my dreamscape.

Secure in his embrace, I smoothed my hands along his broad shoulders, up the slope of his neck. I had envisioned this moment for weeks, since he had kissed me the first time. I wanted to make it last.

Our eyes met. Even that small connection had been prohibited in Oxford.

And then his lips were on mine, and it felt just as good as it had in the Guildhall.

In the darkness, I was nothing but feeling. He tasted of red wine and something else – something cold and lasting, like silver on my tongue. I wrapped both arms around his neck and let myself sink into that kiss.

His dreamscape sent another flame across my flowers. There was still that distant voice in my head as I kissed him, as I whispered his name into his mouth.

Stop, Paige, stop.

I was playing with fire. He belonged to the Netherworld. But with this nocturne playing, the voice of reason was easy to ignore. Even if we fought to stay together, I didn't know how long this could last, but that was true of my whole life. It was nothing if not unpredictable.

We ended up on what felt like a buttoned couch, my legs on either side of his waist. A soft, instinctive sigh escaped me as he cupped my face again.

Part of me had feared this reunion, in case things had burned out between us. In case I felt as stiff and detached as I had with the amaurotic.

I needn't have worried. Being with Warden was as easy as breathing – easier, in this moment. I broke the kiss, feverish warmth in my cheeks, and clasped my fingers at his nape, my elbows resting on his shoulders.

Our auras sang against each other. His palms smoothed over my waist and hips, as if he was trying to commit my shape to memory. I had a mind to let him do that until morning.

My hair was still wet, and cool beads of water seeped under my collar. His lips graced my neck, sending a sweet ache through my whole body as I curled my legs around him, my fingers winding into his thick hair. Now I knew my skin could be as hungry as the rest of me.

When he lifted his face, I framed it. He drew me to his chest and kissed me again, and I opened his shirt, pressing myself flush against him. His sarx felt like satin. The heat of it burned through my nightshirt.

Perhaps this feeling *had* been there before the trap room, out of sight. A quiet desire, growing just below my threshold of perception – held there by the weight of fear, too dangerous to be acknowledged. I didn't know when it had started, but I recognised it now.

Until that night, I hadn't understood how much I wanted him to hold me like this. Now I did, that want filled me. Neither of our worlds had room for intimacy, but here, we had one of our own. The liminal space of our secret, existing only where we met.

Warden stilled when my hands strayed. I met his gaze as I skimmed the ends of the welts on his back. When he nodded, I slid a hand between his shoulders, finding the branching scars. They were cold and waxen to the touch, like the ones on my left hand. The marks of a poltergeist.

'Whose spirit was it?'

He moved a damp curl out of my eyes.

'Its name is no longer spoken,' he said. 'Perhaps time has forgotten it.'

'You never saw its name on Nashira?'

'I was never with her like this.'

I couldn't say I was surprised. They had been consorts for over a century, but theirs had been a political union, designed to humiliate Warden.

'I am grateful for that small mercy.' He touched me just under my jaw. 'I would sooner be your secret than her trophy, displayed for all to see.'

I drew him in close and kissed him, softer. 'I prefer it like this, too.'

'You need not lie for my sake, Paige.'

'I'm not,' I said truthfully. 'I've never had to consider it, but I'd prefer my relationships to be private. It's no one else's business who I'm seeing.'

'Then we are in accord.'

I wanted to spend the whole night exploring this, but I couldn't stave off the exhaustion any longer. My eyelids were heavy, and the wound in my shoulder was aching. Warden traced the edge of the dressing.

'Does it hurt?'

'Yeah.' I leaned against him. 'I should get some rest.'

His chin rested on the top of my head. 'Should I leave you to sleep?'

'Don't you dare.'

Warden reclined against the armrest and drew me to him, letting me perch my knee on his thigh. He was so warm, I doubted I would need a duvet.

'I'll still go out,' I murmured.

'Hm.' He stroked my hair. 'It has no bearing on my choices.'

'It isn't just that. It's every reason under the sun.'

'True.' He nodded to the skylight. 'But we are not under the sun.'

Now I was used to the darkness, I could make out the crescent moon through that window. I smiled into his chest.

With his arm cradling me, it was easy to drift off. Just as I reached the cusp of sleep, someone began to play a piano. I glanced up at him.

'Cécile Chaminade,' he said, eyes on the ceiling.

I tucked my head back under his chin. 'Do you keep a jukebox up there?'

'That would make a fine addition to my dreamscape.' His hand passed over my curls again, stopping at the back of my head. 'I remember all things. Including every piece of music I have ever heard.'

'I'm not sure if I'd like that or not.'

'It is both a gift and a curse, like all clairvoyance.'

I closed my eyes and nestled closer. There was a soft tremor in my core – the same feeling I got when I discovered some rare ornament or instrument at the Garden. The sense that my fingers would slip on its surface. That it would break before it saw the light of day.

'The traitor from the first rebellion,' I said. 'Did you ever see his face?'

'If I did, I may never know. I was not told which human had betrayed us.'

'I've been wondering if it's the Rag and Bone Man.'

'Perhaps.'

It must have eaten away at him for years, not knowing who had done this to him. I rested a hand on his breastbone, my thoughts drifting.

'You are sad.'

'Yes.' I opened my eyes. 'When I betray Jaxon, my life with the gang will be over. They're the closest thing I have to a family. Nick will side with me, but I don't know about the others. I might lose them. And as much as I hate to admit it, I've loved being the Pale Dreamer.'

'Do you intend to kill Jaxon?'

The question gnawed at me.

'Being away from him gave me distance. I see what he is,' I said. 'But even after all he's done, I don't want to kill him, because part of me still recognises him as my saviour. The man who helped me embrace a side of myself I had always feared.' I paused. 'But it is a fight to the death.'

'Are you ready to face him?'

'I think so.' I sat up a little. 'Can I try entering your dreamscape again?'

'Are you not tired?'

'I want to test my silver cord before the fight. You said it had been strained.'

It was no small thing to ask, yet he didn't raise a word of objection. Instead, he turned to face me and gave me a small nod. I grasped his nape.

When I stepped into his dreamscape, the silence pressed against me like a wall. As I walked across the hadal zone, I made out red drapes, swirling down from high above. Those hadn't been there before.

My footsteps echoed as if I were walking through a cathedral. This dreamscape was a floating island in the æther, taking no clear form. I moved between the swathes of crimson velvet, through each wide ring of his consciousness, until I reached the sunlit zone, the very heart of him. His dream-form stood with its hands behind its back.

'Welcome, Paige.'

The red drapes surrounded us.

'I see you redecorated,' I said.

'Apparently.'

Something had changed in this part of his mind. A flower had grown from the dust, sealed under a bell jar. A flower with petals like glass.

'The amaranth.' I knelt beside it. 'Why is it here?'

'I do not claim to know how dreamscapes choose their shape,' Warden said. 'How is your silver cord?'

'It's holding up.'

It trailed into the shadows behind me, while the golden cord was taut and bright between us – undeniable evidence of our connected spirits.

'Jaxon will not have walls as strong as mine,' Warden said, 'but he may have spectres.'

He nodded towards his twilight zone. Twelve faceless shapes had gathered there, held back by the light in the centre of his dreamscape. They took a vaguely human shape, but looked as if they were made of smoke.

'I always thought they were just defences,' I said, 'but Jax says they're ... memories. Is that true?'

'In a manner of speaking. They are projections of certain memories – specifically, memories that have not been laid to rest,' Warden said. 'When something plays on your mind, as you say, it is the spectres at work. They cannot hurt your dream-form, but they may attempt to block your path. You must not tarry, nor let them hold you.'

'Do you know which memory is which?'

'Yes.' He observed his collection. 'I know.'

I had never touched a dream-form when I wasn't in fear of my life. Entering a dreamscape was already an invasion of privacy, and it struck me as too cruel to contemplate – handling the image they held of their own nature. Leaving fingerprints on that image could do irrevocable damage – burst or bolster an ego, shatter a last inch of hope.

Our intimacy calmed my fears. My wanderlust had turned to lust and wonder – a thirst for knowledge, no matter how dangerous. I reached up a little, then paused.

'Can I touch you?'

Warden looked at me, then nodded. I laid my hand against his cheek.

He felt cold and rigid, as if his entire body was a suit of armour. I had to remember these weren't my real fingers, though they looked exactly like the ones I knew. These were my hands only as Warden perceived them.

The golden cord hummed around us both. I let my hands rest on his face for a while, tracing the firm lips and carved jaw. His vision of me, in direct contact with his vision of himself.

'Take heed, dreamwalker.' He lifted a hand to cover mine. 'Self-portraits are as fragile as mirrors.'

He let go of me. I stepped away, and the silver cord cast me back to my body.

When I woke, I sat up, my chest heaving. Doing this without oxygen was still difficult. Warden gave me plenty of room as I collected myself.

'Why do you see yourself like that?'

'I cannot see my own dream-form,' he said. 'I confess myself intrigued.'

'It's like a statue of you, but covered in gouges, like you've taken a chisel to yourself.'

'Hm. My years as blood-consort gouged my sanity, if nothing else,' he said. 'Remember our dance. You can leave some of yourself behind.'

'I don't know if it will work in real combat. I can't split my spirit between two bodies.'

'Do not think of it as splitting yourself, but leaving a shadow behind.'

'You're good at this. You should be a writer.'

'Hm. I would sooner be a musician.'

The piano had stopped. I climbed back into his arms, mounting him again. His fingertips sketched a line from my jaw to my neck, stroking downward to where the collar of my shirt fell open above my breasts.

'You ought to sleep,' he said. 'You must be well-rested for the scrimmage.'

421

'I need you to promise me something first.'

He looked at me. I had asked him for a favour once before, as I faced death.

If she kills me, you have to lead the others. I need you to promise you'll set me free.

'Promise you won't interfere in the scrimmage, even if it looks like I'm about to die,' I said. 'And promise me that if I die, you'll find out what the grey market is. You'll end it.'

Warden tilted my chin up. He placed a tender kiss on my brow, then my lips.

'I vow it,' he said. 'But you will not lose.'

'How do you know?'

'Because I know you. And you will be Underqueen.'

In that moment, I let myself believe he was an oracle. That my future was already set, and all I had to do was chase it.

I had never slept beside anyone, with their aura wrapped around mine like a blanket, or a second skin. My defences kept rising, set on edge by his proximity. I imagined that this was what it would be like to sleep on a ship, adrift on a surface that never stopped moving. More than once, I woke disoriented, warmer than I would have been alone.

The first time, his eyes gave me such a powerful reminder of Oxford that I scrambled off the couch, groping for the knife I had left downstairs. Warden waited for me to remember. Afterwards, he let me lie with my back against his chest, making no attempt to hold me there.

When I woke for good, it was dawn. Warden lay at my side, sound asleep, his arm around my middle. I had never seen him look so human. I brushed his brown hair away from his face, drinking him in.

Downstairs, Nick was moving. Leaving Warden to rest, I slipped out from under his arm, unlocked the door, and left the garret.

My heart was racing. I had told myself to take it slow with Warden, but by touching his dream-form, I had already broken that rule.

I went to the bathroom first. My hair was a crunchy tangle, as expected. As I met my own eyes in the mirror, I shivered, suddenly feeling vulnerable.

Admitting that I wanted Warden had been exhilarating last night. Now I was remembering that encounter with the amaurotic at Dance upon Nothing, and the course of events that had taken me to him.

This was different. For whatever reason, Warden seemed to want me as much as I did him. I hadn't just felt that in his touch, but in the cord.

Some secrets are kept for their sanctity.

For once, I wanted to stop running. There was a warmth in Warden that made me feel alive and strong. Even if it didn't last, I wanted to see where it went. For ten years, I had concealed a vast part of my life from my father, not to mention Scion. Warden was just as good at pretending. We could meet under the rose without alerting Terebell.

Nick was at the kitchen table, reading the *Daily Descendant*. I sat down.

'Morning.'

'Not quite yet.' He gave me a measured look. 'I went out to buy us some breakfast. I also snuck back to the den and got you some fresh clothes.'

'You're the best, on both counts.'

'I know.'

I went up to the bathroom to change. When I got back to the kitchen, bundled up in a thick jersey and trousers, I went for a slice of bread.

'Was that you on the piano last night?'

Nick nodded. 'I took lessons when I was young.'

'I always forget you were a child prodigy.'

'I'm no Mozart. I never had the same knack for music as I do for the sciences,' he admitted. 'But I thought I'd try, to help Zeke sleep.'

'How is he?'

'Warden was right. He hasn't got any worse, and he woke up a few times.' Nick put the paper down. 'We'll tell Jax he has food poisoning.'

'How convincing.'

I pulled the *Descendant* towards me. The front page advised denizens to increase their vigilance in the hunt for the fugitives, warning them to look out for dyed hair, masks, or the scars of back-street surgery. Examples were shown – seams of purpled stitching, often located on the cheeks, near the hairline, or around the ears.

My mouth tightened. I wanted to avoid surgery. Scion had taken many things, but I wouldn't let them take my face, on top of everything.

'I need to tell the others what I'm planning for the scrimmage.' I reached for the coffee pot. 'And find out who they'd side with if I won.'

'Are you going to tell them about Warden?'

I stopped.

'I'm not as sensitive as you, but I am a jumper. My perception goes a bit farther than average,' Nick reminded me. 'You were with him all night.'

After a moment, I poured the coffee, waiting for him to continue.

'I know it's none of my business. I'm just—' Nick seemed to consider his words. 'He's not human, Paige.'

'I'm aware.'

'I'm not going to lecture or patronise you.' His gaze was soft. 'What you do is your concern.'

'It is.'

'I just want you to remember what he did. Even if he never meant to hurt you by keeping you there – even if he wasn't the one who captured you in the first place – you have to remember that he used you.'

'Nick, I'm not naïve. I lived through it.' I met his gaze. 'He could have let me go on the first night. I know that. I also know he put me in danger, that he used me as a weapon. I haven't forgotten – I will never forget – but I see why he did it. Does that make sense?'

Nick looked at me, his brow furrowed.

'Yes,' he said. 'You're taking a citadel on to your shoulders, Paige. If he makes that easier for you, I won't argue. Only you can forgive him.'

'I have.'

'But he's so distant and formal. You're not like that. Does he make you happy?'

'I don't know yet, but I want to find out. He isn't as cold as he seems, Nick. He's just a Reph,' I said. 'Anyway, they do say opposites attract.'

'True.'

'You can't tell anyone,' I said quietly. 'You're my best friend, and I trust you. But if the other Rephs found out, it wouldn't be pretty.'

'For you or him?'

'Both, as far as I can tell.'

Nick grimaced. I covered his hand and gave it a quick squeeze.

'I know you're saying this because you care, and I appreciate it,' I said. 'I'll watch my back. I promise.'

'I'm already terrified for you, Paige. I want you to be Underqueen, but even if you survive the scrimmage, look at what happened to Hector and Cutmouth.'

'Someone has to risk their neck.'

'I have a bad feeling about it.'

'We're clairvoyant. We're supposed to have bad feelings about things.'

He gave me a flat look, just as Eliza came downstairs, hair piled into a messy bun. 'Morning,' she said, stifling a yawn. 'I'm famished.'

'Good,' Nick said. 'I have fresh bread.'

'I adore you.'

She sat beside him and reached for the jam. Nick and I exchanged a glance.

'Eliza,' I said, 'why does Leon Wax have your self-portrait?'

'Because he's like family to me,' she said. 'And he offered to look after it.'

It was rare for any of us to mention the word *family*. Jaxon liked to forget the concept existed, as if we'd all hatched from miraculous Fabergé eggs.

'I was left in Soho with a token around my neck, saying my name and where I was born,' Eliza said. 'The aster dealers kept me so I could be their mule. From the day I turned eleven, I was moving regal between sections. I didn't know any kind of love, any kind of basic kindness, until I was seventeen. That's when I got a job on the New Cut.'

That was where she had been employed when she applied to work for Jaxon.

'I ran away from Soho with nothing,' Eliza said. 'I loved my work as a set designer, but I was on such a low salary that I couldn't even afford a doss. One of the actors – Bea Cissé – found me sleeping under the stage, and I admitted I didn't have anywhere else. She let me live with her for two years. Never asked for a penny in rent.'

'Her name sounds familiar,' Nick said. 'Isn't she a physical medium?'

Eliza nodded. 'She used to let all sorts of spirits possess her – escape artists, contortionists, dancers. A few years ago, she got to the end of her tether. Her joints were shot to pieces, and the barrier of her dreamscape cracked.'

That was a risk for mediums. Their dreamscapes had flimsy defences, sending an open invitation to wandering spirits, but they could only take so much.

'The apothecary at the Garden sells a painkiller that helps, but it's expensive,' Eliza continued. 'Leon wants to move Bea out of London. There are too many spirits here, and they won't leave her alone. That's why they're gone today. They're looking at a place in Kent.'

'That sounds like a good idea,' Nick said. 'How does she know Leon?'

'They're married. She's the reason Leon knows about the underworld, and why Jax trusted him to be involved. He only employs amaurotics if they have a good reason not to betray the syndicate.'

'That night at the Garden,' I said. 'You collapsed a street away from here.'

'I was on my way to visit Bea.'

'Warden might be able to help. He has medicine from the Netherworld.'

'That would be great, if he could.' Eliza rubbed her eyes. 'I've kept this from Jaxon for years. He doesn't know how close I am to Leon or Bea.'

'We all have things we haven't told Jax.' Nick wrapped an arm around her. 'You used to tell me everything when we were the first two Seals.'

'I'm sorry.' She rested her cheek on his shoulder. 'I didn't want to burden you.'

'You could never.'

Nick planted a kiss on the crown of her head. It seemed we had all kept secrets from Jaxon.

'I need to tell you something,' I said to her. 'I'm going for the Rose Crown.'

Eliza sat up, eyes widening. She turned to Nick, as if he could snap me out of this moment of madness.

'I've known for a while,' Nick said. 'I support her.'

Eliza shook her head. 'Paige, don't. You can't. Jaxon will—'

'—kill me.' I finished my coffee. 'He's welcome to try.'

'Jaxon is more than twice your age and has thirteen boundlings. He knows everything there is to know about clairvoyance,' Eliza said. 'And if you betray him—' Her voice caught. 'It's over. Seven Dials is over.'

There was no denying it.

'If I don't win,' I said, 'everything is over. I can't let the syndicate crumble.'

'Jax will—'

'He won't do anything. I asked him time and again,' I said. 'I gave him so many chances. I don't want to fight him, but he's forced my hand.'

Her lips pressed together.

'You can't tell Nadine or Zeke. Nadine wants my position as mollisher – there's no guarantee she wouldn't rat me out to Jax,' I said. 'Dani could go either way. I don't know about Zeke.' I looked at Nick, who clasped his hands. 'Do you?'

It took him a while to answer. 'He wants to fight the Rephs, but he loves Nadine. She's his little sister. Zeke will choose whoever she does.'

'Paige,' Eliza said, 'did Jaxon really say he wouldn't do anything about the Rephs?'

'Yes.'

'Now I've seen them, I don't understand it.' She kneaded her forehead. 'Jax took me in. He gave me a home. I know he's … difficult, but he gave us Seven Dials. He made us, Paige.'

'No. We made ourselves, in spite of him,' I said. 'If you want to stick with him, it's your choice. But if I win, I'd like you to be on my side.'

'Really?'

'Of course,' I said. 'You're my family.'

Eliza managed a smile.

We filled up on warm bread and lingonberry jam. When the floorboards creaked in the parlour, I turned. Warden had come down from the garret.

'Give me a second,' I said, standing up. Nick watched me leave the kitchen.

Warden took his coat from one of the hooks. His gloves were back in place. When he saw me, his eyes burned.

'Good morning, Paige.'

'Morning.' I was suddenly very aware of my skin. 'Did you sleep well?'

I sounded too brisk. I had no idea how you were supposed to talk to someone after spending the night in their arms. There must be an art to it.

'Very.' His gaze flicked over my face. 'Did you?'

'After a while.'

'The Ranthen are outside. I wondered if you might like to put your idea to Terebell yourself.'

Now he mentioned it, I could sense them.

'All right,' I said. 'I suppose I have to learn to negotiate with her at some point.'

'Precisely.'

I stepped into my boots and unlocked the door. Our auras were still pulling apart as I followed him out of the chandlery, into a thin fog.

The Ranthen waited by the arched tunnel, beneath a painted sign reading BEDFORDBURY. They turned in unison to look at us. Pleione said, 'How fares the human?'

'Great.' I raised an eyebrow. 'Thanks for asking.'

'Not you.'

A Reph asking after an injured human. I never thought I'd live to see the day.

'Zeke is okay,' I said. 'He's sleeping it off.'

'I trust you have also recovered from facing the creature. Next time, think before you interrupt a hunt,' Terebell said, arms folded. 'I came to deliver you a warning, dreamwalker. Situla Mesarthim has been sighted in this section of the citadel. I am sure you remember her.'

I remembered Situla very well. A relative of Warden, whose only resemblance to him was her physical appearance. She must be hunting us.

'It would be safest to avoid her attention,' Terebell said. 'We must leave for our safe house in the East End to await your success in the scrimmage.'

'About that.' I tucked my hands into my pockets. 'I have a favour to ask.'

'Explain.'

'I'm sure Warden has told you this, but a few other humans survived the Bone Season. Four of them have been captured by the Abbess, the interim Underqueen, who's working with the Rag and Bone Man. One of those survivors has information I need. Her name is Ivy Jacob.'

'Who was her keeper?'

'Thuban.'

Terebell lifted her chin. 'The palmist.'

'Yes,' I said. 'The survivors have been imprisoned in a night parlour in Kensington. It's called the Chanting Lay. I know a way in, but the building will be heavily guarded. I wondered if you'd consider—'

'You dare imply that we should fetch them for you,' Errai said. 'We are not your thralls or couriers, to be dispatched at your beck and call.'

'You are really starting to get on my nerves, Errai. I told you, you Rephs can't scare me. You did your worst in Oxford.' I tapped my right shoulder, where I was branded. 'You think I don't remember this?'

'I do not think you remember it well enough.'

'You absolute—'

'Peace, both of you.' Lucida held up a hand. 'Arcturus, is this a rational course of action?'

Warden dealt Errai a hard look. 'I believe so,' he said. 'The Rag and Bone Man has knowledge of our presence. His enterprise – the grey market – must be stopped, lest he continue to mock us from the shadows.'

Terebell narrowed her eyes. 'What is the meaning of *grey market*, dreamwalker?'

'I don't know,' I said. 'But I think Ivy will.'

'You expect us to do your bidding,' Pleione said, 'for an uncertain outcome.'

'Yes, just like I did for Warden in Oxford. I agreed to help with your rebellion, even though the first one crashed and burned.' I immediately regretted saying it. 'Look, win or lose, I need Ivy to talk at the scrimmage. If you want me to get you an army, get me Ivy Jacob.'

Terebell regarded me. After a silence that seemed to stretch on for a small eternity, she led the other Rephs away. I looked up at Warden.

'Was that an agreement?'

'I will persuade her,' Warden said. 'Where will the scrimmage take place?'

'I should hear today. I'll leave you a note at the Old Lyre.' I turned to face him. 'Warden, I'm sorry for saying that. About the first rebellion.'

'The truth requires no apology.' He removed two vials from his coat. 'I wanted to offer you these, for the scrimmage.'

One vial was full of ectoplasm, the other of amaranth. I looked between them, hesitating. If I had those on me, I would be almost invincible in the ring.

'Thank you,' I said, 'but I'd see that as cheating. If I can't win the scrimmage on my own merit, I don't deserve to rule the underworld.'

'As you wish.' He returned the vials to his pocket. 'Will others cheat, do you think?'

'Maybe, but I'm trying to change things. I'd like to start off on the right foot.'

'What about the pendant?'

'I'll wear that. It's more like armour than a weapon,' I said. 'The Abbess might have been using a poltergeist to kill anyone who gets close to the Rose Crown. I'd better not face her without some protection.'

'This fight will still push you to your limit. As soon as it is over, I will bring the amaranth.'

'If I'm alive.'

'Yes.'

The weight of his gaze made my skin prickle. He glanced after the other Rephs, whose dreamscapes were retreating. When I gave him a nod, he lifted me, insinuating me between his chest and the wall. A soft heat rose behind my ribs and unfurled all the way through me.

'First a crate and now this.' I twined my fingers at his nape. 'How *will* you account for our height difference next?'

'You will have to survive to find out.' His gaze burned. 'Do this for me.'

'You might think I have a death wish, but I have a vested interest in living.' I looked him right in the eyes. 'I've lasted this long. I'll be fine.'

'Good.'

He brushed my cheek. I kissed him like these were my last hours on Earth.

And I had the sense that I belonged. Not in the material sense, as I belonged to Jaxon, as I had once belonged to Oxford. This was belonging of a different sort, as things that are alike belong with one another.

I had never felt like this in my life, and it scared the living daylights out of me.

'I have every faith in you.' Warden pressed his brow to mine. 'I place our fates in your hands again.' He clasped them for a moment. 'Good luck, Paige.'

He leaned down to kiss me once more – a soft, lingering kiss – before he rounded the corner and vanished. I leaned against the wall and breathed out, letting the morning chill take the heat from my face.

Somewhere in the citadel, a bell began to ring.

Jaxon was locked inside his boudoir when we got back to the den, playing 'Danse Macabre' so loudly we could hear it from the hallway. Eliza and I parted ways on the landing. I waited for a bang on the wall, but there was nothing.

Trying not to make too much noise, I took the hot bath I had been craving, then went back to my room. When I saw what was on my bed, I stopped.

My costume for the scrimmage. Eliza had been working on it for weeks in private. I ran my fingers over it, admiring the fine needlework.

Once I had hung it in my wardrobe, I lay on my bed. I needed as much sleep as I could get before the scrimmage, but I felt wide awake.

A spider had made a web on my window. I reached for my can of oxygen. After two humans, a bird and a butterfly, it was painfully easy to possess.

Inside its tiny dreamscape, I found a delicate maze of silk. I left a shadow in my wake, just enough to keep my body upright while I scuttled around with eight spindly legs – until I lost my balance and whacked my human skull against the nearest wall. Spewing profanities, I took a few deep breaths from my oxygen mask, my vision blurred.

Perhaps it was time to trust in my gift. It had saved my life more than once, even before I knew how to use it. I had trained for six months in Oxford.

I could do this.

'A Bird in a Gilded Cage' drifted through the wall, rustling with static. I lay on my bed and listened to it, the spider crawling on to my pillow.

I didn't know where I would be, the day after tomorrow. Certainly not here, in my little room at Seven Dials. I could be on the streets, a pariah and traitor, banished from the syndicate. I could be Underqueen.

I could be in the æther.

Just beyond the window was a solitary dreamscape. I looked between the curtains, into the courtyard, where Jaxon Hall sat alone under the red glow of daybreak. He wore his lounging robe and trousers with polished shoes, and his cane lay on the bench beside him.

He must have felt me looking. Our eyes met, and he crooked a finger.

Outside, I joined him on the bench. His gaze was on the sky. Its light was trapped in the crypts and furrows of his irises, so they seemed to sparkle with the knowledge of some private joke.

'Hello, darling.'

'Hi.' I shot him a sidelong look, waiting for a rebuke. 'Sorry about last night.'

'No matter. Did you see your glad rags?'

'They're beautiful.'

'They are. My dear medium is an extraordinary talent,' he said. 'Your very first assignment for me was in October, three years ago. Do you remember?'

I couldn't help but smile. 'I do.'

'It was the first time I ever had you do a job at street level. Before that day you were the tea girl, the lowly researcher,' Jaxon recalled. 'And getting quite cross with it, I should imagine.'

'You've no idea. I'd never met someone who drank so much tea.'

He chuckled. Even now, that sound warmed me.

'I was testing your patience,' he said. 'I remember it so clearly, when those two poltergeists were loose. Sarah and Sally Metyard, the murderous milliners, along with their unhappy victim, Anne Naylor. You and Dr Nygård spent the best part of the morning wrangling those three.'

It had been the best day of my life. Earning his approval and respect, along with the right to call myself his mollisher, had filled me with such joy and purpose. I couldn't have imagined a world without him in it.

'I took you to the sundial pillar,' Jaxon said, smiling a little. 'I pointed out the sundial facing this side of Monmouth Street, and I said to you—'

'*This is yours,*' I recited. '*This street, this path, is yours to walk.*'

As if I could ever forget.

'Precisely,' Jaxon said. 'Precisely that.' He covered my hand. 'We are the Seven Seals. Brought together, across seas and oceans, by the mysterious wiles of the æther. It wasn't chance, darling. We were meant to be here. And we shall bring about a day of reckoning in London.'

With that image in his mind, Jaxon closed his eyes and smiled. Looking up at the red dawn, I breathed in the scent of London. Roasted chestnuts, smoky coffee and extinguished fires. It was the smell of flames and life and renewal. The smell of ash and death and ending.

'Yes,' I said.

Or a day of change.

25

THE ROSE RING

1 November 2059

The clocks were striking across London. In the Interchange, every light had been snuffed – but beneath the brick warehouse, in the secret labyrinth of the Camden Catacombs, the scrimmage was about to begin.

It hadn't come as a surprise when Minty revealed the venue. Whatever the Rag and Bone Man and the Abbess were plotting, it all hinged on the scrimmage. Holding it in their domain made perfect sense.

I had left a note for Warden at the Old Lyre, and another in the call box for Wynn. If my luck held out, everyone would arrive at the right time.

Jaxon and I stepped out of our cab. Competitors traditionally wore the colours of their auras, but Jaxon and I were haughtily monochrome. A thin band held my curls away from my face, with a subtle fascinator made from swan feathers and silver ribbon. My lips were black and my eyes outlined, the paint expertly applied by Eliza.

Naturally, Jaxon looked just as resplendent. His hair gleamed with oil, and white contacts bleached his irises. He had cajoled me into wearing them, too.

During the scrimmage, our matching costumes would mark us out as an allied pair. Both of us were in tailcoats, which looked elegant, but allowed us to move. Where mine was ivory, Jaxon wore pure white. His fastenings and cufflinks were gold, while mine were silver. Under our coats were supple trousers, tucked into grey boots with low heels.

I felt confident in this ensemble. Eliza had made it to measure, with her usual attention to detail. She had sewn a few pockets into the coat. Beneath it, a bandolier crossed my chest, full of throwing knives.

A small lace mask helped conceal my identity. Most syndies must know by now that the Pale Dreamer was one of the fugitives, but Jaxon didn't want it distracting anyone from the spectacle of our performance.

'The hour is upon us.' He smoothed his lapels. 'Ready to win, darling?'

'Absolutely,' I said.

'Pity about the setting. I can't imagine why the Abbess would hold it here.'

'Maybe she called a truce with the Rag and Bone Man.'

Jaxon grunted.

The rest of the gang disembarked from their cab. Twenty of our personal guests were already here, waiting to cheer us on as we fought. Chat and Babs were among them. Babs gave me a grin and a wave.

Eliza came first. In her dress of alabaster lace, she might have been an aristocrat from the monarch days. Nadine was in a sleeveless cream blouse and tapered black trousers, while Zeke had gone for a dark twill suit and turtleneck. Danica had scrubbed up nicely in pinstripes.

Other than me, she was the only masked one of us. Nick stood close to Zeke, wearing a black silk waistcoat over a white shirt, barefaced.

'My darlings.' Jaxon linked my arm. 'I shan't make a tedious speech. We've talked enough about this night. First, to battle. Then we celebrate.'

'We're with you,' Nadine said. 'All the way.'

'Yes.' Zeke smiled, but he was sweating. 'You are going to win. I know it.'

Jaxon had accepted the lie about the food poisoning, but it didn't exempt Zeke from the scrimmage. At least Nick was there to keep him upright.

Eliza caught my eye, her brow furrowing. I was trusting her not to betray me.

A Rag Doll opened the black door to the Interchange. As we stepped inside, I recognised his dreamscape, tensing before I could stop myself.

'White Binder,' Hodden said. 'Pale Dreamer.'

His pale lavender eyes bored into mine. I stared him down, my jaw set.

'Welcome to Camden,' he said, as if we had never met in our lives. 'The Rag and Bone Man is honoured to be hosting the fourth scrimmage.'

Jaxon gave him a curt nod. We followed another Rag Doll, who held a lantern.

'Paige.' Jaxon used a soft voice. 'Was he one of the two who tried to kill you?'

'Yes,' I said.

It wasn't strictly a lie.

Another Rag Doll led us down the steps to the tunnels. They had cleared up the crates Warden had destroyed, but the wine had stained the floor.

My ribcage felt smaller. I glanced over my shoulder, finding that the exit was already out of sight. If there was one place I didn't want to be going, it was back into the Camden Catacombs, where voyants could be swallowed up, never to be found. If the Rag and Bone Man had his way, I would never walk out of here alive. I took a few deep breaths.

'Don't be nervous.' Jaxon patted my hand. 'The Rag Dolls won't dare strike tonight. As soon as I am Underlord, I will punish their insolence.'

I nodded.

The Camden Catacombs had been transformed. All the rubbish and rubble was gone, the floors swept clean. The naked lightbulbs had been replaced by strings of stained-glass lanterns, each the colour of an aura. When we entered the central vault, I couldn't believe my eyes.

Grand crimson drapes hung from the walls, turning the space into a splendid theatre. A painting of the Bloody King – our supposed forefather – looked down on us all, holding up a sceptre. A troupe of whisperers played instruments, creating a soundscape that had lured at least a hundred spirits. Red upholstered chairs had been arranged around large tables, each of which had been set aside for a section.

Golden bowls shone here and there, brimming with red wine. Platters of lavish food covered the black tablecloths. Huge game pies, drizzled with thick gravy; gourmet sandwiches with all manner of fillings, from lobster to vintage cheese and walnuts; brisket of beef, boiled with onions and spices; sponge cakes, light as you please, layered with cream and strawberry jam. People were already finding seats, feasting on steamed puddings and flummery and sweet brandy snaps.

Nick had cooked me a square meal to fuel me for the fight. I hadn't been able to finish it, and I doubted I could stomach anything now.

'This is grotesque,' Nick muttered. 'We're about to watch a fight to the death, voyants are starving, and we're throwing a party.'

'Thank you, Nick,' Danica said, her voice muffled.

'What?'

'I've been searching for a long time for someone who is more boring than me. I'm so glad to have found you.'

Nick pursed his lips. He kept a reassuring hand on Zeke, who still looked weary.

We stopped for drinks. While most of the others chose wine, I scooped my glass through a bowl of blood mecks. Real wine could get me killed tonight. I sipped the spiced punch, scanning the vault. A chalk line separated the guests' seats from where the fight would take place.

There it was. The Rose Ring, symbol of secrecy and plague, claimed by the syndicate in defiance of Scion. The old rhyme flitted through my head.

Ring a ring of roses, a pocket full of posies. Ashes, ashes, we all fall down …

One rose had been laid out for each participant, arranged at equal distances in an oval circle, creating an amphitheatre in the middle of the vault. Ash had been poured into it to soak up any blood we spilled.

Eliza touched my arm, lifting me from my thoughts. Jaxon and the others had already gone to our designated table, leaving me to gaze at the ring.

'Are you all right?'

The edges of my vision had turned blotchy and dark. My hands were clammy.

'Fine,' I said. 'I just wanted a look.'

'Come on. Let's join the others.'

She led me to the chair between Jaxon and Nick. I recognised many of the voyants in the vault, but not everyone. Some of them were trailing guardian angels, boundlings or spools. So far, the other participants' costumes all reflected their auras. Jaxon leaned towards me.

'You're quiet, Paige. I do hope you aren't going to faint.'

'No. Just looking,' I said. 'The monochrome was inspired. We stand out.'

'Darling, I would sooner be caught waltzing with Didion Waite than dressed from head to toe in orange. At least you would have had the dignity of matching the roses.' The corner of his mouth flinched. 'Speaking of Didion, I simply must torment him, just once more.'

I raised an eyebrow. 'Are you planning to be nice to him when you're Underlord?'

'You misunderstand me. I must specifically torment him with the prospect of my victory.'

He gave me a light kiss on the hand before he strode away. Didion was in greasepaint and a luxurious periwig, so large I was impressed he could stand upright. He curled his lip when Jaxon sauntered up to him.

The endless crackle of people and spirits was overwhelming my sixth sense. To tune it out, I concentrated on the golden cord. From what I could feel, Warden was calm. Clearly nothing had changed on his end.

Danica tapped me on the shoulder, distracting me.

'About your oxygen,' she said. 'A nasal cannula is less conspicuous.' She brought a coil of clear tubing from her satchel. 'Open your coat.'

She tucked a can of oxygen into one of my inner pockets, attached the tubing, and fed it under my waistcoat. Lifting my lace mask, she looped the tubing over my ears and attached the cannula to my nose.

'With your mask, this should be difficult to see,' Danica said. 'The oxygen will only last so long, so don't go overboard. This isn't a ventilator – it can't breathe for you – but it might keep you from passing out.'

'Thank you, Dani.'

'Okay. Please don't try to hug me.'

'I would never be that stupid.'

I tested the oxygen can. Once I had worked out how to adjust the flow, I pulled on my leather gloves. They wouldn't provide much protection from knives, but they might help me keep my grip on my own. There was no limit on how many cold weapons we could take into the fight, but I only had blades. Anything heavier would slow me down.

Eliza came to sit on my other side. 'Does everything still feel as if it fits?'

'It's all perfect. Thank you.'

I put my mask back on. She took out a small brush and touched up my lips.

It took some time for everyone to arrive. After what seemed like hours, the seats were filled, and rivers of illegal alcohol were flowing. By then, I wanted to be in the ring. The waiting had covered me in sweat.

At last, a psychographer strode from the crowd. Her black coils of hair were arranged in an intricate updo, and a pale wingtip collar peeked above her belted olive blazer, a sharp contrast to the dark brown of her skin. A silver brooch flashed on her lapel, showing the clock and pens.

The Abbess followed her, an arresting presence in absinthe green. You would never think she had killed someone in cold blood two days ago.

'Good evening, mime-lords and mime-queens, mollishers and mobsters, honoured guests,' the psychographer called. 'I am Minty Wolfson, your Mistress of Ceremonies.'

The vault fell silent at once. Minty was petite, but her voice cut straight through the din.

'Welcome to the fourth scrimmage in the history of the Scion Citadel of London,' Minty continued. 'There is no more thrilling or important event than a scrimmage. We extend our sincere thanks to the Rag and Bone Man for allowing us to use his den, the Camden Catacombs.'

A cautious patter of applause followed her words. I stiffened when a figure in a dirty greatcoat stepped out to join Minty and the Abbess.

The Rag and Bone Man wore a mask of yellowed cloth over his face, with a thin slot for him to see through, and a flat brown cap on top. The Abbess turned her face away as if the very sight of him repelled her.

I sensed he was watching me through that mask. Not taking my eyes off him, I raised my glass.

Soon, you faceless coward.

He looked back towards Minty. It was then that I realised why he chilled me.

I couldn't read him.

My stomach tightened. I glanced at a masked voyant on the next table, identifying their gift at once – a soothsayer, specifically a cyathomancer. But the Rag and Bone Man gave me nothing.

He had taken alysoplasm.

What?

'As lead editor of the Spiritus Club, I am delighted to inform you that you will each receive a copy of our brand-new bestseller, *The Rephaite Revelation*,' Minty said. 'If you haven't yet read this story, prepare to be both charmed and gripped by the tale of the Rephaim and the Emim.'

A few cheers went up.

'We have also been granted a glimpse of the long-awaited new pamphlet from the White Binder, *On the Machinations of the Itinerant Dead*. Members of the Penny Post will deliver this sample to your tables after the scrimmage.'

This time, there was a storm of applause, and a few voyants came over to clap Jaxon on the back. He accepted the praise with a faint smile.

'I will now entrust you to the Abbess, who has provided us with steady and courageous leadership in a time of crisis,' Minty said. 'I give you the interim Underqueen.'

She took a few steps away. The Abbess walked into the middle of the Rose Ring, greeted by her own round of applause. I didn't join in.

'Good evening.' Her red lips curved beneath her birdcage veil. 'It has been a bittersweet pleasure to serve as your interim Underqueen. As we prepare to crown a new leader, we mourn their predecessor, Hector Grinslathe. Alas, we must now also mourn his mollisher. Yesterday, the body of Chelsea Neves, known as Cutmouth, was discovered in a squalid hut in Jacob's Island.'

Murmuring from the crowd.

'She appears to have been murdered by her own people, the vile augurs of Bermondsey. We mourn her loss,' the Abbess said. 'We mourn for a competent, intelligent young woman, and what could have been her prosperous reign as Underqueen. And we condemn, with one voice, the actions of her murderers.'

What a performance. The woman could give Scarlett Burnish a run for her money.

'I will now read the combatants' names,' the Abbess said. 'As I call each one, the named candidate should step forward and take their assigned place in the Rose Ring.' She opened the scroll. 'From VI Cohort, the Hare of VI-2, and his esteemed mollisher, the Green Man.'

Jaxon smirked as the pair went forward. One wore a wooden hare mask, complete with ears, while the other had painted himself green from head to toe.

The Rag and Bone Man turned to go. When I stood, Jaxon looked up at me.

'Are you going somewhere, Paige?'

I couldn't even bring myself to think of an excuse. I didn't need to placate Jaxon any more.

'I'll be back,' was all I said.

Nadine eyed me. 'Don't be long, Dreamer.'

Leaving them to watch the parade of combatants, I shadowed the Rag and Bone Man. There would be enough pomp and ceremony for a quick word with him.

Beyond the main vault, most of the Camden Catacombs had been sealed off, leaving me a single path to follow. As I passed a foul-smelling alcove that must be serving as the jacks, a gloved hand grabbed my arm and slammed me into a wall.

The Rag and Bone Man loomed over me, his mask fluttering against his breath. It fell to his upper chest, disguising his face and neck. His greatcoat smelled of sweat and blood.

'Go back, Pale Dreamer.'

The voice sounded too deep, as if it had been mechanically altered. It magnified his laboured breathing.

'Who are you?' I said quietly. 'Are you going to confess that you had Hector and Cutmouth killed, or let someone else take the blame for it?'

'Do not interfere. I will cut your throat.'

'You, or one of your puppets?'

'We are all puppets here.'

He released his iron grip on my arm.

'I'm going to stop you,' I said as he left. 'Your grey market is finished.' When I tried to follow him, two Rag Dolls blocked my path. One of them was Hodden, and the other was La Chiffonnière.

'Don't try it,' Hodden said.

I lifted my chin. 'Off to torture another prisoner, is he?'

'Walk away, Pale Dreamer.' La Chiffonnière wore a burlap sack over her head, with crude holes cut out for her eyes. 'I advise you to die tonight, if you can. You touch the Rose Crown, and you'll find out what kind of death the Rag and Bone Man has in store for you.'

'Do tell me. I'm fascinated.'

'You killed Moreen,' La Chiffonnière said. 'I think he'll let the rats have you.'

'Moreen tried to kill me first. But you know that,' I said. 'Enjoy your last hour of immunity, Chiffon. It won't last when I'm Underqueen.'

She answered by pointing a gun at me. I gave her a swift nose-bleed before I walked away. By the time I got back to the vault, the Abbess was introducing the combatants from II Cohort.

Jaxon seemed deathly calm. As he smoked, he grasped an ebony cane with a solid gold pommel shaped like a disfigured head. The same cane he had used to beat the living shite out of me in Trafalgar Square.

'The Wicked Lady of II-6,' the Abbess read, 'and her esteemed mollisher, the Highwayman.'

More cheering. The Wicked Lady was a favourite among gamblers. With a dismissive wave of her hand, she took her position behind one of the roses.

'Now for the combatants from I Cohort,' the Abbess continued. 'First, Mary Bourne of I-3, and her esteemed mollisher, Falcon Brook.'

Mary and Falcon rose from their seats. Jaxon and I would be called next.

'Remember, Paige,' Jaxon said softly, 'this is a show. I know you could kill them in a heartbeat, darling, but you must *grandstand*. You are a debutante at your first ball. Show them the whole spectrum of your talents, so they will never rise against us. Make them fear you.'

'And of course, my personal favourites,' the Abbess declared. 'The White Binder of I-4, and his esteemed mollisher, the Pale Dreamer.'

The roar of approval was deafening. Jaxon stubbed out his cigar and stood with a wide smile. Nick gave my hand a last press, and Eliza squeezed my shoulder. I stood and followed Jaxon to the Rose Ring.

The joints in my legs felt stiff. Willing myself not to fall at the first hurdle, I took my place to the left of Jaxon, keeping my rose between my boots.

Everything was riding on this. The Ranthen were counting on me; so were the vile augurs, the Bone Season survivors, and every voyant the underworld had ever hurt. It was my only chance to save the syndicate.

I had faced death before, when I walked on to the stage in Oxford. This time, I didn't just have to survive.

I had to win.

'And finally,' the Abbess said, 'our four independent candidates. First, the Maverick Medium. Second, the Bleeding Heart. Third, Nicnevin.' All three of the newcomers took their places, to a smattering of applause. 'And last, but by no means least … Black Moth.'

There was a long silence. The Abbess cast her gaze over the spectators.

'Black Moth,' she repeated. 'Please step into the Rose Ring.'

The silence continued.

'Oh, dear,' the Abbess said lightly. 'Black Moth has fluttered away.' Minty removed the final rose. 'Now we have our twenty-six candidates, I formally open the fourth scrimmage in the history of London.'

Minty offered her an ornate golden hourglass. She turned it on its head.

'When the hourglass is empty, I will call out *begin*,' she told us. 'Until you hear this command, remain still, on pain of disqualification.'

Every pair of eyes were on that hourglass. It was full of ashes.

Jaxon glanced at me. I returned his subtle nod, then fixed my gaze ahead. Opposite me was the Bully-Rook, who wore a rudimentary plastic mask.

The adrenalin must be getting to me. I was shaking like I was electrified. Slowing my breaths, I remembered the final days of training in Oxford, when I had trusted Warden. I imagined a string at the top of my head, lifting my posture, as if I could float off the ground. I tried to remember the breathing techniques, but my body was distracting me – heart racing, ears ringing, every inch of bare skin cold.

I had learned as much as I could about the other participants' gifts. Most of them were soothsayers and augurs, dependent on a numen. They wouldn't be too difficult to overcome.

But there were several – including Jaxon – who could pose a real challenge.

Five seconds. I imagined the six vials that represented my senses, pouring them as I saw fit. My vision flattened and diluted as the æther took over.

Three seconds.

One second.

'Begin,' the Abbess barked, and the Camden Catacombs erupted into chaos.

———

As soon as the last ashes had escaped the hourglass, I charged towards the Bully-Rook. The audience screamed their enthusiasm as the clashes began. At last, the mime-lords and mime-queens had emerged from their hideouts to do battle in the very heart of the empire.

The Bully-Rook was tall and strapping, with upper arms as wide as my thighs. A bold choice for a first opponent, but I needed to show I could fight. I drew my sharpest knife and went for him. The bastard grabbed me around the waist and hurled me right over his shoulder. I managed to land in a crouch, but it slammed the breath from me.

This early in the fight, the spectators' attention was divided, but the nearest of them jeered. I stood, my cheeks hot. Not an impressive start. Compared to some of these hulking combatants, I must look fragile. The Bully-Rook laughed and stalked off to find a worthier first kill.

The urge to use my spirit on him was overwhelming. For now, I restrained myself. I had to prove I could hold my own in any sort of fight. This competition wasn't just about strength – speed and skill could overcome muscle – but Jaxon had warned me not to look weak. A frail leader courted mutiny, tempting cutthroats and usurpers. In any case, killing with my spirit would only entertain and impress the audience so many times. I needed to build up to the grand finale.

The fact that I had to think like this was infuriating. My rare gift, the one Nashira would have executed me to obtain, reduced to a parlour trick.

I swept the æther. Sensing a dreamscape just behind me, I moved. The Knife Grinder lurched as he missed his mark. A machete gleamed in his hand, big enough to cut through my neck in one swing.

He was a macharomancer. While it gave him a knack for all knives, that machete was his numen, the one that made him the most lethal. Turning to face me, he made a point of opening his coat. He had scores of blades in there – ornate stilettos, daggers, even a cleaver. His face tilted, making the light shine on his steel mask. I braced myself.

No sooner had he picked two dark knives than he threw them, one after the other. I barely avoided them, feeling a sting as one of them nicked my cheek. He lunged at me with the machete again, switching between slashes and stabs. I threw out a hand to protect myself, and he sliced across three of my fingers, leaving shallow cuts.

I was back in Book Mews, hunted by the Rag Dolls.

No one was coming to save me.

I didn't mean to dislocate my spirit, but the Knife Grinder shouted as pressure broke on him, stemming from my dreamscape. Grounded again, I ran and dived into a roll. I used the momentum to kick him in the stomach as hard as I could, shunting him into the Maverick Medium.

Someone else took hold of me before I could even draw a breath. Massive arms wrapped around me from behind, pinning my elbows to my sides. I knew from the smell of clove and orange that this was Halfpenny, mollisher to Bloody Knuckles. A talented sniffer, he often used oils or perfume to keep the stink of spirits from his nostrils.

That gift would get him nowhere in the Rose Ring.

Eliza was the smallest member of the gang. I had still seen her put huge brutes on their backs. With just a clever shift of her footing, she could turn the tables to her advantage. She had taught me to do the same. Halfpenny was strong, but when I suddenly widened my stance and swung my right leg behind his left one, his grip on my arms loosened, allowing me to reach the knife I had strapped to my calf.

I had sharpened all my blades for this occasion. When I slashed the back of his knee, the knife ripped through his trousers, drawing blood. As soon as he let go, I slipped free, grabbed his collar, and punched him between the eyes, breaking his nose. The blow knocked him flat.

'Pale Dreamer,' Eliza shouted.

A few cheers rose around her. I hadn't known I had that kind of strength in me. As I caught my breath, my knuckles throbbing, I realised.

I was angry.

If the Unnatural Assembly had been competent, none of this would be happening. I wouldn't be here, risking my neck, just as I desperately needed to live.

Another muscular arm locked across my upper body. A massive paw closed around my bloody knife, wrenching it clean out of my hand.

The Bully-Rook was back, presumably deciding I was worth the bother after all. With a snarl, I tried the same trick, but he must have seen what I had just done to Halfpenny. Evading my attempt to grab his knees, he crossed his arms over my front, trapping me against his chest.

He was crushing my ribs, forcing the breath from my body. His grip woke all my older hurts. I kicked and writhed, to no avail. I could feel his pounding heart against my back.

And I understood why Jaxon had told me to demonstrate my strength. A powerful gift was nothing to fear if the voyant was easy to kill.

The Bully-Rook laughed. As my vision darkened, my spirit flew against his dreamscape like an explosive. He released me with a growl. Wheezing and coughing, I groped in my coat for the canister, increasing the flow of oxygen. It hissed into my nose, and I breathed deep.

Now to bring down a giant without pollen.

My opponent was upright, but dazed, lurching around as if he was drunk. Seizing my chance, I leapt back up. I pummelled him in the chest and stomach, then drove my elbow into him, hitting the weak point under his breastbone. As he folded, I plunged a stiletto deep into his thigh.

He roared and fell to the ground. I should finish him off. Nell had told me how brutal he was, and if he survived, he would seek revenge for every blow. I drew another stiletto, my face slick with sweat.

The Knife Grinder distracted me. Apparently he was developing notions. Seeing the glint of another blade, I ducked. It flew overhead and hit someone in the audience, killing them. The cheering only grew louder.

My left wrist gave a twinge as I straightened. Nick had secured a brace for me, but it was only going to take so much. For now, I would use spirits.

I aimed my blade at the Knife Grinder, who sidestepped it with ease. The distraction gave me just enough time to make a spool. I bowled the knot of ghosts towards him, knocking him over. Bloody Knuckles leapt right over him. He was a palmist, but he seemed keen for a spot of spirit combat, too. He flung a string of complex spools at me.

He was good. Spooling ghosts with ghosts or shades with shades was one thing, but weaving more than one class of spirit – that was a fine art, giving a spool a lot more power. I could deflect them, but it would take more strength than I could afford to waste. Instead, I outran them. I cut straight through the heart of the fray, so the spools tangled on other voyants' auras. I caught sight of Jaxon fighting Ark Ruffian.

With the spools distracted, I closed back in on the Knife Grinder. Just as he rose, I slid to the ground and scissored my legs around his ankles, flooring him again. I got in a few punches before he bucked me off.

Bloody Knuckles was hot on my heels, gathering spools for a second try. I pushed a shockwave of pressure from my dreamscape, breaking them apart in his grasp, making several noses bleed. He stared at me.

Behind me, the Knife Grinder rose again. Before he could throw yet another blade at me, a dagger sank into his neck, and he fell, revealing Jack Hickathrift. He grinned and spun a wooden stake into his grasp.

'How are you, Pale Dreamer?'

'Sure you know yourself.' I watched him. 'You planning to stab me, Jack?'

'Not before I see your face.'

'Jack,' came the adoring cries. He blew the crowd a kiss and took on Bloody Knuckles.

Halfpenny was picking himself up. I gave him a swift kick in the head, and he collapsed without a sound. When I looked up, the Bleeding Heart sprinted at me. He was one of the independent candidates, a haematomancer. Crimson ink followed the veins of his face.

When his aura shifted, I avoided him, imagining I was dancing with Warden. His swing missed me by a foot. As we circled each other, I sent out the barest flicker of pressure, just enough for him to feel it.

The Bleeding Heart was unsighted. From his stricken face, he must have missed my red aura, and now he was realising he had bitten off more than he could chew. He sent a feeble spool at me, made of wisps, so frail I didn't know why he had bothered. I forged a spool of my own and hit back, and he flopped like a boneless fish on the ash.

Definitely playing dead. He must have lost his nerve, and with killers in the ring, I didn't blame him.

The audience seemed to be enjoying my performance, even if I hadn't killed anyone. Supportive cries rose from several tables, and Jimmy O'Goblin tossed something at me. A sprig of mistletoe landed at my feet, followed by scores more. In the language of flowers, it meant *surmounting difficulties* – a message of encouragement and admiration. I picked a sprig up and curtseyed, and the cheering grew louder.

My moment of glory was cut short when Jenny Greenteeth seized me around the neck. Her sharpened teeth sank into my shoulder, breaking skin, pain leaping from each point. The Hare took hold of my ankles, and the next thing I knew, the pair of them were fighting over me. Either that, or they were working together, trying to pull me in half.

Now the fickle audience was cheering for Jenny. Taking a chunk out of the famous Pale Dreamer – who wouldn't be impressed by such a shocking tactic?

Jenny clamped a hand at the back of my head, keeping her other arm wrapped tight around my neck. As she leaned back, she lifted me clean off the ground, choking me. I had moments before I passed out. Gritting my teeth, I grabbed the brawny arm at my throat, using it for leverage, and swung up my legs. The sudden move dislodged the Hare. As I pitched my legs back down, I yanked Jenny forward with all my strength. It threw her balance, and I took her to the ground with me.

She was stubborn. Even after losing her footing and almost falling on top of me, she had me in a headlock. I drew the knife from my left boot and jabbed it into her side, then her thigh, forcing her to release me.

The Hare was already back. I rolled away from him and chucked the knife. To my shock, he caught it. I didn't have time to think before he came at me – as fast as his name – and slammed his brass knuckles into my face.

In the three years I had worked for Jaxon, I had taken my fair share of punches, but there was ambition behind this blow. The Hare wanted to be Underlord, and I was in his way. As my entire skull flooded with pain, he thrust me out in front of him, holding me at the end of his arm. The cheering from some of the tables reached a fever pitch.

Jaxon sneered at suburban voyants. Now one of them was getting their own back, breaking his mollisher. The White Binder had many enemies, and the Rose Ring had given them a clear shot at his weak point.

I blinked away stars, tasting warm iron. After everything I had survived, I was going to be killed by a man in a hare mask. I almost laughed.

The Hare showed me the brass knuckles. As I watched, claws sprang from inside them. *Of course*, I thought distantly. *You're a hare, after all.* They caught the light as he angled the sharp tips towards my face.

So did another blade.

A flash of bright silver, and I was on the ground, along with half a pale arm.

The Hare curled over with a howl of agony. His arm had been severed below the shoulder, and blood was pouring from the end. A collective breath was drawn. I sat up on my elbows, just as Jaxon stepped in front of me, holding a sword. Its blade was glazed with red.

'You dare besmirch my dreamwalker with your foul paws,' he said coolly. 'A creature so low shouldn't breathe in her presence.'

'Binder,' the Hare gasped out. 'What have you done?'

'Not enough.'

With that, Jaxon stabbed him, straight through the eyehole of his mask.

I made an involuntary sound of disgust. Jaxon withdrew the sword, and the Hare collapsed. His spirit fled as blood seeped from under his mask.

Jaxon returned the sword to his cane. Now it was his turn to take a bow. It had been a rotten ploy, but a well-executed one, as stylish as it was precise. VI Cohort booed and bellowed at him, but the roar of approval from the centrals' tables drowned them out. Nadine was right at the boundary of the Rose Ring, cheering at the top of her voice.

I couldn't watch him crow for long. Jenny Greenteeth was back, red on her pearly whites, clawing at my legs. As she tried to pin me down, I shoved back with my bare hands, still reeling from the blow to the face.

VI Cohort had just lost a fighter. Now its voyants were shrieking at Jenny, urging her to rip out my gullet. Spittle dripped from her cracked lips, frothing like suds between her rotten teeth as she snarled at me.

Jaxon could not save my neck again. Once was acceptable – a touching display of loyalty to his heir – but twice would be unforgivably weak.

Time to bring out the big guns.

I wedged my heel against her chest and scooted away from her. As soon as I was upright, I jumped out of my body. Now to see if my new skills held up.

Jenny was no medium. The barrier of her dreamscape was robust, without gaps to exploit. I still broke through it, even in a tired state. For six months, a Reph had been my target practice. I had cut my teeth on stone. If I could breach an ancient dreamscape, I could beat an augur.

I stayed aware of my silver cord as I raced towards her sunlit zone, barely seeing my surroundings. I collided with her spirit, forcing her into a darker ring of sanity. At once, I shot back to my own body, only to find myself falling towards the ashes in the ring. My palms snapped out just in time. My wrist ached as I caught myself, one knee buckling.

Jenny lay in the ashes beside me. She gave the smallest twitch, then stilled.

The spectators cheered, half the vault giving a standing ovation. It was the loudest acclamation of the night so far. It took me a few moments to realise it was all for me. For three years, Jaxon had crowed about my abilities, but this was the first time the citadel had seen me in action.

I had to wonder how the jump had looked to sighted eyes. The crowd must have watched my spirit leave my body and disappear into Jenny, all while my physical form was alive. An unimaginable marvel. A chorus of buskers started to chant.

Pale Dreamer, the jumper, just look at her leap!
The wrath of the dreamwalker will make you weep.
She's got poor sweet Jenny and Halfpenny, too –
watch out for her, Bully, she's coming for you!

The chant ended in more laudation. A few more sprigs of mistletoe soared towards me. This time, I flashed a smile and took a sweeping bow. They wouldn't follow someone who didn't play into their charade.

Even Nick was clapping now, while Zeke punched the air. Behind him, Eliza called 'Pale Dreamer' again, joined by the rest of the central voyants. My smile widened into a grin as I straightened, buoyed by the show of support. These voyants, divided for so many decades, were united in this moment – in their love for the underworld, their delight in the many wonders of the æther, even in their bloodlust. It gave me an ember of hope.

As their attention drifted elsewhere, I scanned the ring, taking deep breaths through my nose. There were still a good number of combatants standing, but for now, I was being given a wide berth. I needed the break. My body was heavy and sore, my head starting to ache.

Redcap was the nearest fighter. She was the youngest mime-queen by far, only a couple of years older than Jos. A crimson beret perched on her dark bob. She had the aura of a fury, but not a type I recognised. The furies were almost as rare and mysterious as jumpers.

Her adversary was the Swan Knight, a mollisher in her late twenties, with a head of white hair. A purple cloak was slung over her shoulder. Like the Knife Grinder, she was a talented macharomancer.

'I'll give you a chance to surrender.' She drew a rapier. 'Don't think I won't kill you, brat.'

'Please,' Redcap said. 'Do try.'

The Swan Knight raised her sword. Redcap closed her eyes, and the æther rippled.

Then she screamed.

The scream was so unearthly that glasses and bottles burst on the tables, eliciting a few yelps from the audience. There were rumours of polyglots who could call out with the might of the æther, but not furies.

Redcap attacked the Swan Knight in a whirl of fists and hobnail boots, howling all the while. She kicked her opponent in the face, knocking her flat, only to pounce on her with a knife. Her face was flushed and contorted. The nearest spirits reeled around her, their movements following hers as she stabbed. I couldn't tell if they were echoing or guiding her. This was taking me back to Trafalgar Square, when I had watched Antoinette Carter fighting off three Rephs. Redcap didn't have quite the same aura, but they were cut from the same cloth.

Jaxon had named their order well.

The Swan Knight stood no chance against the violent whirl-wind. She was still alive when she fell, but bleeding from multiple wounds. Redcap rushed towards a stunned Jack, giving no sign that she might slow down.

'Cool off,' someone bellowed at her. 'Get it under control, Red, now!'

Redcap didn't appear to hear. She kept going, kicking and claw-ing at Jack. He danced away, holding up his stake in self-defence. She brought one hand down like a cleaver, breaking his favourite weapon in half.

All the combatants had stopped to watch, including Jaxon. I used the opportunity to retrieve some of my knives, grabbing a few that weren't mine, too. Keeping my distance from Redcap, I stocked my sheaths.

Redcap roared again. She was staggering now, drunk on æther. Jack fell as she landed a terrible blow to his leg. He fell to his knees, hands raised.

Then, quite without warning, Redcap crumpled. Her head cracked on the stone floor, and her limbs began to tremble. Jack scrambled out of the way, just as one of the spectators came running into the Rose Ring.

Stop,' the Abbess barked.

The voyant froze. His eyes darted around, and his throat bobbed. The Monk strode to the edge of the Rose Ring and pointed a pistol at him.

'Only combatants in the Rose Ring,' the Abbess commanded. 'Leave at once.'

The young voyant backed away, looking with desperation at Redcap. A mix of taunts and cheers went up. Her display had been impressive, but she had no staying power. She must have over-stepped her limits.

Her rampage had halted the fighting. To my right, the London Particular swung at the May Fool, starting it again, but they were slowing down. They buffeted one another with spools, swearing and snarling, until the London Particular knocked his opponent flat with a massive fist. The audience groaned in unison, bored by the dull skirmish.

Redcap was still convulsing. She was too young to have full command of her gift.

I looked around for her mollisher. The Faerie Queene lay in the ashes, a knife in her chest, her aura extinguished. The Maverick Medium was already stalking towards Redcap, spinning a blade between his fingers.

No one could break into the Rose Ring, but a voyant could choose to leave it. They would be disqualified, but they would live to fight another day. I shouldn't help another combatant, but when I looked at Redcap, I saw Sebastian Pearce – tied to a chair, waiting to die.

As soon as Jaxon started fighting again, I made towards Redcap, outpacing the Maverick Medium. Clenching my teeth, I rolled her out of the Rose Ring.

'Redcap is disqualified,' the Abbess said. 'She may not return to the Rose Ring.'

'Dreamer,' Jaxon called. 'Behind you, darling!'

I spun to face the dreamscape and thrust out my stronger fist. It was caught by a bruised Halfpenny, who had managed to rise again, broken nose and all. 'Fucking hell.' I sighed. 'You don't give up, do you?'

'Never,' he said grimly.

Fortunately, the dazed May Fool had seen a chance to prove himself. He slammed into Halfpenny, and the two of them went their own way.

My oxygen can gave a warning beep. I turned to confront the remaining combatants. The harder I fought, the faster I could get out of the Rose Ring.

The Wicked Lady was closest. As I picked one of my stolen blades, she caught sight of me and grinned, spreading her arms wide. The sight gave me pause. I still launched a knife, needing this fight to be over.

In a blur, someone else threw themselves between me and the Wicked Lady – Bramble Briar, an axinomancer, mollisher to the Wretched Sylph. My knife buried itself deep her arm, and a pained snarl escaped her. Before I could absorb what she had done, she sent her bearded axe flying across the Rose Ring.

She had incredible strength. Almost without thinking, I somersaulted out of the way, earning myself some cheers. Better get some flair in while I still could.

Bramble Briar ran for her axe. Faceless appeared on my right. I kept a wary distance. She was a summoner, and a good one, so rumour had it. Dressed in orange silks, she wore a white mask that wiped out all her features. There were no eyeholes, or even a breathing slot.

Behind me, Bramble Briar picked up her axe. The Bully-Rook sauntered towards me, while Bloody Knuckles arrived on my left. I took up a defensive stance. The Wicked Lady smirked, watching them encircle me.

This felt wrong. Jaxon was fending off a single mollisher, hardly breaking a sweat, while I was fighting a mime-queen, two mime-lords *and* a mollisher.

None of these combatants were meant to fight together. They must have agreed to remove a dangerous threat. When Jaxon saw them, his eyes widened. Once they killed me, they would probably target him.

I shot a look over my shoulder. The Rag and Bone Man was watching from the edge of the Rose Ring. He wanted me to die in this chaos of hot blood and grudges, where my death would never be investigated or questioned. He and the Abbess must have orchestrated this ambush.

In a flash, I unsheathed another knife and lobbed it at the Wicked Lady. This time, it was Bloody Knuckles who knocked it out of the way.

Were they *protecting* her?

I had no time to think about it. Faceless was gathering spirits. I held still as a spool formed between her slim hands. She was drawing them from all over the citadel, into the pocket of æther between her palms.

The Bully-Rook had got hold of an iron chain, which he swung in circles. Bramble Briar spun her axe. Bloody Knuckles raised his armoured fists. He had filched the spiked knuckledusters from the Hare.

Faceless unleashed the spool. More so than Bloody Knuckles, she was an artist with them. One of those spirits was a breacher – either an archangel or a poltergeist. A spirit that could affect the physical world.

Unfortunately, it worked against her. My pendant deflected it with such force that I stumbled. It rebounded and hit Faceless, propelling her out of the Rose Ring. I evaded a punch from Bloody Knuckles and sprinted at Bramble Briar. Her expression slid from murderous to shocked when I ducked her axe at the last second. It was already swinging, too heavy to stop. It whacked the Bully-Rook instead.

The blade lodged in his muscular chest. As soon as he screamed, I snatched his chain and slung it around Bramble Briar, taking her down by her neck.

The Bully-Rook was on his knees. He yanked at the axe, but no amount of wrenching would exhume that blade. The audience was baying for blood, like amaurotics at a hanging. Out of nowhere, I remembered Kraz Sargas.

I believe their kind used to force animals to do battle for their amusement. We could make a new sport out of it – human baiting.

'Rotten ploy,' Bramble Briar forced out, while I pulled the chain tighter.

'This isn't,' I told her.

I shunted her spirit, and she stopped moving. Before Bloody Knuckles could reach me, I had flown at him, too. He dropped to the ground.

My nose bled. The canister in my coat beeped again, but oxygen was still flowing. I drew a few long breaths, sweat trickling under my lace mask, my shirt. I was overtaxing myself, but I had no choice.

The Bully-Rook slumped over, the axe still in his chest. Bloody Knuckles was clutching his head and groaning in pain. The Maverick Medium danced past him and rammed a filleting knife straight into the back of his neck, finishing him off.

I rose, my vision blurred. Seventeen combatants were either dead or out of action, leaving nine with a chance of winning, including me and Jaxon.

Last I had seen Jaxon, he had been wielding his boundlings, but now he fought with his sword again. He got the best of the London Particular, unseaming his stomach, to howls of appreciation and one scream of horror from the crowd. I stared as his intestines slopped into the Rose Ring.

'Dreamer.' Jaxon beckoned with a bloodstained glove. 'Fight with me, darling.'

I recovered and went to him, my back pressed to his. 'What's the story?'

'Not far to go. The crown's in the bag,' he said with a laugh. 'Let's take down this fool, shall we?'

I tensed when I saw who he meant. The Glym Lord was walking slowly around the Rose Ring, towing a panicked Falcon Brook by the ankle.

'He's possessed,' I said.

'A physical medium, like the Abbess. He's let some angry spirit puppeteer his body,' Jaxon said. 'I will dislodge the possessing spirit. You will cast his out.'

Glym lifted Falcon Brook by her throat.

'Come back to yourself, you old bastard,' Tom the Rhymer roared. 'You don't want to kill anyone!'

Now Glym was gaping at his friend, while Falcon fought to escape his grip, kicking at his knees. His mouth hung open. I thought of how Eliza looked when she was possessed.

'We don't have to kill him,' I said to Jaxon.

'Do it,' Jaxon said. 'Every candidate left alive will pose a threat to my rule.'

'We can't lose half the Unnatural Assembly.'

'I will choose new leaders.' Jaxon pressed a spot on his left arm. 'Loyal ones.'

But I liked Glym. He had a sense of humour, and had always been decent to me. If I won the scrimmage, I had a feeling he would be a strong ally.

As Falcon fell limp, Jaxon called one of his boundlings – not a breacher, but a powerful shade. His lips moved, and it whipped towards Glym, who crashed to his knees, dropping the unconscious Falcon. Jaxon set his teeth as he steered the boundling, a vessel rupturing in his eye. Glym must have lent his body to a powerful spirit.

'Now,' Jaxon barked.

I pitched my spirit towards Glym.

The possessing spirit and the boundling fell out just as I soared in. I ran to the sunlit zone in one sprint. My dream-form threw out its hand and grasped Glym, tossing his inert spirit into his twilight zone. I burst out of him and rebounded into my own body, waking just as my oxygen ran out. Jaxon was propping me up with one hand.

Glym now lay beside Falcon. The Maverick Medium had been killed, and Nicnevin had fallen at some point. Now only four combatants were standing – me, Jaxon, the Wretched Sylph, and the Wicked Lady.

The Wretched Sylph looked weary. One of her fingers hung by a thread, her white corset was drenched in blood, and tears welled in her eyes, spilling on to her ashen cheeks. I assessed her aura. She was a binder.

'You take the Sylph,' Jaxon said.

'No,' I said. 'I'll take the Lady.'

The Wicked Lady had set her sights on him first, but now she turned her attention to me. She wore a waistcoat over a shirt with billowing sleeves.

Jaxon twirled his cane without argument. He closed in on the Wretched Sylph, who seemed ready for her imminent death. She must be a competent binder, to have lasted this long, but nobody was Jaxon. I walked towards my chosen opponent – the woman who controlled the poorest slums in London, keeping them in poverty and misery.

The Wicked Lady swiped her sleeve across her upper lip. Her blue waistcoat was flecked with blood, and a few lank curls hung around her face.

'Hello, Pale Dreamer,' she said. 'Do we have a feud I missed?'

I circled her, just as Jaxon circled the Wretched Sylph. Both of their mollishers were out cold or dead. We were the only allied pair that remained.

The audience began to shout the names of their favourites, or whoever they had put money on. *White Binder* was the loudest of them.

'No,' I said, 'but I wouldn't mind starting one.'

'Interesting.' The Wicked Lady unsheathed her cutlass. 'Any particular reason, or are you as mindlessly violent as Scion seems to think?'

'Jacob's Island,' I said, keeping my voice low. 'You've left those augurs to rot.'

'Take that up with Binder, not me.'

She slashed at me with her cutlass, and I stepped back, my stomach dropping a notch.

'Odd that you suddenly care about the Island,' the Wicked Lady said, a smile hooking one corner of her mouth. 'Three years you've worked for Binder, and you didn't give a shit. What changed, Pale Dreamer?'

'I think you know,' I said.

I had no oxygen. From here on out, I needed to be careful with my gift. Instead, I drew my finest blade, a French stiletto from the Garden.

'She got a cut too far above her station,' the Wicked Lady said. 'A vile augur at the side of the Underlord, always with her nose in the air. I should have got rid of her sooner. As for the Jacobite, she won't last much longer. He sent her away for betraying him – poetic justice, he called it – but this time, I say he'll open her throat and be done with it.'

'Poetic justice.' I shook my head. 'What the hell are you talking about?'

'You must have guessed, Pale Dreamer. Or are you too noble to have thought of it?'

She pounced. I just managed to stop the cutlass with my stiletto, then ducked another blow and kicked her in the ribs, doubling her over.

'We almost asked you to join us, until you started meddling.' She wheezed a laugh. 'Seems a shame to kill you, honey, but I have my orders.'

She sprang away from my next stab and sidestepped. I had used my spirit too many times to predict her next move, and finally, her blade found its mark. It sliced me from ear to jaw, trailing white fire to my chin.

461

The pain almost blinded me. My hand jerked instinctively to the wound, and a hard jolt of agony flared at my fingertips. Before I could stop it, my spirit dislocated, unleashing a wave of pressure on the Wicked Lady. My head throbbed, but I pushed until her nose leaked blood and her fingers loosened on the cutlass. I wrested it from her grasp and flung it out of the ring. It clattered across the floor and spun to a halt under the nearest table. A courier snatched it up.

Blood smeared my ivory gloves. The Wicked Lady looked across the vault, and her grin widened, giving me a glint of a silver canine. Another rich mime-queen. She was smiling at the Rag and Bone Man.

Wait.

The cut on my face was throbbing. The bright pain scoured away my fatigue, letting me connect the dots. Bramble Briar and Bloody Knuckles had both taken knives for the Wicked Lady, endangering their own performance. That wasn't a quick alliance, made to end a threat.

The Rag and Bone Man and the Abbess hadn't entered the scrimmage. Now I understood why.

They planned to put someone else on the throne. A figurehead to control from the shadows while they went on with their dirty work. Bribing a combatant was easier than risking their own lives in this bloodbath. How many fighters had been conspirators, helping the Wicked Lady to win?

Now it wasn't just important that I won. It was imperative.

I had to knock this pawn off the board.

The Wicked Lady smirked at me. Jaxon had been wrong to put voyants in a hierarchy, but he had made one astute observation – the first two orders mostly had passive gifts, not much use in combat. My opponent was an augur. Without a numen, she couldn't use her gift in battle.

At least, that was what I had always believed – until she whirled a spool together and directed it not at me, but at the candelabra above us.

And the spool *caught fire.*

Five burning spirits came soaring towards me like comets, leaving tails of flame in their wake. I was rooted to the spot. They might have been made of flammable gas.

Shock and exhaustion delayed my reactions. I rolled at the last second, but two ghosts seared across my upper arm, burning through my sleeve, wrenching a scream from me. The spool broke apart like a firework and fizzled out. In the audience, screams for the Wicked Lady doubled.

She was a pyromancer. I had thought they could only use flames to scry.

'Yes,' the Wicked Lady said. 'Not just you who has parlour tricks, Pale Dreamer.' She rolled up her sleeves. 'I knew Binder had oversold your skills. Play dead like the weakling you are, and I might kill you quickly.'

'If you insist,' I bit out.

I left my dreamscape one more time.

The Wicked Lady smoked purple aster. Over the years, it had thinned and fractured her defences. I cleaved through her dreamscape, fuelled by sheer rage, and propelled her spirit into the æther, snapping her silver cord. Just as I had killed a man the night I was arrested.

This time, I did it with intent. I killed her for Vern and Wynn, for Chelsea, and for Ivy. When I returned to my body, I teetered, almost falling over, before I regained my footing. The Wicked Lady stayed upright for a moment, the expression leaving her face, before she tipped to the right and collapsed. Her hair lay around her head like a wreath.

Almost in chorus, Jaxon called on Weeping Sukie. The poltergeist struck the Wretched Sylph, killing her as swiftly as a rock to the skull. Her boundlings fled, soaring away from the Camden Catacombs.

And just like that, Jaxon and I had won the scrimmage.

The spectators broke into thunderous applause, so loud it seemed to rattle the tables. 'White Binder,' they bellowed. 'WHITE BINDER. WHITE BINDER.' They stamped and roared until I thought they would raise the entire warehouse from on top of us. They were calling our names, throwing mistletoe and oak, the sprigs landing in ash and blood. Jaxon gripped my hand and lifted it with a laugh of triumph.

The boy they had called gutterling was king of the whole citadel.

His arms spread wide, embracing the applause. His cane was slick with blood, held aloft like a sceptre – or a wand, made from the branch of a tree.

King of Wands, inverted. Liss Rymore was holding up the second card in my reading, my present. *He controls you. Even now, you can't escape his hold.*

My wrist hung limp in his grasp. My scorched arm had already blistered.

A man shaped by cruelty. He was grasping my bad wrist, which ached inside as he pulled my arm higher. *His expectations of you are too high. You're afraid of him.*

Edward VII, the Bloody King, gazed down at us with frozen eyes, the barest hint of a smirk on his lips. I looked up at him, then back to Jaxon.

If I remained silent, I could still be his mollisher, his beloved dreamwalker, his right hand. I would bask in his favour for the rest of my days. If I only smiled for him, he would shower me in praise and fondness, as my father never had. I would never want for affection or respect or power in this citadel. I would not have to shatter the only family I had.

He wears a crown of many secrets, and the shadows are his throne.

Liss was almost shouting in my ear, as if her spirit was in my dreamscape, even though I had banished her. I closed my eyes and breathed in.

Two psychographers emerged from behind the curtains. One carried a large book; the other, a small cushion, made from purple velvet. On that cushion was the authority I needed, sparkling under the lights.

Edward VII had been arrested at his coronation. According to legend, his crown had been saved by a servant, who had hidden it from the Republic of Scion. Over the next decade, the ermine lining and cap had come off, the precious jewels had been sold, and the grand arches had been gambled away, leaving only a wide openwork band.

At last, after more than a century, the syndicate had come into possession of that band, and a soothsayer had been charged with resurrecting the crown. Along the upper rim, it had been adorned with glass roses, the red of spilled blood, for the voyant who ruled under the rose.

Beneath those undying flowers, the gold band had been padded with dark velvet and studded with ceramic miniatures of the Major Arcana. They were interleaved with real numa, from vole skulls and pearls to tiny mirrors, keys and rings. Those were to commemorate Thomas Merritt and Madge Blevins, a soothsayer and an augur respectively. On this momentous occasion, the Rose Crown was also strung with perishable numa, like fresh blossoms and small icicles.

Minty Wolfson lifted it from its cushion and walked towards Jaxon. A man who would have sneered at Good Tom and Madge Blevins.

'We have a winner,' Minty called. Behind us, a few hirelings were erecting a rudimentary dais. 'It is with great pleasure that I announce that the White Binder has won the scrimmage, earning the right to rule as Underlord of the Scion Citadel of London – and that the Pale Dreamer, his heir, has survived to stand beside him as mollisher supreme.'

Witcher Cully led the mollishers in a huge cheer. A smaller crown was brought out, ornamented with rosebuds. Against my will, I smiled, my eyes prickling.

All I had to do was hold my tongue, and I could accept the lesser crown. I could go back to the den, to my own room, and sleep away the pain.

Minty turned to address the audience. The blood was draining from my face.

'Before I crown our new leader, does anyone know of any reason why this man should not be Underlord?' she asked the audience. 'Why the White Binder may not rule the underworld for as long as he lives?'

I had gone through the rules with a fine-toothed comb, so I knew Minty had to wait for a set time for anyone to raise an objection. Jaxon cast a cool gaze over the quiet spectators, not even suspecting my intent.

My breath knotted in my throat. It was now or never, and I couldn't speak, because he had saved me. Without him, I was alone in the world.

Then I caught sight of Nick in the crowd, right at the front. His mouth was set in a grim line, and he looked worried, but he gave me a tiny nod. I would have Nick, and perhaps Eliza. I would have Warden.

I know you. The memory warmed me. *And you will be Underqueen.*

I had faced Nashira Sargas. I had survived everything Scion had thrown at us. I refused to remain stagnant while the anchor moved against us. I summoned up the woman I had been on that last night in Oxford – when Jaxon's influence on me had loosened, letting me stand up to him.

'I do,' I said.

My voice came out soft, but everyone heard. Jaxon looked at me, his hand vising around my wrist. The audience seemed to have turned to stone.

'Pale Dreamer,' Minty said, after a pause. 'What is the reason?'

'Because there is an active combatant still in the Rose Ring.' I stepped away from him. 'I'm Black Moth. And I challenge you, White Binder.'

Minty slowly put the crown back on its cushion. The Abbess rose from her chair, a flush sweeping into her cheeks. Jaxon wrenched me towards him.

'I do believe you are about to stab me in the back, Black Moth.' His breath feathered on my face. 'Think carefully before you commit to it. You flaunted your independence in Oxford, only to crawl back to me.'

'Not this time.' I held my nerve. 'Trust me. I have thought about it.'

'I don't think you have.' His gaze bored into mine as he spoke, too quiet for anyone else to hear. 'I saved you from the slums. Make no mistake, that is where you would have been – an Irish girl with no meaningful skills, beyond what the æther granted at birth. Just a kern, scrubbing pots in the Old Nichol.' I stiffened. 'You would have been tormented and broken, your pride stripped by your seventeenth birthday.'

The same picture my father had painted, that night when he found me pouring out my heart in Gaeilge. The same rage surged in me.

'I made you special. I made you powerful. I made people want to *be* you.' His grip tightened. 'Not content with that, I mobilised the Seven Seals to save you from Oxford. Had any of them been identified, twenty years of my life's work could have unravelled – but I was willing to risk it, for you. Stop now, and I will forget your ingratitude.'

'What, now I've challenged your authority in front of all these people?' I shook my head, my smile thin. 'Now I've spoiled your victory dance?'

'We can blame it on your exhaustion.'

'No more lies, Jax. You can't shut me up this time. You can't tidy me away.' I stared him down. 'All you had to do was act. You've given me no choice. You saved my life. That doesn't mean you own it.'

'Oh, but I still know your secret.' His grip moved to my right arm. 'Did you forget, darling?'

I smiled. 'I don't know what you're talking about.'

I gave him a subtle glimpse of the skin beneath my sleeve, just enough to show him that the phantom blade was gone.

And it was glorious, watching Jaxon Hall put two and two together. Watching him understand, inch by agonising inch, that he could no longer blackmail me into submission. That words, for all their worth, would not protect him this time. His eyes turned to glass fixtures in his skull.

I stepped back, pulling my arm free.

'I predicted a betrayal,' Jaxon declared, raising his voice. 'You saw it yourself, Mistress of Ceremonies, when you received my posy in October. Did I not place monkshood at its very centre – the flower of treachery, of warning? But did you expect my very own mollisher to turn on me?'

An outbreak of whispering followed.

'This is all very exciting,' the Abbess remarked, 'but is it permissible?' She looked to Minty. 'She fought as the Pale Dreamer. Black Moth ignored my summons.'

'Black Moth was already in the Rose Ring,' Minty pointed out, giving me a scrutinising look. 'I believe the Pale Dreamer – well, Black Moth – has done her reading. So far, no rules have been flouted.'

'She is a wanted fugitive,' Jaxon said, his temper flaring. 'How is she to lead us when Scion knows her face?'

'That didn't seem to concern you when she was loyal, White Binder.'

'A mollisher supreme is not an Underqueen. Do you really want this backstabber to soil your beloved traditions, Minty?' His voice turned silken. 'When it comes to upholding syndicate law, the Spiritus Club is known for its brassbound integrity. By allowing this—'

'Coward,' I said.

Jaxon slowly turned to face me. Other than a few jeers, you could have heard a needle drop.

'Say that again.' He cupped a hand around one ear. 'I didn't catch it, darling.'

The audience was on tenterhooks. This was the entertainment they craved. A mime-lord and mollisher at war. A good old-fashioned revenge tragedy. I had done my homework, just as he had ordered me – I knew this event was unprecedented. I took a step closer.

'I called you a coward.' I shed my tailcoat, leaving me in a ruffled black shirt. 'Prove me wrong, White Binder, or I'll send you to the æther tonight.'

And there it was. The monster in him. A film of ice spread across his eyes – the merciless look I had seen many times, as he struck a pleading beggar with his cane, told Eliza he would cast her out, grabbed me in Oxford like I was his property. Once, I had feared that look more than anything. Many Rephs had stared at me that way, but that cold lack of expression was far worse on a human face.

'Very well,' he said. 'I made the Pale Dreamer. I will unmake her.'

26

DANSE MACABRE

Jaxon Hall wasn't one to waste time when he wanted something done, and he clearly hadn't touched a drop of absinthe this evening. The cane came singing towards me in a gust of dark wood and gold, almost too fast to avoid, but I was ready for him. I had sensed his aura move a split second before his arm.

He was as easy to read as a book to a bibliomancer. For the first time in my life, I could predict his intentions. With two quick turns, I avoided the stab and stopped myself dead, like a wind-up dancer in a music box. I clasped my hands behind my back, a faint smile on my lips.

With arched eyebrows, Jaxon took a second swing for me. I caught the subtle tell again, and the pommel hit the flagstones. There was no time to savour it – the blast of air soon came once more, and the cane struck my shoulder. That was going to leave an impressive bruise.

He had beaten me with this cane once before. If the pommel caught my shin or knee or hipbone, I already knew it would be excruciating.

Jaxon herded me towards the audience. I cartwheeled out of his reach and spun on the spot, back into the middle of the Rose Ring.

A smattering of cautious applause broke out from the centrals' tables, along with some of the others. If Jaxon won this battle, everyone who had supported me would suffer for their insolence.

And yet I wasn't afraid. In Oxford, I had stood up to him in front of a small group of people I trusted. Here, my defiance had more weight. Being double-crossed by his mollisher had already made Jaxon look weak.

He stayed at the edge of the ring with his back to me. It would have been irresistible to most fighters, but I knew him too well to take the bait. Instead, I used the opportunity to peel off my pale gloves and toss them out of the Rose Ring.

'Rotten ploys, Jaxon.' I fit my hands into my other pair, supple black leather. 'Last I checked, no voyant used a cane to touch the æther.'

'You seem to be dancing out of its way.' Jaxon turned. 'If I didn't know you better, I'd say that was a sign of fear.'

'I've been afraid of you for too long.'

'Let me remind you why.'

A few voyants had dived for my gloves, squabbling over the souvenir. With the dark ones on, my transformation into Black Moth was complete.

The audience was murmuring. Nobody knew what to make of this. Where the vault had been full of rowdy shouts, now there was tension, thick as smoke, filling every corner. Jaxon gave my black gloves a disdainful look. He swung at me twice more, and twice more I eluded him.

'Tell me,' he said coolly, 'where did you learn these lovely pirouettes?'

'From a friend,' I said.

'Tall, is he?' His footsteps matched my heartbeat. 'Variable eye colour?'

He made as if to swing for me again, then whirled the cane and thrust the other end towards me, the spring-loaded end of his blade shooting out. Its reach was much farther than I had anticipated, forcing me into an awkward step backwards to stop myself losing an eye.

'Maybe,' I said, ignoring a few laughs. 'Are you seeing him behind my back?'

'I know more than you might think about the company you keep. More than I care to know, my dear.'

It sounded like banter to the crowd, who needed a good show for the finale, but there was meaning underneath the mockery. He knew about Warden.

What else did he know?

Jaxon swung and spun and stabbed. I used my French stiletto to parry between steps. When I looked at his face with the raw clarity of adrenalin, I saw a mask with empty eyes, soulless as a mannequin.

If I can't have you, no one can. That had always been the rule. *No one walks away from me, Pale Dreamer.*

He would show me no mercy tonight.

I stayed on the defensive, predicting his every move, but my sixth sense was overstrained. At some point, I needed to attack. As soon as I went for him, however, he pulled the same trick on me. The moment I committed to stabbing him in his left side, he slid to the right.

'I've been sighted for a long time,' he reminded me. 'Two can play that game, darling.'

He was back to being one step ahead of me, quite literally. Now he was schooling me in front of everyone, reminding them all who the mollisher was.

We came to blows again, moving faster. Now it was harder to watch his aura. I drew another blade. Each time I struck, Jaxon blocked me, wielding the cane with graceful ease. He knocked my right arm and clipped me under the chin. My teeth cut into my tongue.

If the blade had been extended, that move would have killed me. Black Moth might need to grandstand, but Eliza had been right. Jaxon was much older than me, and he wasn't a mime-lord for nothing. I spat blood to one side and took a few steps back, catching my breath.

'Of course, this is a duel – much like the duels of the monarch days, when honour was settled with blood and steel,' Jaxon said, the spark returning to his eyes. 'Whose honour are we settling today, Paige?'

'You tell me,' I said coolly.

'Oh, come now. You know very well that these good voyants will never accept you as Underqueen. Even if you win this little skirmish, you will always be remembered as the mollisher who murdered her own mime-lord, as well as Hector Grinslathe – and Cutmouth, too, I hear.'

'That's a serious accusation, Jaxon.'

'Why not disprove it?'

'The burden of proof is on the accuser,' I reminded him.

'Look at my clever mollisher, reminding us she's educated. Did you know she went to Ancroft, of all places?' Jaxon asked the audience, which remained silent. 'Not only did Scion shape her formative years, but she recently abandoned her own father to Coldbath Fields.'

'They know that, Jaxon,' I said in a drawl. 'Scarlett Burnish already told them.'

I sounded nothing like myself, but Black Moth drawled, apparently. Perhaps I would make her a little more arch than the Pale Dreamer.

'Then everyone can see a pattern emerging,' Jaxon said. 'Black Moth chooses to discard the people who kept her alive – who fed her and taught her, put silk on her back. If she can betray her own father, her own mime-lord, what will she do to the people beneath her?'

'There's the difference between me and you, Jax,' I said. 'I don't see any of these voyants as beneath me, and that will not change when I'm Underqueen.' I raised my eyebrows. 'Can you say the same?'

That won me a few cheers from the spectators, lifting my confidence. I stabbed from below, aiming for his gut. He brought the cane straight down on my wrist. My dominant arm shook under the strain.

'And that wasn't from Ancroft,' I said. 'That was from *A Concise History of Clairvoyance in London*. There *is* no burden of proof under Inquisitorial law, because voyants are always guilty. That rule only applies to the syndicate – which you'd know, if you gave a damn about it.'

'I care very much about the syndicate. I am London,' Jaxon said. 'The waters of the Thames are in my veins; the stock brick of this citadel is mortared to my very bones.'

His next movement was fast and decisive. He shunted my right arm hard with the cane, sprang to the left, and cracked the pommel into my cheek. I reeled away from him, hissing a curse between my teeth.

That was the second time he could have fetched me a fatal blow. He wanted to draw this out.

I was the warning. He was teaching them what would happen if they rose against the White Binder.

'I care just as much about London,' I told him. 'That's why I have to keep her from you.'

'Ah, you were brought against your will, to your conquerors' bosom. How can you love this citadel?'

'That's easy, Jax,' I said. 'You taught me.'

Jaxon snapped out the cane, barely missing my hand. I ducked the next strike and whipped out my leg, almost catching his face with my boot.

'You are not London,' I told him. 'You are Jaxon Hall, and you want London as your throne. You'll sit on it until it crumbles, just so you can say you were its king.' I rebuffed the cane again. 'I will stop it crumbling. I will make it strong enough to force the anchor from its heart.'

'You won't survive it long enough. London does not forget a traitor, nor forgive the weak,' Jaxon warned me. 'It will suck you down, Paige. Into the tunnels and the plague pits, the sewers and the lost rivers. Into its heart of shadows, where all the traitors' bodies sink.'

The end of his cane hit the ground. I waited, my swollen cheek throbbing.

'I think we've both established that we excel in an old-fashioned skirmish,' Jaxon said, 'but neither of us wants to die that way, darling. Our gifts are too exceptional to waste. Let us match them at last.'

'If you insist,' I said.

Before he could attack first, I did. He gritted his teeth against the sudden wall of pressure, a vein standing out in his forehead. My temples ached as I hammered at his dreamscape. I stalked towards him, pushing until blood wept from his nose, a shock of red against his waxen skin. He lifted a hand to touch it, staining the white silk of his gloves.

'Blood,' he said with a chuckle, showing the crowd. 'Just a little blood. Is she no stronger than a haematomancer, this so-called dreamwalker?'

But not many people were buying this. Jaxon had boasted about me for years. It was too late for him to belittle my abilities without looking a fool.

'Binders work with blood, too, Jaxon,' I said. 'You conveniently downplayed that, when you put the vile augurs in Jacob's Island.'

Jaxon wasn't stupid. He knew he was losing the crowd. To distract them, he attacked with his cane again, swinging and stabbing with vicious accuracy. When he aimed at my side, so hard the air whistled in its wake, I brought my blade to meet it, taking some of the force before it could shatter my ribs. It jarred my arm to the shoulder.

My feet carried me away from the next onslaught. A spring of laughter welled up inside me. Some slashes I met with my blade, others with evasion. Amused by the chase, the buskers took up another chant:

> *Ring a ring o' roses, Binder's got a nosebleed.*
> *Defeat her, the Dreamer! She won't fall down!*

'How appropriate,' Jaxon said, chuckling as the crowd gave a cheer. The buskers had got them back into the mood. 'Some say that song refers to the bubonic plague. My first strike will be with my loyal friend, the Plague Doctor, who succumbed to the Leith Plague of 1645.'

I planted my boots apart, grounding myself as best as I could, ready for the hallucinations.

Jaxon let his boundlings wander the section like stray cats. I rarely crossed paths with them, but I did know about the Plague Doctor, a powerful shade discovered in Edinburgh. If voyants spoke ill of Jaxon, he often sent the Plague Doctor to give them an unpleasant warning.

'John Paulitious,' Jaxon sang. 'My mollisher requires a lesson in humility.'

The boundling sailed into my dreamscape. Next thing I knew, I was in a bed, burning with fever. My fingertips rotted with gangrene, and thick swellings bubbled under my skin. The very plague I had been fighting had its claws in me. I staggered, straining to see past the horror – mass graves, red crosses painted on doors, leeches growing fat on blood.

Paulitious was old, which made his apparitions weak, though he was strong. I blinked them away, trying to focus on the vault, but he was still in my dreamscape.

My boundlings are superior, for they carry my strength with them – the will and awareness of the living, giving them a power I imagine is akin to yours, when you take spirit form. I could hear that soft voice, see the bird dying again. *This fortification means they can inflict damage on the dreamscape – even manipulate its appearance.*

All dreamscapes had natural defences, protecting them from intrusion. You fed those defences with sleep, and with time. Being twice my age, Jaxon had much thicker walls. I had slept as much as I could before the scrimmage, but I was tired and injured, losing strength.

Fortunately, so was Jaxon. Though he looked as collected as ever, I could see his cuts and bruises, the way he favoured his right side. Even the White Binder couldn't scrape through a scrimmage unscathed.

As I started to fall, my defences finally surged up, forcing out the Plague Doctor. I moved to avoid Jaxon. Not quite fast enough. As I raised my blade over my head, the point of his sword caught my left flank, leaving a shallow wound from underarm to hip. While I was shocked, Jaxon disarmed me, the cane almost clipping my hand. I rolled to avoid the second blow, and my spirit lashed against his dreamscape.

Jaxon reeled back with a shout of anger. I returned to my body, drenched in sweat, and crawled to my stiletto. Now both of us had a fresh nosebleed.

'Quite brilliant,' Jaxon said, pointing the cane at me. 'Observe her array of gifts. When I bleed, she is dislocating her spirit from its sunlit zone. It pressurises the æther around her.'

I closed my hand around the blade and got back up. My knees trembled.

'But what she did to me just then – that was more. That was projection,' Jaxon informed the enthralled audience. 'You see, my friends, a dreamwalker can leave the confines of her own body. She is the highest and rarest of all seven orders. I stand by that assessment.'

When I continued my offensive, he fended me off with the cane, holding both ends.

'But she forgets herself,' he said, looking me dead in the eyes. 'She forgets that without flesh, there is no anchor to the Earth. To her autonomy.'

With a deft hack and an almighty shove, he knocked my legs out from under me. My left side was soaked, the black silk drenched in blood. It was trickling from my neckline, oozing down my chest to my stomach.

'I do believe it's my turn,' Jaxon said.

Sweat glazed my skin. I readied myself, lifting every defence, picturing my dreamscape with walls as dense and hard as those of an unreadable.

This boundling was a poltergeist. Jaxon couldn't use the London Monster without implicating himself in the deaths of Hector and the Underbodies. He would have already sent Rhynwick Williams to Paris. This was either Weeping Sukie – a murdered girl from Wycombe – or Jean the Skinner, who had killed for Catherine de' Medici.

It didn't matter. My pendant sent the breacher packing; it bolted in panic. As it happened, I let myself fall to the ground with a sharp cry, as if the poltergeist had glanced off my skin. Jaxon narrowed his eyes.

He knew I was faking it.

The pendant was icy, hidden by my collar. Before anyone could notice the deception, Jaxon hurled another boundling. This one cut past my defences like a knife through ribbon.

'Mary Holte,' he said. 'My mollisher requires another lesson. Oblige me.'

This boundling had once been a revenant. It had been torn from its remains, forced to serve a stranger. I could feel that deep tension between its natures, bolstering its strength.

As soon as it reached my twilight zone, it started to manipulate my dreamscape, serving as the brush that painted what Jaxon was picturing. My poppies swayed, and spikes came shooting from inside them, twisted with barbed wire. Jaxon might not be able to use the London Monster, but he could recreate the apparitions it had given me.

My dreamscape was my safe place, shaped to keep me calm. The intruder was tainting and warping it. I breathed hard, breaking a cold sweat. The world seemed to fold itself tightly around me, dangerous and crushing.

As I grew weaker, my dreamscape was slow to lift its defences. My vision flickered between my poppies and the ring, the two places overlapping. Jaxon was fighting to keep the boundling rooted, and now he was raising his cane to strike. One swift blow to my head, and I could rest.

No.

It wasn't just my life that hung in the balance. If I didn't beat Jaxon tonight, everything would be lost. Liss Rymore, Sebastian Pearce, Chelsea Neves – all of their deaths would have been for nothing.

Warden had taught me how to split my attention. Still with the boundling wreaking havoc in my head, I rolled to avoid the cane. I willed Mary Holte gone from my sanctuary, willed it until my dream-form screamed. The earth trembled beneath me, and a rolling wave turned the flowers on their heads, burying their spikes in the earth. Mary screamed back as my poppy anemones bloomed around her. My defences heaved back up, and she was pitched into the æther.

When my vision cleared, Jaxon was motionless, hands folded on the top of his cane. A strand of hair had worked its way loose from the oil, and his breathing was heavy. Still, a smile was playing on his lips.

'Very good,' he said. 'You truly did learn a great deal on your trip, Paige.'

My blade was in one of his hands, the cane in the other. Fury swelled from deep within me.

There were candlesticks near the edge of the Rose Ring. 'Give me that,' I ordered a stunned libanomancer, who quickly threw one to me.

Jaxon was hot on my heels. I used the candlestick to block the cane. When he countered with the stiletto, I knocked it from his hand. Throwing the whole candlestick at him, I dived for the slender blade and brought it around, just as Jaxon caught up with me. A scarlet line appeared above his eyebrow, like paint on a blank canvas, stopping him.

'More blood.' His gloves were more red than white. 'There are pints of it in my veins, I assure you.'

'Is it blood or absinthe?' I caught his cane when he thrust it towards me, fire blazing along my left side. 'Not that it matters. I can spill it either way.'

'I'm afraid I can't let you do that,' he said. 'I need a little more of it, you see. I have one more trick before the finale.'

My hands were slick on the ebony. I kicked out with the side of my boot, catching his knee, and his grip loosened. And somehow, I wrenched the cane against his throat, shooting the short blade from the end.

Both of us grew still. His pupils were tiny dots of hatred.

'Go on,' he whispered.

The blade pressed against his neck. My hands trembled. In that moment, I despised him, right down to the pit of my being. I remembered every time he had browbeaten and sneered at me. *Do it*, the voice of reason said, cool and logical. *He'll come back to haunt you if you don't.*

But he'd been like a father, taught me and sheltered me, saved me from a life spent without knowledge of my gift.

He sees you as property. That's why he saved you.

He had given me a world in Seven Dials.

He wants you to be silent …

My hesitation cost me. His fist came slamming into my chin, right where the Wicked Lady had cut me. I reeled back, almost retching at the pain, before the same fist walloped into my ribs. The crack of bone resonated through my body, and I folded. The audience roared – some cheering, some in protest. Jaxon drew the sword from his cane.

This was it, then. He was going to take my head off and be done with it. I had escaped decapitation in Oxford. Now that death had stalked me here.

Jaxon laid the sword down, like an offering. I looked up at him in confusion. With a crafty smile, he drew his bone-handled blade from its sheath. As he rolled up his sleeve and turned the blade on his skin, he whistled.

He was binding. I clutched my ribs, trying to breathe through the pain. When he showed me his inner arm, I stared at the name, my blood running cold.

PAIGE

His eyes shone with the arch delight I had once longed to see. And I understood. It could only be a theory, but it made a terrible sense.

Once that name was finished, I might be unable to use my gift without putting myself in mortal danger. In the æther, as a spirit, I could be vulnerable to binding. If so, he could use my name to control me. I would be the loyal mollisher he had always wanted, unable to disobey. Clever Jaxon, always thinking, turning my own gift against me.

The knife slid through his skin, creating the next letter. His theory might not be right. This was an experiment. No one had ever bound a living person.

I couldn't risk it. With a scream of effort, I leapt out of my body, into his dreamscape.

Jaxon wasn't a Reph or an unreadable, but his dreamscape was stronger than most. His defences shut me out at once. My body collapsed again. I heaved for breath. Fresh blood dampened my side, and my face dripped sweat. Loud jeers came from every corner of the vault.

'She's finished!'

'Put her to sleep, Binder!'

But there were some cries for me. I couldn't tell whose voices they were, but I heard a distinct holler of my name. My legs were like straw.

'Dreamer,' Nick roared. 'Dreamer, don't give up!'

'Come on, Black Moth! Give him what for!'

'Black Moth!'

'Get up, Paige,' shouted Ognena Maria. 'Get up and wipe the smirk off his face!'

My hand clamped over my injured side. I had survived Dublin. I had survived Oxford.

I could survive Jaxon Hall.

With a tremendous lunge, I went for the fallen candlestick and ran at him again, ignoring the screaming burn in my shoulders. Jaxon let out a chuckle. I swung for him over and over, but he danced out of the way. Pure anger overflowed from me – anger at Jaxon, at Nashira, at the Abbess and the Rag and Bone Man and everyone else who had corrupted the syndicate. The syndicate I loved, in spite of everything.

Once again, his fist collided with my stomach. I doubled over, gasping.

'Sorry about that, darling.' He scored his arm again. 'You mustn't interrupt. This is delicate work.'

My lips were quivering. I could barely draw a breath, but there was only a small window of opportunity to stop him.

'Dreamer!'

Danica tossed me a new can of oxygen. With clumsy hands, I attached it to my cannula.

When I got up again, Jaxon retrieved his cane. I picked up a chair from the edge of the ring and hurled it with all my strength. Jaxon was too surprised to move. It struck him, forcing him to drop his cane. I made a grab for it. He clawed it back into his hand.

I was running out of time. Fuelled by fear, I shucked my flesh and shot through the æther, and finally, I broke into his dreamscape, falling on to the frost and grass of his midnight zone.

In the Rose Ring, my window slammed shut. Outside his dreamscape, the æther trembled. I launched myself back out of him, into my body.

Eyes watering, I looked up at Jaxon, on my knees. He held out his arm for the whole vault to see, and the letters glistened in the candlelight.

PAIGE EVA MAHONEY

Sweat dropped into my eyes. The name must have been finished while I was still in spirit form. All I heard were my own thin breaths.

'Stand, Paige,' Jaxon said gently.

I stood.

'Come to me.'

I went to him.

Half of the audience was chortling now, while the other half looked appalled. Nick was almost grey with disquiet. No binder had ever snared a spirit quite like this. The dreamwalker was a sleepwalker now, defeated by her own pride, and by someone two orders beneath her.

Jaxon took my arm and turned me to face the audience. I was limp and pliant in his grasp.

'There, now. I believe this counts as unconsciousness, Mistress of Ceremonies.' He curled his fingers into my hair. 'What do you say, my boundling?'

I touched my finger to his arm. My lips parted a little, and I tilted my head, as if in childish fascination.

'Yes, darling,' Jaxon crooned. 'That's *your* name, isn't it?'

Howls of laughter followed as people caught on to what he had done.

I didn't say a single word.

All I did was dig my fingertips into his arm, right into my bleeding name.

Jaxon snarled in surprise. I gave him a grim smile.

'You wanted me to be a weapon,' I whispered. 'Have it your way, Jax.'

His defences were weakened by fatigue and premature thoughts of triumph. They snapped up an instant too late, just as I dived into his dreamscape.

———

When we had come to England, my father had anglicised my middle name to Eva. Before that, it had been Aoife, an Irish name that meant *beauty*.

Scion had no regard for Gaeilge. Once it had been outlawed, our names had been mangled by force, replaced with unrelated sounds that sat well on an English tongue.

I answered to Paige Mahoney. I had grown to like Eva. After all, my first name was English, chosen by my mother as she died. For over a decade, no one had called me anything else. It was a quick and living name.

But I had lost another one, and my spirit remembered it. A connection to my family. A name I had once shared with fabled warriors and queens.

Perhaps that was the reason Jaxon Hall had failed to bind me. Or perhaps the White Binder had finally gone too far, in his arrogance and vanity.

Perhaps even his power couldn't override a silver cord.

I sprinted through his dreamscape, over snarls of weeds and twisted roots, whipping branches out of my way. Each branch dripped bloody leaves. As I sprinted, I caught glimpses of the grey slabs that surrounded me. They radiated in circles, right into the depths of his hadal zone, embossed with names that blurred as I passed them. This dreamscape was a sprawling graveyard. Nunhead Cemetery, perhaps, where Jaxon had mastered his gift for the first time.

Spectres were rising from the graves, tall and translucent. Their spindly fingers reached for me.

'Get back,' I shouted.

One of them gripped my dream-form, and for the first time in my life, I looked a spectre right in the eyes. Two yawning pits gaped back at me, full of fire.

Jaxon should be in charge in this dreamscape. His opinion of me should dictate how I looked, but he was either distracted or shocked, or both. Just as I had with Nashira, I imagined myself as a giant, growing too large for the spectre to hold. Its arms turned into smoke.

I shrank again as I ran into his twilight zone, where the grass was thick and the scent of lilies hung on the air. The spectres gave chase, but I was faster. I jumped over another grave and ran towards the glow.

Now I was in his sunlit zone. A statue waited there, slumped in grief over a stone coffin, its face weathered away. As soon as I was close enough, it lifted the lid of the coffin. Jaxon Hall climbed from inside.

'There you are,' he said. 'Do you like my guard?'

Cold black eyes stared at me with odium. His curling hair was like beaten copper, and faint strands of silver fingered out from his parting. This was a stranger, but his face did hold something of Jaxon.

'You look different,' I said.

'So do you. But you'll never know what *my* Paige looks like.' He glanced up. 'Or will you?'

When I tried to move my wrists, I realised they were bound. I looked up to see the long strings above me.

'Poor puppet,' Jaxon said. 'You have no idea of anything, do you?'

'Neither do you.' I pulled my wrists downward, and the strings evaporated. 'Did you get my name wrong, or did you oversell your abilities?'

'No progress was ever achieved through lack of trial and error. I see that you control your dream-form, even here,' he added. 'Your talents continue to impress. How long have you been able to enter human dreamscapes?'

'A couple of months,' I said. 'I learned in Oxford.'

'You kept it from me.'

'Of course I did.'

'And what are you going to do now?' he asked me. 'Make me dance around the ring? Make me cry and whimper, just to show how untethered you are?' His eyes watched my every move. 'Or perhaps you simply mean to force my spirit out.'

'I'm not going to kill you, Jaxon,' I said.

'It would make a grand denouement. Go on,' he purred. 'Prove me right before them all. Prove you're a murderer and a backstabber, darling.'

'I'm not your darling, or your lovely, or your fucking honeybee. But I'm not going to kill you, Jaxon,' I told him. 'I'm going to take your crown.'

That was when I ran.

He was slow. The spectres couldn't enter his sunlit zone, and for all he tried to stop it, his injuries were drawing his attention from his dreamscape. I leapt into the coffin, and the lid slammed down on top of me.

I saw the Rose Ring through sighted eyes. A rainbow of auras surrounded me as I adjusted to the new weight of my host. The spectators' faces blurred and spun, and a dull roar washed in as they shouted our names. Everything felt light, as if I wasn't quite filling this body.

Then I saw why. My own body was still upright. A thin line of blood had seeped from my nose, and my eyes were vacant, but I looked alive.

I could still do this.

Jaxon was trying to wrest back control. With difficulty, I moved his protesting body, so it knelt in front of mine. The weaker I became, the more his limbs weighed, and the harder it was to endure his pain.

'In the sight of the æther,' I called.

His voice came from his lips. I used an English accent, so I would sound like him.

Wait. Now his voice was elsewhere, too. *Stop.*

'I, the White Binder,' I said loudly, 'mime-lord of I Cohort, Section 4—'

Enough. Get out of my head!

'—yield—'

SHUT MY MOUTH, Jaxon bellowed. His spirit was fighting back, pounding the lid of the stone coffin. My hand – his hand – slapped the floor, and I almost lost control of his face, his neck giving a sudden crack. His voice rang through my whole being. *I FED YOU! I CLOTHED YOU! I SAVED YOU FROM SCION! YOU WILL BE THEIRS IF YOU ARE NOT MINE—*

'—to my former mollisher,' I finished, gasping the last words: 'Black Moth.'

With that, my vision was yanked back to his dreamscape. The statue had fished me out of the vault. With a crisp rasp of stone, it catapulted me into the æther. I went hurtling into my own flesh, barely keeping my footing, just in time to hear Jaxon regain control of his body.

The cane was already back in his grasp. I raised my arms to defend myself, just as Nick rushed in front of me.

Eliza hastened to my side, wrapping me into a protective embrace. Nick wrestled Jaxon back, but he was clawing for my face like a wild animal, his white teeth bared. His fingers closed around my throat.

'Stop it,' Nick barked. 'Jaxon, it's done!'

'The Red Vision is right. The fourth scrimmage is over,' Minty Wolfson said, returning to the ring. 'Unhand Black Moth at once, White Binder!'

'You little ingrate,' Jaxon hissed.

The loathing in his voice tightened my chest. I could hardly breathe as it was.

Nick managed to break his grip. As soon as Jaxon let go of me, my knees folded beneath my weight, almost taking Eliza to the floor. A pair of arms came around my waist, lifting me back to my feet. Nick was already back. I gripped his forearm with white knuckles, heaving.

'You did it,' he breathed. 'You did it, Paige.'

It took six people to restrain Jaxon, whose nose was still bleeding. The centrals' tables were divided. Some were booing or demanding a rematch, but frenzied cheers and applause drowned them out. I let Eliza and Nick draw my arms around their necks and help me limp to the other side of the Rose Ring.

My ears rang. I couldn't think straight. It seemed impossible that I had just defeated Jaxon Hall.

I had won the scrimmage.

I was Underqueen.

'Order,' Minty called. 'Order!'

She clapped for attention, but the audience refused to settle. That must have been the most exhilarating and unexpected fight the citadel had ever seen.

Nick got me into a chair. Straight away, he started unpacking his medical supplies.

'Nick,' I rasped, 'do you have scimorphine?'

'Yes.'

Now I was still, the pain was flooding in, threatening to overwhelm me. Eliza helped me unbutton my dark blouse, leaving me in my undershirt, which I had worn to wick off sweat. Once white, it was now soaked in red, most of it stemming from my side and gashed collar. People would be calling me the Bloody Queen by dawn.

Nick stayed calm. He dabbed my upper arm with a sterile wipe and gave me a quick injection. It was a small hurt compared to the rest.

Jaxon was on the other side of the Rose Ring. Nadine offered him a handkerchief for his bleeding nose, while Chat took charge of tending his wounds.

Nick opened a pot of fibrin gel. I hitched up my undershirt, used the wipes he passed me, then slathered the cool gel on to my bleeding side. As soon as it was done, Nick started to wrap gauze around my waist.

'It's going to be okay,' he said, his voice level. 'The scrimorphine will kick in soon.'

I couldn't even nod, I was in so much pain. Eliza saw to my swollen cheek.

'Bring forth the crown,' Minty commanded. 'We have a new winner!'

Nick cursed under his breath. He would have to clean my wounds later. Before I could rise, the Abbess spoke: 'What can you possibly mean, Minty?'

'The White Binder has yielded to Black Moth.'

'It was clearly not a true surrender,' the Abbess said coldly. 'The girl is a cheat.'

'She is a dreamwalker. The scrimmage allows for unlimited use of all combatants' clairvoyance,' Minty said. 'If the æther has gifted Black Moth with any given ability, then it was, and is, her right to use it.'

'And what of her blatant treachery?' the Abbess pressed. 'What of her contempt for her mime-lord, for the hierarchy of this syndicate?'

'There is a *lex non scripta* regarding mollishers' loyalty, but no laws that hold weight,' Minty said. 'You would know this if you had read about the syndicate and its history, Hortensia.'

'You dare,' the Abbess sneered at her. 'You and your hacks are in league with this turncoat, aren't you?'

'I am the Mistress of Ceremonies. My role is to uphold the integrity of this syndicate, and I have done that for twelve years,' Minty said, undaunted. 'My decision is final. Black Moth will be Underqueen.'

The Abbess stared from Minty to Jaxon. She looked across the vault, presumably for her partner in crime, but the Rag and Bone Man had vanished.

A commotion broke out on the other side of the Rose Ring. Chat seemed to have engaged a pair of augurs to help, but Jaxon had shoved one away in disgust.

'Get back,' he bit out. 'I may not be Underlord, but I *will* have my due from this day.'

The augur scarpered out of the way, while Jaxon stood, holding out a hand for his cane. Nadine passed it to him. The spectators fell silent, waiting for a dramatic speech.

'The Seven Seals are broken,' was all he said. His voice was almost too soft to hear, but I heard it.

I heard it.

Jaxon was too proud to see me wear the crown he had craved for almost fifty years, but he wouldn't leave without the final word. He walked across the Rose Ring, his cane making soft *clinks* against the floor.

Nick got up to stand beside me, one hand on the back of my chair. Their gazes locked for a long moment. Jaxon and Nick had been friends for over a decade. They were the founding members of the Seven Seals.

'Do you know, Paige,' Jaxon said, 'I find that I'm rather proud of you.' He looked down at me. 'I believed you would stay your hand in the Rose Ring, like the soft creature you were when you first came into my service, and walk away without a single death on your conscience. But no. You are well on your way to being an Underqueen.'

'I'll let you stay on the Unnatural Assembly,' I said quietly. 'I'll let you keep Seven Dials, Jaxon. All you have to do is accept the result.'

'Oh, darling. I would never reward your betrayal that way,' he said. 'That would do you no good, as Underqueen.'

487

He leaned down to my level. Nick gripped his shoulder in warning as he leaned in close.

'I will find other allies. One day, I will have London,' he whispered in my ear, raising a terrible chill. 'Be warned. You have not seen the last of me.'

When he drew back, I met his empty gaze, my heart thudding. He smiled.

'The new Underqueen seeks your freedom,' he said, for all to hear. 'Soon she will learn that the only true freedom lies in the æther. That is where she leads you all.' He touched my bleeding cheek. 'Enjoy your freedom, when the ashes fall. The theatre of war opens tonight.'

'I look forward to it,' I said.

His smile widened.

He turned away and walked back across the Rose Ring. The spectators parted to let him through. Not even the bravest mobsters dared to taunt him as he left – the White Binder, the man who was almost Underlord. The man to whom I owed so much; who had been my mentor, my friend; who could have been the man to lead us, if only he had shown me that he was prepared to change. I had never known it was possible to feel so much pain in my skin and still hurt more inside.

Nadine took his coat from his seat and went after him, not looking back. At the entrance to the vault, Jaxon stopped.

He was waiting.

On the other side of our table, Danica stayed where she was, arms folded. When I raised my eyebrows, she shrugged and slouched into her seat.

She would stay.

Beside me, Nick was still and hard-faced as a statue. Eliza took a deep breath, tears spilling down her cheeks, but she didn't follow Jaxon.

They would stay.

Zeke rose from his chair. With no expression, he picked up his jacket and pulled it over his turtleneck. Nick reached for his hand, and Zeke squeezed it once before his fingers slipped away. He touched my elbow, then walked out of the vault after his sister, his gait stiff.

Nadine linked his arm without a word. She shot me a glance, one I couldn't interpret. I didn't understand her choice – Nadine had been open in her resentment and fear of Jaxon – but I trusted that she had her reasons.

Jaxon gave us all a final look. His beloved Seven Seals, split down the middle. Then he led Zeke and Nadine away, and they rounded the corner. About a third of our personal guests went after them, including a grim Chat, which I understood. His livelihood was in Seven Dials, and he didn't yet know if I would oust Jaxon.

The others stayed in their seats, including Babs. She gave me a tentative smile.

'Black Moth,' Minty said. 'Please step forward.'

In the time I had been sitting, the dais had been erected in the middle of the Rose Ring. Minty stood on top of it, waiting with the crown.

Nick helped me stand. With the scimorphine, I could manage it. I walked back into the middle of the Rose Ring, stepping over the corpses and blood. Minty lifted the crown.

'Ready?'

My throat was aching, stopping anything I might have said in return. I just nodded. With care, Minty lowered the crown on to my head.

She hadn't asked if anyone knew of a reason I shouldn't be crowned. I supposed it had already been a long night.

'In the name of Thomas Merritt, and in the sight of the æther,' Minty said, her voice clear as a bell, 'I hereby crown you Underqueen of the Scion Citadel of London – mime-lord of mime-lords, mime-queen of mime-queens, and resident supreme of I Cohort and the Devil's Acre.' She took a step back. 'Long may you reign, Black Moth.'

There was a hush. No one cheered or applauded, but it wasn't a foreboding silence.

The Rose Crown was heavy, and slightly too big for me, made for the head of the Bloody King. I straightened, willing it not to slip down.

'Thank you.' My voice came out too soft. 'I vow to serve this citadel as best I can.'

Minty nodded. 'Who is your mollisher?'

'I have two. The Red Vision,' I said, 'and the Martyred Muse.'

'Let me guess,' the Abbess said, her tone pettish. 'She can do that, too.'

'Black Moth has done her reading, Abbess,' Minty said. 'There is no law against a second mollisher.' She picked up the circlet of rosebuds. 'Martyred Muse, Red Vision. Please step into the Rose Ring.'

Eliza and Nick came forward, Eliza with a tearstained face. Nick kept hold of her arm. Minty offered the circlet to them, and they grasped it together.

'The Martyred Muse and the Red Vision, mollishers supreme of the Scion Citadel of London,' Minty said. 'Do you vow to serve the Underqueen?'

'We vow it,' they chorused.

'Then my duty for tonight is done. I surrender the floor to the Underqueen.'

Minty stepped outside the confines of the ring. At last, here was my hard-won chance.

No one could stop me speaking now.

'Thank you for your diligence, Minty,' I said. 'As you can see, I'm not really in a fit state to be talking for too long.' I gestured to my face. 'But I owe all of you an explanation for why I turned on the White Binder.'

After a moment, I took off the crown, holding it at my side. The action raised a few murmurs.

'This syndicate is threatened on all sides. Haymarket Hector ignored this reality. He buried his head in the sand and did nothing,' I said. 'So, to my regret, did the White Binder.'

I had their undivided attention.

'At some point in this month,' I said, 'Scion aims to begin installing Senshield scanners across our citadel. Walking the streets freely and invisibly, as we always have during the day, will soon be a thing of the past. If we don't fight back, the anchor will crush us. We've already been oppressed and brutalised, blamed just for breathing, and Scion has the nerve to call *us* evil – and if we let it continue, there will be no syndicate left by the dawn of the new decade. I cannot allow that.'

'Senshield is a fabrication,' the Abbess cut in, stepping forward. 'There is no evidence that it even exists. Do you believe a word Scion says?'

'In this case, yes,' I said.

'Abbess,' Minty said, 'you will not speak without permission from the Underqueen.'

'As you said, Minty, your duty is done,' the Abbess said. 'I will not submit to this Underqueen. Not only is she a liar and a cheat, but the prime suspect in the murder of our last Underlord. My own glym jack saw her leave the Devil's Acre!'

The crowd descended into chaos. Some were already on their feet, screaming for my head; others for proof, for the glym jack himself to come forward and speak.

'You have no evidence of this, Hortensia,' the Pearl Queen called out in steely tones. 'I said this at our meeting, and I will say it one more time. The word of an amaurotic, without good evidence, is rotten.'

'I believe Grover,' the Abbess said. 'I saw the look on his face when he told me.'

'If you now claim you knew that the Pale Dreamer had killed Hector,' the Pearl Queen said, 'why have you shielded her for all this time?'

'The White Binder convinced me that his mollisher was simply in the wrong place at the wrong time,' the Abbess said. Her smoke-screen of soft charm was evaporating. 'It seems his faith in her integrity was gravely misplaced. She is a backstabber and a cold-blooded murderer.'

'That could be said for several of us,' Jack Hickathrift said, rising painfully from the Rose Ring. 'Did we not just play a blood sport, Abbess?'

'A scrimmage is a different matter,' she retorted. 'I see now that if the Pale Dreamer could turn on her mime-lord, she could never have respected our traditions. She killed Hector. How sad that I overlooked it.'

'You believe your gym jack, Abbess,' I said, 'but I believe in what I've seen with my own eyes. And what I've seen is tyranny built on a lie – the lie that clairvoyants are unnatural and dangerous. That we should despise ourselves enough to give in to extinction. They ask us to hand ourselves over to be tortured and executed, and they call it clemency.' I turned on the spot, addressing the crowd. 'But Scion itself is the greatest lie in history. A two-hundred-year-old façade for the true government of England. The true inquisitors of clairvoyance.'

'Of whom do you speak, Underqueen?' the Heathen Philosopher asked.

'She speaks of us.'

The deep voice came from the entrance to the vault; an outbreak of shouting and gasping ensued. Arcturus Mesarthim stood beneath the archway, flanked by his fellow Ranthen. His timing was impeccable.

'Underqueen,' Ognena Maria said, her wide-eyed gaze on the newcomers, 'do forgive me if I'm hallucinating, but are those Rephaim?'

I smiled, my courage rushing back.

'Yes,' I said. 'They most certainly are.'

27

THE GREY MARKET

Eight of them had come. Some I hadn't seen before – silver and gold, brass and copper, all with burning eyes. They wore heavy black silks and velvets and leathers, as regally magnificent as they had looked in Oxford. Even in the cavernous vault, they seemed enormous.

As one, the entire crowd surged away from them. I stayed in the middle of the Rose Ring, listening to the unnerved whispers and chatter.

'That *is* a Rephaite.'

'Just like the pamphlet.'

At least they knew what they were looking at. My instinct had been right.

Warden stepped forward with Terebell. The other six fanned out on either side of them. Errai, Lucida and Pleione were among the arrivals.

'You have heard of us,' Warden said, 'in the pages of a penny dreadful.' He swept his gaze over the crowd. 'But we are no work of fiction.'

Warden was usually soft-spoken, but apparently he could unleash a stentorian rumble when he felt like it. His words filled the vault. It helped that everyone had fallen silent, including the surviving members of the Unnatural Assembly.

'For two centuries,' Terebell said, 'we have controlled Scion. We have let down the anchor in whichever cities we desired, and reaped clairvoyants from this citadel. Your world is not your own, voyants of London.'

It was a nice little speech. I wondered how Warden had persuaded her to make it.

'Underqueen,' somebody piped up, 'what is this?'

'Clearly,' Didion Waite said, his eyes popping, 'this is an elaborate jest.'

'You're an elaborate jest, Didion,' Jimmy said.

'It's no jest,' I said.

For once, I could sympathise with Didion. It was exactly what I had thought when I first arrived in Oxford.

The scimorphine was spreading through me, numbing most of my body, giving me the vague sensation of floating. I needed to stay conscious until I explained this.

The eight Rephs walked towards me, parting the crowd as they went. When I glimpsed the small group of humans among them, I could have collapsed with relief. The survivors looked tired and shaken, but they were alive.

I stepped down to meet Warden. His gaze darted over me, counting my injuries.

'Is that a crown I see?'

He kept his voice too low for anyone but me to hear. The whole vault watched us.

'It surely is,' I said. 'Good timing.'

'They were being held captive, as you suspected,' Warden said. 'Ivy agreed to address the Unnatural Assembly.' He noticed the Rose Ring, strewn with limbs and corpses. 'Or … what is left of them, in any case.'

'Right.'

I returned to the dais. The Ranthen came to stand on either side of it. Whatever the reason behind the penny dreadful being doctored, it had worked to my advantage. There was fear in my fellow voyants' faces, but it was mingled with curiosity, even wonder, rather than outright hostility.

'These are the Ranthen,' I said. 'They are a faction of the Rephaim. Those of you who've read *The Rephaite Revelation* will know a little about them. Here are the writers.' I motioned to Jos and Nell. 'We were like Liss, imprisoned in Oxford. That's where we learned the truth behind Scion.'

Nobody moved, except for Jimmy, who took a swig from his hip flask. I envied him. I could use a decent slug of brandywine in this moment.

'This faction is willing to help us fight the anchor,' I continued. 'They respect our gifts and our autonomy – but there are other Rephaim in the Westminster Archon that care nothing for humans. They are the true makers of Scion, and they will imprison or kill all voyants if we—'

'This is shameful,' the Abbess cut in. 'Do you take us all for fools?'

'Hortensia,' Ivy said hoarsely, her face contorted, 'if anything in this room is shameful, it's *you*. You and your lies.' Her mouth thinned. 'Our lies.'

The Abbess stared at her. 'How did—'

'They rescued me.' Ivy gestured to the Rephs. 'From the Chanting Lay.'

'All four of us,' Nell said, eyes flashing. 'She had us chained up in her parlour.' She held Jos to her side. 'You lot had better listen to Paige.'

'Come forward, Ivy.' I beckoned her. 'Nobody will stop you speaking.'

Ivy stepped towards the dais. She stood before the spotlight in her dirty clothes and bare feet, head tilted away from the glare. Dark hair was growing back, but the shape of her scalp was still clearly visible.

'If you wish to address the Unnatural Assembly,' Minty said, 'you must identify yourself.'

'Divya Jacob,' Ivy said. 'Most of you won't know my real face, but—' She coughed. 'I used to go by the name of the Jacobite. Until January this year, I was the second mollisher for the Rag and Bone Man.'

A wave of murmurs broke across the crowd. All I could do was wait.

'I was born in Jacob's Island,' Ivy said. 'My mother was a palmist, like me. Her name was Parul. She lived through the gang wars, and they put her in the slum, when all the vile augurs were being locked in there.'

This part was just as I had expected. It was the rest that blindsided me.

'When I was eleven,' Ivy said, 'Chelsea Neves came to the slum. About four years later, we escaped together. I ended up in Camden, working for a kidsman called Agatha Lamb. The Rag and Bone Man noticed me. Once I outgrew the gutter, he invited me to join his gang. The rawhand was inked on to my arm, and I was initiated as a Rag Doll.'

Now I was thinking back to Oxford. To the first time I had ever seen her.

'The Rag and Bone Man didn't have a mollisher back then,' Ivy said. 'He told the Unnatural Assembly he did, but the Wild Hunter never existed. His first mollisher abandoned him, and he refused to take another.'

The Abbess had gone notably quiet. The Ranthen were also silent, watching us.

'He knew I came from Jacob's Island,' Ivy said. 'He claimed he could trust me, because I knew what it was like to be mistreated by the syndicate. When I was twenty, he promoted me. I became mollisher of II-4.'

I folded my arms. 'Did you ever see his face?'

'Never. He always wore his mask,' Ivy said. 'I did the same.' She raised her chin. 'Not long after I became his mollisher, he asked me to join him on an endeavour.'

She closed her eyes.

'Ivy,' I said. 'What was the endeavour?'

'I didn't know it then, but—' She breathed in. 'He was selling voyants to Scion.'

The uproar that followed hurt my ears.

It couldn't be. Of all the things I had imagined, it was the only one that made perfect and immediate sense, but the underworld

– my underworld – could not be that corrupt. Surely even Hector would never have bargained with Scion. Even Hector would kill a rat.

'Silence,' Errai barked.

That shut everyone up. Clearly Errai had his uses.

When it was finally quiet enough for her to continue, Ivy folded her arms, gripping her own elbows tight. Her jaw was trembling.

'He asked me to go across the whole citadel, finding voyants with powerful gifts,' she said. 'He said he was recruiting them to our section. At the time, it made sense. A lot of mime-lords poach from other sections, looking for new blood. But every time I chose someone, I never saw them again. After a while, it began to feel strange.'

I could only listen.

'By then, Chelsea was mollisher supreme. I met her in secret and told her about the endeavour, hoping she could help,' Ivy said. 'She visited the Rag and Bone Man, claiming Hector had sent her to inspect the section, including his den, the Camden Catacombs. She found one of my choices in chains. Of course, she said she had to tell Hector; that an operation like that couldn't go on without his knowledge. I thought Rags was going to kill her, but he agreed to meet the Underlord.'

'Did Hector try to stop it?' the Pearl Queen asked. 'Was that why he was killed?'

'No,' Ivy said. 'He didn't stop it. He joined in with it.'

This time, the commotion lasted an entire minute. I exchanged a silent look with Nick, who looked sick to his stomach. The syndicate was meant to offer protection. Instead, it had turned some of us into prey.

Now I understood what Chelsea had meant by those final words. While Scion had sold us to the Rephs, our own leaders had sold us to Scion.

That was the grey market.

That was the endeavour.

After a while, Minty wrangled the crowd back under control, returning to her role as the Mistress of Ceremonies. This must be the longest night of her life.

'Chelsea and I didn't know exactly what was happening,' Ivy said. 'All we knew was that voyants were disappearing, and each time, our mime-lords seemed to get richer. My gut told me something was fucking wrong, but I was too afraid of Rags to question him. He told me to keep going. I started being more careful about who I chose, and how.'

'How *did* you choose?' I said quietly.

Ivy looked up. 'What?'

'How did you *choose* which voyants to sell, Ivy?'

My tone was sharper than I had intended. To her credit, Ivy didn't flinch.

'Chelsea helped me. We decided to pick wrong'uns,' she said. 'Violent murderers, cruel kidsmen, proper scourges. It was how we slept at night.'

'Who else was involved in this?'

'Hortensia Smythe,' Ivy said at once. 'Otherwise known as the Abbess.' To drive this home, she pointed her out. 'The Chanting Lay is a night parlour, but it's also a trap. She lures voyants into her den and pumps them full of regal and wine before she *sells* them to—'

'Lies,' the Abbess cut in, her voice soaring above the cries of disgust. 'This is outrageous!'

'But the Rag and Bone Man wasn't finished with me,' Ivy shouted, her skin tinged with a flush of rage. 'One night, he called me to these tunnels and stuck me with a needle. When I woke up, I was in the Tower of London. He found out it was me who had reported him to Hector. I betrayed his trust.' She managed a bleak smile. 'Poetic justice.'

In Oxford, Ivy had suffered the most out of all of us. She had also, in all likelihood, helped to send at least a few of the prisoners there.

'You were back in London when the late Underlord died,' Ognena Maria said, a deep crease across her forehead. 'Were you privy to any details?'

'I wasn't there,' Ivy said. 'A few days after Hector was killed, I found Chelsea in Savory Dock. She told me it was the Abbess who did it. Chelsea saw her on the Devil's Acre, butchering Magtooth with a knife.'

The Abbess laughed. 'And how do you suppose I would have killed eight people, alone?'

'Not alone,' I said quietly. 'You used a spirit, didn't you?'

'Do not speak to me, usurper,' the Abbess snarled. 'I do not recognise your authority as Underqueen, regardless of how many bodyguards you have acquired. How very convenient that they brought the Jacobite here to slander me, just as I question your integrity. Even more so that the only person who could verify her account is dead.'

Ivy tensed. 'What?'

'Yes. Your fellow vile augur, Cutmouth, bled to death in Jacob's Island,' the Abbess said, with relish. 'Her spirit is already in the outer darkness.'

Grief wrote itself in small print on Ivy. She gripped her arms until her fingertips bit into her skin.

'Her name was Chelsea Neves,' she said, 'and without her, I can't prove a word of this.'

'Perhaps I can.'

If the Ranthen had frayed my fellow voyants' nerves, they were about to unravel altogether. Wynn Ní Luain Jacob walked into the vault, with Vern at her side. She still wore the pouch of sage around her neck. Ivy let out a faint cry and flung her arms around Vern, who crushed her to his chest, while Wynn strode into the Rose Ring. She looked down at the body of the Wicked Lady with disgust.

'I am Wynn Jacob,' she said. 'And I have a thing or two to say, Underqueen.'

'Another vile augur?' Didion spluttered. 'No resident of Jacob's Island is permitted to speak before the Unnatural Assembly. None but the palmists may give testimony. This cannot be allowed, Underqueen!'

'Go ahead, Wynn,' I said. 'Tell us what you know.'

Didion turned puce.

'Two days ago, a masked enforcer came to Jacob's Island, where Chelsea Neves was in hiding from the syndicate,' Wynn said. 'The gatekeeper said the interim Underqueen had sent this enforcer to us on her business. Apparently,' she shouted over the clamour, 'her business was to cut open Chelsea's throat and slice her poor face apart!'

'These accusations are grotesque,' the Abbess sneered. 'Hector was my dearest friend, though I had no knowledge of this *endeavour*. I could never have killed his mollisher. If you'll excuse me, good people of London, I'll be returning to the Chanting Lay to mourn in peace. I have suffered enough of this false Underqueen and her ravings.'

'No, Abbess,' I said softly. 'You haven't.'

All that could be heard was my footsteps. I came down to stand between the two wings of Ranthen, so they towered on either side of me.

'You were in league with the Rag and Bone Man,' I said.

'No,' the Abbess said. 'I despise the Rag and Bone Man. You know it.'

'We all do, because you've made a big point of it. Too big, arguably.'

'What are you implying?'

'I think you were the Silken, that first mollisher. But I don't think you ever betrayed the Rag and Bone Man. Quite the opposite. I think he sent you off to Kensington so you could make yourself a mime-queen. So the two of you could gain control of I Cohort.'

'None of this is true.'

'The only thing I can't work out is why you killed Hector,' I mused. 'I thought it was to get him out of the way, but if he was in league with you, you didn't need to kill him, or put the Wicked Lady in his place.'

'You are deranged,' the Abbess told me, but her gaze betrayed the truth.

'Maybe, but I'm still Underqueen,' I said. 'Hortensia Smythe, I charge you with the murders of Hector Grinslathe, Chelsea Neves, and their seven associates: Magtooth, Slabnose, Bloatface, Slipfinger, Roundhead, the Underhand, and the Undertaker. I also charge you with abduction, trafficking, sending cutthroats to a rival section, and high treason – that is, conspiracy with the anchor. You'll be placed under house arrest to await trial by the Unnatural Assembly.'

A sea of stricken faces looked between us. The Abbess laughed into the silence.

'The arrogance of you,' she said. 'We are the lawless of London. What prison will you throw me in – or will you kill me now and lay my corpse in Flower and Dean Street? What kind of Underqueen will you be?'

'I hope I can be a just one,' I said.

'Then where is your evidence, Underqueen?'

'You, Abbess,' I said. 'You're the evidence.' I nodded to a courier, who jumped to attention. 'Would you kindly check the Wicked Lady's right arm?'

'Yes, Underqueen.'

He knelt beside the body, which Wynn looked as if she wanted to kick. Ivy and Vern came to stand with her, and she drew them into her arms.

The Wicked Lady looked almost peaceful, compared to some of the other corpses. As we all watched, the courier took out a penknife and cut open her sleeve, exposing her upper arm.

There, for all to see, was a tattoo of a skeletal hand, rendered in black and white. Ognena Maria stepped forward, crouching down to look closer.

'It's the rawhand,' she called to the people at the back of the audience.

'Yes,' I said. 'You'll also find it on the Bully-Rook and Bramble Briar, and everyone else who was helping her in the ring, because all of them were working for the Abbess and Rag and Bone Man. All of them were in on this … grey market.' I smiled at the Abbess, who was starting to look skeletal herself. 'Let's see that arm of yours, Hortensia.'

The Abbess took a step backwards, away from the crowd and the evidence in the ring. In an instant of strange clarity, I saw the tiny shifts in her expression – her lips pulling back over her teeth, the quick flare in her nostrils.

All around us, faces were hardening.

'Arrest her,' I said.

And they obeyed. Anyone who hadn't been standing rose to their feet, facing the Abbess, who kept retreating. There were no

Rag Dolls or Nightingales left in the crowd. Every one of her associates had vanished.

The Rag and Bone Man had abandoned his old mollisher.

'Very well, Black Moth,' the Abbess said. 'Here is the one who truly killed Hector.'

She covered her own mouth with a silk glove. I stiffened.

And suddenly, a poltergeist appeared.

The audience moved away from it. It circled the vault. I watched it rattle chairs and tables, then soar around the chandelier, extinguishing every candle. All the other spirits cowered in its wake. I didn't recognise this poltergeist, and I hoped I never encountered it again.

When the golden cord gave a harsh vibration, I realised four of the Ranthen had seized up. Warden was stooped among them, his eyes burning. He was gripping his shoulder, his other hand balled into a fist.

'Warden,' I said. 'What is it?'

'Kill her,' the Abbess barked.

She pointed straight at me. The poltergeist threw me backwards, right over the dais. Before I could hit the floor, I was wrenched upward again and slammed against the curtains of the nearest wall, held up by an unseen hand. Eliza and Nick ran towards me, shouting my name.

Panic closed my throat and racked my limbs. I was the little girl in the poppy field again. The poltergeist was holding me by the shoulders, but all it had to do was reach for my bare skin, and it would mark me.

Then the pendant was cold on my neckline, and the poltergeist released me, its grip broken. I fell at once, landing hard on my feet. The spotlight cart flickered.

I stood tall.

As if a wire had snapped, the Abbess buckled, and the poltergeist was gone. As our gazes met, her lips formed the word *impossible*. Teeth clenched, she took a revolver from her jacket and aimed it at my heart. My vision tunnelled; my reactions failed me. All I did was raise my hands.

Then the Ranthen were there, closing ranks to protect me. I was their investment now. Warden took three bullets to the chest in quick succession, but managed to stay upright. Turning wildly, the Abbess spun a few spools and blasted the nearest voyants back with them. Her next bullet hit Ivy, who crumpled to the ground. I heard myself shout her name as Wynn and Vern rushed to shield her.

The Abbess laughed again, alone. And a gun went off, but it wasn't hers.

The bullet hit her just under the ribs. Two more shots finished her off, one each from Tom the Rhymer and Ognena Maria, head and heart.

The Abbess collapsed. As silence fell in the vault again, and blood seeped from the small hole in her temple, I drew a deep, shuddering breath. To my right, Nick loosened his white-knuckled grip on his pistol.

He had shot her first.

My ears rang from the gunshots. At my side, Nick seemed to come back to his senses.

'Paige.' He took my head between his hands, bone-pale. 'Paige, that poltergeist. I've never felt anything like it.'

'I know.' I shook my head, drained. 'Can you help Ivy?'

Nick made his way towards her. The Ranthen would recover from the bullets, but I still went to Warden, wishing I could risk getting closer. He gave me a nod, glancing at the pendant.

I turned to face the audience. The remaining members of the Unnatural Assembly, along with their surviving mollishers and loyal supporters, were looking to me to make sense of this madness, but words failed me. Jaxon would have known how to explain, but I had never been much of a storyteller.

'So, Underqueen,' Ognena Maria said, 'here we are. You seem to have won the day. And cleared your name.'

A masked trader nodded to Ivy, who didn't so much as raise her head. 'What will you do with this one?'

'There won't be any punishment without a trial.' I was shivering a little. 'A full investigation needs to be conducted, starting with a thorough search of the Chanting Lay. Any volunteers?'

'I'll take my gang,' Ognena Maria said. 'I know where it is.' She whistled to the Firebirds, and they followed her from the Camden Catacombs.

'Underqueen,' said a footpad, sweeping off his cap, 'the penny dreadful told a tale of these creatures, but are they to be feared or worshipped?'

'Feared,' Errai rumbled.

'Or worshipped,' Lucida chimed in. 'We will not reject tribute.'

'They are to be treated with a healthy degree of caution,' I said, giving her a hard look, 'and certainly not worshipped. I'll gather you all to discuss it in more detail soon.' I picked up my crown from where it had fallen. 'Scion can have their natural order. The White Binder can keep his seven orders of clairvoyance. Since our actions will speak loud and clear to Scion, who would never listen to us speak … ours will be the Mime Order.'

Walk out of the vault. That was all I had to do. They parted for me, the voyants of London. Eliza and Nick shadowed me, and so did the Ranthen.

I made it just around the corner, out of sight of the audience, before my knees gave way. A strong arm came around my waist, and a vial was held to my lips. Just before I passed out, I heard Errai speak.

'Just as I suspected. Life is cheap to them.'

After that, I really have no idea what happened.

I was no longer the Pale Dreamer, mollisher of I-4. No longer a songbird in a gilded cage. Now I was Black Moth, Underqueen of the Scion Citadel of London. I curled up in my dreamscape, drenched in the warm blood of rebirth.

The damage to my dreamscape wasn't quite as bad this time. A few chinks in my mental armour, which the amaranth was already healing. Jaxon was a powerful binder, but not as powerful as Nashira Sargas.

My body had endured far more. Even in my dreamscape, I was aware of the distant pain.

When I could finally lift myself from the shadows, I cracked my eyes open. I was lying on a rug, my head on a faded red cushion. My bloodstained clothes had been replaced with a sleeveless nightshirt.

My throat was parched. I coughed.

A scorching pain ripped through my ribs. Other pains flared all over the place, erupting from my knuckles and legs, shooting bolts into my head, searing like hot steel in my left side. A scream blazed up my throat and burned out before it reached my lips, emerging as a weak groan.

Jaxon wouldn't wake up in half as much pain. I knew that, because I had been in his body. He might still be nearby, in Seven Dials. Wherever he was, he would already be plotting to pull the syndicate out from under me.

Let him try.

A paraffin lamp shone to my right. As soon as I made out the ceiling, I knew where I was.

Outside, the underworld must be rippling with the repercussions of my surprise victory. I sensed the Rag and Bone Man wouldn't just lie down and accept defeat. By killing the Wicked Lady, and by not dying myself, I had flung a spanner into his plans. Sooner or later, he would seek retribution, too.

I was going to have a long reign on my hands.

Even when the worst of the throbbing had subsided, I dared not move again. Instead, I just lay on the stage, too sore and parched to sleep.

After a while, I roused myself to move again, opening the nightshirt. There was a dressing on my neckline, and bandages encircled my waist, holding a thick gauze pad against my side. The burns on my arm had been covered, and deep purple bruises had bloomed on my ribs and stomach. I let my head fall back with a sigh.

I must have dozed for a while. When I opened my eyes, Warden had come to sit on the edge of the stage, just beside my makeshift bed.

'Good evening, Underqueen.'

'Not feeling that regal,' I rasped.

As soon as I spoke, a line of fire jumped from my jaw to my ear. He took out a hip flask.

'The Abbess shot you,' I said, noticing his fresh shirt. 'Are you all right?'

'Yes. Bullets do no lasting harm to our bodies.' He offered the flask. 'It has been almost three hours since the scrimmage ended. Dr Nygård will not be pleased that you are awake.'

'I was thirsty.'

With difficulty, I sat up, letting him help me. He tipped the flask to my lips. Even swallowing was painful, and the water tasted of blood.

'Thank you.' I kept hold of the flask. 'Why are we in the Old Lyre?'

'Eliza and Nick have gone to Seven Dials to collect your possessions. Nick wanted you to be nearby,' Warden said. 'When he returns here, Eliza will join Ognena Maria to search the Chanting Lay.'

Nick had good sense, and the foresight I should have expected from an oracle.

'I doubt they'll find much,' I said. 'The Abbess was just a vessel for the poltergeist.' I looked up at him. 'It was the one that scarred you, wasn't it?'

'Yes.'

'How is that possible?'

'Nashira controls that spirit. She could only have allowed the Abbess to wield it.'

The implication settled over me. The grey market might not just send voyants to Scion. Somehow, it must also be a direct pipeline to the Rephs.

The world was suddenly too big for the cramped little cup of pain inside my skull, and I closed my eyes to block it out. I could think about this when I was clear-headed. If I faced it now, I would crack.

'She wasn't alone,' I said quietly. 'The Rag and Bone Man will be back.'

'And you will be ready.' Warden studied me. 'Once again, you have faced great odds and surmounted them. You never cease to impress, Paige Mahoney.'

I managed a smile. 'Did you catch any of it?'

'We arrived just before you turned on Jaxon. I thought it best to wait.'

'You did well. Very dramatic speech.' I took another drink of water. 'I'd better take a look at my battle scars. Any chance of a mirror?'

'Yes.'

He brought one to me. As expected, my entire face looked awful – grazes and bruises, split lip, puffy cheek – but the wound the Wicked Lady had left was the most conspicuous by far. Nick had stitched the red and swollen cut, which curved down from my lower ear and traced the shape of my jaw, ending just shy of my chin.

It would scar, but I found I didn't care. If this came to war, scars of all kinds were on the horizon.

On the other side of the stage, three shapes were curled under blankets. Nell, Felix and Jos, all huddled together, the way people had slept in the Rookery to ward off the cold. I could tell from their dreamscapes that they were dead to the world, unable to hear a word.

'The Abbess gave them white aster,' Warden said, following my line of sight. 'They remember very little of their time in the Chanting Lay.'

'Did Ivy make it?'

'Yes. Nick treated her,' Warden said. 'Wynn Jacob is speaking with her in the Camden Catacombs. They will join us here before sunrise.'

'I wish we could make a new den in those tunnels. They'd make a perfect hideout,' I said. 'But we can't risk using any places the grey marketeers know about. Not when they've been in league with Scion.' I breathed in, making my ribs hurt. 'I can't believe Ivy was involved.'

'She has already paid a heavy toll for her mistake.'

It was a good point.

'I suppose we'll stay here for the time being, then,' I said. 'Where are the Ranthen?'

'They have left to spread word of your victory. On that note,' Warden said, 'I hear your new subjects have been marvelling at your abilities. Not only did you demonstrate your dreamwalking, but you repelled a poltergeist.'

'That wasn't me.' I touched the winged pendant. 'Thank you for this, by the way. I'm losing count of how many times it's saved my skin.'

'It is yours to keep for as long as you wish.'

'How *does* it repel poltergeists?'

'The metal is sublimed – that is, imbued with ectoplasm. It belonged to Azha Mothallath,' he said. I raised my eyebrows. 'Terebell was reluctant to give it to you, but she eventually agreed that you needed it to face Nashira.' He touched it. 'I ask only that you keep it safe. It is one of the few heirlooms from our ruling family.'

My heart thumped. Probably best not to mention how close I had come to hawking it.

'Of course,' I said.

His hand moved to my hair. I gazed at his face as he stroked my tangled curls back. How far we had come in the space of a few weeks.

'Jaxon is gone,' Warden said. 'You did well to defy him again, Paige.'

'It was harder than it should have been.'

'You gave him every opportunity to choose a better path. He refused.'

'Yes.' I let my eyes close, savouring his touch. 'Not that I'm in a much better position now. I was dependent on Jax, and now I'm dependent on Terebell. Like you said, this isn't going to be an easy alliance.'

'I will do what I can to facilitate it. Besides, you may only need our patronage during the initial period of change, to win your voyants' trust. In the end, loyalty will outweigh greed. When they have hope.'

'Is hope enough?'

'Hope is the lifeblood of revolution. Without it, we are nothing but ash, waiting for the wind to take us.'

He spoke with quiet conviction. I didn't have much choice but to believe it – that hope alone would be enough to get us through these early weeks.

But hope couldn't sustain the underworld. It wouldn't bring down the Westminster Archon, which had stood for two centuries. It wouldn't destroy the Rephs inside it, who had watched the world for far longer than that.

Not alone.

'I will get your next dose of scimorphine,' Warden said. 'Nick said you would need it soon.'

He made to stand, but I reached for his arm, keeping him where he was. Wordlessly, I leant into him, so my brow rested against his. We lingered there for a long time, silent and still, human and Rephaite. I could have stayed like that for hours, just breathing him in.

'I'm glad you're with me,' I said softly.

Fire played in his eyes.

'This would seem an appropriate moment for me to kiss you,' he said, 'but I fear it would hurt.'

'Give it a try.'

Warden considered my face. I smiled as his lips grazed my forehead, just at my hairline. After a moment, he placed a kiss on the end of my nose.

'I know the syndicate must always come first,' he said, his voice very soft. 'I will be there to meet you in the interludes, Paige Mahoney.'

'I look forward to it.'

Seeing that he understood lifted a weight from my shoulders. I might have named myself Black Moth, but I was still in my cocoon, forming into my new self. I didn't know what kind of woman I would have to become to control the underworld.

'You should rest,' Warden said. 'I will keep watch.'

'I will, but don't give me the scimorphine yet. I'll sleep for too long,' I said. 'I want to speak to Ivy when she gets here. Will you wake me?'

'As you wish, Underqueen.'

On a whim, I kissed his cheek before I lay down and closed my eyes, oblivion already closing in around me. He dimmed the paraffin lamp.

I slept fitfully. Warden woke me with a touch to the arm, and I glanced up at him, my cheek throbbing. Now I could feel the deep ache in my strained muscles, from the sheer physical exertion of the fight.

'Ivy is here,' Warden said. 'Are you in pain?'

'A little.' I sat up and clutched my ribs, puffing. 'Never mind. A lot.'

'I can ask Ivy to come to you.'

'It's fine.' I was breaking a cold sweat. 'Could you just help me stand up?'

He grasped my elbows and slowly lifted me. I clenched my jaw as he propped me on my feet, sending a fresh wave of discomfort through my body. After a moment, I nodded and walked down the steps from the stage. The scimorphine had worn off, but I would have to stomach it.

Ivy didn't move when I sat beside her. She had chosen a seat on the back row.

'You look awful,' she said.

'So do you.' I took a deep breath, adjusting to the pain. 'How are you?'

'The Abbess was a good liar, but not such a good shot. The bullet grazed my leg,' Ivy said, patting her right knee. 'Nick says I'll be all right.'

'Do you remember anything from the night parlour?'

'Some of it. Hortensia didn't use much blank on me. She used regal,' Ivy said, using the street names for white and purple aster. 'That's why I told her—' Her voice wavered. 'That's why I told her where Chelsea was hiding. I didn't know what I was saying.'

'It wasn't your fault. And you got your own back,' I said. 'Without you, I couldn't have exposed her. It was brave of you to tell the truth.'

'Brave.' A huff escaped her. 'Nah. I'm a yellow-jacket.'

A code understood only by those who had lived through the first nightmare.

She wore a sleeveless top. It exposed her upper arm, where her rawhand must once have been. Now there was a shock of pink and scarlet that ploughed through the smooth brown of her skin.

'He burned it off,' I said.

'For my betrayal.' Her fingers dug into the scarring. 'I used to beg Thuban to kill me. Rags didn't tell Scion I had been involved in the grey market, but after I broke out of Corpus, Thuban guessed I was a syndie. He tortured me for information. He asked me about you.'

I waited for her to go on, listening.

'When Nate got me out of Corpus, I considered not getting on the train with you,' she said. 'I had no right to it, after what I'd done. And I was sure Chelsea had stabbed me in the back.'

I considered this. 'You thought she told the Rag and Bone Man about your report.'

Ivy nodded.

'After you told me she was looking for me, I found her on Savory Dock. That's where she was hiding, before she went back into the Island,' she said. 'She told me she'd passed my report to Hector, and he was the one who told Rags. When I vanished, she thought Rags had killed me. She was distraught, but I couldn't forgive her for ever trusting Hector. I left her, thinking she'd be able to get back into Jacob's Island and be safe with Wynn. I left her alone and went back to Agatha.'

'You escaped the Island as children,' I said. 'How?'

'It was her. She persuaded the gatekeeper to let her out, and she refused to leave without me,' Ivy said. 'She fought her way to Hector to become his heir, so she'd be Underqueen one day. So she could free our family from the Island. When she joined the Underbodies, I told her not to lose herself, but … the power turned her into someone I didn't recognise.'

The violent woman I had known. She must have felt she had to behave that way, to satisfy Hector. To keep hold of his approval.

'We've all made questionable choices for power,' I said. 'Present company included.' I looked her in the eye. 'I'm going to do exactly what Chelsea wanted to do as Underqueen. Minty has the names of all the spirits that guard the Island. It will be disbanded within the next few days.'

'You're serious?'

'Yes. Anyone who tries to hurt a vile augur on my watch will be punished.'

Ivy regarded me. 'Did you know about Jacob's Island?'

'Not when I first agreed to work for the White Binder. When I heard about it, I let myself think—' I stopped. 'No. I *didn't* let myself think. I closed my eyes to everything he'd done, because I wanted power, too. I wanted enough power to be safe, like Chelsea did.'

'Because you're Irish,' Ivy said slowly. 'You would have found it really hard to get a job.' I nodded. 'Me, you and Chelsea, all tearing ourselves to shreds for bad men. It's not easy, being a mollisher.'

'No,' I said quietly.

'I turned up on time to see you fight Binder. That took some real brass, Paige.' Ivy breathed out. 'I forgive you for working for him. Can you forgive me for not working out what Rags was doing?'

'I already have, Ivy.'

She dredged up a tired smile.

'I have to do things properly,' I said. 'Once the Unnatural Assembly gets back on its feet, you'll be given a fair hearing and a trial by jury. The Rag and Bone Man will also be charged for his crimes.'

'That's all I can ask.' She held my gaze. 'I want to see his face, Paige. Before the end.'

'I'd be curious to see it myself.'

My body was starting to hurt too much for me to stomach. With difficulty, I got to my feet.

'You did get on the train, Ivy,' I said. 'You chose to live.'

'No. I'm just too much of a coward to die,' Ivy said, her smile turning mirthless. 'It's funny. Even though we're voyant – even though we know there's something more – we're still afraid of death.'

'None of us know what waits in the last light. Even dreamwalkers can't see that.' I looked at her. 'Ivy, Chelsea died in my arms. She told me to tell you that you were everything to her, and that you had to make it right. Stick with me, and we'll do that together, as best we can.'

Ivy pressed her lips together, and the unshed tears finally seeped down her face. She nodded, her face tightening. I left her to grieve in peace.

On the stage, I lay down and rested a hand on the Rose Crown – the symbol of the underworld, the weapon I would use to bring

Scion crashing down around Nashira Sargas. Warden came to sit beside me again.

'Would you prefer to give yourself the scimorphine?'

'I don't want to move for a year.' My eyes fluttered shut. 'Do you mind?'

'Hm.'

He chose a spot on my upper arm and gave me the injection, careful with the needle. As soon as the pain faded, I slipped back into a deep sleep.

It didn't last long. Before I knew it, a different hand shook me awake.

'I'm sorry, sötnos,' Nick said under his breath. 'You really need to see this. Now.'

28

THE MUTUAL FRIEND

Danica's laptop sat on the floor in front of me – a clear glass screen with a delicate silver keypad. I pushed my weight on to my elbow, unsteady. The scimorphine was still slithering through my blood.

'What is it?'

I blinked, looking around. Nick, Eliza and Danica had gathered around the laptop, surrounded by bags and suitcases. They must have just returned from Seven Dials.

Beside me, Warden was leaning towards the screen, his eyes scorching in the gloom. Nell and Jos had come to look, too, while Felix was still out cold.

'It started about half an hour ago,' Eliza said. 'We think it's a live broadcast.'

The screen displayed the Lychgate, the place of execution. There was no commentary from ScionEye – just the anchor, rotating in the lower corner of the screen.

The condemned stood in a row, nooses around their necks. Their faces had been left uncovered. I recognised Lotte Gordon, one of the performers who boarded the train from Oxford, dressed in the black shift of a condemned prisoner. Her hair was bound in a knot, while her neck and forearms were stippled with fresh bruises.

I pressed a finger to the screen, zooming in. Charles was on her right, bruised and bleeding, and on her left was Ella Giddings, whose shift was caked with dried vomit. She was painfully thin, and her eyes stared into nothing. Lotte was writhing against her bindings.

'Paige.'

The voice was far away, somewhere I wasn't. As I watched, the screen flicked to a message with a plain white background. The anchor kept rotating in the corner.

PAIGE MAHONEY, SURRENDER TO THE
WESTMINSTER ARCHON. YOU HAVE UNTIL 07:00.

'No,' I whispered.

Lotte and Charles had escaped the Tower, but Scion must have hunted them down. Either that, or they had been in custody for the last two months, their executions saved for exactly the right moment.

'It's half past six,' Eliza said. 'We got here as fast as we could.'

Pressure rushed from my dreamscape, leaking into the æther. Before it could touch the others, I suppressed it, cramming it down until blood ran from my nose and flooded my mouth with the taste of metal.

It couldn't be a coincidence that Scion was making this open threat now. There must be a spy in the syndicate, who had told them I was Underqueen, making them understand the fresh threat I posed. If I entered the Westminster Archon, I would never come out – but if I failed to answer the summons, all three prisoners would die, and every voyant in London would believe that I had done nothing to save them. A swift and effective way to undermine my rule.

Nashira had acted quickly.

The other Bone Season survivors had been woken by the commotion. They had gathered around the laptop as well.

'Paige,' Jos said, 'are they going to die?'

'Shh.' Nell gathered him into her arms. 'Of course not. Paige won't let them.'

'Paige can't hand herself in,' Eliza said, staring. 'That's exactly what Scion wants.'

'We have to help them,' Nell pressed. 'We already lost Liss, and now—' She stopped, her jaw shaking. 'Paige, you weren't a performer. Don't treat us the way the Rephs did, like our lives didn't mean anything. Almost none of us escaped. We can't lose three more.'

'Eliza is right, Nell,' Nick said. 'If we lose Paige, we lose any influence we have over the syndicate. We lose this war before it's started.'

'Paige,' Eliza said, her voice much harder than usual, 'you can't do this. You're Underqueen.' She grasped my shoulder. 'I left Jax because I believed you could lead us. Please don't make me regret it.'

'You have to try, Paige,' Nell insisted.

'No,' Jos said, tears in his eyes. 'Lotte wouldn't want Paige to die.'

'She wouldn't want to die herself, either!'

'It's too late,' Ivy said. She had come to join us. 'Look at them, Nell.'

Nell looked away, her teeth gritted. I kept watching the screen. All three of the prisoners' mouths were sealed with dermal adhesive.

'I'll go to the Archon,' I said.

'Paige, no,' Nick said hotly, echoed by Eliza. 'They won't let you walk out of there alive.'

'Nashira will be counting upon your altruism,' Warden said in a soft voice. 'If you go to the Westminster Archon, you play into her hands.'

'You stay out of this, Reph,' Nell burst out, rounding on Warden. 'You might have stopped Liss dying, but you left the rest of us to rot, so you can—'

'I said I was going,' I said, louder. 'Not that I was going in person.'

There was a brief silence.

'It's too far,' Nick murmured. 'You've already overstretched your-self today.'

'Drive me to Westminster, then. Keep my body in the back of the car.'

Nick looked at me, his mouth thinning. 'I don't think it will save them, but at least you'll have tried.' He took a deep breath.

'Danica, Warden, you come with us. Eliza, can you stay here to meet Wynn?'

'Paige is hurt,' Jos said.

'Paige is just fine.' Nell watched me. 'She knows what she's doing.'

Danica picked up her backpack of equipment without complaint. I pushed myself into a sitting position. Sickening pain punched a fist through my skull, poured fire down my side, and branched across my ribs, breaking the loose grip of the scimorphine. Nick lifted me into his arms, supporting my head with one hand, and we followed Danica to the car, Warden bringing up the rear. He sat in the back with me.

In the passenger seat, Danica took out my oxygen mask and a fresh canister. Nick locked the doors and drove along Catherine Street.

'Nick,' I said hoarsely, 'have you handed in your notice, so to speak?'

'No. I'm on leave,' he said, eyes on the street. 'I've been withdrawing cash for the last few weeks – as much as I can without tripping alarms. I have an appointment at the Bank of Scion England tomorrow, so I can make a larger withdrawal. I'll walk out of there with as much cash as they'll let me take in one go.'

'What excuse are you giving?'

'I'm buying a second property in Sweden, and the owner will only accept cash.'

'What if they ask to verify that?'

'I'll think of something,' Nick said. 'As soon as I have the money, I'm going to break into the labs and steal as much equipment and medicine as I can carry. Then I'll disappear.'

'Nick, this sounds dangerous.'

'I'll be fine. Don't worry. I've played this game for a long time.'

I looked at Danica. 'Are you planning to leave your job, too?'

'Absolutely not,' Danica said. 'One of us needs a steady income.'

Nick kept driving, passing squadrons of night Vigiles. The car was moving too quickly for them to glimpse our auras. My wounds throbbed.

'I'll park under Hungerford Bridge,' Nick said. 'You have to be quick, Paige.'

I already knew this was a lost cause, but I needed to try. Not just for Lotte and Charles and Ella, but for every voyant who had been killed in our escape. For the victims of all twenty of the Bone Seasons.

The theatre of war would open tonight. I was Underqueen now, with the might of the syndicate at my back. The grey market had poisoned the syndicate from the inside, leaving it to rot while they ruled over our citadel.

There had to be something better than this. Something worth the price we had paid. I was tired of quaking in the shadow of the anchor, of fighting for survival in the shadows – every minute, every hour, every day of our short lives. I would tell Nashira I was coming.

Nick braked under the bridge and parked on the pavement, close to where a pleasure barge twinkled with blue lanterns, full of laughing amaurotics. Behind them, on a screen no one was watching, the prisoners stood on their scaffold, waiting for me.

Danica put the mask on for me. 'Are you going to leave your body?'

'Yes,' I said, 'but I can try to keep breathing. I can split my focus now.'

'Good.' She showed me the can. 'There's about ten minutes' worth of oxygen left in here. I'll shake your body when it runs out, but it might not work when you're so far away. Watch the clock.'

'Okay.' I could hardly think. 'Warden, do you mind if I lean on you?'

'No.'

I gave him a nod, which he returned. His would be the last face I saw, the last face in my mind, before I stepped into the nest of the enemy.

Danica started the flow of oxygen. I pushed through the blinding headache, taking a deep breath before my spirit twisted free of its restraints and rose into the night. My body slumped against Warden.

In my spirit form, where my vision was no longer fixed to my unsighted eyes, London was a galaxy of tiny lights – millions of minds, bound together by a web of arcane knowledge. Each spirit was a candle in the glass orb of a dreamscape.

Identifying buildings was usually difficult in the æther, but I knew the Westminster Archon. I had passed it many times. Approaching it, I latched on to someone, passing into their dreamscape. When I opened my eyes, I had a new body – shorter legs, thicker waist, an ache in the right elbow. But behind these new eyes, I was myself.

I took a moment to concentrate on my own body, far behind me. If it could breathe when I was asleep, it could keep breathing now.

All around me were sleek walls and gleaming floors and lights too bright for these new eyes. My borrowed heart was pounding. Even though I was disoriented and afraid, part of me enjoyed this feeling. I had shucked a familiar set of clothes and laced on a luxurious dress.

With some effort, I moved my host. When I caught sight of myself in a gilded mirror, I could see that she was walking like the puppet she had just become – jerky, drunken, graceless. The sight entranced me. I was myself. I was not myself. The woman looking back at me was about thirty, and a thread of blood was leaking from her nostril. My suit of armour.

I was ready.

The Vigile I had possessed was a commandant. I could tell by the three anchors on her uniform. When I turned on my heel, her squadron marched after me. My steel-capped boots fell on the red marble floor of the Octagon Hall, the central lobby of the Westminster Archon. I knew it from my classes at Ancroft. Twisting pillars rose high above me, stretching to the ceiling, where gilt shone in the light of a chandelier.

This was the seat of the Republic of Scion. All around me, vast arches were set into the walls, housing the stone likenesses of every Grand Inquisitor in history, as well as Lord Palmerston, the last Prime Minister. They looked down at me from their lofty heights, their faces full of shadow and judgement, as if they knew I was an interloper.

I will destroy your doctrine of tyranny, I told them in my head. *I will cut the strings from the limbs of the puppets.*

Leaving them behind, I walked up a flight of steps and down a long corridor, where the eyes of granite busts watched from all sides. The paintings melted into waves of dark oil and gold.

'Wait here,' I said.

My guard stopped at the threshold of the Carmine Gallery. Alone, I walked under the archway.

I will rip the anchor from the heart of London.

Four figures stood at the other end of the gallery. On the far left was Scarlett Burnish. Her hair was the red of the carpet. To her right, Gomeisa Sargas towered in his high-collared robes, a chain of woven gold and amber strung between his shoulders, hair drawn back from his gaunt face. Frank Weaver was beside him, stiff as a corpse.

And there she was. Nashira Sargas, the Suzerain, standing with two humans as if they were her equals – as if these marionettes were her friends.

Seeing her rooted me to the spot. The last time I had faced her, I had come very close to dying.

'You have not been summoned, Vigile,' Nashira said. 'I hope you have the fugitive, or I will have your eyes put out for your insolence.'

Her voice called to me from a dark part of my memory.

'Hello, Nashira,' I said. 'It's been a while.'

To her credit, she didn't look surprised.

'Good day, 40,' she said. 'Or perhaps we should call you Black Moth.'

'Call me whatever you like. This is still Paige Mahoney, present-ing herself at the Archon,' I said. 'Have you something to say to me, Nashira?'

'You must think yourself exceptionally clever.'

'I've fulfilled your condition. I've even arrived by seven in the morning.'

Even as I said it, Big Ben knelled the hour. Nashira waited for it to finish before she spoke: 'I am pleased that we finally have your attention, but I have no use for you in this body, as you are well aware.'

'We were prepared to show clemency,' Scarlett Burnish said. Her voice was somewhat cooler than it was on ScionEye. 'If you had surrendered in person, we would have considered freeing the survivors.'

'Oh, Scarlett,' I said. 'Don't you think you tell enough lies?'

She fell silent.

Frank Weaver said nothing. Nashira walked down the steps, her long black dress spilling behind her.

'Perhaps I misjudged you after all,' she said. 'Do you not have the courage to give me your life in exchange for theirs, Underqueen?'

'You'll spare theirs,' I said, 'or I'll take his.'

The Vigile I had possessed carried a standard-issue handgun. In a single movement, it was in my hand and aimed at Frank Weaver. He made no sound as a red dot hovered on his chest. Burnish moved towards him, but I fired the pistol between them, stopping her.

'Shoot if you wish,' Weaver said. 'To prevent Scion from falling back under human control, I am willing to lay down my life, Paige Mahoney.'

'Good,' I said. 'I'm willing to lay down your life, too, Inquisitor Weaver.'

He really did mean it. This man was ready to die, all to make sure the Rephs had the power to oppress us. It shook me to see the resolve in his eyes.

'It seems you were wrong, Nashira,' Gomeisa said. 'She is willing to kill for her own ends.'

'For all the lives he's taken at your bidding,' I said.

'Even if you topple this pawn where he stands, you will not stop what is coming. Our influence is already deep in your world, rooting us like an anchor to this Earth.'

'I'm a dreamwalker, Gomeisa. I recognise no anchor to this Earth.'

But I had lost. The Sargas had made no attempt to shield their Grand Inquisitor. If I shot him, all they would do was find another willing servant.

I had no leverage.

'If it helps to allay your guilt,' Gomeisa said, 'you were right. We would have done this regardless.' His yellow gaze flicked to a giant screen on the wall behind me. 'These three lives are for the one you stole in Oxford, but they are worth nothing in comparison. You will pay this debt for as long as you live, with as many lives as I see fit.'

Kraz Sargas had been his blood-heir. The Reph I had brought down with a vial of pollen. After a moment, Burnish touched her earpiece.

'Lower the anchor.'

I turned to face the screen. The Grand Executioner walked towards the lever that had murdered so many voyants. The lever that would open the trapdoors built into the Lychgate, sending three survivors plunging to their doom.

As he reached it, Lotte wrenched her arms from behind her back and cut right through the binding on her lips. Blood unfurled from her mouth, but her eyes shone with furious triumph.

'BLACK MOTH RULES IN LONDON. STAND WITH HER AGAINST THE ANCHOR,' she screamed at the camera. 'SENSHIELD IS COMING. VOYANTS, DO YOU HEAR ME?'

The broadcast cut off.

Another three of us, gone.

'How interesting. Someone in the Tower must sympathise with your organisation, 40.' Nashira watched me. 'Be assured, that act of rebellion has not saved your friend. As we speak, her corpse hangs by the neck from the Lychgate. That is the fate that will befall your so-called army. It will end only if you surrender to me.'

A terrible sound came from my host. A laugh, thick and mangled and hollow.

Voyants, do you hear me?

'It will end,' I said, 'when there are no Sargas loyalists left on this side of the veil. When you rot with the rest of your world.' I took a few steps towards them both. 'Lotte just proved you wrong. You'll never be in full control. You *are* afraid of the syndicate, as well you should be. We're in league with the Ranthen now, led by Arcturus and Terebell. Your past is coming for you, rising from the underworld. The moths are out of the box, Gomeisa. Tomorrow, we will be at war.'

A word that most syndicate voyants would never use. Even *gang war* didn't have quite the same weight as that word when it stood alone.

'Your threats continue to hold little weight. The Ranthen are a broken relic of a fading past,' Nashira said. 'I would almost believe that this syndicate of yours did not exist, were it not for the voyants we historically received from certain members of the Unnatural Assembly.'

Do you hear me?

'Like the syndicate, the grey market was never supposed to exist,' she said, 'but I am not too proud to admit that it has proven useful. The voyants we received through that channel were often far more powerful than those that Scion plucked from the street. Even if we did not require them, Scion used them to bolster our military, or the NVD. The Rag and Bone Man has been our ally for many years, along with the Abbess, Haymarket Hector, and the Wicked Lady.'

'Three of those four are dead.' My vision flickered. 'Looks like you'll have to make some new friends.'

'Oh, but I have an old one,' Nashira said. 'One who returned to me in the early hours of this morning, after twenty long years of estrangement. One who does not recognise you as Underqueen, despite your … association.' She looked to Burnish. 'Do kindly summon him, Scarlett. 40 ought to meet our mutual friend in person.'

Burnish walked across the room, swift and poised, and opened the double doors. A sound echoed through the hallway beyond. The clink of metal against marble.

When he arrived, I knew his face. I knew it very well.

Words, my walker …. words are everything. Words give wings even to those who have been stamped upon, broken beyond all hope of repair …

As he came through the doors, I turned as cold as the æther. I had predicted many things, but I was no oracle. As he smiled, and

523

the sight of him sank in, I finally understood the mistake I had made – what a fool I had been to trust him, to care for him, let alone allow him to live.

'You,' I whispered.

'Yes.' His hands were gloved in silk. 'Me, O my lovely.'

Glossary

Æther: [noun] The spirit realm, which exists alongside the physical or corporeal world, Earth. Among humans, only *clairvoyants* can sense the æther.

Adamant: [noun] A metal from the Netherworld.

Alysoplasm: [noun] The blood of the *Emim*. It can be used to conceal the nature of voyants' gifts, or to hide their dreamscapes in the æther, making them undetectable to a *dreamwalker*. However, it also prevents them from being able to use their clairvoyance for a time.

Amaranth: [noun] An iridescent flower that grows in the Netherworld. Its nectar can heal or calm any wound inflicted by a spirit; it can also fortify the *dreamscape*.

Amaurotic: [noun *or* adjective] A human who is not clairvoyant. This state is known as amaurosis, from an Ancient Greek word referring to a dimming or dulling, especially of the senses. Among voyants, they are known colloquially as *rotties*.

Anchorite: [noun *or* adjective] A disparaging term for people who work directly for Scion, or are especially committed to its message. It can also be used as a descriptor, e.g. *anchorite propaganda*.

Angel: [noun] A category of *drifter*. There are several known sub-types of angels:

    – A *guardian angel* is the spirit of a person who died to protect someone else, and now remains with the living person they saved

- An *archangel* protects a single bloodline for several generations
- A *fallen angel* is a spirit compelled to remain with their murderer.
- All sub-types of angels can be *breachers*.

Apport: [noun] The movement of physical objects by *ethereal* means, derived from Latin apportō ('I bring, I carry'). Among spirits, this ability is unique to *breachers*. Rarely, clairvoyants or Rephaim may be able to use apport.

Aster: [noun] A genus of flower. Certain kinds of aster have *ethereal* properties:

- **Blue** strengthens the link between the spirit and the dreamscape. It can sharpen recent memories and produce a feeling of wellbeing
- **Pink** strengthens the link between the spirit and the body; consequently, it is often used by voyants as an aphrodisiac
- **Purple**, highly addictive, is a deliriant that distorts the dreamscape
- **White** causes amnesia

Augurs: [noun] The second order of clairvoyance according to *On the Merits of Unnaturalness*. Like the *soothsayers*, they are reliant on *numa*. The so-called vile augurs, who use the substance of the human body to connect with the æther, were persecuted by the syndicate for many years.

Aura: [noun] A manifestation of the link between a clairvoyant and the æther, visible only with the *sight*. Since the Netherworld began to deteriorate, *Rephaim* have required human auras to sustain their own connections to the æther.

Binder: [noun] A type of clairvoyant who can compel and tether spirits. A spirit that serves a binder is called a *boundling*.

Blood-consort: [noun] The consort of a *blood-sovereign* of the Rephaim. Following the Rephaite civil war, Nashira Sargas forced Arcturus Mesarthim to be her blood-consort for two centuries, treating him as a war trophy.

Blood-sovereign: [noun] The leader of the Rephaim. There are always two – a male and a female. Nashira and Gomeisa Sargas are the incumbent blood-sovereigns.

Bob: [noun] Slang term for a pound. The Scion Inquisitorial Pound is the official currency of the Republic of Scion, used across all nine countries.

Bob cab: [noun] An unlicensed cab, generally used by clairvoyants.

Boglander: [noun] A hibernophobic slur in the Republic of Scion.

Boundling: [noun] A spirit controlled by a binder.

Breacher: [noun] A category of spirit that can affect the corporeal world, e.g. by moving objects or injuring the living. The ability to breach is usually related to the manner of a spirit's death – a violent death is more likely to produce a breacher. The most common types of breacher are angels and poltergeists. When breachers touch either a human or a Rephaite, they can leave cold scars and a profound chill.

Brogue: [noun] A hibernophobic slur in the Republic of Scion, referring to an Irish accent.

Busking: [noun] Plying a skill for money in public. For clairvoyants, this is a type of mime-crime.

Buzzers: [noun] See *Emim*.

Card sharp: [noun] A specialist in cheating at cards.

Cartomancer: [noun] A clairvoyant who uses cards to connect with the æther.

Clairvoyant: [noun] A human who can sense and interact with the spirit world, the æther. They are identifiable by their aura.

Cold spot: [noun] A portal between Earth and the Netherworld, which manifests as a perfect circle of ice. Humans cannot pass through a cold spot, but *Rephaim* and *Emim* can.

Costermonger: [noun] A street vendor.

Dead drop: [noun] A secret place where letters and other items can be left and collected. All dominant gangs in the syndicate have a dead drop.

Denizen: [noun] A resident of the Republic of Scion.

Dreamscape: [noun] The house or seat of the spirit, where memory is stored. The term is often used interchangeably with 'mind' by clairvoyants.

The dreamscape is thought to be how the brain manifests in the æther, and often resembles a place where an individual feels safe. Clairvoyants can access their dreamscapes at will, while amaurotics may catch glimpses in their sleep. The dreamscape is split into five zones or rings:

- **Sunlit zone**, the centre of the dreamscape, where the spirit is supposed to dwell. The *silver cord* fastens it in place
- **Twilight zone**, a darker ring that surrounds the sunlit zone. The spirit may stray here in times of mental distress. Only dreamwalkers can go beyond this zone without injuring themselves
- **Midnight** and **abyssal**, the next two zones
- **Hadal zone**, the outermost and darkest ring of the dreamscape. Beyond this point is the æther. There may be spectres – manifestations of memory – in this zone

Dreamwalker: [noun] A contraction of *dreamscape walker*, referring to an exceptionally rare and complex form of clairvoyance. Comparable to the esoteric concept of astral projection, dreamwalking involves the dislocation and projection of the spirit from the dreamscape. Dreamwalkers have an unusually flexible *silver cord*, allowing them to not only walk anywhere in their own dreamscape, but possess other people.

Drifters: [noun] Spirits that have not gone to the *outer darkness* or the *last light*, instead remaining within reach of the living. They are broadly divided into two categories: breachers and common drifters. Within these categories are numerous sub-types of spirit, including angels and *ghosts*.

Ectoplasm: [noun] The Rephaite equivalent of blood. It is luminous and slightly gelatinous, and considered to be molten æther. As such, it heightens clairvoyant abilities.

Emim: [noun] Large and violent creatures that have infested the *Netherworld* and are now venturing to Earth. Like the *Rephaim*, they were named after a race of Biblical giants by the Victorian government of Lord Palmerston. They are known colloquially as Buzzers, due to a distinctive sound that voyants hear when they appear. They feed on human flesh to sustain their earthly forms, and are also believed to devour spirits.

Ethereal: [adjective] Pertaining to the æther.

Fibrin gel: [noun] A medicinal substance that helps seal cuts and lacerations.

Floxy: [noun] A brand name for scented and enriched oxygen, inhaled through a cannula. Served in most entertainment venues across the Republic of Scion, including dedicated oxygen bars. It is considered a legal alternative to alcohol and recreational drugs, both of which are forbidden under Inquisitorial law.

Flux: [noun] A colloquial name for Fluxion 14, a deliriant that has a particularly intense effect on clairvoyants. One of the key ingredients is purple aster. The number refers to the version of the drug.

Ghost: [noun] A spirit that prefers to dwell in one place – often their place of birth or death. Moving a ghost from its *haunt* will upset it.

Gilet: [noun] A sleeveless jacket.

Glossolalia: [noun] The language of spirits and Rephaim, distinguished from the fell tongue. Usually shortened to *Gloss*. It is impossible to acquire Gloss; one can only be born with it. Among humans, only polyglots are capable of speaking it.

Golden cord: [noun] A connection between two spirits. It creates a seventh sense, allowing the linked individuals to track one another and share their emotions.

Grand Inquisitor: [noun] Leader of a Scion country. Each has its own Grand Inquisitor, but they all submit to the authority of the Grand Inquisitor of England, currently Frank Weaver.

Grand Raconteur: [noun] The main propagandist of a Scion country, who makes public announcements and reads the news. News reporters are known as little raconteurs.

Greasepaint: [noun] A slang term for makeup.

Gutterling: [noun] A young homeless person, or a child who lives with, and works for, a kidsman. They may go on to become hirelings for the syndicate.

Haunt: [noun] A place occupied by a spirit – typically a *ghost* – for a long time.

Inquisitorial: [adjective] Referring to the authority of a Grand Inquisitor, e.g. Inquisitorial law.

Jarker: [noun] A forger of documents in the underworld, employed to provide fake travel papers and identity cards, and to send clandestine messages across Scion. Some jarkers also specialise in making counterfeit money. They may be clairvoyant or amaurotic.

Kern: [noun] A derogatory term for Irish defectors to the Republic of Scion, from Old Irish *ceithern*, referring to Irish or Scottish soldiers.

Kidsman: [noun] A person who employs children, who are known as gutterlings.

Last light: [noun] The end or heart of the æther, the place from which spirits can never return. What lies beyond it is unknown.

Ley lines: [noun] A term for the trade routes between the various underworlds of the Republic of Scion.

Macer: [noun] A slang term for a cheat.

Mecks: [noun] A non-alcoholic drink. Comes in white, rose and blood (red) to imitate wine.

Mime-crime: [noun] Any act involving contact with the spirit world, especially for financial gain.

Mime-lord *or* **mime-queen**: [noun] A high-ranking member of the clairvoyant syndicate of London. Generally heads a dominant gang of five to ten followers, but maintains overall command over clairvoyants within a section of the citadel. Together, the mime-queens and mime-lords of London form the Unnatural Assembly.

Mollisher: [noun] The heir and second-in-command of a mime-lord or mime-queen. The Underqueen or Underlord's mollisher is known as the mollisher supreme.

Muse: [noun] The spirit of a person who specialised in any sort of art or music. Eliza has several muses, who frequently possess her.

Netherworld: [noun] The home world of the *Rephaim*, which once functioned as an intermediary realm between the æther and Earth. At some point, the Netherworld was overrun by the Emim and began to fall into decay, forcing the Rephaim to relocate to Earth.

Numa: [noun] [singular: numen] Objects used by soothsayers and augurs to connect with the æther, e.g. mirrors, tarot cards and bones. The term originates from the seventeenth century and refers to a divine presence or will.

Off the cot: [adjective] A slang term for mad.

Oracle: [noun] One of the two categories of jumper. Oracles receive sporadic visions of the future from the æther, often experiencing intense migraines at the same time. They can also learn to make and project their own visions. Like dreamwalkers, they have red auras.

Outer darkness: [noun] A distant part of the æther that lies beyond the reach of clairvoyants. Spirits sent to the outer darkness are rendered incommunicado, but may be able to return through sheer force of will. See also *threnody*.

Penny dreadful: [noun] Cheap, illegal fiction produced in Grub Street, the heart of the clairvoyant writing scene. They are often serialised horror stories.

Performer: [noun] In Oxford, this term referred to humans who had either been evicted from the residences or received the *yellow streak*. Performers specialised in various arts to entertain the red-jackets, and were under the command of the Overseer.

Psychopomp: [noun] A spirit that once led the spirits of the dead to the Netherworld, before the Waning of the Veils. Many psycho-pomps now carry messages for the *Ranthen*.

Querent: [noun] A person who seeks knowledge of the æther. They may ask questions or offer part of themselves, e.g. their palm, for a reading.

Ranthen: [noun] A group of Rephaim who supported the doomed Mothallath family during the Rephaite civil war. The surviving Ranthen see the Sargas family as usurpers and do not wish to subju-gate humans.

Red-jacket: [noun] The highest rank for humans in Oxford. Red-jackets were primarily responsible for patrolling Gallows Wood to protect the city from the Emim.

Regal: [noun] Purple aster.

Rephaim: [noun] [singular: Rephaite] Humanoid beings of the Netherworld. Among humans, they are known colloquially as *Rephs*. Since their proper Gloss name is untranslatable in the fell tongue, Lord Palmerston named the arrivals after the eponymous Biblical giants, referencing their imposing stature. (The alternative names Titans, Manes and Ettins were proposed.) The word may also be used to refer to the shades of the dead who dwell in Sheol. Since their world fell into decay, the Rephaim have been forced to use human aura to sustain themselves.

Rookery: [noun] A Victorian slang term for a slum. In Oxford, it referred to a shantytown on the Broad, where the performers lived.

Rottie: [noun] See *amaurotic*.

Ruffler: [noun] A syndicate criminal who specialises in physical intimidation and robbery.

Sarx: [noun] A name given to the skin and substance of Netherworld beings. Rephaite sarx is slightly metallic and more durable than human skin, showing no signs of age. While Earth-made weapons may pierce it, it will heal quickly, while breachers and Netherworld metals cause significantly more damage.

Scimorphine: [noun] The most effective painkiller in Scion.

Scrying: [noun] The art of seeing into and gaining insight from the æther, especially through numa.

Senshield: [noun] A form of ethereal technology, which Scion claims will be able to detect clairvoyants.

Seven Orders of Clairvoyance: [noun] A system for categorising clairvoyants, first proposed by Jaxon Hall in his pamphlet *On the Merits of Unnaturalness*. Despite its controversial implication of higher and lower sorts of clairvoyance, the system was adopted as the official method of categorisation in the London underworld, resulting in a spate of gang wars and the persecution of the so-called vile augurs.

Shade: [noun] A type of drifter, older than a *wisp*.

Shew stone: [noun] A type of numen used by seers. Like a crystal ball, a shew stone can offer glimpses of the future.

Silver cord: [noun] The link between the body and the spirit. The silver cord wears down over the years and eventually snaps, resulting in death.

Soothsayers: [noun] One of the seven orders of clairvoyance according to *On the Merits of Unnaturalness*. Broadly agreed to be the most populous order, soothsayers are reliant on numa to connect with the æther.

Sovereign-elect: [noun] The leader of the Ranthen, currently Terebellum 'Terebell' Sheratan.

Spirit sight: [noun] Sometimes referred to as the *third eye* or simply as the *sight*. The ability to perceive the æther visually, indicated by one or both pupils being shaped like a keyhole. Most voyants are sighted, but some are not. Half-sighted voyants can choose when to see the æther, while full-sighted voyants must see it all the time.

Spool: [1] [noun] A group of spirits; [2] [verb] to draw spirits together. All clairvoyants are capable of spooling.

Strides: [noun] A slang term for trousers.

Summoner: [noun] A clairvoyant who can call spirits across great distances. Jaxon classifies summoners as part of his own order, the guardians.

Syndies: [noun] A slang term for all voyants who are members of the syndicate.

Syndicate rent: [noun] A monthly sum of money paid by London clairvoyants to their local mime-lord or mime-queen, to buy a place on their turf.

Syndicate tax: [noun] A monthly sum of money paid by clairvoyant business owners to their local mime-lord or mime-queen, on top of syndicate rent. After receiving both rent and tax, the mime-lords and mime-queens give a sum of their money to the Underlord, known as the rose tax.

Syndies: [noun] Members of the clairvoyant syndicate of London.

Threnody: [noun] A series of words used to banish spirits to the outer darkness. There are many threnodies, developed by clairvoyant communities across the world.

Underlord *or* **Underqueen**: [noun] The head of the Unnatural Assembly and mob boss of the clairvoyant syndicate of London. The incumbent Underlord is Haymarket Hector.

Unnatural: [adjective *or* noun] The formal name for clairvoyants under Inquisitorial law.

Veil: [noun] A word used to describe the boundaries between the three known planes of being – the corporeal world, the æther, and the Netherworld.

Vigile: [noun] A member of the police forces of Scion. Day Vigiles are amaurotic and work for the Sunlight Vigilance Division (SVD), while night Vigiles are clairvoyant and work for the Night Vigilance Division (NVD). Night Vigiles agree to be euthanised after thirty years of service.

Voyant: [noun] A common shorthand for clairvoyant.

Waitron: [noun] A gender-neutral term for anyone in the service industry of the Republic of Scion.

Windflower: [noun] A red flower, also known as the poppy anemone. In Greek myth, it grew from the blood of the hunter Adonis, a lover of Aphrodite. Though named for its short-lived fragility, its pollen can inflict serious damage on Rephaim.

Wisp: [noun] The weakest type of drifter. Wisps are often used in spools to bolster their strength.

Yellow-jacket: [noun] A rank given to humans in Oxford if they showed defiance or cowardice. Earning a yellow tunic three times was called the yellow streak and usually resulted in permanent eviction to the Rookery.

A Note on the Author

SAMANTHA SHANNON is the *New York Times* bestselling author of the Bone Season series and the Roots of Chaos series. Her work has been translated into twenty-eight languages. She lives in London.

samanthashannon.co.uk

@say_shannon

A Note on the Type

The text of this book is set Adobe Garamond. It is one of several versions of Garamond based on the designs of Claude Garamond. It is thought that Garamond based his font on Bembo, cut in 1495 by Francesco Griffo in collaboration with the Italian printer Aldus Manutius. Garamond types were first used in books printed in Paris around 1532. Many of the present-day versions of this type are based on the *Typi Academiae* of Jean Jannon cut in Sedan in 1615.

Claude Garamond was born in Paris in 1480. He learned how to cut type from his father and by the age of fifteen he was able to fashion steel punches the size of a pica with great precision. At the age of sixty he was commissioned by King Francis I to design a Greek alphabet, and for this he was given the honourable title of royal type founder. He died in 1561.